GIRL, GODDESS, QUEEN

GIRL, GODDESS, QUEEN

BEA FITZGERALD

PENGUIN BOOKS

PENGUIN BOOKS

UK | USA | Canada | Ireland | Australia
India | New Zealand | South Africa

Penguin Books is part of the Penguin Random House group of companies
whose addresses can be found at global.penguinrandomhouse.com

www.penguin.co.uk
www.puffin.co.uk
www.ladybird.co.uk

First published 2023

005

Set in 13.25/19pt Adobe Jenson Pro
Typeset by Jouve (UK), Milton Keynes
Printed and bound in Great Britain by Clays Ltd, Elcograf S.p.A.

The authorized representative in the EEA is Penguin Random House Ireland,
Morrison Chambers, 32 Nassau Street, Dublin D02 YH68

A CIP catalogue record for this book is available from the British Library

HARDBACK
ISBN: 978–0–241–62427–2

INTERNATIONAL PAPERBACK
ISBN: 978–0–241–62790–7

All correspondence to:
Penguin Books
Penguin Random House Children's
One Embassy Gardens, 8 Viaduct Gardens, London SW11 7BW

To S1,
without whom there would be no light, no book and no me.

A NOTE FROM THE AUTHOR

While this book is a work of fantasy fiction, it is grounded in many aspects of our world and addresses concerns about our reality. And, though it covers some serious topics, my hope is that it will ultimately be a fun and enjoyable read. To enable that, I want to give a brief summary of things in this book that might be emotionally draining or difficult to engage with, depending on your own lived experience. There are certainly topics I am affected by, some of which have been unpacked in the writing of this book, so if any resonate with you I send my love and best wishes. Be gentle with yourself, and please take care of yourself – whether that involves talking to a loved one, a trusted adult, a doctor or referring to another resource – and know that you are not alone.

- This book contains discussions and references to rape culture and sexual assault. There are no graphic scenes of this content.
- A character navigates war-related trauma and suffers undiagnosed PTSD.

- A character experiences emotionally manipulative, coercive and abusive parental relationships. There is no physical abuse.
- References are made to physical harm and injury. There are no graphic or explicit scenes of this content.

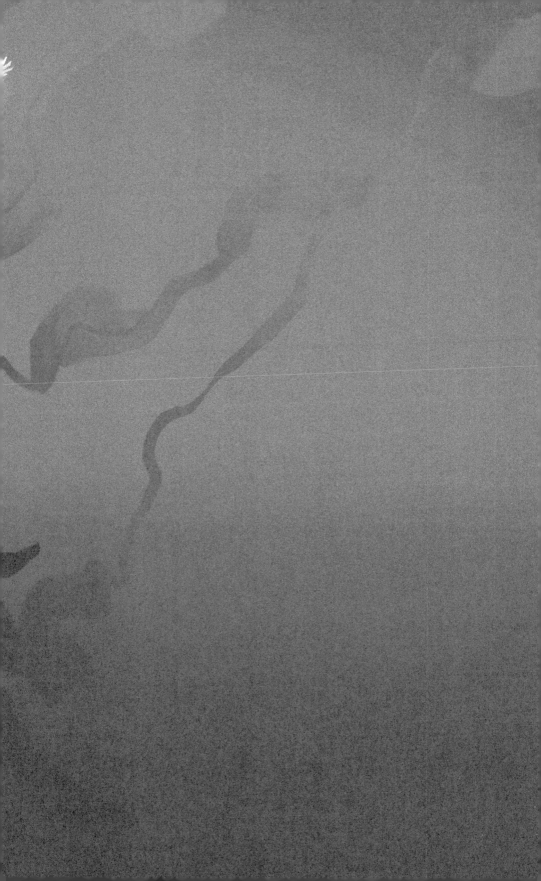

CHAPTER ONE

WHEN THEY ASKED ME WHAT I wanted, I said: 'The world.'
'And what would you do with the world?' my father
asked. His words were lined with sharp edges but I didn't
catch their threat until Mother squeezed my shoulder. Her
fingers were too hard to be a comfort – a warning, perhaps? Or
a threat of her own?

I stared from god to god, no one giving me any indication of
what I'd done wrong. They had asked me a simple question. I
had given a simple response. Now everyone watched me from
the shaded porticoes of the megaron, their faces distorted in
the reflections on the bronze pillars that ringed the throne
hall. I had no idea what they wanted, no idea why everyone
suddenly seemed tense. A few people glanced to my father,
whose glower was so fierce he could have passed for one of his
own statues.

I considered his question, my mother's nails digging deeper
with every passing second that I remained wordless.

'I'd fill it with flowers,' I decided.

A heartbeat as the words landed.

Then my father laughed. Long. Loud. The kind of noise that had me shrinking into my chair. The assembled gods joined in a split second too late.

I wanted to turn to my mother, to see if I'd answered correctly, but her hands held me in place, though her nails were less piercing.

She hadn't let me out of her sight all evening.

'It is good practice to be wary around strangers, my child,' she had said. But these people weren't strangers – at least not to my mother. They were her sisters and brothers, in arms if not in blood. They were gods she had known her entire life.

I'd wanted to know more, but 'Don't ask questions, my child' was Mother's favourite saying.

Still, at least all this 'my child' nonsense would stop soon. I was eight years old – or thereabouts. It's hard to keep track when you're immortal, and all the other gods had, until that point, been locked in a war against the lord of time, who shifted it about as he pleased.

But regardless of my age, it was my amphidromia, the day a child receives their name. And, as I was a goddess, I was also due to receive my domain – the aspect of the world that I would be responsible for.

'Very well,' Father said, rising from his throne. The laughing strangers fell silent at once. 'Let it be so.' He paused, the corners of his lips twitching as he took in the concerned expressions of the other gods, particularly the other members of the council who sat either side of him. They were his advisors, and now they nudged each other and whispered, keen to hear his judgement.

Then Father smiled, though nothing about it eased the tension. 'Goddess of the flowers it is.'

My jaw dropped and my mother's grip became vice-like once more, holding me back. She knew me well enough to sense I was just shy of screaming, my rage intensified by the confusion of having asked for something so large and received something so small. All my hopes, all my lofty ambitions crumbled away. But I kept my mouth closed and curled my hands into fists that I hid in the folds of my dress. My anger was not worth challenging the king of the gods.

'And I name you . . . Kore.'

My eyes widened as the meanings of the name ran through my head: *pure, beautiful maiden, little girl.* Apparently that was all I would ever be to him.

'Goddess of the flowers and of beauty –' Aphrodite made an almost imperceptible noise of discontent before Father continued – 'in nature.'

As the ceremonial fire was lit, I fought back tears.

This felt like a punishment.

And I had no idea what I had done wrong.

I'm thinking about my amphidromia now, while trying not to wince as Mother tugs my hair into place. My thoughts often return to it. There was a lot at play – and I've had years to unpack it bit by bit. But now my thoughts linger where they rarely have before: on the sea of faces lost in the shadows.

Mother told me certain things about them back then – things to keep me safe, but also stupid. Now that she's told me more, the memory is drenched in fear.

So many people, all watching me. Two of the three courts gathered, gods from Olympus and Oceanus surrounding me. None from Hades, of course. I hadn't been near that many people before, and I haven't since. Now, in a matter of days, I'll be married to one of them – and I can't even remember them well enough to imagine who might be waiting for me at the end of the aisle.

According to everyone I know, it's natural to be nervous before you are married, but no one has told me whether it's natural to be terrified, filled with such abject horror at the thought that you can't breathe properly.

'Please hold your head still, Kore.' Mother sighs, her fingers loosening the tangled mess of my hair.

My head is attached to my hair, Mother. Pull it and the head goes with it.

'Put whatever sarcastic comment you're thinking out of your head.'

In her weary words lies the echo of the lecture she's given a dozen times: *'Men don't take sarcasm well, Kore. They take it as a challenge to their authority.'*

I wonder if her lessons will ever sink in or if they'll forever ring through my mind in her voice, oil on water, condemning my actions without helping me stop doing the things that so annoy her. The things that apparently make me undesirable.

I've tried. Fates know I've tried.

'Demeter, are you sure you wish for such a tightly coiled look? The fashion now is much looser,' Cyane says from the doorway, the only space left with Mother and I both crammed into my tiny bedroom. She is the nymph ordinarily entrusted with the important and arduous task of combing my hair, and, from the way she's worrying at the edges of her own tightly coiled curls, I assume she's quietly livid that Mother has decided to interfere on such an important day.

Gods forbid my hair looks a mess – the universe might end. Or curse shame upon my household at the very least.

I grit my teeth as Mother's fingers catch on another knot.

'Loose?' Mother sneers, as expected. 'What would that imply about her? No, a traditional look is best. She will look beautiful but still virginal, precisely what is needed.'

'Yes, because if I don't look virginal how will the fine suitors know that the girl whose name literally means chastity and who has lived her entire life alone on an island is pure?'

'None of *that* today, Kore.' Mother sighs again. The sound has become so common that my name feels odd without it.

Still, there's something about hearing her sigh on a day like today that pulls at a cord in my chest. I'm disappointing her, even when I'm agreeing to the biggest thing she's ever asked of me.

She puts the final pin in place. 'There, you look just as beautiful as all the rumours claim.' She holds a looking glass up and I take in her work: my thick, unruly hair pinned tight against my scalp, frizzy black strands already trying to escape. Hair aside, I try to see myself the way a stranger might, the way my future husband might – smooth olive skin and a long straight nose, thick eyebrows and hollowed cheeks. Eyes that are just a bit too big, too dark, that always look inquisitive and naive, like those you'd expect of someone named 'little girl'.

She's right. I'm beautiful. Of course I am. We're goddesses. We're all beautiful.

What I notice isn't my beauty, it's how defeated I look. Like I have resigned myself to my fate.

In other words, I look perfect.

'We'll have you a husband in no time,' Mother chirps happily, setting the glass down. It clatters on the table a little too roughly and when she pulls her hand back I see it's shaking. I don't like seeing evidence of her fear that I won't get a good match. Especially when I'm terrified of getting one at all.

I tug at the ridiculous dress Mother has forced me into: a monstrosity of lilac silk, draped and twisted again and again to hint at the body on offer while obscuring enough to keep my modesty intact. It's less an outfit than gift wrapping. It's also too long to be practical, trailing along behind me. Considering how shallowly I'm having to breathe, I suspect it's been designed to stop me running away.

I nearly trip down the stairs following Mother to the kitchen. Cyane stays behind to tidy up but she must have been cooking before she joined us because the kitchen is steamy – worryingly so in a house made almost entirely of wood and several twisting trees – and the smell of bread is crushing in so small a space. Normally I'm too impatient to wait for the bread to cool down, burning my fingers as I tear it into chunks, but my dress is cinching my stomach so tightly that the very thought of eating is nauseating. My fingers fumble, trying to loosen the strands that tie it all together.

Mother swats my fingers away and straightens the bow instead. 'You should always look your best for your husband.'

What would you know? You aren't married, I want to scream. 'Will he always look his best for me?' I ask instead.

Mother jumps, glancing around like an Olympian could be lurking round the corner, like she hasn't spent the last decade weaving intricate magic to bar the uninvited from our island. 'Don't say things like that, Kore!' she scolds. 'No one will believe that a woman who talks of attraction is virginal. Do you want people to believe you're a whore?'

'Well.' I feign consideration, the *naive little girl* role I slip into for self-preservation. 'If they did then no one would want to marry me. Maybe I *would* like that freedom.'

Mother's face falls and she takes my hands in hers. 'That's not freedom,' she says gently. 'Men see a reputation as an invitation.'

'But I don't understand,' I say, blinking vacantly though I understand perfectly well. 'I thought you kept me on this island to keep me away from men. But now I have to marry one? Is sex okay then, if it's with your husband?'

'Yes, but only then.'

'But you weren't married when you had me.' I furrow my eyebrows to really drive home my confusion. *Remind me of how I was conceived, Mother.*

'That was before the goddess of marriage became queen of the gods. Rivers of Hell, I might not like Hera but at least she gained power somehow. She made marriage mean something, enough to bind even her own husband.'

Gods, not Hera as an example again. How is my stepmother the shining hope of marriage? My father forced her into it and they're both miserable.

'Hardly,' I snort without thinking better of it.

'Marriage is *protection*, Kore. A ring on your finger binds you to one man and that's all the gods respect.'

'Another man's property?' I sneer. I can't stop myself now that I've started.

'Yes,' she snaps, mirroring the vitriol in my own voice. 'By the Fates, Kore, I didn't design this system, so stop blaming me for it. If I have to arrange a marriage to keep you safe then I will.'

'I'm safe *here*. Why can't I just stay on Sicily?'

'Oh, *now* you want to stay here – funny, Kore, you've spent the last decade begging for me to let you visit other lands.' She shakes her head but when she speaks again it's without the bite of her anger. 'You're safe here because we've been lucky. The wards won't last forever, and certainly not now you're of age. Do you really think that if I had the power to keep you safe myself, then I wouldn't choose to have you by my side forever?'

'No, actually, I don't.'

That's not true. I know it's not. But I want to hurt her.

It works. I see my words land, the wince across her brow, her outstretched hand faltering. I don't even feel guilty when tears spring to her eyes. I want her to cry. I want her to feel a fraction of the pain the thought of marriage causes me. I want her to realize just how much I don't want this.

Her hurt turns to anger in seconds. Good. I want her to shout so that I can scream. 'For your entire life, everything I've done has been for your protection. Stuck on this island, begging charms and wards off the other goddesses, barely going to Olympus, rarely leaving – all to keep you safe.'

'I never asked you to do that!'

'And I did it anyway! Anyone else would be grateful, Kore. Every single god thinks they're entitled to take whatever they want, and that includes you. The only thing gods respect is each other. Do you not see that marriage is the only way to protect yourself? I'm sure I don't need to tell you the fates of other girls who thought they could survive alone.'

I don't care, I want to snarl but my words falter on my tongue as I remember myself. There is no point in arguing and, worse, it could undo everything. All this time, I've been pretending I'm fine with this arrangement so she'll lower her guard and give me the opportunity to escape, and here I am, pushing her barriers back up at the last moment for the sake of an argument I'll never win.

I know my mother will never understand because what it comes down to is this: safety isn't enough for me. I'd rather perish, rather be another tragic tale for a mother to use in warning, than become a long, drawn-out sigh in a hymn, an immortal life spent in misery.

But my safety – and my reputation – has and always will be my mother's priority.

'I know you're scared,' she says, her anger cooling at the opportunity for a lecture. 'I know if you had your way you'd go off exploring the world, planting flowers, probably wearing a vastly inappropriate outfit and no shoes. But you can't. The world is too dangerous.'

'You can,' I say quietly, defeat heavy in my voice.

'Kore. I'm only going to say this once and you need to listen to me.' She steps towards me again and strokes my cheek. 'I love you, my dear, but you are not powerful. There are gods out there with untold powers and Zeus gave you flowers. How do you plan on keeping yourself safe with petals? Our lives are not the same. I'm one of the first gods, the goddess of sacred law, nature, the harvest – all powerful domains. Even then I'm not powerful enough to protect you, because Zeus gave all the more powerful things to men. By the Fates, when the war ended he awarded whole realms to the boys and one of them was ten years old.'

'To be fair, you would never have wanted the Underworld.' Too cold, too dark, too full of horrors.

'That's beside the point,' she says. 'The only way you get more power and carve some space for yourself in this world is by aligning yourself with a powerful man in marriage. Give the others something – or, rather, someone – to fear. Do you understand me?'

I swallow and my hands are trembling, but I manage to keep my expression neutral. I want to scream that she's wrong but I honestly don't know if she is and I think if I try to say anything I might end up crying.

'I understand,' I whisper.

'You cannot stay a girl on an island forever.' At least we agree about one thing. 'I know you're scared but I'm the goddess of vegetation. There is no place on Earth you could go where I would not be able to find you.' I know that too. 'You won't be leaving us forever.'

I press my hurt down, push it to where all my fear and rage coalesces into an impossibly heavy nothingness.

'You're a woman now.' What an arbitrary word. I don't remember much of a transformation on my birthday but apparently the whole world saw one. 'You're too old for these tantrums. Promise me you won't be like this when your father gets here.'

There it is. Her disappointment sucks the final dregs of anger from me.

My eyes fall to the floor. Even that is enough to hurt me. I stare at the orange tiles I might never see again, the home I'm leaving – one way or another. 'Yes, Mother.'

'You're beautiful, Kore. And you're wonderful, so accomplished, *normally* so obedient and gentle, so easy to love,' she says pointedly. 'Keep that up and any man would be lucky to have you.'

They'd be bloody blessed.

'Are you only looking at Olympians?' I manage.

'Of course. I'm going to find you a good match. With an Olympian you'll still be a part of this court. Besides, I don't trust anyone under the rule of Poseidon to be the sort of man you marry.'

Right, because Zeus's rule is so much better.

'What about the court of Hades?'

Mother laughs sharply. 'Hilarious, Kore. I know you think I'm sending you off to a fate worse than death but I wouldn't send you to the actual realm of it.'

'Okay,' I say, not wanting to continue this conversation and cursing myself for even bringing it up. 'Can I go see my friends now? Before Father gets here?'

'Oh,' she says, a little wary. 'I really don't want you to muddy your dress.'

'Oh please, Father's the one who made me the goddess of flowers. He can hardly be surprised by a bit of mud, can he?'

'I'm the goddess of the harvest and you've never seen me with straw in my hair, have you?'

Yes, actually. Once. She was two bottles of wine into a 'mothers' evening' with Selene and Leto. Mother loves inviting other goddesses over to regale me with horror stories about the men she's protecting me from. They would gather round, tell me the worst things I've ever heard in my life and then give me tips for staying safe. '*Don't wear a gown if you have to travel,*' from Aphrodite. '*Disguise yourself as a man if you can and at the very least travel as part of a group.*' Or Athena patting my head, telling me the places to hit a man to break free of him if, gods forbid, one ever made it on to the island and took me away. Hestia isn't much older than me, but she would harp on about how it was always safest to stay at home – though admittedly, I assumed she'd say as much as goddess of the hearth. She'd say that if I ever found myself stranded I should march straight to the nearest palace or estate and request xenia, a bond of hospitality of her own creation that would make anyone there unable to hurt me without consequence. They could still hurt me, of course, but there would be consequences. Before xenia, men could do whatever they liked to those foolish enough to be unprepared for their advances.

'I'll be gone in a few days,' I plead. 'Who knows when I'll next see my friends.'

'You know I don't like you spending time with those girls,' she says, gnawing on her lip. 'Oh very well, I can hardly say no, not with . . . everything else.'

Which I suppose means if she's forcing me to bind myself to a man I've never met, then stopping me from talking to my friends is a moral line she's unwilling to cross.

'Cyane!' Mother calls and the nymph appears at the foot of the stairs. 'Go with her to the river, but if the girls start corrupting her I'm counting on you to stop them.'

Oh, Mother, they corrupted me long ago. And a good thing

too, or I'd be heading off to my wedding night with no idea of what goes where.

'Be back soon,' she calls when I'm already halfway out the door. 'Your father will be here in an hour.'

An hour. I can practically hear sand trickling through an hourglass – counting away my last moments of the only life I've ever known.

CHAPTER TWO

I FEEL BETTER THE SECOND I'M outside. My ever-present itch soothes, calmed by the gentle hum of the flowers around me: carnations, snapdragons, crocuses, marigolds, fuchsias, the buttercups and daisies nestled in the grass. And that's just in the clearing our cottage is tucked into. When I venture to the meadows, that feeling swells until I'm giddy.

Cyane is in front of me before I can take another step towards the nature calling to me. Her golden eyes search me for some clue to my unease, fine lines creasing the russet skin around them, which is impossible because nymphs don't visibly age but apparently I've worried her so much I've caused wrinkles.

I want to break down in her arms. I want her to hug me and tell me it will be okay. Who knows when I'll next have that? Whatever happens today, whatever choice I make, no option contains comfort.

Instead I smile. 'I'm okay.'

'I know it's hard.' Cyane rubs my arm.

'Let's get away from here,' I say, in no mood to pretend she could comfort me and unwilling to risk tears again so close to the house. My whole life I've found it too small, something to run away from. Especially after seeing the impossible heights of the buildings of Olympus, built by gods of craft rather than desperate nymphs seeking to shelter a pregnant goddess in the middle of a war. The very roads in Olympus are gold, and our roof leaks. But now . . . now I'm not sure. I love it and hate it in equal measure.

We head through the grove and I let the smell of the pine and oak and cypress trees wash over me. I strain my ears for the humming insects and whistling birds. I glance around like if I look hard enough I'll be able to take it all in, to carry it with me wherever I go.

'Your mother argued with him, you know,' Cyane says. 'She pleaded for another few years. He refused. Apparently, there's something of a competition for you.'

'Great,' I mutter.

'The mythic Kore? Not seen since she was a girl, raised on a mystic island to keep her purity intact? You're a legend among the other gods, and a prize above any other.'

I might be sick.

'That's *good*, Kore,' she insists, her worried eyes flitting across me. 'With everyone vying for you, your parents will be able to choose the best of the best. You'll have a great match.'

That's what all of this is for, right? All the accomplishments, the styling, the holding my breath and keeping my mouth shut. Be perfect, get a larger pool of options, increase your chances of a nice and decent husband.

Then keep being perfect to keep them nice and decent once you're tied to them.

'Why didn't Mother tell me she didn't want this either?'

I finally manage, guilt twisting in my gut. 'I wouldn't have fought with her.'

'Yes, you would,' Cyane says with a glance at the house. 'Because you can't fight with Zeus, can you?'

No, I can't.

Even thinking about disobeying a direct command from the king of the gods has that ache in my gut swelling, a chasm inside of myself that I wish I could vanish into.

'I think Demeter thought that if you believed it was her idea then it might feel easier for you.'

'Nothing could possibly –' I cut myself off. If we keep talking I'll say something that will undo everything. Thankfully, that's the moment we crest the trees and reach the river, where nymphs start squealing and rushing towards us.

Cyane is a river nymph too, a naiad, but one Mother favours. As a general rule, Mother doesn't like nymphs very much. Their ethics don't align with hers and that scares her.

But they also helped her when she first arrived here, scavenged tinder and helped her build a shelter. They made this island a home. I doubt Mother imagined she'd stay here after the war she fled was over, but I also doubt she imagined all the things the gods would do when they won, the things she's protected me from by keeping me here.

I suppose she sees my friendship with the nymphs as a sacrifice, something she puts up with in exchange for keeping me on this island with no one else for company.

Eudokia and Myrrha reach me first, squeezing me and shrieking in delight.

'Kore,' Eudokia gushes. 'Can you believe this is finally happening?'

'Oh, I can't wait to meet your man,' Myrrha says. 'I bet he'll be gorgeous, all swollen muscles and glistening skin and wavy hair.'

'I simply hope he is kind,' I reply. What else can I say? Any agreement with them will get back to my mother and I'll get another round of lectures about desire.

'Come on, hope for more than that!' Eudokia says, twirling her thin blonde hair round her finger wistfully. 'I think he'll have the most stunning eyes; they'll be the colour of the sea and he'll have hair the colour of the sun.'

'So you want me to marry Apollo?' I ask dryly. Eudokia has been going on about him since we were children.

Eudokia's pink, sunburnt nose wrinkles. 'I wish, but you can't very well marry another child of Zeus.'

It hasn't stopped gods before. There are even rumours that my parents are siblings, though they're unfounded. My grandfather Kronos overthrew his own father to become king of the Titans and was so scared that someone else might grow up to steal his crown that he snatched children from the other Titans and swallowed them whole. Then he had his own son and decided to eat him too. But his wife, Rhea, tricked him and managed to smuggle their child, Zeus, away to safety. When he was older, Zeus tricked Kronos into throwing the other gods up. Kronos had used all his powers to freeze the children within time before he swallowed them. They came out perfectly preserved.

Baby Hera woke first, the woman who would go on to become queen of the gods. Months later, my mother and Poseidon, king of the court of Oceanus, gasped in their cribs. I think everyone had almost given up on Hades and Hestia when they finally woke screaming years later. The other gods had grown by then, and were weary with battle. Hades and Hestia were still children when the war ended and Hades was made king of Hell and Hestia goddess of the hearth.

I like Hestia, I do. But I kind of hate her too.

I think my father wishes she were his daughter instead of me. Goddess of the hearth and happy to be – she'd rather be home than anywhere else. Hestia asked my father to be allowed not to marry, and he agreed so quickly that when I found out I burned a meadow down in my rage. I'd begged for that, pleaded, and received only his laughter in return, his assertions that he'd already lost two daughters to eternal virginhood; another and the gods of the court would rage. It took all my talents with flowers to revive the meadow's dead, charred remains. Hestia is who I could be if I just accepted my role in this world, never chafed against it. If I was just perfect.

And she's not stupid either – she knows there's power in the home. It's just power that Zeus overlooked. Xenia is one of the most powerful bonds in the world, second only to an oath on the river Styx.

Hestia wanted power and she found it in what my father gave her – unlike me, too headstrong to think about being subtle.

'Well, at least that means you can leave Apollo for me,' Eudokia continues, unaware of the way I'm spiralling.

'Why, so you can end up being another Daphne?' I ask. Poor Daphne, turned into a tree to escape the predatory pursuits of Apollo. I'll say many things about Mother, but the threats she's protected me from all these years are very real. Daphne's story was taught to me as a fairy tale – better to be a tree than defiled. That's what passes for a happy ending in the court of Olympus.

Eudokia scowls. 'Please, like you'd turn down Apollo.'

'Besides, why was Daphne even on the bank if she didn't want Apollo's affections?' Myrrha asks. My stomach turns.

'Come on, we have so many other things to chat about! You must be so excited,' Amalthea says. 'Come, sit with us a while.'

It's a beautiful day, the sun shining so hot the air ripples, the water and sky a shade of blue I've never been able to replicate in flowers. The breeze catches the scent of the ocean and everywhere I look there is life. The goddess of the harvest and the goddess of flowers trapped on an island with only nature spirits for company? It's paradise.

I miss it already.

I never want to look back.

'Do you know which gods your mother is meeting with?' Amalthea asks.

I shake my head. 'No, it's not my place to know.' A line, verbatim, from my mother's mouth, though it sounds like something my father has said to her. 'Besides, I'm sure Mother's judgement in this is better informed than mine. Her choice will be far more sensible.' That one's all Mother.

'A sensible choice,' Eudokia jeers. 'Do stop it. I want to know how hot the options are.'

Gods, I used to be so close to these girls. But that all stopped when I started saying I never wanted to be married and they said, 'Oh, you're just worried Demeter will set you up with one of those ancient gods. Don't think about that! Think about the good ones you might get instead, like Eros.' As though imprisonment in a marriage would be tolerable if the man controlling me had good cheekbones.

And: *'But you'll make such a good wife! And mother!'* Like the reason I don't want to marry is that I think I'm lacking the skills to successfully do all that's expected of me. Seeing it all laid out, every step of my life planned – it feels like horror. A very obvious trap.

And: *'Of course you want to get married!'* This is one of their favourites, as though just by refuting what I say they can change my mind.

No alternatives. No understanding. Nothing.

And, if Mother has me terrified, they have me confused. They're all so aggressively positive about sex that they think not wanting it makes you a freak, or at the very least a repressed prude. They can't imagine a world where you'd say no and mean it.

'Is it just the court of Olympus she's looking at?' Myrrha asks.

'No,' Eudokia tuts sarcastically. 'Demeter's going down to Hades to fetch a lava monster from the river of fire itself. Kore, make sure you bring an aloe vera nymph to the wedding.'

'I didn't mean Hades, *obviously*. Although, to be fair, some of the gods down there are –'

'Terrifying? Depressing? More likely to stab you with a sword than with their –'

'It's just Olympus.' I interrupt their squabble.

'Why?'

Cyane jumps in. 'Demeter was saying she had so many people interested that it was easiest to cut Oceanus out of the mix altogether. And … well, I think Zeus wants to keep a close eye on her. He wants her in his court.'

I might find his pettiness amusing if it weren't ruining my life. I am forever suspect because as a child I asked for too much, threatened his authority, marked myself as something to be watched.

Knowing it's only Olympians vying for my hand doesn't make things better. Oceanus has always been the most consistent threat to our island given it surrounds it, waves crashing on the shore like it's only a matter of time until the court swallows the place whole. If one of Mother's horror stories did come true, I always imagined it would be an Oceanic god stealing me away. But Olympians are just as bad.

The very queen of Olympus, Hera, was made to marry the man who forced himself on her – my father. It's not exactly a happy union but she's the goddess of marriage so he can't divorce her – though he can cheat on her, beat her, hang her in chains when she rises up against him, and make her swear on the Styx never to fight him again.

When I point this out to Mother – that perhaps the safety of marriage is not worth it, that being protected from many men for the sake of one is a risk all the same – she simply says one is better than many and, besides, she'll marry me to someone far better than my father. She says that's why she's choosing and not me – because she made mistakes in her youth, my father included, and I must learn from them.

But she's also jealous of Hera – despite everything – because Hera got a crown with her marriage. After the gods defeated the Titans, the Fates decreed that only one snatched by Kronos could rule. Father only considered the boys threats, and he attempted to appease Poseidon and Hades by splitting the world in three and making them kings of their own courts so they would never come for his crown. Never mind that Kronos chose six children, three of whom were girls.

As one of those girls, Mother has never forgiven the slight. Technically she's an Olympian too. She's even on the council of twelve, the body that oversees the courts. But she stays here with me most of the time. She says this is for my own safety but it's also because as a single, unwed mother she became a social outcast the second Hera married Zeus and the goddess of marriage became queen of the gods. Mother's friendships became something to be hidden in hushed whispers and quiet reconciliations away from Olympus.

Sicily is beautiful, but it's a prison. For us both.

The nymphs are still speculating about potential suitors and I tune out, staring at the sun dancing on the river, the flowers that fill every inch of soil. If Father wants me married to an Olympian, does that mean he wants me on Olympus? The court is beautiful – huge arched gates open on to a city of palaces, golden roads winding between them, ambrosia so thick in the air you can taste it. Muses sing on the streets, the marble gleams whiter than the clouds, and the buildings sit atop bronze plinths. Everything is shiny and gleaming and perfect.

And then the acropolis! The whole court is on a steep mountain, but the higher up you go, the more you realize you're not walking on stone any more. Beneath your feet are the stars themselves and there, where the very tip of the sky arches, is the palace of Zeus. I practically skipped up to it for my amphidromia, awed by all the beauty the court had to offer.

I haven't thought about Olympus much since; my memories always linger on my naming ceremony.

But now I try to imagine living in the court, gods round every corner, and my heart pangs for something else. Trapped on this island, I've always wanted to see this world. I thought perhaps it might be the one thing that could make marriage bearable, if I married a husband who lived near snow-capped mountains or forests too thick to see through, near a desert maybe or a jungle – something different, something new, something so very of this realm I love.

Olympus is far from this world.

And I can't remember seeing a single flower there.

'Look!' Myrrha gasps, pointing at the sky, and I know it's too late. I know there's only one thing she could be talking about before I even look up and see his chariot racing above us, four horses dashing their hooves against the air.

My father is here.

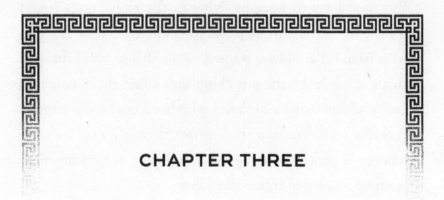

CHAPTER THREE

I ALMOST COLLAPSE WHEN I REACH home. My suspicion that it's impossible to run in this dress was correct.

'Kore,' Mother scolds when I burst through the door, rushing to me and soothing back strands of my hair. 'What are you doing charging about like a raging bull?'

'Father –' I manage.

'Oh Fates.' Mother brings a worried hand to her mouth. 'He's early. Step back. Let me look at you.'

I do as she asks, taking in the spread she has arranged for my father's arrival: feta-stuffed artichokes glistening in olive oil, dried chickpeas dusted with flakes of salt so large they catch the light, tarts with creamy cheese and pickled vegetables, flaky pastries with dollops of raspberry jam and a dozen breads with flowers baked into the top – decorative edible ones that I created because I thought they'd make my mother happy, flowers and domesticity in one.

But it's all for show – Father won't be staying to eat any of it. He'll make a few withering comments, put me in my place and then dash off to pay attention to his favoured children or the future mothers of them.

'All right, you look fine,' Mother says to soothe herself. 'But, Kore, you need to behave when he gets here. Don't rile him up. I need to . . . Look, he's going to want to marry you to the god who offers him the most cattle, or bows lowest, or, gods, I don't even know what. I'm already going to have to push to choose someone who will treat you well. Don't make him angry enough to spite you with a different choice.'

'Yes, Mother. I'll behave.'

I'm not an idiot.

'Good girl,' she says, pressing a kiss to my temple as the door slams open.

I wince at the noise. Father likes to be loud – everything about him is thunderous. He likes it best when his voice is loud enough to have people cowering. As he enters our home, the air itself tenses, crackling with the static of something other than his lightning. I fall to my knees as he enters, head bowed.

'My king,' I mutter, my voice echoed by my mother on her knees beside me.

'Rise,' he commands.

I keep my eyes glued to the floor as I do, wishing I could sink into the tiles. Mother edges forward, her shoulder brushing mine as she positions herself in front of me as subtly as she can.

He snorts. 'You've done a decent job, Demeter. She looks somewhat tame.'

My cheeks flush with anger but I hope he mistakes it for an embarrassed blush.

'Indeed. Now, shall we go?' Mother asks.

He ignores her, and begins stepping round me in a long, languid circle.

'Yes,' he finally says. 'I imagine we will get quite the offers for her. I've already had several in, trying to hedge their bets. Kore.' He shouts my name like I haven't been able to hear him, and I jerk my gaze up.

'Father,' I answer with a delicate nod of my head.

'Are you looking forward to your wedding?'

What to answer? If I say yes he'll sell me as a woman who's *up for it*, who can't wait. If I say no, there I am, being obtuse, refusing him.

'I'm excited for my marriage, my king.'

'Last time I was here you were begging me not to have one.'

I've done that so often I can't even recall the specific time he's referring to. 'My highest wish remains as always to follow your commands. If you want me to marry then I am excited to do so.'

He hums his amusement. 'And what else do you want?'

It always comes back to this. I'm not sure he's angry any more, just satisfied to break a stubborn girl down into a subservient woman. Like if he crushes me he'll be able to crush every person on the planet who ever challenges him.

'What would you like me to want?'

His eyes start crackling, lightning racing across them, and he takes a step forward that has me jumping back. He laughs so loudly they must hear it on Olympus. 'That, Kore. I want that – for you to never forget who has power here. When you're on Olympus, making your husband's house a home as a good woman should, I want you to remember that I'm the one who put you there.'

My teeth grind. 'Yes, my king. Whatever you want.'

'And you won't feel sad to leave this place? To maybe even leave this world?'

'I'm simply the goddess of flowers, Father,' I say, relieved to be on familiar ground. He likes this, me making it clear that I am settled in lacking the power I once craved. 'What more could I possibly offer this world?'

'Excellent,' he chirps happily, stepping back and turning to my mother. 'Come, let's get this over with. There's a tournament in Ithaca I'd be awfully loath to miss.'

My mother turns to me. 'I'll be home soon, Kore,' she says, her arms hanging limply by her sides like she wants to reach for me but doesn't know if she can. 'Finish your bridal quilt while I'm away and when we return –'

'Now, Demeter,' Father snaps.

My mother looks me in the eyes. 'It'll all be okay, Kore. Just be good while I'm gone.'

Then she leaves. I don't get a final hug, a final kind word – or at least one not shaped for my father's ears. I don't get a proper goodbye.

And I don't know when – or even if – I'll see her again.

I wait until I hear the sound of hooves on the ground vanish as they race up to Olympus, and then I wait a few more moments just to be safe. Then I take a shaky breath and head outside.

Cyane is waiting just outside the door. She rushes up to me and pushes my hair out of my face, searching for a sign that something is wrong.

'Dear?' she asks.

I smile but it's not so much a reaction as a reflex. 'I thought I might pick some flowers for my betrothed.'

I was going to head down to the beaches and then to the groves, to say farewell to all the nymphs of this isle: the nereids, alseids, dryads, aurai, leimoniads and nymphs so specialized we don't even have names for them. The thought of not hugging Syrinx one last time, of not seeing Egeria again . . .

But I know myself. And if I don't do something now with this rush of emotions flooding through me I'll push it all down and ignore it, and the next thing I know I'll be married. If I'm going to do this, if I'm really going to disobey them all like this, then I need to do it now.

'What flowers were you thinking of gathering?' she asks.

'Anemone and statice,' I say without missing a beat. I gave flowers meaning in a vain attempt to make them more interesting, and the meanings for these two are *hopelessness* and *sympathy*.

Cyane frowns and I don't want that expression to be my final memory of her. 'I do not think your mother would be best pleased with that.'

'I'm only joking. I was thinking daisies, freesia and gardenia.' *Purity, purity and more purity.* What else would be suitable? 'There are some in the meadow by the rockpool cove.'

'That's too far for me to stray from my stream,' Cyane says. 'Will you be okay to go alone?'

I nod and wrap my arms round her before I think better of it. 'I'll be back soon. I love you.'

If she thinks my display of affection odd, she does not mention it. Maybe she just thinks it's because I'll be leaving soon.

Although some of us know it will be a lot sooner.

'I love you too, dear,' she says, letting me go.

With that, I turn and walk away from the only life I've known. Once I'm out of Cyane's sight, I run from it.

I can sense the flowers, though they aren't the ones I told Cyane I was going to.

I think of my naming day and how I'd wanted more.

I still want more.

I love flowers; it's true. I love them so much the thought of leaving them behind makes me want to reconsider this whole thing. I love the way they smell, the way they look, the way they change. Mostly, I love the way they make me feel, like I'm connected to something so much bigger than myself.

I have done the best with what little I've had. I've made flowers to please the eye and aid nature. I've made flowers in intricate shapes, constructions more complicated than the architects of Mount Olympus could dare hope to create. I've given flowers meanings, shaped them into language to make them more than anyone could ever have thought they would be.

I've given roses thorns and made flowers that sting, that bite, that can kill a man in seconds.

And I've made tools too, spades and pitches and shears that I take to my dress now, slicing through the binding laces, tearing off inches at the bottom, the muddy hem that has been threatening to trip me this entire time. The ripped edges tickle my ankles – a much better length. If this fails, at least my mother will be furious. That's something. At least my husband will know he is marrying a wild spirit and not a dutiful little girl.

Oh, and I made sickles, small curved blades to cut flowers,

but I imagine they have other uses. I strap one to my thigh with a length of fabric. It never hurts to be prepared.

I cannot believe I'm doing this.

I've been thinking about it for years, ever since I first heard the stories of a boy who ended a Titan uprising without even picking up a blade. Ever since Mother told me horror stories of rivers of woe and lamentation, of a pit so deep it was all that could contain the vanquished Titans. All I could think was that I wanted to see it for myself.

I've never stopped thinking about it, a world where even gods fear to tread. Some part of it has always played on my mind, like it's daring me to come, daring me to take the risk. Mother said my safety was dependent on their dread. So, if I need to give the gods something to fear, then very well.

I'll give them Hell itself.

'There is no place on Earth you could go where I would not be able to find you.'

Mother owns the land; Father the sky. I do not trust my chances in the ocean with a court full of grasping gods, Poseidon the worst of them all.

But there is someone who I can go to, somewhere none of them will be able to find me.

A thousand tales of death and darkness and not a single story of a stolen woman.

I'm risking everything for fables. But staying feels the bigger risk.

I thank the Fates as I cross the meadow that its nymphs are elsewhere. In the middle there is a bare patch of land. I reach down, dig my fingers into the dry dirt and focus. I let all my fear and desperation pour out of me and into the flowers I create. White, curving stalks spring from the ground, their roots running deep into the earth, deeper than anything I have made before, something that links our domains.

'I name you asphodel,' I say, addressing the blooms. 'You shall be lain at graves, you shall honour the dead and their memories. I name you in honour of the god Hades, king of the Underworld and all that lies beneath this Earth.'

I find the biggest, most beautiful flower I can. It's stunning; the ivory petals on it are perfectly imperfect, not symmetrical but balanced. This flower is like chaos in nature. It's one of my best creations.

I tear it from the earth and shred it between my fingers. 'And, Hades,' I call, 'we really need to talk.'

Then I wait, hoping, feeling nothing but the gentle breeze rustling my skin.

I let the ruined flower fall and, as it hits the ground, the earth erupts around it.

I smile, and leap into the darkness.

CHAPTER FOUR

There's something you should understand.

I'm good. I'm really good. It's pretty much my defining characteristic.

What a good girl. What a pretty girl. Isn't she beautiful? Such an angelic child.

I have other characteristics, of course. I'm very accomplished. I can weave almost as well as Athena (I'd say better but Arachne doesn't spin webs for nothing). My voice could bring armies to heel – when I sing, of course, not when I talk. Good girls should be seen and not heard, after all. My needlework is as detailed and fine as any other and you should see me spin a pot.

Do you see it yet? What I'm trying to say?

When Mother entertained her friends, I sat quietly and prettily and ate delicately. I declined second portions even while my stomach growled, and the adults beamed and complimented my mother and said how perfect I was and how could they ever have expected anything less from Kore?

I rubbed honey into my hair to make it shine, even when it attracted insects, and I mixed sand with olive oil to take the hard skin off my body, even when it bled. I bled a lot: on the loom, on a needle, in the garden, between my legs as my mother smiled and said I was becoming a woman and then she cried and added another layer of protection to this island and swore the nymphs to secrecy. *Just in case*, she said. *Just in case*.

I was pretty, always pretty. It's what they told me again and again until the very word came to mean pain. And still I went on, tearing and pulling and hurting until I was prettier still.

When Mother told me to curl my hair I wrapped it so tightly round coiled fabric that the strands ripped. When her friends told me to sit up straight, I jolted. When they said I was a 'growing girl' in that tone, I thrust my plate away. When they said I would be prettier if I smiled, I beamed.

I was good. I was obedient. I was *fucking* perfect.

So when I finally snapped, I snapped hard.

When I finally said no, I screamed it from the mountaintops.

Or from the Underworld, as the case may be.

CHAPTER FIVE

I AM FALLING FOR MILLENNIA AND I am falling for seconds.

When I crash down, I know – with a knowing beyond logic – that I'm somewhere *else*. I can feel it in my very skin. I can't breathe. I'm suffocating from the shock of losing the nature that has always surrounded me. The flowers ripped away. And then something else settles on me, winding me enough to draw air into my lungs. Something heavier. I feel soil that is not my own, a new connection threading.

For the first time in my life, I am far from home. And I have no way of returning, not of my own volition at least.

I take in another shaky breath, and stand as gracefully as I can, having fallen from such a height.

'I'd explain yourself quickly,' a voice commands, deep enough to reverberate off the walls. 'Before I come to my own conclusions about your . . . insult.'

Shivers arch down my spine and I force myself to push through. Fear is, I remind myself, something I can work with.

I toss my hair out of my face, smooth my dress down and look up.

It's blinding: fires blaze in torches on a dozen pillars, the light bouncing off the bright white walls and the luminous golden floor. The bronze columns are long and winding, the frescoes so detailed they must have been carved with a needle. The edges are ringed with porticoes and a hearth crackles behind me in the centre of the room. It's breathtaking and incomparable – except, of course, that it is completely comparable. It's the megaron. It's the acropolis. It's Olympus.

Which means in the centre of the Underworld there is a replica of the palace of Zeus. And that means that Hades sits on a replica of my father's throne.

I wasn't expecting this, to have to beg at the same seat of power that damned me so many years ago.

Only it's not the same, because everything *feels* different in a way I could never mistake for my father's court.

I force myself to turn – and my throat closes.

I'm not sure what I was expecting. Power, probably, but a power built of swords and crowns and sceptres. And Hades has that – a rustic blade at his side, one that's clearly not for decoration; a bird-tipped sceptre with a beak so sharp it could slash throats; a crown that ends in jagged, uneven points. But his power is more primal. His power is the kind of terrifying that roots you to the spot. The kind of power that has you falling to your knees and begging for mercy.

Waves of pitch-dark smoke emanate from him in coiling tendrils, like all that he is cannot be contained. I retreat from their touch, and I hate myself for it. He clocks the movement and smirks, but who knows what all that darkness might do to me.

And I see it's not my father's throne at all – no cloth-padded marble atop a plinth. Hades' throne is an enormous slick stone of a black so dark I can barely make out its shape.

I try to look past it, to focus on him. He is everything the nymphs would adore: a face made of sharp lines, deep brown skin tinged gold under the torchlight, shoulders broad and rigid on his throne. Striking – it's the only word that comes to mind.

At my silence, his eyes narrow with suspicion.

'Well?' he pushes.

I hesitate, trying to work out the best approach. My father would be shouting by now, of that I have no doubt. He would not be sitting still on his throne, but across the floor waving a thunderbolt in my face or demanding I bow before my king. But Hades doesn't seem angry – there's an edge of irritation but, beyond that, there is curiosity.

'Hades.' I nod, playing into his intrigue as though it might make him forget how rudely I requested this meeting. 'Thank you for bringing me here.'

He raises an eyebrow.

'It is not often a deity creates something in my honour,' he says carefully. 'It is even less often that they destroy it a second later.'

'I required an audience.'

'I can think of other ways to request one.'

'It worked, didn't it?' I ask. 'I couldn't risk you ignoring me. I was desperate.'

'Evidently, if you're here at all,' he says. 'So do hurry up and tell me why that might be.'

I consider my options. I could plead, drop to my knees and beg him. Would that stroke his ego enough? Or would he see an opportunity to exploit? I could demand it, but would he react with dangerous anger? So many hundreds of paths open before me. I thought myself silver-tongued, able to navigate Cyane and the nymphs and my mother, always knowing what they want to hear even if I don't always say it. Especially when I don't always say it. Knowing what is wanted makes saying the opposite all the more enticing. But not now, not when I'm talking for my life.

Honesty, then. Until he reveals more of himself to me.

'You've met my mother. You know the wards that bound the island.'

At this, the corners of his lips twitch. 'Yes, no uninvited person may walk the land of Sicily.' He examines the sceptre he holds. The sharp metallic tip catches the light and I wonder if this is a threat, as subtly as he can make one. 'I assume she expected people to search for loopholes, though I doubt she thought her own daughter would be among those who did.'

I cast what I hope is a withering look. 'She assumed much.'

Hades laughs. It is a short, quick laugh but one that reassures me I am, at worst, not far from the right path of conversation. The darkness emanating from him shrinks ever so slightly.

'You are the daughter of Demeter then? The infamous Kore of the flowers?'

'I never did like that name much,' I say dryly and Hades smiles once more.

'Yes, I heard all about that little encounter at your amphidromia.'

My whirring thoughts pause. I hesitate, not sure how to voice my question but realizing whichever answer comes will help my case.

'You heard? You were not there?' I ask.

'Of course not,' Hades says. 'I was busy learning how to decapitate Titans.'

'But the war was over. That's why we were divvying up their domains.'

'Sure,' he says with heavy condescension, like I'm wrong but he doesn't have the energy to correct me. 'I must say Hermes could barely stop laughing when he told me – how tense and worried dear Zeus had become at the thought of his eight-year-old daughter upstaging him at the ceremony. How pleased he had been with himself to put her in her place.'

'That's Father.' My smile tastes bitter but he seems bitter too – that's it, then, that's how I present this to him.

'Quite. Well, I suppose in the extenuating circumstances of your situation I can forgive your insult.'

'That's gracious of you.' He won't kill me. At least not right now. I exhale with relief, however slight. This whole encounter was a roll of the dice: that angering this man would not be the end, that he would bring me here, that he would listen to me, that he would agree. 'And, on that note, I have an opportunity for you.'

'An opportunity?' he repeats sceptically.

'Yes.'

'I am quite content in this world of mine. I want nothing more. What could you possibly offer?'

I laugh as derisively as I can. 'Contentment? When was that ever enough for anyone?'

'Do not presume to know me,' he says, anger edging back into his words. Smoke clings to him, traces tendrils along his skin like a live beast. Whatever false sense of comfort his ease had given me vanishes. Foolish, really, not to be on edge around a god – and a mistake I won't make again.

'Hades, do you know where my mother is right now?'

'Should I?'

'On Olympus, at my father's decree, arranging my marriage,' I say, trying to tear the emotion out of the words. I've been injecting my sentences with fake feelings for years, so I think I do a passable job.

'So congratulations are in order?' Hades asks. His voice is dry and sarcastic but beneath it all I sense he is genuinely confused. I don't think he has the slightest idea why I am here.

'I don't want to get married.'

Hades blinks. 'I see.'

'Do you? Let me be clear: I do not want to marry *at all*, certainly not to some man I have never met who will claim me as his own,' I say. *Come on*, I think. *Don't let every story I've heard of you be false.* By all accounts he is so different from the Olympians.

I can still remember when Mother's stories stopped being about his worthlessness – she couldn't believe Zeus had gifted Hell to a child who wouldn't even pick up a sword – and started being about his haughtiness. '*He thinks he's better than us, refuses a position on the council, ignores our summons – for what? To hide in that miserable little realm of his? The insult of it, that the dead might be better company than the Olympians.*' I can feel now the echo of what I felt then: the first spark of hope I'd known in years. Because, yes, wouldn't that be better? The Underworld better than the Olympians? I guess the idea stuck.

Slowly, Hades begins to nod. 'I do understand but if you think I can talk sense into Zeus –'

'Oh Fates no, that would be impossible,' I say. 'I know he is set. I know my mother will never defy him. And I know there is nowhere on Earth I can hide from her.'

'Indeed.'

'And Father has the sky so that rules out various other places.'

Hades nods once more.

He still doesn't get it. By the Heavens, have I not made myself clear? I had hoped to make him think this was his idea, but perhaps not.

'I want to stay here,' I say bluntly.

'Here?' he asks, looking around the palace. 'This is no place for a mortal.'

I would roll my eyes if I didn't think it would undermine every single argument I have.

'I'm no mortal.'

'This is no place for the goddess of flowers,' he corrects, though the tone of his voice tells me he doesn't see much of a difference.

Fine.

'You weren't at my naming ceremony,' I say. 'You weren't at anyone's.'

'I do not see how that relates.'

'You're not invited to ceremonies or festivals or celebrations.'

Hades glowers. 'If there is a point you are trying to make, I suggest you get to it.'

'This is the point,' I say. 'I stay here where no one else can find me. In return, you get the knowledge that my presence here is infuriating every Olympian who ever wronged you.'

Hades smiles patronizingly. 'You think I want revenge.'

I shrug, like my entire existence does not depend on his answer. 'Maybe, maybe not. But you do not need revenge for spite to be a viable option.'

'So I give up my solitude by harbouring a goddess in order to spite the Olympians?'

'Precisely.'

'No.'

My mouth is dry. 'Why not?'

He throws his head back as he chuckles, like this is so very funny. 'I don't need to explain my decisions to you.' With that he rises. He's tall, and on the throne's plinth he towers above me. His black robes cling to him in ways they never did while he was sitting and my eyes fall again to the sword at his hip. 'Now, if that's all —'

'No, that is not all,' I snarl, my anger bursting from me before I can even attempt to get it under control. 'You know exactly what horrors you're condemning me to. You at least owe me an explanation.'

'I'm condemning you to nothing,' he snaps back, the crawling darkness clouding his eyes until the white vanishes altogether. The haze creeps closer to his skin, contracting like it might burst forth, an explosion of deathly power. His attempts to intimidate me only infuriate me more and perhaps he recognizes this because he blinks and the darkness vanishes, as does the full force of his anger. 'Your father has done that. I am merely refusing to interfere with the will of the king of the gods. Quite simply, you are not worth angering the Olympians.'

'You don't wish to anger the Olympians?'

'And have them retaliate in an endless cycle?' There's a condescending tone to his voice and his features are contorted with derision. If he pays any attention to my curling fists and burning eyes, it is only to let my hurt spur his indifferent cruelty on. 'No, I do not wish to anger the Olympians. I wish for them to leave me alone.'

'It seems like they're already doing that,' I say, unable to keep all the bitterness from my words and honestly not sure that I'm trying to.

I prefer his anger to his disinterest, to his treating this refusal like a trifling matter and not the end of my world.

But he seems bored now. He examines his sceptre again. *At least look me in the eye, you coward.*

'Indeed, and, as I said, I am perfectly content.'

'Well, what a thrilling way to spend your immortal life.'

'You're not going to change my mind with an argument.'

'Perhaps not,' I acknowledge. 'But I don't need to change your mind.'

Hades frowns.

'Please remember that I did ask nicely.'

'You didn't actually ask –'

'I invoke xenia in the name of Hestia,' I say. It seems impossible that there could be a breeze down here but I feel it nonetheless. The hearth behind me crackles louder, Hestia's power filling the room. My hair lifts, my gown flows behind me, and the words fly to my tongue before I can think them, like Hestia herself has offered the incantation. 'I am far from home and under your roof, and I request safety. I request hospitality and a place at your hearth.'

Before I can finish my sentence Hades is in front of me, a foot away, and that dark cloud surrounds us. His face is twisted with a kind of fury I've never seen before, like I've wronged him in the worst possible way.

'Is this really how you want to do this, goddess of flowers?' he asks, voice low, and I'm not sure if he means it to be threatening but it is. His jaw is tight. His hand shakes round his sceptre. The torches flicker until the smoke blocks them from view and the ground tremors beneath us. I step forward, closing the little space between us and staring right up at him, as challenging as I can be, twisting my delicate features into a sneer. This feels incredible. Power. Gods, so many years regretting asking for it and I was right all along. This is what I want.

'I tried another way,' I say. 'So, are you going to show me to my room now?'

His nostrils flare with every sharp breath he takes. I have trapped him and he knows it. Forsaking xenia would lead to a curse no immortal would risk, even if the alternative is the wrath of Olympus. But now I fear he may be just as likely to spite me with his answer as Zeus.

'Mark my words, you will regret this,' he says.

I think of the smarmy men begging my mother for my hand in marriage. I think of regret, and I smile. 'I don't see how.'

'Flowers don't last long in the Underworld; I doubt you will either.'

Hades snaps his fingers and the wind swirls, pushing me a step back.

'You may have your safety,' Hades says. 'You shall have shelter and I'll even dismiss the court. I will tell no soul of your whereabouts. But I make no claims on the spirits of this realm, so if safety means that much to you I'd suggest you keep your head down. If you step from this palace you do so at your own risk. And I suggest you avoid me for the duration of your time here. I do not take kindly to being extorted.'

With that he turns. The wind roots me to the spot until he has swept from the halls.

And Mother likes to call *me* dramatic.

CHAPTER SIX

THE SECOND THE DOORS SLAM shut behind Hades, those strange winds stop holding me in place and start pushing me towards the same doors that just closed, huge wooden arches that I remember opening before me at my amphidromia to reveal a room full of gods. They swing open for me, and from the marble hallway I hear voices. *The court.* Which Hades is dismissing. Fates, I didn't even think of that. How long have I been planning this and I didn't once think about the other inhabitants of the Underworld? I've been so focused on whether or not Hades is a threat that I didn't even think of the rest of his realm.

I'm dragged in the opposite direction. I stumble down twisting corridors, the wind only stopping when I'm standing in front of another door – a much smaller one. It doesn't open itself but, the moment I try to step away, the wind pushes me firmly back towards it.

'What are you?' I ask the empty hall. 'An aurae?'

I can't imagine there are wind nymphs in the Underworld but whatever it is doesn't reply so I relent and open the door.

It's a bedroom – my bedroom, I suppose. I wonder if this too is a replica of a room on Olympus. It's not large but compared to my tiny room in my ramshackle cottage it feels enormous. The bed itself could fit three bodies; two wardrobes stand with doors open, revealing empty insides; and a small table is tucked in the corner, two chairs drawn up to it. Everything is white: pale wood, cold sheets, marble walls and hazy curtains. It smells stagnant and dusty. I don't imagine Hell gets many guests.

I catch sight of myself in the mirror of the vanity table tucked beneath the curtained window. Only a few locks of my hair remain in Mother's tight pins and the escaped strands are already knotting round them.

I run my fingers along the door, searching for a latch, and breathe a sigh of relief when I find a sliding bolt. It won't keep Hades out in his own realm but it is reassuring nonetheless.

When the door is secure I collapse against it and let myself feel, just for a moment, the weight of what I have done. When it threatens to overwhelm me I push it all back and cross to the window.

Twitching the curtain open, I see nothing but darkness. It's night, then. I should sleep, start fresh in the morning, let my hurt wash away overnight. But I can't. If I want to survive here, then I have work to do.

By morning, my hands are raw from the pokes of the needle. I couldn't exactly pack a bag so I've made clothes from bedsheets I hope Hades won't miss. Unfortunately, they're all white. Any plans I had to distance myself from my virginal curse of a name are scuppered by dressing like its embodiment. Still, the dresses contain pouches and pockets to hold food in case I need to run quickly – and huge slashes so I can reach for my sickle if it's needed. I hope it isn't. There are goddesses that are good with weapons, but I've never done anything more than wave a stick at an imaginary enemy – hardly Athena born on to a battlefield fully armed.

The wind blows the door open and carries with it a bowl of hot, soapy water that I wash my face and hands with. The door is left ajar, which I take as an invitation.

When I step out a shadow is thrown down the hall and it takes me a moment to recognize it as my own; in the torchlight it is darker, longer and more grotesque than I've ever seen it. I glance at the walls, the impressive heights and intricate designs. It's like living in a mausoleum.

I wind along hallways, past rows of shut doors. Whenever I encounter a fork, only one way is lit. I'm being led somewhere. Instantly, I want to go in the opposite direction, to see what I'm not supposed to, but I might as well find out what I'm being guided towards. The torches linger on a stairway and at its base I find an arch. Irises and gardenia are inscribed into its sides and I trace them, wondering whether they were Hades' choice or part of an Olympian decoration. It seems strange for Father to decorate his palace with the very thing he insults me with, the domain he bestowed on me, but then perhaps not. Flowers are for decoration, pretty things to stare at and nothing more. I wonder if that's how he's pitching my hand in marriage.

'Well, don't just stand in the hallway.' Hades' voice shoots down my spine and my hand flies from the wall. My eyes flash around the room while my hand skips to my sickle, and I force myself to calm down. I am safe. From direct attack at least.

I pocket the fear instead, let it inspire the right performance. I think of every time my mother's words have rooted me to the spot and every time I have bitten my tongue, shown her a smile instead of baring my teeth. What am I, if not an expert at maintaining a facade?

I turn into the room. It's long and narrow, lit by candles in a chandelier and the crackling flames of a fireplace, warmer light than the torches in the rest of the palace. A mahogany table fills the space, long enough for forty and set for two. Hades sits at the end and it's difficult to look at anything that's not him. Last I saw him he was hissing in my face. Now he does not even deign to look up from the parchment he reads, not even while he reaches for a grape. His aura lingers but it's dimmer, clinging close to his skin like a shroud of darkness.

I stand in the doorway, watching as he picks at the food. Hesitantly, I take a step into the room. I am not exactly faking my uncertainty but I'm definitely exaggerating it and at my movement Hades' hand flicks from the empty plate beside him to the fireplace.

'Hospitality. Hearth. I'd say help yourself but isn't that exactly what you're already doing?'

A retort rolls to my tongue but I simply nod my head. 'Thank you,' I say, which isn't a lie. I am grateful. I just may have been more so if he had been a willing participant in all this.

It appears that's the right thing to say because Hades finally looks up. He looks younger without the heaviness of the smoke and the menacing torchlight. I forget, sometimes, that Hades and Hestia were frozen in time for so long that I was born mere months after they finally broke free.

All I know of most gods are stories – and Hades has so few. Born in the middle of a war, just like I was. And then nothing until the war ended, when, still a child, he was awarded Hell, made king of the Underworld. Resurfacing a handful of years later, a little older, he stood on a battlefield in Thermopylae, hands spread and palms wide, not a sword in sight as waves of undead crested the hill behind him, rushing to attack the Titan forces. There were no more uprisings. Then he disappeared to the realm named after himself, only the occasional whisper surfacing – tales of gloom and shadows, monsters and violent rivers. But nothing that would strike true horror into the heart of a girl, not like the stories of the gods of Olympus and Oceanus.

I take a seat and scan the food in front of me, my stomach begging me for haste, to reach for whatever is closest. I did not eat last night and I've been up half the night sewing. From the corner of my eye I can see Hades examining me. I wonder whether dark shadows beneath my eyes and messy, frizzy hair is what greets him.

Every single cell in my body is on alert, but the thought that my mother is telling tales of my beauty while I sit looking the worst I ever have pleases me.

I don't look up, just keep my eyes glued to the fruit and hope Hades will fill the silence. The less I speak the less I have to pretend. A lesson from Mother: *There is nothing a man loves so much as his own voice, Kore. Make him think you are a blank slate to be filled with his ideas.*

Unlike surviving a marriage, surviving Hades is a temporary measure, but my mother's advice still unsettles me. What happens if all this fails?

'For the sake of the Styx,' Hades barks. 'Don't force me to provide hospitality and then refuse it.'

I jump. I'd expected his anger but not this bluntness.

I glance at the food, then at him.

'I read that food consumed in the Underworld binds you to it.'

'And where did you read that? Are they making travel guides for my realm now?' He's watching me so intently that I'm scared of blinking in case he gets the wrong impression. He doesn't wait for an answer, which is just as well as I wasn't planning on giving one. 'That only applies to food grown in the Underworld. This is from the surface. Pedasa, I believe.'

I still don't reach for anything. I'm not sure if lying is outlawed by xenia but I'd be a fool to simply trust him.

He glares. 'By the Fates, the last thing I want is you here for eternity. Nor would I break xenia in so mundane a way.'

Then how would you break it, Hades?

He does, I suppose, have a point. He doesn't want me here at all, let alone forever. This feels like a test, like he wants to see whether I will believe him or not. I reach for the nearest bowl and find it contains pomegranate seeds. I'm not a particular fan of pomegranates but this feels too important a moment to be picky, so I shove a spoonful into my mouth.

He doesn't look like he cares.

'So, how long *are* you planning on staying here?' Hades asks. 'What's your plan?'

I almost laugh. This *was* my plan – just getting here. Everything beyond that is improv. But, if Hades wants to think of me as some genius with a masterplan to avoid Olympus, I'll let him.

He looks at me expectantly, like I'm about to give him a departure date.

I reach for the apples and choose silence.

'Very well. I'm sure you'll have requirements. A loom, a lyre, whatever it is you wish to fill your day with. The aurai are almost always around.' So they are wind nymphs then, rushing around the halls, acting almost like servants. 'They'll be able to get you paints or thread or whatever it is you require.'

I'm so glad living with Mother has made me an expert at biting my tongue. The thought of me running off to Hell to find a quiet place to sew is too funny, though he won't get that from my carefully neutral face.

'Whatever keeps you busy and away from me.' He smiles but it's more of a cruel twist of his lips. 'Of course, given xenia so carefully specifies I give you a place at *my* table, I'll see you at mealtimes. But other than that I would much prefer you stay as far away from me as possible. A whole realm away is my preference but, then again, my preferences don't hold much sway here, do they?'

'I'm sure you'll cope,' I mutter. I'm furious with myself a moment later. It's like he's pushing me, like he wants me to break, and I refuse to give him the satisfaction of doing just that.

'What was that?'

I smile demurely. 'I'm so sorry for the inconvenience, my lord. I hope I do not burden you too much. Perhaps with time you might find my company tolerable, possibly even enjoyable.'

His jaw tenses and the smoke ripples along his skin.

I get the feeling he's not taking it as a genuine apology, which is rather satisfying, even if it would be much better for me if he swallowed the lie.

'Doubtful.'

I take a sip of water. It would be so easy to fight, to argue or to irritate him further, but I'm not sure what loopholes exist within xenia and I don't need to give him cause to search them out. Maybe he'll calm down in a day or two. If I'm as unobtrusive as possible, he might forget I forced his hand. He rolls his parchment up angrily. 'You were quite happy snarling at me yesterday. And today you have nothing to say?'

If he wants a reaction, I could give him one . . .

'I was scared yesterday,' I say instead. 'As you so rightly pointed out, I'd have to be desperate to be here. No one runs to Hell if they have other options. I'm sorry to put you in this position, truly.'

Hades stares at me and I do my best to look as sincere as possible. I suppose I am *slightly* sorry to inconvenience him.

No, actually, I don't think I am.

If he doesn't want to help someone in my position then he deserves much worse than an unwanted guest under his roof. The Underworld's famed river of fire springs to mind.

But I don't want to provoke him. I can hate him quietly, I'm sure.

'I don't know why you're really here,' he says. 'But, whatever the reason, I suspect you'll be sorely disappointed.'

I clutch the table to stop myself from cursing. What does he think I'm doing here, if it isn't escaping an unwanted marriage? Is being scared and hopeless so unbelievable?

'You're free to roam the halls but you won't find anything of interest,' he says. 'So, by all means, stay in this palace, enjoy my hospitality. But leave me alone.'

I don't know why he thinks I'd be so desperate to be in his

company. Has he met himself? He can't think this is anyone's first choice.

But I nod. 'If that's what you wish.'

He glares one final time and leaves the room. When his heavy footsteps sound far enough away, I sigh and my eyes catch on the food on the table. I realize there's no one to deny me second portions here.

I'm not sure it's enough to make all this worth it, but it's a start.

CHAPTER SEVEN

I'S EASIER TO THINK WITH a full stomach but it's not enough to unravel the mess I've found myself in. Hell is not a permanent solution. I have mere days before my parents return to Sicily and realize I'm gone. It might take them longer to realize where I am but they *will* realize. If I figured out the Underworld was the only realm I could hide in, eventually they'll work it out too. And Hades might have sworn not to tell anyone, but that doesn't mean he'll stop them dragging me back to the surface when they inevitably come for me.

I had hoped that when I left the island things would become clearer, that maybe I'd step foot in this palace and think of an escape. I'd work out a way towards the life I want. Or, at the very least, I'd work out what that life is, rather than what it isn't.

Instead I have a moody king trying to provoke a fight at breakfast and the promise of wind nymphs with art supplies.

I'd love nothing more than to go back to bed and contemplate the many ways I'm screwed, not least because I hardly slept last night and I'm exhausted, but I don't have time to waste.

I have a week at most. Which on some level is all I am looking for – a bit of extra time. But, here it is, my extra time, and I have no idea what to do with it. There are two options, I suppose: use this week to figure out how to be free forever – unlikely, given my lifetime of ruminating on the matter has provided no solution; or enjoy a final week of freedom – real freedom, no Mother scolding my uncouth behaviour, no nymphs reporting to her – before they haul me back to the surface, back to Olympus, and down an aisle.

One week of freedom. I could see anything, go anywhere. Only of course I can't because my parents would find me or someone far worse would. Unless I explored the Underworld. Are there places to see here? I know there are at least rivers – the Underworld is famous for them. A river of hate, one of pain, of fire, of forgetfulness, of screams . . . The last sort of thing a nice young girl would want to see, and yet I long for the sight of them, for the sight of anything new.

Beneath it all, I ache for something else. It takes me a moment to recognize what I'm yearning for because, in my whole life, I've never been away from them: flowers.

I could laugh. Of course that's what I want. Although, thanks to Father binding my life to them, it's less a want than a need – a hunger.

I rise from the table and go in search of the front door to the palace. I can't really remember the layout of Olympus from my amphidromia. I remember the big palace doors and the arching gates to the megaron with its blazing hearth and towering throne, but I can't recall the path between the two. Still, there are only so many places a front door could be.

Hades told me not to go outside but I'm willing to take the

risk. He might have only barred his court from the palace, not the realm, so there's a chance someone might see me and report back to my parents – but I'd take a day discovering this new land over a week locked behind its doors.

I take mental notes of the layout of the palace as I walk. I used to run around my island making maps of everything I found. I wanted so badly to be an explorer, to find new lands, meet new people, see new flowers. I forced the nymphs to bash sticks against mine and pretend they were swords, to teach me words from languages they'd heard from the wind and ocean nymphs who'd brushed against our shores before leaving again as quickly as they'd come.

Perhaps this week I can live like that dream is possible, even if the Underworld is only a tiny sliver of all I want to see.

Eventually I find what must be the front doors. They're three storeys tall with huge golden hoops for handles. I have to lean my whole body against the weight of one to push it open. As I do it reveals more darkness.

I step out, a bitter, acrid smell burning in my nostrils, the ground crunching loudly beneath me. There's no sun, nowhere at all for light to come from – but despite that I can see grass stretching for miles, burned brown and spun like thread. I crouch to touch it and it crumbles to dust beneath my fingers.

Interesting.

A desolate land, nothing but drab grass meeting inky sky. No – that's not right. There's one of those infamous rivers on the horizon, so dark I thought it was part of the sky but now I see it's churning too quickly, crashing into itself so loudly I can hear its rage from here. Styx, I realize: the river of hatred.

I am halfway towards it when a screech grates my skin,

shatters against my ear drums and leaves my body shaking. My chin snaps up and this time my hand isn't just reaching for the sickle, I'm holding it before I even think to summon it.

Here is a fact my mother does not know: it is no accident that the sickle doubles as a weapon. I created it that way.

She's the goddess of agriculture so you'd think she'd have figured that out but, honestly, I don't think the idea of me being violent has ever crossed her mind. Not because I haven't been, obviously. Mother might be pressing me into a meek little mould, but I'm still the bloody daughter of Zeus. There is lightning in my blood just as much as there is earth.

And one day I grew tired of stories about followers of my brother Ares hurting innocent people and blaming it all on the demands of war. I wanted to give the people who were just trying to grow things something to defend themselves with.

But, even though I was the one to sharpen the tool for their hands, I'm still startled to see a blade in my own. More startled than I am by the winged creature that soars overhead, continuing to crow. One of the demons of Hell. A Fury, maybe. It does not seem like a threat but, as the person who added petals to the poisonous belladonna, I know better than to trust appearances.

The creature flies into the horizon and slowly I lower the weapon. My arm is shaking.

I turn round because annoyingly Hades was right: I can't stay out here. It's too dangerous. And then I catch my first glimpse of the outside of his palace – and stagger back. This part of the realm is not like Olympus at all. It towers in spires and peaks, obsidian black that gleams against the sky, the turrets jagged twists torn to sharp points. And layered one over the next like some kind of grotesque weave is blade after blade. Primordial blades, to be precise – Titan blades.

These are more than the fallen weapons of a failed uprising – these are trophies of a war I never knew. A war that supposedly ended before Hades was old enough to fight in it . . .

What have I done?

More urgent than my confusion is my fear. Does each blade mark a life? I'm stuck here with the man who made such a display. I have sought refuge in a realm I thought might be safe because of – what? Stories? And here is the evidence that I am not safe, not safe at all.

I step back, startled – and flowers bloom where I tread, as they often do when I'm anxious. The tether connecting me to this world lurches and the flowers spread, rippling along the fragile grass. I realize I can feel the bond growing, solidifying, even stronger than it was on Earth, like this land is begging for life, like the absence of living things has paralysed it and a single flower is enough to have it gasping, screaming for more.

I don't know how I'll explain this to Hades – his land has demanded life and is taking it for itself. I'm not sure how he'll see this as anything other than me impressing myself on a world that is wholly his. I know what it is to challenge a king's power. He'll see it as an attack. But despite everything, despite the very terrifying blades before me, the thought of him seeing something so harmless as an act of aggression appeals.

I think of this morning, all his taunts and snide remarks. Am I really scared of someone like that? And, more importantly, am I really this petty?

Yes. Apparently, I am.

Hades might claim to be above spiting other gods but I am not.

I turn towards that empty expanse and the river in the distance seems to beckon me closer. Well, if I'm going to do this, I may as well do it right.

Up close the water slows, rippling gently, and I find myself entranced by the patterns it makes. I never thought all this darkness could be beautiful, but I find myself wanting to translate this, to create petals whose surfaces dimple, whose colours are black as pitch. I want a flower that twists like the surface of the river and reaches down rather than up, closer to the water. Its roots would run deep, to suck all that it needs to survive here, in this land without a sun, from the river itself.

My irritation is soothed by the peace of creation. The comfort of finding inspiration in a place like this, with a blade at my thigh and a thousand more coating the palace behind me. Looking at the river, I think maybe there is a life for me here. At the very least, there will be *some* life here, something living in this land of the dead.

I shove my fingers into the soil and am about to bring my flower to existence when I rethink. Why make more darkness when there could be colour instead? Wouldn't all the black look darker beside something bright?

I think of fluffy pink petals, the sort of thing Hades would hate, folding on themselves like tissue paper. Almost a peony but not quite. Big, round blossoms striking against the wine-dark waters.

I feel roots flow from my fingertips and when it is finished I whisper its name like a caress. *Styx*, like the river itself.

I suppose that makes it mean hate, but what is hate but passion? A promise? Gods have sworn binding oaths on this river for as long as I can remember.

And, of course, there's the hate Hades will have for me taking any form of joy from this land. I hope it irritates him, puts into perspective how ridiculous he is – angry over a girl seeking refuge? Over something as simple as flowers in his realm?

Maybe he should be.

Fingers still buried in the soil, I feel every flower in this new meadow. I close my eyes and tell them to bloom and seed and spread. I'll cover his realm in a thousand flowers.

I'll ensure Hades can't even look at his domain without seeing mine.

CHAPTER EIGHT

RUSH BACK INTO THE PALACE, letting my flowers multiply. I'll explore more of the realm tomorrow, when I can see how far they've reached. It's astonishing – I've never known power like it. Creating a meadow of flowers takes energy. Usually it tires me. But this time I feel energized. It was so easy. Maybe the realm's hunger for life helped, like it wasn't just my own power I was drawing on.

I spend the rest of the day scoping out the palace. At first, it feels like spying on my father, if these rooms really are an exact replica of his. But I soon realize they can't be. The structure, yes, but the contents must be different because this place feels practical – filled with libraries and meeting spaces, empty council chambers and tidy offices. I may not have seen it, but I know my father's palace is designed for far more leisurely pursuits. There's likely a lot more furniture one can be horizontal on.

I notice it at first by accident. I'm trying to work out where a fireplace leads from one floor to the next, and I realize the room I'm looking for is missing. Then I realize more are missing, too.

It's subtle and clever and, if I hadn't spent so long making maps of my island, I likely wouldn't have the awareness of space to put it together – but enormous rooms on one floor are tiny cupboards on the floor above.

Which means Hades has places he's hiding, likely filled with *things* he's hiding. And, as I don't encounter him all day, I can only assume that's where he's spending his time.

It's possible, I suppose, that his powers are immense and he can pull a room from existence in seconds, but that seems unlikely. He is king of the shades, receiver of the dead, lord of the Underworld – his powers shouldn't stretch to manipulating architecture. The palace would have to be designed this way. Which means he didn't hide these spaces when I got here, they've been hidden for a while – a secret he's keeping from his own court.

In my explorations, I find a somewhat dusty study and wonder which god of the court normally occupies it. The shelves are mostly empty – a few lingering documents detail the number of souls entering the Underworld on any given day. The ceiling is low and the candles lining the walls make it feel close. In a desk drawer I find an old petteia board and sit playing, spinning the board round to become my own opponent.

Dinner must be soon – I should go back to my room and attempt to run a comb through my hair, though I'm sure I'll fail quite miserably. Cyane always insists on doing my hair, holding it at the roots so she can tug the knots out without hurting me. She'll know I'm missing by now. She might even have found a way to get a message to Olympus. My mother might –

The door behind me opens with such force it slams into the

wall. I turn to see the air shimmer and solidify as often happens with wind nymphs, but I'm still waiting for her to fully appear when I realize the process is complete. Nymphs look human until they sink into the nature their spirit connects to – but this woman is translucent, tinted grey with wild, frizzy hair and a dress that clings like mist.

'Hades has requested your – what was it he said – "grating company" at dinner,' she says, her voice straining, like finding the air to speak is a struggle.

'I'll be down,' I say. 'Sorry, I didn't catch your name.'

The woman glares, apparently incredibly irked to be in conversation with me. 'Tempest.'

I'd offer mine but it feels especially wrong down here – a name for a naive child, not a woman so attuned to the world's horrors she ran whole realms to escape them. 'And you're, what, Hades' servant?'

'If you like.'

'And you're a wind nymph?'

She folds her arms across her chest. 'Yes. Do you have any other inane questions? Perhaps you'd like to know if Hades is king or if you're an unwanted interloper in this land?'

I think I should be hurt but I can't help it, I laugh. I've never met a hostile nymph before. They're nature spirits and most are so many years old their moods take seasons to change. Tempest lifts her chin and watches me through careful eyes.

'Sorry,' I say. 'But you're a wind nymph in the Underworld? How did that happen?' Nymphs don't have immortal souls. They fade and reform, a constant cycle.

'I'm a storm nymph.'

'Ah – and storms die out?' I guess.

'Dying is how most of us end up in the Underworld,' she says bluntly. 'I'll be a breeze again in a few years. It would be longer but Hades offers us a deal: serve him for our time here and he'll make that time considerably shorter.'

A wave of repulsion washes over me. 'Serve him as in . . .'

'As in tell spoilt goddesses to get to dinner.'

I don't know if she's being obtuse or if she doesn't understand. I never thought I would have to explain innuendo to a nymph.

Frustrated with my silence, she throws her head back and answers what I'm really asking. 'Urgh, no. Serve him in domestic tasks only. I don't know if he's not interested, we're not his gender of choice, or half-corporeal nature spirits just don't do it for him but, as far as I'm aware, that's never been part of the deal.'

I nod but my mind is whirring again and I have to remind myself that if Hades was going to press that advantage with me he'd have done it already.

'Are you done with your interrogation now?' Tempest demands.

'Most servants don't speak like this to guests,' I muse, though it's clear I'm not bothered.

'Hades makes no demands on our bodies and none on decorum either.'

'Really?' I ask, unable to keep the surprise from my voice.

She shrugs. 'He says he doesn't care for false platitudes or anyone debasing themselves for his benefit.'

That is definitely odd. The other kings – Poseidon and my father – love nothing more than people debasing themselves. They raise themselves up by forcing others down. Why wouldn't Hades do that?

'Well, that is something,' I say, finding myself smiling.

'I'm glad you're pleased.'

I shouldn't be. Seeing Hades in any kind of positive light could be ruinous so I clutch at what I can show disdain for. 'So you serve him for the sake of spending fewer years down here?'

Tempest doesn't only glower, her whole being turns a darker shade of grey. 'A year in this place feels like an eternity. It can take centuries to cycle through to a gale again. I agreed to enter his service when I could stand it no longer.'

'And Hades is so kind that he allows you the honour of serving him in exchange for shortening that pain?'

'It's not like that,' she protests. 'His magic is an exchange. It needs a sacrifice on my behalf to work.'

'Whoever told you that could have been lying,' I say. 'Was it him?'

Tempest's lips part but she says nothing, as though the thought had never occurred to her.

'It was, actually,' Hades says, appearing at the door frame. He seems impossibly at ease, eyebrow quirked and challenging. I run my eyes over him looking for signs of Mother's rare, icy kind of anger. I prepare for whatever hell he might have planned for someone who says treacherous things about him in his own halls. How long has he been there? How much has he heard?

'I thought I'd come see what was taking so long,' he continues, tendrils of dark smoke clawing along his shoulders and rippling down his arms. 'And I find you interrogating my servants. Tell me, have you discovered anything interesting?'

He doesn't seem angry, but he does sound pleased to catch

me out, ready to wheedle apologies out of me not because he's offended but because it amuses him to do so.

'I was simply curious about the existence of aurai in the Underworld,' I say, trying not to show my unease. 'I meant no offence.'

'Really? So what was it you were trying to ask?'

'Can I leave?' Tempest interrupts, glancing between us.

Hades nods. 'Of course.' His voice softens as he speaks to her, the edge that always seems present when he talks to me vanishing.

She disappears, fading into the very air, and Hades turns back to me. 'You're quite right – if I were lying, it would be a brilliant fabrication. But it's the truth. You cannot create something from nothing.'

I think of every single flower I have popped into creation. Of course you can create something from nothing. I'd argue it's the main hallmark of the gods.

But he seems to be enjoying himself, correcting my assumptions, or perhaps he thinks he has me convinced that he is not manipulating the nymphs with his lies.

'Of course, Hades.' I nod in what I hope is a respectful fashion. 'My apologies for the misunderstanding.'

'I see. I suppose forgiving misunderstandings falls under xenia, though I wonder what the bond of hospitality has to say about accusing your host of something so uncouth,' he challenges.

'I'm sure xenia was designed precisely because of such accusations,' I say. 'I can think of no one more in need of protection than a host hearing cruel barbs.'

For a moment he seems lost for words and I rise before he

can find them. 'Did Tempest say dinner was ready? I'll just go wash up and join you there.'

Hades hesitates before stepping aside to let me pass. 'Yes, well, do hurry. It's bad enough being forced to dine with you. I'd hate to make it worse by letting the food grow cold.'

'Of course,' I say, allowing myself to grimace now that he's safely behind me. 'What greater struggle could one face than lukewarm vegetables?'

If I didn't know better, I'd say his huff of annoyance sounds almost like laughter.

CHAPTER NINE

HADES IS ALREADY SITTING AT the table when I finally arrive. I half expect him to start up our earlier argument but he barely glances up as I enter. He's once again focused on a sheaf of paper and his plate is already depleted.

If I'd started eating before Mother sat down she would have been furious. *I can't believe you, Kore. How gluttinous, how greedy. A good woman always makes sure everyone is fed before herself. You'll understand when you're a mother – then you'll put everyone else first. Just like I do for you.*

My hand tightens on the door frame. There are multiple places set and I don't know where to sit. For so much of my life it has been just Mother and me. It makes sense that I think of her so often. But every time I do it jars because I know how angry she will be when she finds out I'm gone. My throat constricts. *I can't believe I did this.*

'Don't eat the bread. The wheat was grown here,' Hades drawls. He sounds distant, his voice echoing in the background of my deafening thoughts.

I have no idea how she will react. Not knowing is almost worse. I have never, ever done something like this before.

Gods, I can't believe I did this.

I think I'm more afraid of Mother finding out than Father. He'll punish me but he would have done that anyway, for far lesser infringements. Mother, on the other hand, might never forgive me. She's lived her whole life for me and I've betrayed her. I'm the worst sort of daughter, the worst sort of person, and I'll never be able to make this up to her, to earn her forgiveness and her love –

'Are you quite all right?' Hades asks, watching me carefully but less with concern and more with judgement.

'Where?' I ask, stepping forward quickly.

'Excuse me?'

'Where was the wheat grown? I went outside earlier and could barely feel a whisper of any living thing.' I take the seat next to him. The moment I do, I think that maybe all of these place settings were meant as a test. I'd interpret my choice as a powerful one, saying that I'm not scared of him. But I wonder how he'll interpret it.

'Away from here,' he says after a moment, clearly deciding not to press whatever it was he thought he'd picked up on. 'I told you not to go outside.'

I pile my plate with everything that's not bread but the baked rolls are the only thing I can smell. My throat feels choked and the shining fruit on my plate looks fake. 'No, you told me you couldn't protect me outside. I took my chances.'

'You –'

'How does the rest of the food get here?'

'What?' He scowls, apparently thrown by my refusal to drop the topic. 'I don't know. I delegate it. Hermes sorts that sort of thing. I suppose I'll still have to ask him to do it while court is adjourned. Funny, isn't it, how your request for hospitality is draining me of it?'

'Who grows the wheat down here?' I press. I dip a carrot into the garlicky yogurt and pay no heed to his insults. I find myself strangely fascinated by the machinations of his court and all its moving parts. Father always claimed running a realm was hard and tiresome work but it seems straightforward enough to me, especially if asking someone to order food is the most taxing problem. 'I wasn't aware there was an Underworld god of wheat farming. When court is summoned does he sit beside the god of nightmares and the ferryman of the dead?'

'There are several farming gods, actually,' he says curtly. 'They oversee the humans who grow the food.'

'The dead humans?'

'Would you expect any other type to be found down here?'

'I'm not sure any more, not after the aurai,' I say matter-of-factly. 'And I'm not sure the idea of live human farmers in the Underworld is any stranger than dead human farmers.'

Hades shrugs. 'The dead forget who they are. For some that means becoming fixed on routine. Farming is what they did when they were alive so it becomes what they do in death.'

I swallow a mouthful of chickpeas. 'Doing in death as was done in life? That's depressing.'

'I'm not sure why that's a surprise. I never intended the world of the dead to be advertised as the tourist destination it's evidently become,' Hades says pointedly and I surprise us both by laughing.

I quell it quickly but Hades has a strange way of ignoring me that makes me feel watched. His eyes are on his paper again but I still feel like he's studying me.

I'm normally so careful, so assured in my performance that I don't even realize I'm doing it. Back straight, eyes down, demure smile and I am an idle decoration, a pleasant painting brightening a room. But I can't make my mind empty when it's still grappling with the surging panic brought on by my earlier thoughts of my mother and, without all the pretence, I feel raw and exposed and, gods, I'm running from her but I miss her. I want her hands on my hair as she tells me how beautiful I am, how proud I will make her. Or more specifically I want that feeling, the warmth that comes with her smiles, her compliments, her approval. The joy of doing everything I should be doing. The feeling that makes me forget the free-falling crush of letting her down.

The tight knot in my stomach reminds me that I shouldn't be here. She wouldn't want this.

'How far are the humans?' I ask, searching for anything to keep me from my spinning emotions.

'Why? Do you have more flowers to plant?' Hades retorts without tearing his eyes from his papers.

'You saw?' I ask over my cup of wine. Internally my smile is more of a smirk, but he sees the excited, giddy one I use with the nymphs when I'm feeling low so that they don't ask me what's wrong. 'Did you like them?'

'They're certainly something. Was that a new one by the Styx? How very bored you must be.'

It's about as much of an answer as I was hoping for.

'I felt bad about getting your attention by destroying the asphodel. I really did mean for it to honour you.' I take a careful sip of wine because the sentimentality, even if fake, is literally difficult to swallow.

'I'm touched.'

I'm impressed – I don't think even I could manage words that dry.

'But, no, I was thinking of visiting the humans tomorrow,' I say bluntly. I have no issue with sneaking around, but I want to know how he will react to something verging on my real interests.

He looks up from the paper with mild interest. 'Well, I certainly don't recommend that. As I say, you're safe only within these walls.'

'I'm happy to take the risk.'

'The humans aren't the only thing you have to worry about.'

I think of the winged creature I saw earlier. 'I know.'

Hades picks at his food and I realize I've never really seen him eat, just pick distractedly in the same way he talks to me.

'You do not need to know where they are.'

'Are you forbidding me? Is that it?' I ask assertively but not so aggressively that he will get angry in return.

'I'd say I'm not your mother and have no interest nor right to forbid you to do anything, but that wouldn't really hold much weight, given you're disobeying her right now.'

My face is blank but my muscles are tense.

He continues, 'Unless, of course, you're here for something else entirely.'

'What are you talking about?'

He gives me a long look, then shrugs. 'Perhaps it doesn't matter. You're here now.'

'I'm here because I don't want to get married.' I'm unable to keep my anger from my voice, unable to rein myself in. 'I thought I made that perfectly clear the first hundred times I said it.'

'Of course.' It's obvious he doesn't believe me at all. 'But it's no matter. Seeing your flowers made me realize how bored you must be without your mother to entertain you.' My breath hitches. 'You have no need to visit the dead for entertainment. I believe entertaining guests falls within xenia.'

What?

'That's not necessary,' I rush.

'Nonsense, of course it is. Are you done with your food? I shall give you a tour of the halls.'

I am nowhere near done with my food and I have my own map of the halls. But something about my twisting stomach makes saying no impossible.

'Very well.' I stand.

Hades stands too, and I am reminded of how tall he is. Height isn't something I've ever considered before. I have no idea if he is tall or short in relation to other gods. The nymphs all hover around five feet, and Mother and I are seven inches taller than that. Hades is a head taller than me but, oddly, it doesn't make me feel intimidated. His venom has never been threatening, just irritating . . .

Although that could change in a second.

The way his chiton and himation drape round him hints at muscles like those I remember of the statues on Olympus; finely chiselled shadows that are almost more revealing than nakedness would be. I'd have to be quick with a weapon if he chose to attack. Hestia would have to be quicker still with xenia's curse.

Our footsteps echo in the enormous empty palace and my mouth feels dry. I find myself thinking about what Tempest said, about where Hades' interests lie. I suppose I can recognize his objective appeal, and not just because he's the ruler of a kingdom. I eye his tunic again and the artful draping of the cloak on top. Whenever the nymphs mentioned men's clothing, it was to explain how to strip it off and now I find myself blushing. I never dared fantasize along with the nymphs – but I reluctantly admit I can see what they would like about Hades. They were always going on about muscles and strong jawlines and everything else he has in spades.

If my parents hadn't wanted to keep me a part of the Olympian court, Hades might have been part of the line-up for my hand in marriage. He's my age, he's a king . . . he's a far more appropriate choice than most of the Olympians, though just as unpleasant a thought.

'Did you know my mother well?' I ask, without thinking, or rather having thought too much.

'Outside of sharing the same stomach, you mean?' Hades replies.

'I . . .' I have no idea how to respond to that. Being a deity, I'm used to a lot of weird things but a power-hungry Titan eating babies he's scared will grow up to destroy him has always been a tale I've struggled to come to terms with. Especially the way it was presented: *Oh yes, Kore, I'm such a monster for making you work on your embroidery. Real monsters eat babies. I would kill for the life you have.* When your low point is being swallowed, it's pretty easy to make anyone grateful for almost anything.

Hades smiles. 'I joke. It is not as though any of us can remember that.'

Hades is joking now? I glance at him warily, trying not to be too obvious about it. What's he up to? Where is he leading me?

'Demeter was a woman grown long before the hold time had on me faded, and she was already on your little island with you before I was old enough to form memories. She'd visit sometimes, though – come to the training camps to lecture us about the war. All the gods who fought would. They'd tell us of the glories of battle, the importance of it all.'

'Father said the war ended years ago, when we were still children.'

'Zeus says a lot of things.'

I nod, thinking of those swords. That Hades fought in the war feels an undeniable fact, but it's at odds with everything I was taught and all the tales I've heard. How could the gods of Olympus be running about terrorizing mortals when the war was still raging? How could I have been complaining about lyre recitals and dance routines when people were dying on sword points across the ocean?

'Why would he say the war was over when it wasn't?' I ask. I do not want to admit the gaps in my knowledge but I need to know. I wonder what else my father has lied about.

'What does Zeus love more than instant gratification?' Hades scoffs. 'I hear he was incredibly confident when he challenged Kronos for the throne. He thought the war would be won in moments. Zeus grew weary of fighting after mere weeks and, between time unfreezing us, his own rampant

promiscuity and the gods' ability to burst free from anything –
their own heads included – Zeus finally had enough bodies to
fight for him. Isn't that what real power is – getting others to
do your dirty work for you? But then he couldn't step back,
could he? Victory had to be *his*. He couldn't let someone else
win for him. No, much better to declare the war won, start
dividing up the spoils and when the rest of us are dying on a
battlefield in a war that's supposed to be over he can sip wine
on Olympus and call it a little uprising – nothing to worry
about.'

'But that's so . . .'. Cowardly? But then Father bullied me for
years because I dared speak out of turn – it's hardly a surprise
he keeps his power with tricks and cruelty. 'It's over now, right?'

'Yes,' Hades says darkly. He seems tense and he's not looking
at me any more. He's staring into the distance.

'*You* won it,' I realize. 'That story about you and the
uprising . . . it wasn't an uprising at all. You summoned an
army of the dead and the Titans surrendered.'

'I ended the war; Zeus won it. After all, he freed me from
Kronos, he put me in the training camp that raised me to fight,
he gave me my powers over the Underworld. I'd be nothing
without him.'

'You can't really believe that.'

Hades turns suddenly, eyes piercing. 'Whether I believe that
or not is beside the point. It's the line you'll feed back to your
father when you finally return to him.'

I flinch like he's slapped me, my questions knocked out along
with everything else.

'I think that's quite enough talk of that,' he sneers, picking
up his pace as we walk the hallways. 'I wouldn't want to abuse

your delicate sensibilities with further discussion of so unladylike a topic.'

My jaw clenches in my efforts to keep my mouth shut and I can feel my eyes burning with deistic rage. If he were mortal and not another god he would be cinders right now.

'Anyway, I called in some favours,' he says, pushing open a door. I was in this room earlier. It was empty then. 'You must have been too shy to ask the aurai but, no matter, it's arranged now.'

I blink at the loom and my fingers twitch in protest. They are pained enough after sewing all night.

'I hear you are quite the accomplished weaver.' He turns and a smile plays on the corners of his lips. I would like to tear it off with my needle-damaged hands. 'And if that does not suit you there is an art room across the hall, and a music room with a lyre down there.' He points each door out. 'I assume my library won't interest you so I had some poetry delivered through here. In short, there is much that ought to occupy you and save you from the need to venture into the rest of the realm.'

I swallow the acidic response that springs to my tongue and instead hiss, 'How lucky I am to have found xenia with a man who would go to such lengths to provide such tailored entertainment.'

He grins, his joy rising with every glare I throw his way. 'While you were freshening up for dinner, I asked the nymphs if they would accompany you from now on. You seem to have much to say to them, after all. They'll stay in their wind forms until you want them but, don't worry, they'll be at every door to make sure you are never without anything you need.'

I was raised on an island, alone, in the middle of the Mediterranean. I know a trap when I hear it. And this is a trick right out of Mother's book – nymphs to spy on me and report back.

Why? Punishment for the flowers? Or for being here at all? Maybe he just doesn't like a girl doing as she pleases.

'I shall leave you to enjoy it.' Hades waves a hand in farewell before turning down the hall.

I stare at the open doors and step away, back towards my room, to prepare for tomorrow.

Because if Hades doesn't want me venturing into his realm, then that's exactly where I'll go. And he can get a thousand nymphs to spy on me if he likes – I'm not making this a secret. I'll strut out of those doors right in front of him, middle finger raised. The only thing he's managed is to make me hate him as much as he apparently hates me.

So perhaps I ought to add doing something about him to my plans for this last week of freedom.

CHAPTER TEN

ADES ISN'T AT BREAKFAST THE next morning. For a moment, I revel in the relief of being alone, of a meal where I don't have to bite my tongue more than I actually speak. But then I remember the nymphs are watching me now, and I find I can't look away from the doors as I try to catch dust in the air, light refracting in strange ways – anything to indicate the presence of a watcher.

Finally, I give up. 'Can you at least join me at the table?' I ask. 'It would be less weird than you hovering.'

Tempest shimmers into existence with a shrug and, despite being incorporeal, manages to throw herself heavily into a chair. She says nothing but watches me with a growing frown.

'What is it?' I ask.

'Hmm?'

'You keep looking at me.'

'Just trying to figure you out, I suppose. You seem pretty straightforward to me. I'm not sure why Hades is so puzzled by you.'

'Puzzled' feels too soft for the vitriol I've felt from him. But

I doubt Tempest will be inclined to shed light on what she means, so I ignore her stares and focus on pooling honey in sticky waves on to the yogurt before me.

'I should tell you that I plan on going outside the moment I've finished here,' I say.

Tempest simply shrugs again. 'Hades told us to tell him what you did, not stop you doing it.'

'And did he tell you to tell me that?'

She blinks. 'No, but I really don't care enough about any of *this* –' she waves at me – 'to be all that bothered.'

After breakfast, Tempest disappears back into a mist, though I'm sure she's with me still, and I start towards the main palace doors. Which is when I hear the shouting.

'I'm not leaving here until you tell me where she is!' It's a high-pitched voice with something gravelly beneath it, like silt on a river bed. I don't think it's a nymph.

'I will not repeat myself,' Hades says. He's not shouting but the walls are shaking again and I imagine, wherever he is, that aura of darkness is stronger than ever.

'You're lying to me. To *me*, of all people! You absolute –'

'I would be careful how you speak to your king.'

'I'm not one of your other subjects, Hades. I'm your secret keeper. Lie to me again. I dare you.'

'You of all people should know I'm not lying when I say that I took nobody.'

'I know what I saw,' the stranger insists.

'And you really think so little of me that you believe I would kidnap a woman?'

'Maybe the other kings finally got to you. Maybe I should gather the other members of the court and see what they think.'

No. I can't have more people knowing where I am.

I rush out and the woman Hades is arguing with turns at the movement. She doesn't look much older than me – all big, round eyes and long black hair that's damp and plastered to her corpse-pale skin.

She immediately pushes past Hades to grasp my shoulders in her clammy hands. Her dark eyes race across my face and her concern reminds me so much of Cyane that a lump forms in my throat.

'Are you okay? Has he hurt you?' she asks urgently.

'Rivers of Hell, you know me better than that,' Hades huffs.

'No, no, I'm fine,' I stutter, panic surging. 'Please don't tell anyone I'm here.'

The woman blinks.

She turns from me to Hades, who holds his hands open like he has no idea how to explain this.

'Kore,' she says after a moment, 'you and I are going to take a walk.' She points an accusatory finger at Hades. 'And I'll talk to you about this later.'

Hades nods, glancing between us like he's not sure whether he should be concerned at what I might say or pleased that I've saved him from her wrath. 'Tempest,' he finally calls. 'Would you stay here, please? Let them talk privately.'

'You've got aurai tailing her?' The woman gapes at him. 'All right, we're definitely having words later. Come on, Kore.'

Outside, I have to rush to catch up with her. She's not much taller than me but she's slight and spindly. Her long hair and legs make her look stretched and I have to half-run to match her stride.

'I'm Styx. The river,' she says, which explains her general demeanour of having been dredged up from the bottom of a swamp. 'You made flowers for me. That's how I knew you were here. You're Kore, right? Hence the flowers?'

I nod, dejected. Is she . . . Is this it? Am I going to be shipped off home at any moment?

'Hades adjourned court and he's never done that before, so I thought it was to . . . to . . .' She seems confused, blinking rapidly and shaking her head.

'To hold me captive without anyone stumbling across me?'

'Yes. But that's not the case? You want to be here?' I can see her struggling to rewrite the narrative she'd assumed.

I suppose it's nice to know that if Hades *had* kidnapped me, this woman would have fought her own king for me.

'I asked him to help me. I couldn't think where else to go. My mother and father want me to marry, and I . . . well, I won't do it.'

'Marry who?'

'I don't know yet,' I say. 'It's just . . . it's not what I want. I want to see the world and meet people and learn and . . . It doesn't matter.'

'Of course it matters.'

I shake my head. 'All that matters is what I *don't* want – and that's home and hearth. I don't want to be locked up in a house and then . . . I mean, I don't even know if I ever want children, let alone right now. And aside from my father I hadn't even met a man before Hades. Well, there were some at my amphidromia, but I barely remember them, and Mother expects me to . . . and . . . Father just wants to control . . . I just . . .'

It's all coming out of me quicker than I can make sense of it.

But it's difficult to put words to the deep-rooted feeling in my gut that has me struggling for air when I think of my future.

And I don't know why but I don't want Styx thinking Hades took me. He might be an irritating, obnoxious arse but he isn't the sort of monster I was raised to fear. He didn't drag me here, hasn't blackmailed me, hasn't hurt me. Forced looms and spying nymphs aren't the sorts of things that make it into the stories Mother tells. They're actions that deserve spiteful flowers and thinly veiled insults, not your subjects believing you kidnapped someone.

'Gods, this is a mess,' she says, pushing her hair back from her face. It's so damp it sticks into shape. 'So you ran here because Zeus is making you marry someone? And Hades is . . . protecting you?'

I nod. 'He doesn't want to but I bound him by xenia.'

'Smart,' she says. 'But you can trust him.'

'You were the one screaming at him two minutes ago. Clearly you think he's capable of some terrible things.'

'I'm the goddess of hate.' She shrugs. 'I can get carried away. Xenia forces him to give you a roof to stay under, not keep your presence secret. He's doing that of his own volition.'

'And the nymphs he's got following me?'

'Hades can be paranoid. For good reason – you should hear some of the things the other gods swear on my waters.'

As we walk, I see the asphodel has spread even further, and the Underworld's acidic smell is replaced with the fresh floral scents of so many flowers that I don't even notice we're near her river until I see styx blossoms running along the banks like foam on a wave's edge.

'How long have you been here?' she asks.

'A couple of days.'

'Fates, that's what I was afraid of.' She sighs. 'Not long at all. If I've found out already then soon other gods will too. I'm the oath keeper – that's why people swear on my waters. But the others won't keep things secret like I will. They are loyal to Hades but if they think it will win favour with Zeus . . .'

'I know,' I say softly. Hades and Poseidon might rule courts but Zeus is king of the gods. He claims they're all equal but it's a lie everyone pretends to believe because no one can bear another war. My father has the most power here. 'I'm trying to figure out what happens after. I just need some time.'

She nods. 'All right, I'll have a think. But if this is all the time you have . . . make the most of it.'

I nod. 'I am. Or, at least, I'm trying to. Actually, about that, do you know where the humans are? The dead ones, I mean.'

She gives me an appraising look. 'Yes, but you won't get much out of them.'

'What do you mean?'

'Their souls decay the moment they enter this realm. Most of them are little more than memories at this point. But follow the waters of my river that way until it meets the Lethe and across that you'll find them. Keep close to my banks if you don't want to run into any other gods; they quite literally hate being near my waters. Enjoy – and we'll talk soon.'

She takes a step towards the water but her eyes catch on the flowers again and she bends to pluck one.

'These truly are beautiful,' she says, twirling it between her fingers. 'I feel like I should hate it – pink isn't quite my colour. But you've made the petals ripple. It feels like home.' She offers a smile. 'Thank you.'

She reaches forward to tuck the flower behind my ear. 'There,' she says. 'It's like I'm with you, keeping you safe.'

And then she disappears.

My throat is dry and I take a shaky breath. I am safe. I am not being hauled back to my parents. The flower's petals tickle the edge of my cheek and, though I know Styx will not be able to keep me safe, it feels like she could – at the very least it is kinship and companionship and I ache with how much I've missed that. A whole life on an island so focused on what I lacked I never thought about what I had: companionship, friendship, love.

Before my fear can morph into sadness and before the tears escape, I start following the river, not quite running but definitely moving like if I walk quick enough my feelings might be left behind.

The soil beneath my feet thrums in welcome and slowly my anxieties fade. At home, nature feels comforting. Here, it is celebratory, like it's thrilled I'm finally here. There are other nature deities in the courts of Olympus and Oceanus but clearly none in the Underworld. I focus on the feeling and blossoms spring where I step.

I'm not walking long before I see another river trickling to meet the Styx, its waters twisting like mist. As I get closer any sense of it being water at all feels wrong. *The Lethe.* The river of forgetting.

It pulls like a magnet, beckoning me closer through soft whispers and a gentle tug.

I step back. This river is even more dangerous than the dark waters of the Styx.

I scan the horizon for any sign of how far the rivers might run but I can't see an end. The Lethe is not wide where it cuts across my path, more of a stream. I don't know how potent it is. One drop of it might be enough to pull my memories from me.

Before I can think it through further, I run and soar across it in one bounding leap.

Reckless. Impossibly reckless.

But I'd do it again if it gets me where I want to go.

On the other side, the asphodel is thick and above it rolls a hazy grey mist.

Suddenly, I am knocked off my feet. Images flash across my mind – and then more than just pictures: sounds and smells and emotions. It's like I'm actually there, slamming my hand on the wood of a table, my voice rising above others as they fall quiet. Then the shouting continues and I'm left with the impression of an explosive clamour of noise like someone else has shoved the feeling into my brain.

I jump up, sickle in hand.

And there's a human.

A dead one, obviously, hazy and insubstantial like Tempest but worse. This human's life source isn't slowly replenishing like hers but fading. All that is left of his life is a sense of noise. A politician maybe, or a lawyer. A lot of time spent somewhere loud and chaotic.

He staggers forward aimlessly before slowly straightening, a scowl appearing on his lips.

He must have walked through me. That's why the memories were so strong.

If I concentrate, I can tune back into them. I see rows of people slowly becoming clearer.

It's me, I realize. My divine presence is giving this human more life than he has had before – at least in this realm.

I turn and run before his pull on my power goes too far, but even when I get further away my skin is covered in goosebumps. I have never experienced that before – other people's memories, whole lives, felt first-hand. But I wanted to know the world and what better way than seeing it through those who lived there?

And then I realize – that's no mist in front of me at all. It's humans, gathered like herds of cattle and wandering aimlessly. They stretch as far as I can see, grey and hazy. Part of me feels like if I step near them I'll start disappearing too.

But a bigger part of me is desperate to reach forward, to be among them, to learn of their lives.

I steady myself for a moment, and then I plunge in among them.

Salt spray on my lips, rough waters scratching at my hands, rope digging into the soft flesh but always the horizon, always the promise of possibility.

Soft skin against every inch of my own, my mind spinning, so much longing to be closer, needing to be closer.

Hunger gnawing at my gut, too weak to lift myself up, insects biting at my skin.

Blood on my hands, power surging through me, satisfaction unfurling on my lips, my muscles bending to my will, unstoppable as people fall like trees before me.

Blood on my hands, pressed to my stomach, suddenly empty, my whole body caved in two and I'm desperate, dying but desperate to know whether my baby survived.

Blood on my hands but it doesn't stop the fists from raining down on me. I'm choking on my own teeth. There's so much red.

It's too much.

I'm staggering now, almost at the edge of the crowd of

humans, almost out. I need to escape them and their pain and their feelings and all that they are. People condensed into a single moment, a memory, a feeling. It's too much. And there's so much blood.

Terror. My heart stops. My thoughts falter. Flashes of blood and pain and exhaustion but above it so much terror. I fall to my knees in the mud.

It's not mine, it's not mine. I chant like it will keep me sane through all of this delirium.

But it *is* someone's.

The thought snaps me from the terror and I see a woman stumbling in front of me, staring around manically though there's no one else around. There's *nothing* else around, not even asphodel. How far have I come while trying to escape the mortal souls?

She's drawing power from me and it's taking everything I have not to fall into her memories again.

'It's all right,' I choke. My voice is hoarse but she blinks and her eyes focus on me.

Every second she is near me she becomes more of herself.

'What?' She shakes her head like she can shake the confusion from herself. Instinctively I reach for her, taking her hand and she jumps.

'You can touch me?' she asks. 'I . . . I can feel you.' She stares at the arm that slowly forms beneath my touch. 'Who are you?'

'That doesn't matter,' I say. 'But I won't hurt you.'

'Where am I?' she asks, staring at the emptiness around us – black earth meeting black sky unbroken all around.

Will this break her? I don't think so – nothing could be worse than her fear.

'The Underworld,' I say simply.

Realization dawns on her face and she nods like this all makes sense. 'Of course. I remember now.'

'What's your name?'

'Larissa.'

'Why were you so scared, Larissa?'

She looks up and she's terrified. Of course she is. Whatever terror she faced in life was so strong it's all she became after death.

'You don't need to ask me,' she says. 'You can do whatever you did before to . . . see my memories.'

'But do you want me to know?' I ask. Entering her mind feels like an invasion, even if her memories are almost unavoidable. My head is pulsing with the effort of keeping them at bay but me touching her, purposely rather than as before, seems to have restored her to a fully rational being.

She startles at the question. After a moment, she nods, and I lower my defences.

Her memories smother me. I do not witness them as an observer but feel them, understand them.

I breathe in the life of this woman and I feel her suffering. I see every inch of the terror of her life and, as her memories bleed out again, I feel her terror still. Something here and now is terrifying her.

I pull free of her memories and bring a shaky hand to my cheek but my eyes are dry. I cannot leave her like this. If I do she will be reduced to pure terror again.

'I can make you forget,' I say, because it is all I can offer her. I can show her to the Lethe's waters.

'That's not . . .' She struggles to find words and I don't

understand. Why would she want to remember this? The feeling of her memories still lingers. What is the point in being a god if you can do nothing about the things humans do to one another?

Then again, my father coerced his own wife into marrying him after forcing himself on her, something to save her reputation. I think of all the other people he's hurt: the girls running as fast as they can; Prometheus chained to a rock, his guts torn from him again and again.

What is the point in being a god if it is the evil who escape all the pain in this world?

'I do not wish to forget,' she says. 'My memories aren't the problem – it's that *they're* here. The people who hurt me lived longer and hurt other people too and now they're here, in the same field as me for the rest of eternity.'

I glance down at the asphodel, the horror of what she's saying dawning on me. Here, forever, a single feeling of terror for the rest of eternity as your soul decays, constantly encountering the thing you fear.

But this would be so simple to fix. It would be easy in this large empty land to create another space to put the cruellest humans, to save the rest from them. Their souls are decaying anyway – you could create a gentle place for them to fade away without facilitating needless suffering.

Unless Hades doesn't care to do it.

'I have to go,' I say, a coldness to my voice that I have never heard before.

'No! Please don't,' she says. 'This is the first time I've felt like myself in . . . I don't even know how long.'

I pause. Of course. This isn't about me and it's not about Hades. Just yet. But, by the Fates, it will be.

Right now there is one thing only I can do.

I offer her my hand and she takes it. I close my eyes and think about my flowers. I imagine her rushing back to herself: her thoughts, her personality, all that she was. I think about them sticking, about her wandering free again.

It works. I have no idea how I know, I just know that it has. Like a flower taking root.

When I open my eyes I realize it worked better than I thought it would. She is full colour and solid once more, her black hair melting into the sky and her skin dappled by non-existent sunlight.

'There,' I say. 'You'll be fine now. I'll be back soon and we can talk further.' I think I've found my reason for being here, a purpose for my extra time. 'First, I need to give a god another reason to be paranoid.'

For a moment, she looks confused. But then she glances warily in the direction of the other souls.

'I'll make this better,' I promise, wincing as I do.

Too many stories start with gods making promises they can't keep.

CHAPTER ELEVEN

STUMBLE BACK TO THE PALACE in a daze, dragging my feet like all the pain the humans have to offer is weighing on me. When I finally crawl back across the threshold of Hades' palace, I nearly collapse. I wonder whether those spirits were building strength by draining me of it.

Or maybe my exhaustion has more to do with the images that have been crowding in my head ever since. The feeling of hopelessness in my gut.

'Where have you been?' Hades asks. I glance up and see him standing in the doorway of the library, framed by the glow of the fire and his shroud of smoke. 'Surely Styx didn't keep you all this time.'

There's something about his exhalation before he speaks that reminds me of Mother's relief when I'd come home. I wonder what he feared I was doing, what invented slights he's now going to blame me for.

'I can't do this right now,' I say. I want to escape to my room to lie down until my head stops pounding.

He scowls. 'Can't do what?'

'This,' I repeat, waving my hand as I wince at the light coming from behind him. 'Whatever this is. This conversation.'

'Yes, well, conversation would require more words than you currently seem able to form,' he says with a taunting smile, and all this patronizing superiority from a man who's let such misery happen grates on me. 'One of my subjects accused me of kidnapping you, Kore. I think the least you can do is discuss it with me.' If I close my eyes I can still see all that blood. 'I'd even go so far as to say you owe it to me.'

'I don't owe you a thing,' I snarl. 'And I'm not doing this song and dance where you're an arsehole and I pretend I don't care.'

I regret it immediately. What's the point in biting back everything I ever want to say if I just give up the moment I have a headache?

Hades laughs and the sound freezes me.

I glance up at him warily. A laugh can mean too many things.

'You really *can't* do this right now,' he acknowledges and then he looks at me far too attentively.

I feel every muscle in my body tense because I'm not sure what pretence I should plaster on. I can't focus. Even while I stand here, how many spirits are trapped and terrified in this realm? How many are in pain? How many are caught in a perpetual loop of sadness? How many humans walk the Earth, living the horrors they will one day repeat for all eternity?

'What did Styx say to you?' he asks.

'Nothing.'

His eyes narrow. 'Where were you?'

'Goodnight, Hades.'

'You were with the spirits, weren't you!' For a moment he sounds excited to have figured it out. Then his expression darkens. 'I told you not to go and see them. Now look at you – they've dragged you down just as I knew they would. Why would you go there when I told you –'

'Will you shut up?' I snap. 'I don't care what you told me.'

'Well, you should. You look dreadful and it's precisely because you did the one thing I told you not to do.' He's not even raising his voice and it's enough to make me want to scream.

'I'm fine,' I hiss.

'You aren't fine – what was it? A starved peasant? Some murdered child?'

I shouldn't be surprised any more but I step back with the shock of it. I'd prepared for his indifference, not his callousness.

'What is the matter with you?' I demand. 'How can you just so casually mention those things?'

'Ahh – so the child?'

'Fuck you.'

Every inch between us suddenly becomes tangible, the distance the only thing keeping me from trying to tear his eyes out.

Hades has the audacity to laugh. 'My, my, now this is more like it. Kore of the flowers showing her thorns.'

'Is this all just a game to you?'

'Darling, what else would it be?'

Bastard. All that sadness and pain morphs into a rage so hot it's all I can do not to scream – and then I can't stop it all. 'Is this what you do?' I yell. 'See all the pain and anguish and laugh at it? Then come back up to your palace and just sit and read your scrolls and feast on the food they grow for you? What a petty existence.'

I'm no longer leaning against the door to support myself but halfway across the atrium.

'Excuse me?' he scoffs but his facade is crumbling, irritation clipping sharp corners into his words.

'You like to pretend you're different, sitting down here instead of up there with the rest of them. Smiling to yourself that you're better than the Olympians – and for what? So you can ignore the world you've created just like they do? So you can jeer at the humans and revel in the righteousness of being a god? You arrogant arsehole, name one way you're superior.'

Hades laughs but it's weaker, forced, and then he drops the veneer of his amusement altogether. He takes a step towards me and tendrils of smoke reach out menacingly, clawing even closer. 'Please, Kore. Your very name means "naive". Let's not pretend you have any idea how the world works. Why don't you go plant some more flowers and stick to what you know?'

But I'm too far gone to stop now. 'You're supposed to be one of the greats, one of the originals stolen by Kronos! You were gifted an entire realm. You're supposed to be powerful and this is what you do with that power?' I snipe, almost breathless with anger. 'It's pathetic, Hades. *You* are pathetic.'

His eye twitches and he takes another step. He's right in front of me now, drawing himself up and growling words with such venom he can barely get them out. 'You spend your whole life on an island, swallowing your father's lies and –'

'So either you're a truly and deeply hideous person,' I shout right into his face, his efforts to intimidate me only incensing me more, 'or you're just terrible at your job.'

'Cutting,' he jeers. 'Your insults need work, my dear.'

By the Fates, I want to break him.

'You don't deserve a thing you've been given,' I spit. 'Maybe someone should take it from you.'

'You dare,' Hades seethes, his words deathly quiet and icy cold, clashing with the fire of my rage, 'challenge me in my own halls.'

His hand shoots out towards my face and I don't hesitate. My sickle is pressed flat against his throat.

I'm shaking. I have been angry before, so angry I thought I could tear the Earth apart with my bare hands. But this is the first time I have truly felt I could hurt someone.

'I do,' I say.

Hades' chin tilts up, away from the weapon, and he raises his palms in surrender, the flower he snatched from my ear clutched in one hand. I suppose it should be a relief to know he was reaching for that, not me, but *how dare he?* He must have known what I would think he was doing. After everything that has happened today my anger comes crashing down into a rage that goes beyond rashness to the kind of prolonged fury that requires plotting and revenge and war.

He glares down at me like he's perfectly in control. He crushes the flower in his hand and drops it before returning to his mocking surrender, yellow pollen streaked across his palm. He arches back so he can see the edge of the weapon still pointed at him.

'You're quick with that thing.'

'I can be quicker.'

'Is that a threat?' he asks.

I open my mouth to make my threat far more explicit, when my breath catches in my throat.

Because we are bound by xenia. Whichever one of us breaks it will be cursed. And Hestia may not have handed out a rule book, but threatening the life of your host definitely seems like it would break the pledge of hospitality.

'No,' I say, my anger finally breaking as I slide the sickle through my fingers and let it clatter to the floor.

Something flashes in Hades' face and I realize what's been missing all this time: real anger. Everything until now was an act. And now he is incensed, indignant and truly furious.

I step back as it all slots into place.

'But you want it to be, don't you?' I say. My eyebrows knit together and I stare from my fallen weapon and crumpled flower to his irritated sneer as his arms fall to his sides. 'That's all you've wanted. You want me to break xenia.'

Hades snorts. 'I was hoping the poetry might push you to the brink.'

'Why?' I ask and I hate how emotional my voice sounds, how hurt.

He gestures vaguely. 'All this, I suppose. All of your supposed meekness over the last few days, from when you first appeared in my halls with demands and sly propositions. You had me half convinced I'd imagined it. Tell me, are you sure you're the child of Zeus and not Dionysus? You're quite the accomplished theatrical performer.'

'*Why?*' I ask again and this time my voice is harder, my emotions throttled.

'I thought I just explained why?' Hades tilts his head.

'I haven't done anything. I've avoided you, tried not to be intrusive, suppressed everything I've wanted to say, tried to be invisible.'

'An invisible intruder is still an intruder.'

'Worthy of the curse of breaking xenia? Why would you do that to me?' I can't stop looking at him, this stranger who I know even less than I thought I did.

Hades looks at me with narrowed eyes. 'Kore, why are you really here?'

'Do I need to bloody spell it out for you? I don't want to get married!'

'No one comes here,' he says. 'Ever. And the first person who does is the daughter of Zeus? Tell me that's not suspicious.'

'Maybe no one comes here because you treat guests like this.'

'Are you a guest though? Or are you your father's spy?'

It's so ridiculous I burst into hysterical laughter. 'I'm sorry, have you met my father? You think he'd trust me with something like that? I've thought you are a lot of horrible things, Hades, but this is the first time I've thought you stupid.'

'It seems a viable offer for a girl who's made it clear just how desperate she is not to be married – spy on a rival king and stay unwed.'

'You're right. I just sent my report about your overcooked lentils and haunting decor.' I shake my head. 'This is the most foolish thing I've ever heard.'

'I never thought for sure that you were; I simply acknowledge the possibility,' Hades snaps, clearly annoyed at me dismissing his grand conspiracy theories with ridicule. 'I wanted you gone for the simple fact of your unwelcome presence in my home.

You had no right to insist I harbour you – to take my choice in the matter away.'

'You have no idea what it's like, do you? That's why you so readily believe I am lying about why I am here. You can't even entertain the possibility that I might be telling the truth. Then you would have to confront how bad it is for the rest of us.'

'I know exactly –'

'But you don't.' I cut him off. I don't care to hear his excuses, his protests. I don't care for anything he has to offer, actually. 'They're just words to you and if they're not on one of your little scrolls then you don't give a damn. I can't believe I came in here like I could change your mind – you don't have an opinion in the first place.'

'I have no idea what you're talking about.'

'Oh, believe me, I know,' I say. 'You have dominion over a realm of humans. You could change the world if you wanted to but you don't. You have all this power and you don't care to use it.'

'The Underworld is fine,' he says abruptly, his lip curled like enough contempt might dismiss my entire argument.

'No, it isn't. You have people here who have been beaten, abused and murdered right alongside those who inflicted those crimes. So why wouldn't the humans on Earth fight and steal and hurt people when there are no consequences. Consequences *you* could provide. You could change everything but you don't know why you should. You don't deserve your power or your throne. You don't deserve any of this.'

'Why should I care about humans hurting each other?' Hades asks like it's ridiculous.

'That's the saddest thing I've ever heard. Why should you try to minimize the pain in this world? Why wouldn't you? I was going to try to convince you to change things around here, but I don't care what you think any more. Someone has to run this place and clearly it's not you.'

'More threats. Are you planning on taking my realm from me, *Kore*?' he says my name like it's an insult because that's precisely what it is.

'I don't need to,' I say because I can already feel this realm pulsing beneath my fingertips, like it's been begging for someone to do something with it. If Hades won't, then I will.

'And what exactly is it that you plan on doing?' Hades asks with a wry smile. It's so condescending that my temper flares yet again.

'Something. Anything. Which will be a first for this place and better than all you've done. I'll do more than allow truly evil beings to simply wander fields for eternity.'

'You have the stomach for delivering punishment, do you?'

'Yes, I do,' I say and he stares at me a while.

I'm not sure what he finds in my eyes but it's enough that he concedes the point and hurries on like he's searching for anything to say. 'You don't even know where to start.'

'Of course I do.' I'm surprised to find I'm telling the truth.

'Are you a fool?' Hades steps forward, anger returning. 'You think usurping my power won't break xenia?'

I laugh and it's like a whip cracking in the air. I think of all those spirits under the control of this man. I can hardly help them if I am too. 'I don't care any more. You wanted me to break xenia? Well, why don't I do you a favour? I revoke my request for safety, for hospitality and hearth.'

His anger falls, knocked off his face by the shock that replaces it. 'You *are* foolish,' he says quietly.

'Go ahead, hurt me,' I say, picking up my blade from the floor and flipping it casually in my hand. 'I would love to see you try.'

I do not run from the room. I walk slowly, giving him every opportunity to change my mind. But change is clearly not something he is interested in.

CHAPTER TWELVE

'**Y**OU REALLY WERE SERIOUS,' Hades says the next day. He's standing in the arched doorway, his aura completely gone, leaning against one side of the door frame. His clothes drape in such a way that I can see the sharp angles of his hip bones and the angular slant of his shoulders. This man is all lines and smooth planes and, again, I find I can't deny there's something about it that draws the eye.

I force myself to focus on his quirked, condescending eyebrow instead, and feel my irritation spike. That is at least the sort of response I can rationalize.

I have no idea what time it is. I don't know how many meals I've missed. Time has seemed to drag while I've been reading these scrolls. I might have worked through the night or I might have skipped a whole day. I'm having to squint through creased eyes, like without sleep they've decided to find their own alternative.

'Of course I was serious,' I say. When I meet his gaze it feels like a challenge and I refuse to break away. I am not quite scared and not quite angry but something very similar to both.

He doesn't make any signs of leaving so I add, 'You won't stop me.'

'Oh, I have no intention of stopping you. They're just humans. You can do what you like.' He shrugs.

Like I need your permission, you insufferable ass.

'Excellent, then we will have no further problems,' I chirp, like nothing he says, no matter how dry and dismissive, can get to me.

He scans the chaos of the room. So many scrolls are rolled to particular paragraphs. Some scrawled scraps of parchment are pinned to them; others litter the floor. I am sprawled on the floor too, in my crinkled dress, despite the library having a sizeable desk. I've never tried to put my own hair up and I was too embarrassed to call for Tempest's help, so I ended up twisting it into a knot round a paintbrush. I must look dreadful.

Hades' eyes linger on a discarded scroll as he weighs up saying something. He's such a hypocrite. I've never seen him at a meal without one of these boring things – if only he cared as much about the humans as he does the words they've written. I can't design an afterlife for the humans if I don't know what they want, and I can't stop the decaying of their souls to ask without draining myself like I did yesterday. So here I am, desperately reading anything I can get my hands on that might offer a glimpse into their minds.

He clearly decides against commenting and says instead, 'You need to eat.'

'I do not,' I reply, turning back to the work at hand.

'Whatever research you've taken it upon yourself to do is hardly going to be optimal if you're weak with hunger.'

'Let me make one thing very clear.' I look up. 'I'm doing this despite you and that means I do not in any way want your opinion – on anything.'

My breath catches as I finish speaking. Talking this way is a thrill that goes beyond saying words I would never utter before my mother. It's the determination that deems them necessary, driven by the first sense of purpose I've had in my entire life. It's the freedom of feeling contempt and showing it, pushing it out into the world instead of somewhere deep inside myself. It's in not having to think first, in letting myself be true – even when that truth is cruel.

Hades listens without moving but when I finish his smirk has deepened and he nods. 'Noted.'

'Then go away.' I can't focus with him here. He's too infuriating. Too distracting.

Hades nods again, that bloody smile still on his lips. 'I see xenia was restricting you substantially. I had no idea politeness could be such an act.'

'Goodbye, Hades.'

'Very well. But, for the record, and I know you don't care for my opinion, I much prefer you without the pretence.'

I scowl at his retreating form long after he's disappeared from view. If Hades prefers me volatile it almost makes me want to be calm.

Food appears not long after he leaves and I'm not sure whether it's a coincidence, Tempest's decision or, scariest of all, something Hades requested.

I glare at the offending fruit. Is it possible he's done something to it, now that he can? It seems too cowardly, poisoned food, especially for a god who fought in the Titan war. And, as he pointed out, killing me would only mean I'd be here to annoy him forever. I take a bite. It's tough and dry and swallowing it hurts but it doesn't taste deadly.

'You revoked xenia?' Styx is back, leaning in the doorway where Hades stood just hours before.

'It doesn't matter,' I say. 'Like you said, they'll find out sooner or later. And I don't want to owe Hades anything when they do.'

She takes in the chaos of the papers. 'So you're going to spend your remaining moments of freedom reading?'

'I'm going to do some good while I can . . . or I'm going to try to at least.'

'And what exactly are you trying?'

I sigh, pushing the pages in front of me away. 'It's so barren out there. The humans are just standing in an empty field for all eternity.'

'It's not empty. It has asphodel now.'

I wave her comment away. 'You know what I mean. And, some of them, they're . . . some of them deserve better and some of them deserve so much worse. I want to give them that.'

'How?' she asks, walking over and crouching before my hastily scrawled notes.

'That's what I'm trying to find out,' I say, pointing to the pages I've written. 'All this research. I need to know how to create more than just flowers. Humans used to be mud before Athena breathed life into them so it can't be hard.'

'Athena is the goddess of wisdom.'

'Yes, which is why I've decided research is the answer. But I don't know where to start. And, even if I did, I need to figure out exactly what I want to create – what sort of thing the humans would want or hate, and how to decide who gets what afterlife. There's so much to organize and so far all I've managed to find is an account of some mortal war in the Peloponnese and a rather fanatical description of every breath Athena has ever taken. It can't be this difficult.'

She turns to me, lips pressed tight like she's reluctant to ask. 'Have you asked Hades about it?'

'He's not going to stand in my way.'

'I meant have you spoken to him? He knows how this realm works so he could probably help with your first dilemma. And, as these scrolls are his, he probably knows where the ones you need are. And, actually, he's probably already read them and could tell you.'

'He's hardly going to help me change his own realm.'

'He might.'

'He's up to something.' What does it matter if she's trustworthy or not? If she's not then she's already told my parents I'm here, which is far worse than anything she could do with me voicing my concerns about Hades. 'He's being nice to me. He sent me fruit.'

She laughs. 'Oh yes, quite the vessel for an ulterior motive.'

'It's not exactly in keeping with the king of Hell.'

'You'll find that not a lot of what he does is,' she says. 'But good luck. I'd help but I'd only slow you down. However, if you need assistance, I know a certain tall, dark and handsome god who knows his way around a library . . .'

'Gods who try to trick me into eternal curses aren't exactly my type.'

'But you admit he's handsome.'

I admit nothing of the sort but the blush that touches my cheeks says otherwise.

'He doesn't care about all this,' I say, getting back to the matter at hand. 'He's said so himself.'

'Hmm, well, come visit me later. You can't spend all your time in here. You need a break. You need your flowers.'

She's right. It takes me another few hours before I give up for the day, having come up with little more than the vaguest outline of what the afterlife might look like and a few suggestions of how I might create it. I stand, stretching as I do. My back aches from spending so long on the floor, but the desk wasn't large enough for all the documents and it made me feel stifled, like I needed more room to think.

Right now I need air, proper air. I've been inside the whole day – I'm not sure I've ever spent so long away from the outside world. I need to feel petals under my fingertips and dirt beneath my toes.

As I start towards the front of the palace, I pull the paintbrush from my hair, my scalp aching. The strands fall in a knotted clump that I relish leaving be instead of running my fingers through to detangle it before Mother gets home. My hair is a mess, my dress is worse, I have creases and bags round my eyes, and my fingernails are gnawed and covered in ink. What a relief it is, to be hideous without consequence.

'Kore,' Hades calls as I reach the entrance hall, his voice bouncing off the marble so that I have no idea where it came from.

I groan, my eyes closing. Maybe if I can't see him he's not really here. I was so close to being out of the building.

I turn and there he is, striding quickly towards me.

'I'd like to show you something,' he says.

A hundred reactions race through my mind, from confusion to annoyance to an odd sort of touched. Settling on long-suffering exasperation, I nod and follow him like a parent whose toddler wishes to show off yet another drawing.

He leads me through a door I'd somehow missed, which reveals stairs that lead to a basement I'm certain doesn't exist in the Olympian palace. It's only when we're halfway down that I realize I didn't just miss the door – it is part of the unexplained room absences.

Do the nymphs have access to these places? And what else is Hades hiding?

'As you noticed earlier, I'm pretty tired, Hades. This had better be worth it.'

Hades doesn't reply.

The steps level out into a dimly lit cavern, smooth marble turning into rough rock. The majority of the space is taken up by a small lake, irregularly shaped, that reaches right up and under the wall opposite. The air feels too close; an acrid smell clings to it that sticks in my throat.

'If you brought me down here to drown me, I'm going to kill you.'

He ignores me. 'This lake is formed of all five rivers of the Underworld.'

'So?' I ask, but even as I stand here my longing to be outside fades, replaced by a desire to step closer to the lake's edge. I step towards the water, my skin prickling in recognition of the magic of our godly powers, and the surface doesn't ripple so much as blur.

'I came here last night,' Hades says and there's something about the way he's looking at me that has me unable to look away. 'I owe you an apology.'

I scoff. 'I don't have time for whatever this is.'

'Just give me one moment. Please.'

I'm so startled by the politeness that I nod without even thinking about it.

'After our discussion I could not stop thinking about what you said – about how I did not understand. I came down here to prove you wrong but . . . well, you're right. I don't. I spend so much time by myself and, whether I like it or not, you're here now. I have no desire to hurt you, which means I couldn't get rid of you even if I wanted to.'

Sure, Hades, I believe you. My fingers inch towards my sickle. If this is all a set-up, I refuse to let him catch me off guard.

Hades hesitates. 'Anyway, I now know why you're here.'

'I've told you.' It's a wonder I can get the words out, my teeth are so tightly gritted.

'Yes, but . . . I had no idea, truly. I believe it would be easier to show you.' He crouches by the water and, before I can say anything about how dangerous a lake made of the rivers of fire and hate and pain and other terrible things must be, he's dipped his hand in. The water twists and swirls like it's weaving together at Arachne's touch and as the threads shake my mother appears.

She holds a golden caduceus in her hands. The winged staff is such a bright gold it practically shines. Two metallic snakes coil round it and she barely looks at it before passing it to my father, who excitedly snatches it from her and examines it closely. I suddenly feel quite nauseous. I'm watching my own auction – the competition for my hand in marriage.

'Hermes,' I say, because who else would offer that gift?

Hades nods solemnly.

And then my sorrow morphs into panic. Hermes ventures into the Underworld sometimes. He might find me. He might use finding me to secure my hand in marriage. And being married to the god of mischief can hardly be a good thing. There are too many stories of his cruel tricks.

'Don't worry,' Hades says softly. 'I have banned him from the realm. I did that the day I sent the court away – when you arrived.'

'What? Why?'

'Because it's barbaric.' Hades shakes his head and looks at the ground. 'Look, I never believed you were really here for the reason you said you were, but on the off chance you were telling the truth . . . I wasn't going to take that risk. I dismissed the court. I told Hermes to return to Olympus until further notice. All that because I knew vaguely how bad it might be, but to see it like this? It's so much worse than I imagined. To hear them discuss you so blatantly –'

'Is it adequate?' a voice interrupts, and I start before realizing it's Hermes in the lake. I glance at him, trying to imagine him as he could be – my husband standing at an altar. He is slight – a thin frame and wispy black hair, freckles scattered across his warm brown skin. But his eyes alarm me – they're alight with excitement, greed and the sort of unhinged euphoria that makes you worry something's on fire.

'I will consider it,' Mother replies coldly and I flinch so hard I actually step back from the pool. But then she turns her shrewd eyes on him and asks, 'Why do you want to marry my daughter, Hermes?'

The god laughs jovially. 'The same reason everyone else does, I imagine. No one has seen her in years. Rumours of her beauty are one thing, but who could resist such a mystery?'

'And when she is no longer a mystery? When she's the wife you come home to every day?'

Hermes blinks. 'What about it?'

'A staff is hardly enough for Kore, is it?' Father declares, throwing the thing aside. 'You've just said what a prize she is – surely you know she's worth more.'

Hermes eyes him warily. 'Like what?'

'Oh, I don't know. Secrets. Promises. Something to make your offer worth my time.' Father manages to show all his teeth as he leers from his throne. 'You're smart, my son.' I recoil at the reminder that Hermes is, technically, my half-brother and Hades jolts too, his lip curling. 'I'm sure you'll think of something that will sway me towards giving her to you.'

Hades lunges towards the water and with a brush of the surface it all disappears. He's muttering a string of angry curses at my father.

I feel like an incredibly heavy stone just settled into my stomach. And I very deeply resent feeling this vulnerable in front of Hades.

'It's a vile practice,' he declares. 'If it were to happen to any of the goddesses of the Underworld I would be outraged. As I say, I understand why you're here. Truly this time.'

If I don't lash out I'll cry. 'I told you all of this,' I snarl and he startles like my anger is the last thing he expected. 'I've told you so many times. One of the first things I said to you was that I don't want to get married. And your big revelation is that I don't want this? That I object to the fact I'm being bartered like a piece of meat?'

Hades stares at me, blinking like all of this is a surprise. Like he thought I'd be overcome with gratitude and he can't understand what I'm doing.

'Well, yes,' he says. 'But it's different to actually see it.'

'You could actually see it before now,' I snap. 'Wasn't there enough evidence in the fact I ran to a man I'd never met because the thought of getting married was so horrific? You're apologizing for not believing me while still saying you don't believe *me*. You believe *yourself* and what you've seen. And you thought you had to show me that horrific auction to do what, exactly? To prove you believe me now?' His face falls as I rant but it only spurs me on. Good. He should be miserable. He should be grovelling. 'Did you even think about how upsetting that would be for me to see, or were you just too focused on proving whatever damn point you're trying to make? Why should I care whether you believe me or not?'

'Because you're running around my halls with a blade. You think I'm like them,' he says. 'And I'd do anything to show you I'm not – not for my own sake but because you deserve to feel safe here.'

'Great job of that.'

'You're right,' he says. 'And I'm sorry. I apologize for not believing you and I apologize for believing this over you. And I should have . . . prefaced what I was showing you. I'm sorry.'

'What's your play here?' I demand.

'Excuse me?'

'What is it you want from me? One moment you're trying

to trick me into breaking xenia and the next you're . . . doing all this.' I wave my hand vaguely. I'm so confused I can't even put what's happening into words.

He frowns. 'That's what I'm apologizing for. Trying to trick you was an adolescent move. I wanted to be alone, which was selfish. I thought no situation could be so bad that you'd come here willingly, so you must be here for something else. But obviously it very much is that bad and I'm sorry.'

'Do you realize how stupid I would have to be to believe you?'

Hades nods. 'Which is why you don't have to.'

Before I can query this notion he's rushing to speak again.

'You cancelled xenia. Fine, so be it. But I won't have you living under my roof with a weapon strapped in constant reach because you feel so thoroughly under threat.' He swallows and glances to the lake. 'I'm not like them and I don't want you to believe I'd hurt you. I certainly don't want you fearing it. So I swear on the Styx not to harm you. I swear not to force myself on you nor to turn you over to your mother.'

I step back, the rock wall scraping against my hands. My heart is racing, the urge to flee pressing on me harder with each passing second. I don't understand why he's doing this and that's terrifying.

'What are you doing?' My voice is scarcely more than a whisper.

'Something I should have done the moment you arrived.'

Breaking xenia is a curse. Breaking an oath sworn on the river Styx? There's a reason Styx is called the oath keeper – a promise on her waters is binding. Breaking that is something we don't even have a word for. Something beyond damnation.

'Is there anything else I have missed? Anything else you fear?' he asks.

Maybe he's lying but I manage to churn through the words of his oath anyway. 'You will not turn me over to *anyone*,' I correct.

He swears it.

'I still don't understand why you're doing this.'

'Why would you?' Hades laughs like everything up to this moment has been some joke between us. Like just yesterday he wasn't screaming at me while I pressed a weapon to his skin. 'You don't have to like me, Kore, but I'd really prefer you weren't afraid of me.'

I bite my lip, feeling so fragile that it's all I can do not to bolt up the stairs. I need to sort through my thoughts alone. I can't talk to him until I get them straight or his words will run circles round me just like my mother's do.

'How many men so far?' I ask and at his frown I add, 'My parents. How many men have they spoken to?'

Hades' eyes fill with a look of such sympathy that I want to hit him. 'Thirteen,' he says. 'Four of the twelve, even.'

I didn't think it was possible to feel more afraid. But I'd never seriously considered that any member of Zeus's council would vie for my hand. They're the most powerful gods and my father's advisors – there's no way my mother will be able to choose who I marry if they're in the running. The only hope I had left was that my mother would at least pick someone kind, but Father won't only choose someone to spite me, he'll choose someone forever in his pocket, who will do anything he asks of them.

'How is that possible?' I mutter, breathless. 'Only three are unwed.'

'Hephaestus has offered to divorce Aphrodite for your hand.'

I almost choke.

'What?' I splutter. This just gets worse.

'He offered a necklace made in his forge.'

'No, no, no.' I bury my head in my hands. 'I can't add Aphrodite as an enemy, what with everything else.'

Hades smiles apologetically. 'Then you won't want to hear that Ares, too, promised to stop sleeping with her in order to marry you? He offered a spear and his breastplate.'

I had thought men the threat, but Aphrodite is one of the most vengeful goddesses out there. Only Hera is worse and, given I'm her husband's bastard, she already hates me.

I swear and Hades chuckles.

'I'm glad this is all so amusing to you,' I spit.

'No, I didn't mean it like that,' he hurries to clarify. 'I'm just . . . amused at how chaotic this is getting.'

I shake my head. The world just became even more terrifying. 'I'm never leaving here.'

'Very well,' Hades says and I'd roll my eyes if it weren't beyond that level of ridiculous. Just yesterday he was trying to trick me into leaving and now he's swearing oaths on the Styx. It's a ploy. It must be. He must have left a loophole in the oath that I can't spot. He must be getting me to lower my guard so that he can hurt me.

'And Apollo, I'm assuming?' I have to know what I'm up against.

'He's offered his prized lyre,' Hades says.

'The one Hermes gave him?'

Hades nods.

'The bastard thinks he can regift something for my hand in marriage?'

Hades laughs properly and, after a moment, I smile too. This whole thing is sort of ridiculous. It's just far more horrifying than it is amusing. Besides, I'm seconds away from bursting into tears. I'd jump into the Phlegethon, the river of fire, before letting Hades see that.

That must be what he's doing, showing me all this so that he can evaluate my response. It's what I would do.

I force a smile. If this is some strategy of his then I'm not going to let him think it's working. 'Apollo, Ares, Hermes and Hephaestus? Tell me, is anyone who isn't my half-brother trying to marry me?'

'You know the gods don't see it that way,' Hades says.

'The nymphs do,' I say, almost too quietly for him to hear. But it's true. I was raised with so many that, no matter how many loopholes the gods concoct, I'm revolted.

'Zeus was in different forms each time. Genetically, you are all different.'

'It's still disgusting.'

'I agree,' he says, then he hesitates with such a meaningful look I'm sure this is the real reason he brought me down here. 'May I ask – and I mean no offence – why you do not just refuse to get married? Your parents could not force you.'

I stare at him, trying to work out if he's joking or not. Has he not heard a single story of what happens on the surface? My father is the king of the gods. If he told me to jump off a cliff I'd run straight off it. The alternatives are too horrific to consider. He'd chain me to a rock for a sea monster. He'd turn me into an animal or shoot me with an arrow for my hubris, maybe make me fall in love with a beast. Gods have done all these things before.

Horrible things happen to girls who say no to my father.

Hades continues to watch me, eyes all innocent like he just wants to understand.

Either he's a manipulator who can drown himself in the River Styx for all I care, or he really doesn't know and I'm not going to be the one to tell him how the world works.

'You've never even spoken to a single human down here, have you?' I say. If he had, if he'd experienced even an ounce of the misery in that field, he'd understand.

'No,' he says, voice distant.

Well, I'm not explaining it then. 'I need a nap,' I say instead.

His face falls but after a moment he bites his lip and nods. 'Very well.'

I wonder what's really happened to him – and, more importantly, what he's going to do next.

CHAPTER THIRTEEN

COLLAPSE INTO SLEEP THE MOMENT I reach my bed,
dropping like a stone to the bottom of the ocean.

I dream of my mother.

It is a memory, actually. I am young, maybe just a year
or two past my amphidromia. Mother is bandaging my
arm, wrapping linen round it so tightly that I am scared to
breathe in case the movement breaks her concentration and
angers her.

'You have got to be more careful. I've never known anything
like this,' she tuts. 'You're a goddess – how uncoordinated do
you have to be to break a bone?'

'It was an accident,' I protest but my eyes burn, tears
threatening to leak not only from pain but also indignation at
being scolded when I am hurt and confusion at clearly having
done something wrong without knowing what. I do so many
things to make Mother happy. How have I failed without even
noticing?

'One waiting to happen when you rush about like that. You
can't keep doing things like this, Kore. You're becoming a

young woman – you need to start behaving like one. No more racing the nymphs.'

I blink, trying to puzzle it out. Finally I ask, 'But why?'

'Why what?'

'Why can't I race the nymphs? It's fun.'

'I should think why would be quite clear enough,' she says as she ties the final bandage, a slight smile on her face. I relax a little but then her smile falls. She pushes her shoulders back and looks me right in the eye. 'Those sorts of things are all well and good when you're a child but you're not any more. Running around the island, cartwheeling in the grass – it's not appropriate now. They'll think you a wild nymph, not a respectable goddess. They're already telling stories of your grace on Olympus. Don't you want that? To be a mature, elegant young lady? Don't you want to make me proud?'

I know the correct answer and I'm nodding before she's even finished talking, but something inside me is withering like a flower thrust into the shade.

'Good girl,' she says, kissing my forehead and patting my shoulder affectionately. 'I love you so much, Kore.'

And I feel it, that glow of her approval. But, when I go to bed that night, my pillow is wet with tears – and I'm not sure why they are falling.

I wake to damp linen on my cheek. Blinking back sleep, I feel the bafflement I did as a child. It always felt like the rules were shifting. I could never predict what wouldn't be allowed until I got into trouble for it. Eventually it just felt like anything that brought me joy was wrong.

I love my mother. All she's ever done is protect me.

But there must be a reason I'm thinking about her so much – and why every thought fills me with such fear. What I wouldn't do to talk to Cyane about all this. Though I know what she would say: 'Your mother loves you and that means wanting what's best for you.' That is always Cyane's answer: 'She loves you, she loves you, she loves you.'

But can you really love someone when you're trying to change everything about them?

Guilt takes over. How could I even suggest there are faults with my mother's love after watching her with Hermes? She's fighting my father to buy me some small measure of protection. I should be thankful for everything she's done for me – her whole life on an island to keep me from the Olympians, all the sacrifices she's made . . .

I throw the blankets aside and push my sticky hair from my face.

This is all Hades' fault. He probably wanted me to have exactly this sort of emotional breakdown by showing me what he showed me. And what have I discovered, exactly? I already had the outline; he's just given the picture some detail.

There are more pressing things that need my attention.

Hades is in the library reading my notes so intently that he doesn't even notice when I walk in.

'What are you doing?' I demand.

He starts, properly jumping back, and his aura flickers along his skin before disappearing again. For a moment I'm frozen. Either he's a better actor than I've given him credit for or his reaction was authentic, and more disarming than anything he's done so far.

'Sorry,' he says. It seems less a genuine apology and more a reflex, which surprises me from a man who wears a crown. Then that cocky smile returns to his face and he leans back in the desk chair with all the confidence of a man who owns a realm. Which he does, obviously, but I still don't like it. 'As I said yesterday, I'm not going to try to stop you.'

'You couldn't if you tried.'

'Yes, yes, you quite made that point. And I may not care about the humans but I do care about my libraries. This place is a mess but it's nothing compared to these notes.'

'Excuse me?'

'You're excused – you just have much to learn.'

'I –'

'Don't have time to learn? Yes, you've also made your intent to rush this clear. So I've decided to help you.'

'I don't need your damn help,' I snap, finally managing to get a word in.

'Yes, Kore, yes you do.' And he looks . . . disappointed, which is the last thing I thought I'd see when he looked at me.

'You've had this realm for years and done nothing with it. Now you want to help?'

'I told you: I don't care about the realm; I care about my scrolls. So I'll take notes for you and keep this place tidy as you're obviously incapable of keeping anything in order yourself.'

'Why would I trust you to do that?'

'I don't care if you trust me. Watch over my shoulder the whole time for all I care. But look, Kore.' He jabs a finger at a scroll. 'You've ripped this one, and this one has ink on it. It's a good thing you revoked xenia because you would have broken it with this.'

I'm suddenly aware that I'm staring at him, and I scramble for a response to this absolute madness – what sort of tactic is this? 'I don't think xenia was created with slightly marked parchment in mind.'

'Well, if it doesn't take that into consideration then the entire concept has gone down in my estimation. So, come on, tell me what to do and I'll do it. Just stop hurting my books.'

I consider this. It's probable he's here to spy on what I'm doing. But I don't particularly care. I'm not keeping my plans a secret; I'm flaunting them in his face and saying he can't stop me at every opportunity.

Of course it's also possible he's telling the truth, and he does want to help, and he really does just love his scrolls. It's unlikely, but I glance away, a warm feeling fluttering in my stomach. I do not have the time to explore why the thought of this man, a god of a literal realm, caring so much about a library is appealing to me. I have bigger problems. Problems so large that my warm feeling turns to nausea. It's at least safe to look up again.

'Well, I'm not using the books today anyway,' I say. 'We don't have time. Something needs to happen now.'

I realize as I turn from him that I said *we* and I really, really hope Hades wasn't paying attention.

'What?' Hades is chasing after me like this isn't his realm. A smile twitches its way on to my lips.

'Not the whole thing, obviously,' I say. 'But for now I need to get victims away from their oppressors.'

'I'm not sure all of humanity can be easily sorted into victim or oppressor,' he comments dryly.

'No, obviously not.'

I swing the palace's front door open but before I can leave Hades is pushing it closed again, leaning against it with his arms crossed. He's so close to me that I have to make a conscious effort not to jump back. I wonder if he knows how intimidating this is and then almost slap myself because of course he does.

Well, I won't let him push me back.

'Do you even realize how audacious it is to march into another god's realm and change things without so much as consulting them?' His eyebrow is quirked and his smile is so patronizing that my retort flees from my mind as I concentrate on not slapping it off his damn face.

Condescending git.

'Yes, I do. Next question?'

His other eyebrow joins the first, both shooting towards his hairline. He laughs uncertainly and I take a moment to relish the fact that that's the only laugh I seem to hear from him. I've considered myself a lot of things. *Pretty. Obedient. Demure. Unsettling* might just be my favourite.

'You've never been one for politeness but this is an excessive lack of it, even for you,' he says.

'Ah, so despite me yelling that I was going to do all this, me actually doing it without talking to you bypasses some baseline of respect you thought you were owed. Is that it?' I ask. The energy has shifted almost imperceptibly. It feels . . . taut. I want him to push back, want to rile him up, want to win. There's something almost electric in how close he is, all that tension directed my way. Like I'm playing with fire.

'I believe being informed of your proposed changes to my realm would be the bare minimum, yes.' Oh, his tone has managed to reach a level of condescension that surpasses the one achieved by his smile. A milestone.

'Well, let me clear that up for you. I don't respect you, Hades. In any way, at all. So I don't care to pay you even that modicum of respect. Now will you please get out of my way?'

He chuckles like he's enjoying this. 'Have you actually thought this through? How exactly are you going to separate the thousands of complex humans that live in my domain into only two categories? Humans hardly exist in a binary.'

I swear, if he talks down to me one more time I'm going to throw him in Tartarus, the deepest, darkest pit in Hell.

'I'm going to use fear as a mediating and, most importantly, traceable factor to separate those who trigger it from those who feel it. It's a temporary solution to get those souls who are reduced to a state of pure terror somewhere safe while I work out a more permanent arrangement.'

Hades blinks and something crosses his face. He seems to remember himself, to remember that he's not supposed to be trying to annoy me any more, that he wants some sort of civility between us. A laughable concept, really, as we've just proved, but if he wants to start grovelling to get us on to somewhat decent terms, I'm definitely not going to say no.

'Any more questions?' I ask with a saccharine smile, trying to bring his infuriating smugness back. It's so much easier to deal with than whatever he was trying to do when he was offering help earlier.

'Why? Why do you want to do this?'

'Because people are suffering and, unlike you, I care.'

'Kore,' he says. This time his voice is soft and the gentility is worse than the condescension.

'Stop calling me that,' I snap. It's not the real issue, I know that, but it's what comes out of my mouth anyway.

'What?' He frowns. 'It's your name.'

'Only technically,' I say. 'Now get out of my way.'

'Will you just wait one moment, please?'

'Have I not waited enough moments, Hades?'

He takes a breath. 'Look, I didn't mean for things to get out of hand like that. I just have some questions – I really do want to help.'

'I can answer them afterwards.'

'It will take you hours to reach them using this door. There's a quicker way,' he says.

That makes me stop. I'm suspicious but nothing in his face is a tell and the promise of saved time is too tempting to dismiss.

'Two minutes,' Hades says. 'And then I'll take you to the other exits.'

'How is it possible to have doors that shorten distances?'

Hades shrugs and his lips twitch with a smile. 'It's my realm. The laws of physics do whatever I want them to.'

'Fine, two minutes,' I reluctantly agree.

Hades gestures to a side room. This place has so many needless rooms. It's one of the Olympian duplicates that seems to exist only to fill space: a few chairs, a few tapestries, a few holes in the walls for scrolls to sit. Incense burns in a holder and I gag on the sickly sweet scent of it.

Hades' nose wrinkles and I get the feeling he regrets choosing this room, but he's either too awkward to suggest moving or he doesn't want to risk my ire.

'Listen,' he says, ducking his head. 'I wasn't entirely honest earlier.'

'I'm shocked.'

'I do care about the humans – or I did. When I got here, I tried to do things for them but their spirits decayed so quickly that nothing I tried worked. I put my energy into making this place better for the gods of the court instead. But if you see an opportunity then I want to help you. On top of that, as *you* keep saying, you don't exactly have the time to do this alone. Days, at most. You will need all the power and help you can get.'

I think of what Styx said, about how Hades must know a thing or two about this realm, and I hate that she's right. Of course she is. It's his world to command, no matter how little he deserves it. One or two pages of reading is hardly going to give me the expertise he has. Besides, what's the worst he could do? Lie about what he's found out? Fact-checking his research would still be quicker than trying to do it all myself.

'Fine. Help me if you want to. Can we go now?'

'No. Because you haven't told me why you're doing this.'

'For the sake of the Styx.' A weird phrase, actually, now that I know her. 'Is this the new "why are you here"? How many times must I tell you I'm doing this to help people who are suffering before you'll believe me?'

'I do believe you – but, like with "why are you here", I think there's more to it. You didn't come here begging for my help to escape a marriage at first – you came here offering me an opportunity to spite Zeus.'

'Yes, because I thought it might convince you to help me. But *I'm* not here to spite Zeus.'

'Aren't you? Just a little bit?'

I freeze.

'It might not be precisely why you came here. But I've seen you – the real you, hiding behind that ridiculous facade – so don't tell me a part of you doesn't love the fact that he'll be furious about his plans being foiled.'

The worst part isn't that he's right but the fact he says it all so confidently, with a hint of admiration.

Despite a thousand lies, I've been seen. And I don't like it.

'Power,' I say, which is part confession, part a need to see how he reacts. 'I'm doing this for power.'

He doesn't so much as bat an eyelid. 'Mine?'

'Of course not. What would I want that for? So that I can hide out in this house and ignore the rest of the world like you do? No, the other gods of Olympus control everything under the sun – including the actual bloody sun – but what do they care about?'

Hades snorts. 'Sex?'

'Pretty much actually, yeah,' I agree, to his surprise. 'Who's having sex with who is their be-all and end-all. And sure they're interested in which gods are getting together or which nymph they're all fawning over – but honestly that's old news, because right now they're obsessed with humans. It's like they're using the humans to further their own legacies. Cyrene, Europa, Alcmene – these mortals they're chasing are founding cities, and their offspring are heroes. The gods are utterly besotted. Humans are their route to power and they want to know who they can seduce or favour, make a hero or a king, use to destroy cities or found new ones in their names. Humans are everything to them.'

'Yes, and sometimes they just want a mortal plaything to

make their immortal lives more interesting,' Hades says, lips twisting with disgust. 'You aren't wrong but what exactly does this have to do with my realm?'

'I'm getting to that. The humans worship the gods and imitate them, copy all their worst behaviour because if their idols are doing it then why shouldn't they? They end up hurting each other more than the gods do. But if we show them that there are eternal consequences for those actions then they might change. If the good are rewarded and the bad are punished then maybe they'll stop hurting each other quite so much. And if the humans are too scared of eternal punishment in the afterlife to kill and rape and cause such pain, then why would they worship gods who regularly do all these things? Maybe they'll stop caring for gods that play so recklessly with their lives.'

'The gods will have to change if they still want to be worshipped,' Hades realizes. 'Which they will, because they're gods.'

I nod. 'Exactly. What's a god without followers? I'm doing this to help the humans, but taking away the power of the gods? Forcing Olympus and Oceanus to be better? Well, it's some extra motivation to make it work.'

I'm not sure I explained that well enough, and I hold my breath waiting for his reaction. I'm not sure why it matters so much to me but it does.

His forehead creases as he thinks and I can almost see each thought land. After a second he looks at me in a way that makes me squirm. He's seeing me again. No pretence, no bitten tongue and no fear of consequence. Maybe that's why every millisecond without an answer hurts.

'It's brilliant. It's genius,' he says. When he looks at me, it's with something close to awe. And when he smiles I find myself mirroring him.

'So you're in?'

'I'm in.' He stands and offers me his hand. 'Let's go divide the realm.'

CHAPTER FOURTEEN

I T DOESN'T WORK.

Which shouldn't be a surprise, but it hurts anyway.

I don't think I'd ever *really* believed I would be able to split the Underworld in half, but I had definitely been hoping. And now that hope comes crashing down.

I crouch on a ledge overlooking the humans and bury my fingers in the dirt. I can feel it, the realm pulsing beneath my fingertips. It's so similar to the connection I feel with the flowers that, overconfident, I urge the whole thing to just 'move'.

All I get are tremors.

'Well, that's new,' Hades says as the ground shakes beneath us.

I grit my teeth. It's one thing to fail, another to fail while he stands there.

I close my eyes and try again. This time a crack runs towards the souls, a couple inches deep at most. Nowhere near deep enough to be of use.

I stumble back, gasping for breath. A strange sort of tiredness washes over me, like I've run the length of my island and collapsed on the sands at the furthest edge. It's a weariness so strong I can hardly lift my heavy limbs twinned with a heady exhilaration that leaves me breathless.

'What are you doing?' Styx stage-whispers behind us.

'She's taken an interest in the humans,' Hades says. I try to ignore them and concentrate. Whatever grip I had on the realm has slipped and I'm desperate to find it again. 'And she has decided to divide the Underworld in two.'

'She can do that?'

'That remains to be seen,' he says. 'But she's made an impressive start for a goddess of flowers.' From the corner of my eye, I see Hades gesture towards the crevice.

I shut my eyes, trying to focus on the land before me, but the disbelief in Styx's voice pushes through. 'I don't think flowers should be able to do that,' she says. 'Kore, love, are you all right?'

'Don't call her that,' Hades says quietly but I still catch it.

'Love?'

'Kore. She doesn't like that name.'

Styx snorts. 'Fair enough. Who would?'

'Urgh.' I stand, dusting the dirt from my hands, and face Hades. 'It's not working.' It pains me to even ask but this is too important. And it's his realm, after all. 'Can you try?'

Hades gives a doubtful glance at the rift I've created.

'Ha, I knew you'd convince him to help you. How did you do it?' Styx asks.

'I damaged his scrolls, apparently.'

'She did. I'm still furious,' he says, pacing along the cliff edge and examining the world below.

'Ah.' Styx nods. 'I understand.'

'You do?'

'Well, no,' she says. 'He is weirdly anal about his scrolls –'

'May I remind you that I am literally your king.'

'Sorry, *his maj* is weirdly anal about his scrolls –'

'I hate you.'

'No, you don't. Goddess of hate here – I'd be able to tell.'

I realize with a start that I'm smiling. Have I given a real smile down here? I must have – but perhaps not this easily.

'Are all your subjects like this?' I ask.

'No,' he says firmly.

'All his other subjects fear that terrifying reputation of his,' Styx explains. 'But Hades gets his servants to swear his secrets on my waters. I get all the juicy tidbits and don't believe that reputation for a second.'

'Which Styx takes to mean she owes me no respect whatsoever,' Hades says. 'Never mind that I'm still her king.'

'You may be *my* king but I'm *your* closest friend.'

'Knowing someone's secrets isn't the same as friendship.'

'Do you have anything better?' Styx asks.

'I fought alongside half the court. They're my comrades in arms.'

'So that's a no then.'

Hades glares at her. It's rather easy to listen to their back and forth while I'm too worn to contribute much myself, but now I grin and ask, 'So what secrets are we talking about?'

'You will never know,' Hades says curtly. 'Weren't we discussing tearing my world apart?'

'Swerve,' Styx coughs.

'Can you try to create a divide?' I ask Hades. 'You're right – the goddess of flowers really can't do this.'

Gods can do some limited things outside their areas of expertise: turn mortals into plants, curse cities or even twist their own forms into other shapes – though I've never had much luck with that. But this is too big, too expansive. It needs the connection to the land that comes only from a specific godhood. It needs Hades.

'Well, you've done more than I imagine I can,' Hades says.

'Oh come on, I'm not going to beg.'

'I wouldn't expect you to. I'm just not sure I can help.'

'You literally said this is your world and you can manipulate the laws of physics if you want to.'

Styx cackles. 'He said what?' Hades glares at her but she just howls louder, doubling over with her hysteria. 'Somebody's mighty full of themselves. Or are you just bragging in an effort to impress –'

'That's enough.'

Styx lowers her voice into an awful impression of Hades. 'I'm the king of Hell and I control physics now. It's not a whole realm full of gods who make it run. Nope, I do it all myself because I'm the king and I have a big crown that doesn't fit on my big head.'

'He said he could shorten distances,' I say.

'Oh, you mean those magical doors that Hermes, god of travel, installed?'

I turn to Hades and he just shrugs. 'I didn't have time for the full explanation – you were running out of the front door.'

'So what can you do?' I ask. 'Other than your little smoke hands?'

Styx doubles over again, clapping her hands over her mouth.

'I can certainly try to help you,' Hades says, in what I can only assume is an effort to change the subject before Styx gets her breath back. 'But I don't think I can split a realm by myself.'

'Would you care for my assistance, my king?' Styx manages. 'I am but a lowly goddess of a river that runs through a realm controlled by a mighty and all-powerful being but –'

'Okay, you've quite made your point. Will you do me the honour of assisting us with this?' he asks.

'The honour is mine, my liege.'

'You can stop it now.'

'Oh, I absolutely will not.' She winks at me and I feel guilty at my startled laugh. We're here to help trapped and terrified souls – it doesn't feel right to be having fun while we're doing it.

'Can we just do this, please?' I ask. I'm not sure I have the strength to remain standing much longer, let alone exert some godly force over this realm.

'It will be difficult,' Hades says. 'Impossible, even. I do not say this to offend, but your impetuous manner may be better re-placed with patience. The rift you've made is incredible but even the strongest gods would struggle to do more in a single day.'

'We need to at least try,' I insist.

'All right.' He nods, meeting my eyes in what I can only take as an effort to be sincere. 'Tell us what you found – and how you did what you've done so far.'

I feel foolish saying it out loud, making clear how little I garnered from research before my impulsiveness took over. 'Not much. I just read something about Athena creating an olive tree for Athens – it was less about creating the tree and more about finding a link to her own domain: intelligence. The tree was a clever thing. She created something they could use – a plant that makes oil they can burn in lamps, use in ceremonies, make into soaps and perfumes, even eat. You need to link whatever you're trying to do to your own domain. So I guess this one is easy for you, Hades. Styx, maybe think about diverting a stream from your river to run between the two halves? I was thinking of flowers, imagining their roots stretching down, and then I felt something else. It's hard to explain.'

'No, that makes perfect sense,' Hades says.

'Your flowers must be pretty powerful,' Styx says, casting a sceptical glance at the rift.

'Not powerful enough,' I say. 'Come on.'

I crouch to the ground, burying my hand in the dirt again to better connect myself to the roots. Hades stays standing, shadows shivering along his arms, then stretching out and fading into the air of the realm like he's merging with it. Styx heads to her river a few metres away and slips her hand into its waters.

I close my eyes, trusting the others to do the same.

My flowers have spread this far so connecting to them is easy. Their thin, fragile stems flutter against the edges of my mind, and their fragrant scent floods my senses. I push past them to the roots and the mud and the earth beneath. And then I search further, past the nutrients they need until the flowers stop being relevant altogether. Dry dirt and acidic sting and there – I feel it, the pulse of this land that first begged me to fill it with flowers.

I latch on to it before the feeling can escape.

'I can't do it.'

I hear the voice distantly. It must be Styx. I can feel the land stretching round her river, and it's more than just the land – it's the realm. I can feel her river too and the air crackling round Hades as he pushes against it.

I hear whispers that swell and rise into a crescendo – the souls, the humans. Which means . . . yes, there – the rift I created. Petty, inconsequential, hardly deeper than ink on parchment.

'I'm not feeling whatever it was you described,' Hades says. His breath floats on the air, the sound of his voice surrounding me, every vibration dancing on my skin.

A spark, two flickering flares, one near and one further, tangible and enticing, like I might burn myself if I get too close. I reach out and grasp them both anyway.

Power – their power – arches through me like my father's lightning and before I can get lost in the swirl of this world I reach for the rift and I tear it apart. Styx gasps and I take her river and I push it forward. It floods in, filling the rift separating the two lands.

'Stop,' Hades gasps, his hand on my shoulder, but I'm too aware of too many things and my body hardly registers him.

I reach towards the whispering souls and I search for their fear. The moment I hear a single fearful voice it starts screaming – not out loud, but in my head – until their fear is all I am aware of. The souls that are screaming are so easy to find among the others. I flick my wrist and in one fathomless leap they fly across to the other side of the river.

My body shudders and I feel my own tiredness like an echo.

I wrench my hand from the earth and cut off my connection to the realm. My own senses collide and I am on the ground with Hades above me. My head is pounding, my lungs ache, and I've never felt better in my life. I feel like I could do anything, even as I struggle to my feet.

Hades grasps my arm and I jolt as a flare reignites. I recognize it as him – I felt him and his energy. I used his own power to rip his world apart. He looks exhausted but still he helps me up, then he lets go of me like it's an afterthought.

'What just happened?' Styx asks, staggering back to us. Then she sees the land beneath and gasps. 'It worked?'

'Apparently,' Hades says, eyeing me warily.

'Thank you,' I say, my tongue clumsy and heavy in my mouth. My words slur. 'For sharing your power. I couldn't have done that without you both.

Hades and Styx exchange a look I can't read. 'You collapsed,' he says. 'You weren't moving.'

'I was focused. It's fine,' I say. With every second, my tiredness ebbs away.

'I've never felt anything like that.' Styx shakes her head.

'I think you were right,' I say to Hades. 'We were stupid to try to do it all in one day but we got it done, didn't we?'

We did. I stare at my work, the rift between the humans.

It's such a tiny thing. The human souls are still decayed remnants of thought, and the Underworld is largely unaffected – just this tiny part where humans linger split in two. But it's important. Already their fear is fading. It's not disappearing entirely, but they're no longer afraid of running into those who caused them such terror. A tiny thing, yes, but important. The first important thing I've ever done.

If my father snatches me away now, at least it will have been worth it. And he would be so angry, more furious than I can even imagine, because he'd have to admit that, despite all his efforts, he could not contain me.

Who's your little girl now?

I'm done. I'm not answering to that bloody name any more.

'Styx, you heard that too, right?' Hades asks. His jovial tone sounds forced. 'She said I was right?'

'I heard it.'

'I can admit when you make a valid point,' I say. 'You simply make them far too rarely.'

'I'm going to go lie down for a few hours,' Styx says. 'I need a very, *very* long nap.'

She practically falls into her river, the current now forking into two separate streams that reunite on the other side of the humans.

'Come on,' I say to Hades. 'This is just the start. I need to get back to the library and work out what to actually do with this space.'

'You can't be serious,' Hades says. 'Whatever we just did exhausted me.' He raises his hands to show the sputtering smoke he wields. It barely clings to him before vanishing entirely. 'Don't you need to rest?'

I did, but not any more. I can still feel that whisper of the world against my ear. I feel eternal.

'Not really, no.'

Hades sighs. 'Very well. I suppose I won't be resting then either, not if my library is under your attack.'

I'm still not sure I trust him to help, but, after all that, the thought of being trapped in a library with him feels a far simpler matter.

CHAPTER FIFTEEN

DAYS SPENT IN THE LIBRARY crawl by. The exhilaration of rending land apart powers me through only a few hours of research. Soon counting the bricks of the fireplace is more appealing – ninety-six, I establish on my third day surrounded by these shelves.

Hades doesn't talk much. He just sits there, dutifully reading whatever I hand him, taking notes to condense it all for me, never giving anything else away.

I'm never there alone. If I'm in the library, he is too.

He must really love those scrolls.

Admittedly, he's not as frustrating as he could be. I might even venture so far as to say he's rather helpful. He reads scrolls quicker than I do and makes neat notes in summary. After I check the first twenty for lies and they come back clean I decide to just spot-check.

When Hades notices, he smiles in a way that feels decidedly intimate. His eyes glint with amusement and his lips are pressed in so thin a line it's like he's suppressing the smirk. 'Why, does this suggest a semblance of trust?'

'Be quiet,' I tell him, shuffling my papers like I'm trying to concentrate and not struggling to think of an appropriately sassy response.

His notes find their way pinned to my own scrolls, his writing all bold lines and swift marks. I find myself watching him write them more than once. I've only ever been frustrated by his reading – because it was previously done to ignore me – but now his concentration is like gravity, drawing me in.

The texts are boring. It's the only excuse I'm willing to give for why I'm so easily distracted, for why staring at Hades might be at all preferable. Right now I'm reading an unbearable description of triremes – and I'm yet to find any indication of whether such boats exist out of necessity or if the mortals actually like them and might want some in their afterlife. And, if so, do they want to build them or row them or see them on the edges of an ocean? Why don't they make all this clear in the stories they write?

Hades is not particularly interesting, but he's more interesting than this.

And his presence feels like an itch.

Maybe working out why Hades is so committed to this research is all that's distracting me. Maybe it has nothing to do with the way he bites the edge of his quill when he's concentrating.

Or maybe being stuck in this tiny room with him for hours at a time is wearing away at my sanity.

A few days later, Hades unearths a diary from a human. It's a treasure trove of hopes and dreams and fears, and we're so excited it pushes everything else out. We're still poring over it at dinner.

'Where do you even get all these?' I ask, putting the final page down.

'Hermes brings them.'

The messenger of the gods is also the god of thieves and I have no doubt that some of the texts – especially the diary of the scholar we've been studying – are stolen.

'Does Hermes hate you?'

Hades laughs. 'Possibly. But as far as the scrolls are concerned he knows I like to read.'

What does that even mean? Reading is something you just do, not a hobby like music or weaving. 'You enjoy those documents?'

Hades shrugs. 'Well, I'd prefer to read poetry but they're okay, definitely interesting. You don't enjoy them?'

'No, I don't.'

'You could just leave it to me then. I can do the research and you can talk to the humans.'

No. I can't face that tiredness again, can't risk restoring the humans in order to talk to them. Splitting the Underworld was incredible, a high I never thought I'd achieve – what if that's where it ends? What if I go and I try and nothing works? I'm not ready for my new-found confidence to come crashing down.

So instead I give a withering look that I think I might have learnt from him. 'No, I don't think I'll be doing that.'

'Your trust is a fickle thing.'

'Earn it and we'll talk.'

Hades laughs and for once it's a genuine, true laugh. The sound sends a shiver down my spine.

'You wound me,' he says, hand to his heart like he's been shot.

'Good.' I grin.

Hades nods at my smile. 'That's unnerving.'

I grin even wider because there it is again, me unnerving him. 'Did they kick you all the way down here because you're a sarcastic phallus?'

'Interesting. Is this what your mother meant when she told your suitors you have a beautiful command of language?' he asks.

I snort. 'Oh, I'm sure that's code for me knowing a few poems and, more importantly, knowing when to keep my mouth shut.'

'Keeping your mouth shut? Really?' He feigns surprise.

I snatch one of the grapes from the table and throw it at him. 'Arse,' I say decidedly.

'Appalling aim.' He laughs as it bounces off the table. 'Let's hope your mother isn't off bragging about your skill in grape throwing. You'll have the suitors even more devastated when they discover you've taken yourself off the market.'

'I think only Dionysus will be upset that I can't bolster his god of wine status,' I say with a calm smile that betrays none of my panic. Throwing grapes, insulting Hades, chatting with Styx – I've become too comfortable in the Underworld.

I've had longer than I thought – too long. I'm relaxing when I should be all the more terrified. The only thing that could delay them like this is a deluge of offers for my hand – potentially the sort of offer that might sway my father beyond my mother's reach. And even if every god of Olympus wants to marry me, they can't be bartering much longer. My parents will find out I'm missing any moment now.

And it's going to ruin everything.

CHAPTER SIXTEEN

EMPEST APPEARS IN MY ROOM two days later while I'm mid-plait.

'Hades wants to see you,' she says.

'I'll just be a moment,' I say, finishing the final twists of my hair.

'No, now – he said it was an emergency.'

'Tempest?' Hades' voice rings down the hallway. He does sound quite panicked. 'For the sake of the Styx, I said I needed to talk to her, not go get her!'

I'm not sure whether *her* is better than *Kore* but to be fair I haven't given him any alternatives.

Maybe I'll name myself after a flower. The idea has a lovely cyclical feeling to it, given I named the flowers in the first place. I'm still considering my options.

'What's the difference?' Tempest mutters.

'The difference is that I am capable of using my own legs and don't need to summon people all the time,' he says from outside the room.

'You have the hearing of a bat,' I call.

'Are you decent?' he asks. 'May I come in?'

I smile at the innocence of such a question, especially considering all that I was scared of when I first came here. But then I catch myself in the mirror and see I look ridiculous, like a nymph swooning at the very thought of a man.

Which I'm obviously not doing.

There's just something about the respectfulness of the question. Even within his castle I am entitled to my own space. Mother would just march straight in.

'You may,' I confirm, turning in my chair to face him and giving up on the plait. It's a lot harder than Cyane made it look and, given I had ink smeared across my face for most of yesterday, I doubt Hades will care that my hair isn't styled.

He looks so out of place in my room, his black robes stark against all the pale fabrics and gleaming white surfaces. This palace is so cold, everything simple and clinical, the gold floor of the megaron the closest thing to colour I've seen. For the first time, I'm hit by a pang of longing for the messy warmth of my cottage with Mother.

Then I catch sight of Hades' face and the tight lines of anger I have seen only once before – when he watched Hermes vie for my hand.

'They know,' Hades says, but I already knew that's what he would say and my heart dived even before he spoke. 'Your mother knows you're missing.'

I clutch the table for support. I'm glad I'm already sitting down so I'm not staggering back in shock.

'I'm going to leave,' Tempest says.

Neither Hades nor I say anything, our eyes locked on each other. I'm moving slowly, processing too much, but within all that I have to wonder why I'm seeing echoes of my own despair mirrored back to me in Hades' face.

'Show me,' I say, squeezing past him and starting down the hall. Hades' quick steps follow me.

I've had so much more time than I thought I would get and my disgust swells as I think about how long my list of potential suitors must have been – four of the twelve, even. All those men desperate for me to be bound to them . . .

When we reach the Lake of the Five Rivers, the vision shows Mother on our island, screaming at the sky for Zeus to take notice. Nymphs run about behind her in a frenzy and I can see the terror on their faces.

Oh. I didn't even think about the consequences for them.

Mother howls and a group of nymphs fall under her out-swept hands, shrieking in agony as their legs meld together, fish scales racing up their arms and their voices turning to the scratch of salt water.

My hand covers my own startled shriek. I've seen Mother turn nymphs to sirens before, always as a punishment.

But this is *my* punishment, taken out on them.

You stupid, stupid little girl, Kore.

Either Zeus is ignoring her or he's not paying attention. I watch silently as Mother returns to the house she has already torn apart, or perhaps the nymphs did. And what for? In case I was hiding in a cupboard?

She grabs some seeds from a drawer and runs to the ocean. She dips her fingers in the foam of the waves and screams for an audience with Poseidon. There are tears in her eyes but she blinks rapidly, refusing to let them fall.

'What's all this hysterical nonsense for?' a gruff voice says, and there's Poseidon, king of the court of Oceanus, weathered and tanned skin, and wild, sea-matted hair and beard.

'Someone has taken Kore,' Mother says and I'm startled because she doesn't say *She's missing* or *She's gone* – things with many possibilities. She's certain she knows the story.

I shrink back and feel rough rock behind me. My eyes flit for a second to Hades. I am painfully aware of the vulnerability I am showing.

'They couldn't have,' Poseidon grunts. 'The wards on the island are too strong.'

Mother's lip curls in disgust. Poseidon's ocean realm has crashed against the shores of my island my entire life. He has evidently tested the strength of my mother's wards.

'I need you to make enquiries,' Mother says. 'Your realm is vast and someone might have seen something.'

'Come now, surely there's no need for all this fuss.'

'Fuss? She's *gone*,' Mother snarls.

'So?' Poseidon shrugs. 'Say someone did take her – she's a woman grown. It's no matter. They're both having some fun, so what? You kept her contained too long, Demeter. She's probably screaming with delight on some lucky man's lap. Leave her be.'

I think I might be sick.

Hades mutters a string of unintelligible curses, glaring at the lake like he might leap through it to throttle Poseidon himself.

'I was going to bribe you,' Mother says as she drops the seeds and crushes them underfoot. Wild weeds sprout beneath her as they always do when she is angry, just as flowers spring from me when I'm nervous. 'But I think I'll try threats instead.'

Poseidon snorts. 'Your domain is land, Demeter. Good luck with that.'

He turns and Mother calls after him. 'My domain is harvest and fertility, you insatiable prick. Let's see how the creatures of your world cope when I cause the corals to wither and die, when every plant in the ocean curls in on itself.'

'You wouldn't – you couldn't –' Poseidon stutters. Surely no one has spoken to him like this before.

I stare at my mother. This anger is something else. And I'm . . . impressed. For years she's ranted about the world Zeus created, the power he gifted Poseidon and Hades instead of her – and here she is, threatening those men with the very power they disregarded.

But it's also a betrayal. My whole life she's taught me the only way to survive is to keep my head down, make pretty things and nod when a man speaks. But *she* gets to be angry? She gets to make threats? I know she has more power than me but how is that fair?

'Make the enquiries, Poseidon. I want every nereid, fish and single-celled-bloody-organism looking for her.'

Poseidon waves his hand dismissively. 'Very well, if you insist.' Like he's doing her a favour, uncoerced. 'I guarantee the girl is fine, probably better than she's ever been.'

His form bursts into seawater as he returns to his palace, just as another voice enters the fray.

'What's all this about?' My father has finally appeared, adjusting the draping of his richly dyed himation. 'Apollo said he heard you screaming like a harpy.'

'Zeus – someone's taken Kore,' Mother rushes. 'We need to find her but we can't let word get out too far. If her reputation is soiled then the union could be in jeopardy. I need you to –'

'Demeter!' Father scolds. For one stupid moment in which my brain hasn't quite caught up to the fact that this is Zeus, I think he might reprimand her for being more concerned about my marriage prospects than my safety. 'There's no need to panic. We had so many offers that –'

'Every single one of those is in trouble, you dolt.'

My hand shoots out and it's not until Hades grips my palm back that I realize I've reached for him.

Then I think it doesn't matter at all. He's one of the few people who might possibly be on my side with this. And, even if he's not, he's a person and he's here and right now I just need someone. Congratulations, Hades, you finally passed the minimum requirement for something.

'You forget yourself, Demeter.' Father's voice contains storms.

Mother freezes and I see her struggle to bite her tongue. Her fists shake at her sides but she ducks her head sheepishly. I'm so tired of these power plays within my own family that I'm not even gratified by my mother finally behaving as she says I should. I'm just weary, exhausted to my very bones.

'Forgive me, Lord Zeus,' Mother says. 'As I'm sure you can understand, this is a very upsetting time.'

Father nods, paying no attention to the fact Mother's fists have tightened.

'Yes, well, I can put out some feelers. She can't have got far.'

'The nymphs say she's been missing since the first day of our appointments,' Mother says. 'Anything could have happened to her.'

'More like she could have happened to someone,' Hades mutters and I bark out an unexpected laugh. It sounds watery, like the tears I'm choking down have found their way out through alternate means.

'I will handle it,' Zeus says with finality. 'Now get some rest. You look like a disaster.'

And then he's gone, leaving nothing behind but a slight crackling in the air.

Mother's back snaps upward and she glares determinedly in front of her. 'Cyane,' she calls. 'Come help me pack. I'm going on a trip.'

I've had enough and I don't think there's much I could learn from watching her gather her possessions. I try to force myself to believe she only made my prospects her focus because she thought it would convince Zeus. But everything I just heard is ringing through my head and I don't know what to believe any more.

'That's enough now,' I say, releasing Hades' hand and feeling cold the moment it slips away.

Hades steps to the lake edge and trails his fingers through the surface.

'Are you . . .'

'No,' I answer. 'But I will be.'

'What will you do?' he asks and I can't stand the softness in his voice. I'm hurt and scared of what will happen now and everything about him is a confusing cacophony.

'I'm going to plant a garden,' I say.

I leave the lake's cavern and detour to the room we dine in. I snatch the nearest bowl. Pomegranate seeds. They seem as good a place to start as any.

'Is there anything I can do?' he asks. I turn to face him and he looks so sincere that I break.

'What are you doing?' I snap. 'Why are you being so nice to me?'

Hades smirks. 'Because I'm a delightful person.'

'You aren't though. You were a condescending cock when I first got here and now you're . . . well, still a cock sometimes. But you're also respectful and you care about what I think and how I'm feeling and I just . . . I don't understand it.' There are tears in my eyes and I'm disgusted with myself. 'Please.' Now I'm even more disgusted with myself. My voice sounds so pitiful. 'I can't take any more of these games.'

He steps forward, almost like he's coming to comfort me, and I have a sudden image of myself folded into his arms. It might be nice, to lean my head against his shoulder. To relax for once. Instead my glare makes his stumbling feet halt.

'I'm not playing games, not any more,' Hades says. 'I'm sorry I ever was.'

'But *why*?'

'Because I actually quite like having you around.'

'Why? I'm just as horrible to you as you ever were to me.' I snarl the words, like if I can bite them out then what he's saying can't land and seep into my skin. I don't need more lies.

He laughs and it's light and uncertain, just like always.

'Yes, but your insults are witty – and I can't fault you for them. I'd be on the defensive too in your position.'

'I'm not –' My words falter at the look he gives me.

'You're smart. You're ridiculously determined. You're kind – maybe not to me, but to the humans and the nymphs. How many other goddesses would deign to talk to the servants?

Styx loves you and she's a very good judge of character. And I think maybe we believe in the same things. You're creating an afterlife that will shape human morality away from that of the gods. Why wouldn't I want to help with that?'

'I don't understand.' And I really, really don't. I don't recognize myself in any of those things he just said.

'Why are you so certain you can change the world until the moment someone agrees with you?' His voice is softer now and that's almost the worst part. I can guard myself against harshness; this is more insidious somehow.

I swallow, my mouth dry. It's a valid question, I suppose. Why do I do that – stop having faith in myself the moment someone else believes in me? Because I'm not used to having someone agree with me? Because the parts of me he apparently likes only appear the few times I'm not performing? Because I don't know what he wants and that scares me?

I shake my head. I need flowers: they're where I belong, that's where my expertise is, they're it. They're all I have.

'I'm going to go outside until I can think again,' I say, grabbing handfuls of anything that looks like it can be planted and throwing them into the pomegranate bowl. 'This conversation isn't over.'

It's not until my fingers are clawing into the soil that I feel like I can breathe again. I do not plant in rows but haphazardly. I am already straying from flowers – farming and cultivation are my mother's territory, and there is a pleasure to the randomness rather than her neat rows and rotations.

So I close my eyes and I dig until I forget myself and all that matters is the life beneath my fingertips.

CHAPTER SEVENTEEN

MY HANDS ARE RAW AND bleeding. I've been planting for hours. My desperation to feel dirt under my nails kept me from picking up the tools it would have been sensible to use.

I stare at the palace before me, the icy metal and sharp blades. For a moment I try to be like it – file down my edges, turn myself cold. But, when I've been emotional, I've got answers. And I'm not sure I can handle another moment without this confrontation.

Before I can overthink it, I'm pushing through the door.

'Hades?' I ask Tempest and she nods.

'I'll go get him.'

There's no point looking for him; he's never anywhere I can find him. Not that I've looked for him all that much before.

A bowl of water appears in the middle of the hall.

'Tempest!' I call.

'You need it,' she yells back.

Looking down at my dirty, bloody hands, it's hard to argue. I'm drying them on a towel when my stomach knots and I know I'm not alone. The king of the Underworld moves like a shadow and part of me feels him before I see him, like a cloud passing over the sun.

'Hey,' I say, my voice unnervingly gentle. Exhaustion, perhaps? Maybe I've had my defences raised for so long I didn't even notice when they started to crack.

'How are you feeling?' He's standing in the doorway of one of the many libraries. Seeing him, I relax ever so slightly. It hits me just how desperately I want to trust him. I don't need more gods to be at war with. If Mother and Father know I'm missing, I need all the allies I can get. And he's . . . I've seen the way he is with Styx, even the way he is with me sometimes.

I've been clinging to how horrible he was when I first got here because trusting him is terrifying. Now I have to trust him; without someone to lean on I'm going to fall.

But he needs to trust me first.

'Tired, confused, scared, angry. A lot of other things, I think.' I rub at my eyes. If I could only wake up a bit more. If this exhaustion were something physical, I could process it better.' I can't stop thinking about the nymphs she turned into sirens.'

Hades smiles and it's gentler than usual, not the usual cocky smirk or unnerved grin. 'With everything your mother, Poseidon and Zeus said, you can't stop thinking about the nymphs?'

Maybe it was his intention, but my tiredness lifts and I glare at him. 'I care an awful lot about them.'

'Yes, and the humans – who don't you care about?'

'The gods?' I suggest.

Hades shrugs.'Understandable.'

'Why don't *you* like them?' I ask. 'Kronos chose you too. Zeus gave you this world. Why are you so different from them?'

He shrugs again. 'Well, I'm not the only one – plenty of the gods of the Underworld feel the same. And who knows how many gods of Olympus and Oceanus are performing roles they feel forced into. But the others? I don't know . . . Some of the things they did in the war, the war itself, even . . . well, the Underworld seemed like the furthest place to go to get away from them – to forget about them all.'

I scowl. 'Mother said Zeus randomly allocated the domains to those stolen by Kronos.'

Hades snorts. 'He thinks he did.'

I nod. After all, I came to the same understanding – that there is no better place to escape. 'Is everyone in this realm a runaway?'

Hades laughs. 'More or less.'

I must look at him a little too long because he sighs.

'You don't feel safe here, do you?'

'Nowhere is safe from my father.'

'That's not what I meant. You still don't feel safe around me.'

My nails bite into my arm. 'I don't think you're going to hurt me. And I know you swore the oath. But every time I so much as laugh around you I think: what do you get from it? What do you get from being nice to me? From getting me to trust you?'

He shakes his head. 'I don't like that you're on edge all the time.'

'Well, can you blame me? You spent days snapping at me and trying to get me to leave. And then you decided that I wasn't actually here for some nefarious purpose and you did a complete personality switch. Why wouldn't I feel on edge around you? I have no idea who you are.'

'You switched personalities too.'

'I was trying to be polite for my own safety.'

'And I was trying to be an arsehole because I wanted you gone.'

'And what's to stop you wanting me gone again?' I ask. But what I mean is: *Would you stop them? If they tried to take me back?*

But how could I possibly expect that?

Hades pauses for a moment while he thinks before nodding slowly. By the Fates, there's something irresistible in that little action. He looks so contemplative, the sharp edges of his jaw accentuated by the movement, his slight frown etching lines into his skin. I'm surrounded by the most beautiful marble structure in the universe but none of it means anything in comparison to the way he looks when he's thinking.

'Very well then,' he says, emboldened. 'If that's the price of your trust. I thought if I could frustrate you into breaking xenia, you'd be gone before you could discover certain things.'

'Your secrets?' I ask. 'The ones Styx mentioned?'

He nods. 'I'll tell you them. If you know what I'm keeping hidden then you don't have to fear me wanting you gone before you can find out. You can relax. My secrets for your peace – that feels like a worthy trade.'

'You don't have to do that.'

'Yes, I do,' he insists. 'Come with me.'

He starts down a hall and I follow, wondering where he's going – searching for a quiet place for us to talk? Does he have so many secrets I'll need to sit down for their reveal? And then I realize he's not going to tell me, he's going to show me.

'The missing rooms,' I say as it dawns on me.

He turns, half laughing with surprise. 'I should have known you'd work it out. No one in the court has even noticed.'

'Presumably no one in the court feared for their safety in these halls like I did.'

'Well, I should hope not,' he says, stopping beside a section of wall. At his touch, a rectangular outline appears, a handle twisting out that he grasps and turns.

I don't know what I'm expecting but I chuckle when I see it's yet another library.

'Is this where you keep your more arousing tales? Shall I expect the next room to be filled with painted vases of randy satyrs?' I joke before freezing. The only people I have heard that kind of talk from are the nymphs, who are all innuendo and not much else, and now here I go. And with a man too . . .

Thankfully Hades laughs and it soothes the tense lines of my shoulders.

'It's poetry, actually.'

I turn to him but he hurries on.

'I told you I enjoy it.'

'But this much?'

'Yes,' he says almost wistfully, like he wishes the word could be a simple answer.

The next room is enormous, containing not only several different kinds of spinning needles but delicate, stone-weighted looms for more detailed tapestry work. What's more, they're all in use.

'The goddesses of the court?'

'No,' he says and his voice is strained, like it could break at any moment. 'They're all mine. Everything I'll show you is mine.'

I wander to the nearest and see a work so detailed I find myself lost for words. It's so beautiful it could have ended the Arachne-versus-Athena weaving debate in seconds. This is clearly superior. It almost sparkles and it's not even finished.

'It's beautiful,' I say, and it is but that seems like such an understatement. *It's real*, would be a better compliment, but even then I'm not sure the real world glitters like this. I have no idea how he managed to weave moonlight into his threads, or the smell of pine trees, or the touch of cool lake water under my fingers, but I feel it all as I look at it.

When I face him, he's scowling, watching me carefully like he thinks I'm fabricating my awe.

'What?' I ask.

He shakes his head and we move on to the next room. It's narrow with a long table upon which lie various quilt squares in differing stages of completion.

'I can't believe you gave me such a rickety old loom,' I quip but he doesn't smile, just stares at me instead. 'What?'

'Is that really all you have to say?'

'What do you want me to say?' I ask. 'I could shower your work in compliments if that would please your ego.'

'Please don't mock me, not with this.'

'Hades,' I say, confused. 'I'm being sincere. I've never seen work like this.'

He frowns and looks around the room sceptically.

'Well . . .' he says, shaking his head. 'Did you want to see the others?'

More doors appear right where my maps say they should be. The next room is enormous, with vaulted ceilings, huge blocks of stone and chisels waiting to be used. In another, the walls themselves are slick with paint: a mural so detailed I long to step through it and into the forest he's created. Behind more doors I find easels, crafts, writing desks, glass shops, ceramics and clay, metal forges, woodwork and finally a room full of needles and thread. There's no half-finished project in here, just rows and rows of neatly stacked spools collecting dust.

'I didn't actually enjoy this one very much,' Hades says dryly. 'Embroidery wasn't for me.'

'But the others are?'

He nods, folding his arms across his chest. 'I'm not ashamed, you know. I'd rather be here weaving tapestries and making pots than up there destroying lives and causing wars.'

'I didn't say you should be ashamed.'

He's still looking at me in that weird way. 'Yes, I did get that feeling. Why?'

'Why what?'

'Why aren't you . . . I don't know, judging me?'

'I am judging you – these are amazing! This is basically everything my mother has ever tried to make me do – well, except the sculpting and carpentry – and I am terrible at all of it.' I'm not, not really. But nothing was ever good *enough*. And certainly nothing was this good.

'Exactly. It's everything your mother wants *you* to do.'

Oh.

'So you hid this because you thought I'd ruin your manly reputation over it?' I ask.

'My reputation is a tricky thing. It's not my ego that protects it. As far as that's concerned, people can say what they want,' he says. 'But I have this crown because Zeus believed Kronos chose the most powerful beings when he snatched Poseidon and me – the men who might grow to be a threat. Zeus thought that if he gave us some modicum of power we'd never rise against him. But if Zeus found out I did all this – that I'm not the shining example of masculine power he believes me to be, not a threat in the way only a man could be – he'd take the crown back. And being a king is the only thing that gives me the security to do all this in peace. Even the other gods of the Underworld don't know about this. That's why it's hidden.'

'But Hephaestus crafts.'

'He builds machines, not jewellery – unless Aphrodite insists upon it.'

He's right. Hades' metal shop is full of delicate, stunning sculptures and jewels. Nothing built for use but for aesthetic. Art for art's sake.

'Apollo, he –'

'Strums a lyre – it's not the same.'

I understand. The muses are women. Men can be artistic but not like this, not with thread and paint. I realize what he means, why he expected my scorn. I can almost hear the nymphs giggling, the insults they'd throw his way. Mother, gods, Mother – how often has she ranted about the Underworld being given to Hades? How much worse would it be if she knew this is what he does with that power? She would be so cruel. This is not what men do.

Everything my mother has ever forced me to do to improve my marriage prospects is apparently something Hades loves. But how is this any different from me climbing out of my window when I should be weaving? Having to keep my true interests hidden because I'm not supposed to want those things?

Hades leans against the wall but his arms are folded, like even with my reassurances he's still scared I'll be harsh. Hades has never seemed vulnerable to me. But now it's taking his every effort to even meet my eye.

I don't think I'm the only one suffering under Zeus's order. I don't think it's just us girls chafing under its restraints.

'Besides,' he continues, 'I don't care for being the best like they do. I just enjoy it. I would never be allowed all this if everyone knew.' He's so rigid it's like every strand of his body is tensed.

'That's why the palace is covered in swords,' I realize. 'It's a disguise.'

'They think I'm the dark, brooding god of the dead, vanquisher of the Titans who longs for nothing more than isolation in the gloomy depths of the Underworld,' he says. 'It stops them from looking too closely at what I'm really doing.'

'Which is this?'

'Which is this,' he confirms.

'And that's why you wanted me gone? In case I found all this out and used it against you?'

'Yes. I'm sorry.'

'I'm not blaming you.'

'I was terrified. If you were sent by Zeus, like I thought, then you stumbling into the wrong room could have destroyed everything. You had such incredible power to ruin me.'

Power that he's now handed me by telling me all this.

'You have too high an opinion of my father if you think he'd listen to anything I have to say on the matter. I could probably go with a full report and he'd still ignore it.'

'Trust me, few people could manage a lower opinion of Zeus than the one I hold.'

'Is that a challenge?'

He sighs but there's amusement there and the tension dissipates, just a touch. 'Not everything is a competition. That's the point.'

'All right, but most things are. You're just grumpy I won and you couldn't scare me off.'

'I think I did a remarkable job, personally. Acting the part and everything.'

'All the theatrics . . .' I realize. 'The smoke and the tremors . . . they're all an act too, right?'

'They always have been.' He smiles and the smoke appears. Then it turns pink, then blue, then stops being smoke altogether and becomes flowers instead. 'The first beings Zeus rescued in the war were the cyclopes. In return, they made things for us – Zeus's thunderbolt and Poseidon's trident. I was given a helmet that rendered the wearer invisible. Before Zeus took the throne and dished the domains out as spoils of war, the domain used to claim the god. The moment that helmet touched my head, some form of magic claimed me. I think I'm the god of illusion, really, or something like that. I was a child training for war when I was given this realm. If I'd veiled myself in ocean spray I imagine it would be Poseidon down here now. But I wanted the Underworld – what was it you said? – somewhere to run away to. So I wreathed myself in a shroud of darkness and the whispers of the dead and Hell was mine.'

I stare, unable to do much else. It's one thing after the next.

'I'll swear on the Styx,' I say. 'Like the nymphs do. I won't tell anyone.'

'You don't need to swear to it. I know you wouldn't tell anyone.' I must show my disbelief because he laughs. 'You found a loophole in wards made by a dozen deities, ran to Hell without telling anyone and presumably kept much of who you are a secret your entire life. I can trust you with this, I think.'

I nod. 'Right. I won't say a word. Come on, it's my turn now.'

'What?'

'Well, did you want to see my plans for this realm or not?'

'I . . .'

'This is a lot, Hades. Thank you. So . . . yes, if you can trust me with this, I can trust you in return. Let's go talk about the afterlife.'

I show him my idea. Three separate parts: a paradise, the details of which I'm still filling in; a deterrent, filled with terrors I'm still ruminating over; and something in between.

Spoken aloud, it's more than I thought I had.

Leaning over the documents, we've become a little too close and I think of his hand in mine earlier. Is it worrying, how natural it's becoming to gravitate towards each other?

'I like it,' he says simply.

I don't think I realized how much his approval means to me. It's more than just his favour: I'm being encouraged rather than dissuaded from the sort of thing I've always wanted, supported rather than told it's beyond me to make a difference to this world.

Just three little words — and they mean everything.

CHAPTER EIGHTEEN

WHEN I RETURN TO MY room after breakfast the next
morning, a painting hangs above the bed. It's stunning,
as all of Hades' creations are. It's both lifelike and too
iridescent to truly replicate life – deep, like he's captured
something more than an image in the paint.

And it pictures a field of asphodel. The flower I created
only days ago. Which means he's painted this while I've been
here.

I bite my lip but I'm not able to stop my smile. When did he
work on this? When did he decide to share it, no, give it to me?
The gift feels even more intimate than yesterday's revelation
and I immediately begin to spiral. Why has he done this?
What does he want from me in return? What does it mean?

Then I take a deep breath and allow myself to simply
enjoy it.

On closer inspection, I see Hades has used thick, clumpy
paint so that the petals are raised from the surface. He's made
the pollen black, even though asphodel's real pollen is orange,
and now I wish I'd chosen this more striking colour. The paint

is pure and pitch. It's darker than Hades' eyes but nonetheless it reminds me of them, like if I stare hard enough I might get sucked into the shadows.

It's actually very annoying that the painting is so good. It doesn't seem right for someone with their own world to be this talented. Every time Mother put a brush in my hand, I'd dip my fingers into the paint instead and leave, spattered, with thousands of ideas brimming of new flowers to create.

Hades would make the perfect daughter. Though I only mean it with snide humour, the thought sobers me. This genuinely is all Mother ever wanted from me. And then what? If I had been talented like this would she have seen it? Would she have praised me until the thought of doing anything else was sickening? Or would she have seen the raised bumps I find so wonderful as flaws to be sanded? Would she have found something else to pick at? And, even if she hadn't, what would I have been other than a bundle of skills she could market? Would my father look at my work with a satisfied nod? Would he agree this is what I am good at – all I am good at – and wonder how he ever could have worried I might challenge him when I'm only a little girl good with a brush?

I suddenly feel a lot more confident about my ability to change this realm simply because my parents would never expect it of me. And it seems I am very good at doing the things they don't expect.

'It's almost creepy, you know.' I'm grinning when I join Hades in the library but his eyebrow quirks and he barely looks up from his papers.

On the Styx, him and his papers.

'You hung the painting *over the bed*?' I ask.

Hades laughs. 'Tempest's choice.'

'Sure it was, Hades, sure it was.'

'I thought you might like it.' Now he's definitely staring at the paper.

'I do. Thank you.'

He meets my eye and that cocky smirk is back in place. 'Why, that was almost genuine!'

'I believe I've thanked you plenty, Hades,' I say. Even when I thought he was an insufferable arse, I was still thankful he wasn't worse.

'That's true. Not that I need your thanks this time – consider the painting a thank you for the asphodel.'

'Well, it's nice to have confirmation that you like it.'

'Of course I like it. I like it less now it's spread across the realm but it's still . . . a very nice flower.'

'I was wondering how you felt about that,' I say. 'When I spread the plant you were still being a prick.'

'Well, it was hardly a subtle act on your behalf. The floral equivalent of a dog pissing to mark its territory.'

I don't exactly laugh – more cackle. Hades looks pleased with himself.

'I want to argue but yeah, actually, I did spread them out of spite.'

'I know. A nice flower, though, with the spite removed.'

I remove the spite the next day and fill the entire palace with bouquets of asphodel, along with a few other flowers I've managed to grow. I'm not sure whether Hades has seen the styx blossoms yet, so I place a large bouquet in the library.

'I'm not watering these,' Tempest grumbles as she reluctantly hands me a vase. I realize that the vases must have been made by Hades. The flowers work well with his intricate designs.

'More territory marking?' Hades asks when he joins me in the library. We have yet another day ahead of trawling through scrolls, looking for any clue of how this world works. He moves to stand beside me and examines the flowers. He leans in to smell them with a small smile playing on his lips.

'No.' My own smile feels different around him, almost embarrassed. 'Not this time. A marble palace is all very well and good, but it's not exactly the most inviting place to live.'

'Are you critiquing my hospitality now?'

I know he's teasing and before I know what I'm doing I playfully push him away. I flush and turn from him so he can't see. I wasn't expecting such hard muscles beneath that cloak . . .

'Of course not.' I stumble over the words. 'But you can never have too many flowers.'

'The lands of Hades might disagree.'

'Do you?' I challenge.

'No,' he acquiesces. 'I actually quite like them.'

'What's all the fuss about then?'

Hades shrugs. 'Well, I can't make it too easy for you.'

Styx can barely understand all this when I tell her – after checking with Hades what she knows. Everything, apparently.

'He gave you a painting? I . . . right, okay.'

'I guess he's never had anyone to do that for before. He was probably excited,' I say. 'It's a gorgeous painting.'

'I'm sure.' She gives me a look, one I can't decipher.

'I filled the halls with flowers in return,' I say. 'I wish I could give him something permanent to remember me by when I'm gone.'

'Don't talk about that,' she scolds.

'It's true.'

'I know but I don't want reminding.'

'Aww, you like me!'

'Yeah and apparently I'm not the only one.'

I laugh. 'Sure, he doesn't even yell at me any more. He must like me.'

'He shared secrets with you that most people have to swear an unbreakable oath to be privy to – he likes you.'

'Yes, well, being at each other's throats was beginning to get in the way of research.'

Styx sighs. 'Whatever, dear. All I'm saying is that he doesn't need anything to remember you by. He's not going to be forgetting you in a hurry.'

Hades hovers over my shoulder while I take more notes on potential afterlives.

'You think that's paradise?' he asks sceptically.

'What? Why not?' I turn to face him. 'I loved it when it rained on Sicily – I'd go running out and play in the mud and –'

'Because you're a goddess! You had servants for –'

'You have servants!'

'Yes, and I am literally the king of Hell – kings get servants. My point is that many of those humans were not kings, and none were goddesses. They probably died because they were out in the rain and caught a disease or something.'

'How do you know?'

'I'm the king of Hell. I mentioned this.' Hades has gone from trying to annoy me into breaking xenia to annoying me simply because it's fun. The worst part is that our growing familiarity means he knows precisely how to get under my skin. Actually, the worst part is that I think a part of me enjoys it. I go into our conversations like I have a point to prove, like beating him means something.

'You've never even spoken to them!'

'Of course not, but –' he waves his hand – 'I get the gist. And I've spoken to people who have, Charon and –'

'You're ridiculous.'

'And you're spoilt. You have to acknowledge that you're in no position to know what humans want.'

That brings me up short because, damn it, he's right. I've spent my whole life on an island with nymphs. I've never even met a live human.

I glance at the notes I've been taking. I've been so absorbed trying to work out what the weather cycles are like in lands outside Sicily that I never stopped to consider whether the humans actually like them, whatever they are. 'We need to talk to them,' I decide. 'We've done all we can with notes. Come on, let's go.'

I know it will be tiring, healing souls enough to talk to them, but it can't be harder than creating a rift in the land itself. And now that my parents know where I am, it's a risk I have to take. I might be hauled to Olympus at any moment – I'll suffer the tiredness.

'What?' Hades scowls. 'No, you talk to them. I'll do all the research, as I suggested, and you can meet the people you're designing an afterlife for.'

'Come on, you're supposed to be helping me.'

'I am helping – these books were written by mortals. You talk, I'll read.'

'Why don't you want to go near them?' I ask. The entire time I've been here, he's never once mentioned visiting them. Even with the souls decayed as they are, surely Hades' curiosity as ruler of the land would take him there?

'You know what their memories are like, bleeding out of them. They're inescapable and so many are miserable.'

'Exactly, which is why we're doing this. You can't just ignore their suffering.'

'I've got enough suffering of my own, thank you,' he says with a pointed glance in my direction. I refuse to rise to the taunt. At my judging glare, he continues, 'I have no desire to add their memories to my own.'

'You're a king – I thought we covered this. What memories do you have of suffering?'

For a second, he hesitates. Then he sputters: 'I was eaten!'

'Oh, you can't even remember it. You are not playing that card again.'

'Playing that card? I was bloody eaten!'

'You're changing the subject. Come and talk to the humans with me.'

Hades throws his quill down and stands. 'I'll come with you but only because I haven't seen Cerberus in a while. I'm not talking to the humans.'

'Fine. Wait, who's Cerberus?'

*

Cerberus, it turns out, is a three-headed dog the size of my cottage. Hades whistles loudly then grins as the beast bounds over the hill.

'Cerberus. Really?' I say. The word means hound of the Earth. 'Was "Underworld Puppy" too on the nose?'

'I thought it suited him,' Hades says simply.

When the hound sees Hades (with all three heads), he comes charging over with such speed that he knocks Hades to the ground. I expect Hades to reprimand the animal but instead he beams and rubs one head.

'Go talk to your humans then,' he says from the ground. 'I'm quite all right here.'

So I do. It's like the sun hitting my skin, the first breath of clean air after being shut up inside. It brings me back to myself.

My concerns about fatigue turn out to be baseless. It's easier to bring the mortals back this time because I know what I'm looking for. Whatever connection I've found to this land comes rushing back. I get through dozens of souls before the tiredness hits. I stop, cutting myself off before I can push it too far. I'll come back every day that I can and heal as many as I can in my time left. Hades will be so excited when I tell him it worked.

Larissa returns to my side the moment I appear in the human realms and waves away my attempts to apologize for taking so long. I'd thought I could do more good in the library but now I'm not so sure. Staring at souls in full colour – nearly opaque once more, talking to one another, almost *alive* again – it's difficult to believe I should be anywhere else. And they have so much to say! And it's so easy. So much easier than the scrolls. I curse my fear of exhaustion because I could have been doing this the whole time. I can imagine it now, every land I have always wanted to see, created in the Underworld from the stories the humans tell. I might not be able to see the world but I could bring the world to me.

In my final days of freedom, I could have everything I ever wanted.

CHAPTER NINETEEN

'YOU CAN'T LIVE DOWN HERE,' Hades says, and for a moment I think he means the Underworld – then I realize he means the cavern with the lake whose waters I am staring into.

Mother has known I am missing for five days now, and she's not stopped searching for a moment of them.

He's beside me, suddenly, and I start as his hand brushes mine.

'You're freezing,' he scolds, pulling his himation off and draping the heavy fabric across my shoulders. He is left standing in his thin tunic.

It smells of him – bergamot tea and peppery soap – and I find myself pulling it closer, burying my chin into it and breathing in. I must have been colder than I realized.

'How long have you been down here?'

'I'm not sure,' I say honestly. It can't have been long or I'd be sitting on the edge, as I have done every day after dragging myself back from talking to the mortals. Tired from healing too many of them and from hours spent in conversation, I sit and watch my mother and try to work out how close she is to finding me.

At the moment she is raving at my father, sometimes commanding him and other times begging him to do something to help find me.

'She's your daughter – don't you care? She could be hurt!'

'Demeter, I'm handling it. Calm down,' Father says dismissively.

'What of the suitors, hmm?' she tries. I don't blame her – from what I've seen it's the angle that gets the best results when she speaks to my father. 'Word has already spread that she is missing. Everyone knows.'

'I know.' Father rubs his temples. 'It's been pandemonium on Olympus. "Kore"? I should have never named her "little girl". Had I the powers of prophecy I would have thought "chaos bringer" more appropriate.'

Hades snorts beside me. 'You're telling me.'

I elbow him in the side. 'Excuse you.'

Mother is less impressed. 'Ares has already retracted his offer!'

'You and I both know that if Ares cared about virginity he would not be with Aphrodite.'

'As a mistress, not as a wife! It's different now. You can thank your own wife for making marriage so ... difficult,' Mother snaps.

Zeus laughs. 'Well, Hera was no virgin when I married her either.'

Hades and I stare, shocked that even the king of the gods would go so far.

Mother glares at him with such ferocity I'm surprised he does not combust. 'And whose fault was that?' she seethes.

'Demeter,' he growls in warning.

'Oh, I'm sorry.' She's shaking with such fury I'm sure somewhere crops are withering away under the heat of her anger. 'It must be horrible to be called a rapist when you rape someone.'

'How dare –'

'I don't care!' Mother shrieks. She flings her hands above her head and I'm swarmed by guilt. She is the goddess of sacred law and look at her, unravelling by the second.

'I should never –' I start but Hades cuts me off.

'No,' he says. 'We are not doing this again. Entering a marriage you didn't want is not better than this.'

I'm not so sure. I love my mother. How can I watch as I cause her this much anguish? She does not even know it is me causing it – she thinks I was taken.

She tries a different tack. 'What does it say about the king of the gods that someone can seize his daughter? Someone can take her and do whatever they please with her? Hurt her? Steal her away from a marriage *you* ordered? What will it say about you when she returns and no one will take her?'

'It will say nothing.' He stands from his throne and lightning crackles around him. 'Because she is little more than nothing. I have a dozen daughters, Demeter. Yours is special only in her continued insolence. I've seen her traipsing across that island, practically asking for something like this to happen. The only slight here is that fair payment was not made. I will find who did this and I will demand recompense. The gods may whisper but I assure you any damage to my reputation will be swiftly repaired when I haul whoever has taken her before the court and have them beg for my mercy. Which I'll eventually give and all will believe I am a powerful yet generous king. I'll marry Kore off to whoever's left. Someone will be interested – even ruined, she's my blood. That will save *her* honour. Which means the only reputation taking lasting damage is yours,' he sneers at my stony-faced mother, who withdraws into herself with every word. 'Find another way to claw your dignity back because finding your daughter isn't it.'

Hades waves the water away.

'This isn't healthy,' he says.

I'm staring at where my father's face just was. Despite Hades' cloak, I'm suddenly icy cold and shaking. I never considered that my father simply might not care all that much. I didn't think he had the ability to hurt me but his indifference is worse than his anger, worse than a lifetime of being put in my place. It's like, for once and for all, any threat I might have offered has been vanquished and he has washed his hands of me. And my mother, my poor mother, having to hear him say all that . . .

'Listen to me,' Hades insists. 'Zeus is a horrible, horrible person. That isn't new information to anyone, but it's not healthy for you to listen to continued proof of it.'

I turn to face him and my hands curl at my sides. 'You think I don't know that?' I demand, baring my teeth but floundering for words to follow. 'I know it's damaging but I'm hardly taking it in. I'm just trying to predict their next move.'

'Are you?' he demands. 'Because every day you watch this nonsense you become . . . less you.'

'What does that mean?'

'You become less annoying, for example.'

'Go screw your–'

'I'm serious!' he shouts over me. I scowl, realizing he is truly angry, truly arguing the topic. 'Every single second you spend watching your parents talk, you close off more of yourself. I like that you come annoy me when I'm reading, and that you think you're far funnier than you are, and that you fill the house with flowers without asking. I like all of that.'

'It sure sounds it.'

'Please,' he says and his voice breaks. His despair startles me. This is not bickering, not a light-hearted, surface-deep argument. This is real. Hurting myself like this is hurting him. I feel the heaviness of his cloak draped across me. I feel the hollowness that has been growing inside of me.

'You're right. I don't know why I watch all this when it makes me feel miserable.'

'Then don't.'

'They know I'm missing, Hades. I have to know if they're close.'

'And what if they are? What if they do discover you are here? Your mother can't come down here. Zeus would never dare risk the fragile peace between himself, Poseidon and me. Even Poseidon would fight to defend you if he thought Zeus was daring to trespass on one of our realms. More likely Zeus would cover it up, and where better to let everyone forget you exist than the court of Hell? You're safe here.'

'What if I'm not? What if nothing I do keeps me safe?'

He takes a half step forward, his hands lifting like he is reaching for me before he thinks better of it.

'Then I will do it.'

I hesitate before offering a condescending grin, pushing my fear down and replacing it with something more manageable.

'That's cute but I already assumed that if I couldn't do it then you obviously couldn't either.'

He laughs, glad at least that my mood has lifted.

'Then we shall try it together.' His smile falls. 'Actually, that gives me an idea.'

'What?'

'You won't like it.'

'I don't like much about this.'

His eyes meet mine, the intensity of his gaze making me feel untethered before he even speaks. 'Marry me.'

Everything stops: my breath, my thoughts, the very ichor racing in my veins. The silence is a physical presence I can't move against.

And then all at once everything rushes back in a surge of energy.

'What?' I half yelp, half demand.

'Marry me,' he says. 'If you want to stay here and the only argument they have revolves round marriage, then marry me.'

I scramble away from him, trying to put some distance between us.

'I . . . I did all this to escape marriage. I don't want . . . just because I like you doesn't mean I want to marry you!'

'You like me?' Hades grins teasingly. 'I shall remind you of that next time you call me an arse.'

Everything is spiralling, spinning out of control. I'm not merely falling any more, I'm plummeting.

'I'm not joking!' I screech. 'I don't want to marry you!'

His nose wrinkles. 'I don't particularly want to marry you either.' He still thinks this is amusing. 'I've seen what your hair looks like in the morning.'

'I'm trying to turn down your proposal, you arse. Can you stop joking?' I'm verging on hysteria.

'Well, that took all of two seconds. You want to stay here forever. You don't want your parents dragging you back. Tell me how this is a bad idea?'

'I don't want to fuck you,' I snap. I recoil at the crude language but what else would it be? Certainly not the lovemaking that the nymphs always dream of. I think of hands holding me down, my sobs silenced by kisses – images that have always haunted me are now fears with a face, and it's the face of the one person I thought might understand.

Hades winces and all humour falls from him like he's been hit by a physical blow. 'No! By the Fates, no, that's not what I meant. At all.' He steps forward and I flinch back. His lips pull into a tight line and the fury in his eyes could level nations.

I tense.

'Please,' he says like I might break. Maybe I will. I feel like I could. At any rate, I hate the implication I will. 'You know what I swore on the Styx. I won't harm you. I won't force myself on you. That would hold even within marriage. But it's very important to me that you know I would never do that, with or without an oath. *Never.*' He stresses the final word so intently it echoes in the cavern, a dozen desperate and insistent pleas.

I close my eyes and, slowly, I nod.

I do know it.

I've heard him rant enough about those who would – which is every god. That's what they do. That's half the stories. And Zeus is the worst . . . That's what happens when you let the king do as he pleases and never hold him to account. The others follow suit.

But not Hades. Never him.

'Now that I've made that clear, would you like me to get down on one knee?' Hades asks, cocky grin tentatively sliding back into place.

'No, Hades. I don't want to marry you.'

Although it's not quite that. More that I never want to be married at all. I didn't fight for all this to simply end up married anyway.

'It would be a marriage in name only,' he says, like he knows what I'm thinking. Of course he does – he knows me well enough now to put together why I don't want this. But then he smirks again, like a new thought has just occurred to him. 'It would mean fooling everyone else, which, come now, must excite you somewhat? I know you adore a performance.'

I wish performances weren't necessary, but, yes, I suppose that's true. But marriage is too powerful and too risky. I'm not binding myself to someone else, even as a hoax.

He sobers. 'I wouldn't touch you. I wouldn't even hold your hand.'

'People would know it was a sham.'

'Fine, I wouldn't touch you without your permission,' Hades says. 'Consider this. I enjoy your company. I believe I have made that clear.'

'That's not a reason to marry someone,' I say.

'Of course not,' he says. 'But, when you enjoy someone's company and the king of the gods himself is threatening to take that person away – worse, to force them to do something against their will – and it could all be stopped with something as simple as a marriage? That's a damn good reason to get married. If you want to stay here and marriage is the only way you are free, then make that choice yourself and put a bloody ring on my finger already.'

Marriage as freedom? I'd never considered such a thing was possible.

But here it is. Somehow, impossibly, Hades has managed to redefine the institution that has haunted me my entire life.

'Stay with me. Marry me,' he says, like the two statements mean the same thing.

I duck my eyes. I can't look at him right now.

'Thank you,' I say, and he looks up almost hopefully. 'But no. Marriage has haunted me my whole life – it's too much for me, even as a lie.'

He nods. 'Okay, I understand. And . . . are you all right? That was . . . far more intense than I meant it to be. It was just a passing thought. I believed it might solve something. Maybe stop your permanent terror of being found, at the very least.'

By the Fates, I'm so glad I chose to run away to this realm. I'm so glad I met this man.

'I know. I understand.' It's not what I want to say. I want to tell him how much he means to me, to show just how much I value him and his friendship and the fact he would offer such a momentous thing to me. But I've never put such sentiments into words before, and all I can manage is: 'Thank you, really.'

He smirks and just for a moment I imagine what it would be like to say yes to him. Something jumps in my stomach. I'm not sure if it's a good or bad feeling and that uncertainty alone is reason enough to say no.

'Well, if you change your mind, my offer remains open, *Persephone*.'

My head jerks back up and I can't tell if he's joking. 'Is it bad that I actually really like that?'

Because, among the horrific things my father said, there was something that's been echoing through my mind since: *I would have thought "chaos bringer" more appropriate.* Yes, Father, I think so too.

'Persephone it is, then,' Hades says, like it's that simple. And maybe it is.

Gone is *little girl. Kore.*

I am *chaos bringer.*

Persephone.

CHAPTER TWENTY

STYX COMES OVER AND WE spend the evening down in the lake room. It was her idea to come here but I still can't shake the dread. I've spent too long using it to spy on my parents and just being here unsettles me.

'This feels so weird,' she says. 'My river is not happy at being mixed with all these others. The Phlegethon is so polluted.' She wrinkles her nose.

'I guess that's why it's on fire.'

'Hmm,' she agrees. 'But Hades tells me you haven't been using the Lake of the Five Rivers for its best purpose.'

'And that is?'

'You have access to a whole planet of entertainment, and you've been eavesdropping on your parents? Come on, *Persephone*.' She grins at the name. She's very enthusiastic about the change. 'There's a festival for Dionysus happening in Athens right now. And that means theatre.'

Styx waves her hand in the water and performers appear in the lake.

Sitting on a pile of blankets, we spend the evening watching the show. The play is a little odd – it starts with a net over a house – and my vision keeps drifting to the humans watching. They're enraptured, delighted, and the few who aren't seem to enjoy their discontent. They whisper to their neighbours and sit up a little straighter with the superiority their contempt gives them. Theatre – the afterlife should definitely have a theatre.

At the end of the show, I turn to Styx. 'Hades asked me to marry him.'

'I beg your bloody pardon,' she gasps. 'And you let me sit through all that without saying a damn thing?'

'He said that, if I want to stay here and I am worried about my parents stopping me, we could get married and they wouldn't be able to drag me back to the surface.'

'Oh, this is so exciting,' she squeals. 'When is it happening?'

'It's not,' I say. 'I didn't say yes.'

'Why not?' she asks. 'You like him. He likes you. What more do you want?'

'Love?' I suggest. 'And I do not "like him".'

She simply looks at me and I scoff. 'I don't know what you're trying to imply but it's untrue, whatever it is.'

'Sure.'

'Besides,' I say slightly louder. 'I'd like to actually *want* to get married if it's going to happen.'

'Yeah, but this sounds less like a marriage and more like a scheme, and you love schemes.'

'But I'm not getting married for one.'

She shrugs and stands. 'Well, I think we should all get drunk anyway. Come on.'

She marches upstairs and we search the empty halls of

the cold palace until we find Hades at a potter's wheel, so focused on the clay in front of him that he doesn't notice us enter.

'I made a new type of soil from that.' I nod at the clay.

He startles but grins sheepishly. 'How was the theatre?'

'You're proposing without talking to me about it first?' Styx demands.

Hades carefully presses a final line into the clay and doesn't even look up at her. 'I do many things without talking to you about them first.'

'And how many work out well for you?'

'Most.' Hades shrugs.

'I can see why you didn't want to marry him,' she says.

I nod with feigned sadness. 'He never showers me in the appropriate number of compliments. Why would I marry him?'

'I was under the impression your refusal was less about me and more about your general thoughts on marriage.' He dries his hands on a towel.

'Well, yes, marriage is gross.'

Hades points at me. 'That argument would work on your parents, I'm sure.'

My smile falters and from the way his own smile falls I know he's caught it.

'Well, successful or not, an engagement was proposed today and I think we need to drink to it,' Styx says, gleefully unaware of the sudden dip in my mood.

Hades shrugs. 'Very well. I trust you know where the wine cellar is.'

Styx's eyes go wide. 'I'm sorry, you have a whole cellar dedicated to wine and this is the first I'm hearing of it?'

Hades gives a rueful shake of his head. 'Of course, I was keeping that from you for a reason.'

'Keeping secrets from your secret keeper.' She pouts. 'That's so mean.'

'Is it as mean as denying a proposal from a man who only wishes to make you happy?' He glances longingly into the distance, hand clutching his heart.

'Show me to the wine first,' I say. 'You can cry afterwards.'

We spend the rest of the evening drinking and celebrating and laughing so much that my sides ache. At one point Hades shows us his music room and attempts to drunkenly serenade me into marrying him, which would have stood a better chance of working if he were any good. It seems that music, like needlework, is not where his talents lie. He only stopped when Styx requested rotten fruit to throw.

The next morning my head throbs like nothing I've ever felt before and I'm not sure there's enough water in the world to quench my thirst. I've drunk before – been drunk before – but not like that.

The nymphs have gone all out this morning – the usual fruits and breads are joined by buttery pastries, fluffy eggs, honey-glazed meats and creamy cheeses studded with rosemary and whole cloves of garlic. I'm not sure I can sit in front of it without being sick. I ache to both fill a plate and thrust it all into the fire.

Hades groans into his tea, staring at it like it's the Lake of the Five Rivers.

'I haven't drunk that much since I got to this realm,' he says.

'A partier in your youth?' I tease, though it would be more satisfying if we weren't practically the same age and the room wasn't spinning.

He doesn't answer, which I might mistake for some effect of the alcohol if he weren't also avoiding looking at me.

Well, now I'm interested.

'What is it? Does it have something to do with what you said about trying something with the humans when you first got here?'

'Fates, Persephone, is it not bad enough that I'm hungover? You want me to discuss that? Not happening.' He lifts his cup to his lips.

I shrug and reach for the water jug. 'Fair enough.'

'Why do you always do that?' he asks, staring at me with shrewd curiosity.

'Do what?'

'Ask a very pointed question and then drop the point when I don't want to answer?'

'Because I trust you,' I say like it's obvious. 'If you don't want to tell me that's your choice – I trust you have a reason.'

He considers and says carefully, 'I can't help but feel like it's because someone spent an awful lot of time telling you not to ask questions.'

'I do a lot of things my mother tells me not to do.' My throat tightens though and the words are difficult. Maybe he's right. Maybe I don't resist my mother's teachings as much as I think I do.

'You can ask me anything, Persephone.' He's looking at me so intently I feel trapped by his gaze. 'I just might not always answer.'

I nod.

'The war,' he says simply. 'The war is probably the answer to every question you have about me. It's why nothing I tried with the mortals worked – I couldn't go near all those horrific memories of theirs. It's why I briefly tried drinking. I wanted to forget everything that happened, everything I went through and everything I did . . . not that it worked. All it did was make the nightmares worse.'

I go to say something but he steels himself and keeps going. 'You've heard the rumours, I'm sure. Before the final battle – or the "uprising", as Zeus has labelled it – I believe I was known as "the biggest mistake Zeus ever made". Which is hardly a surprise – I'm not exactly made for a battlefield. The whispers of "*How could he give a realm to a child?*" soon became "*How could he give a realm to a boy who flinches at the sight of blood and holds a sword like he's afraid of it?*". On the cusp of adolescence, the others couldn't wait to get on to the battlefield. But I dreaded it, almost like I knew it would scar me in the way it eventually did.' He laughs a little ruefully. 'A life spent training for war and the reality of it still fractured me.'

'Hades –'

'Anyway,' he continues, 'I found other ways to distract myself from my own head. A dozen other ways, it turns out. The memories aren't such a struggle when I'm lost in a project. So I suppose the war is also why I like keeping myself busy.'

It's a deep conversation for so early in the morning and for a hangover this bad.

'I'm sorry,' I say.

'What for?' He scowls, pulling his gaze from the distance to me.

'That you went through that.'

Hades snorts. 'That's a first. Zeus wants to pretend we all nobly and valiantly charged to battle the threat of the Titans.'

'Didn't you?' After all, what else was it?

Hades contemplates the question. 'The Titans were hideous creatures – not all of them, obviously, not the ones who fought on our side. But the things they did . . . Kronos killing those who disagreed with him and eating their children in case they grew up to claim revenge? It barely scratches the surface of the things the Titans did. I suppose fighting them was noble and valiant. I'm sure you've worked out by now that I didn't actually charge the battlefield with the undead.'

'An illusion.'

'Exactly. Enough smoke and hellfire and people will believe you actually have the stomach to kill. Although I did that too . . . hence the nightmares. Anyway, a big-enough army of the undead and even the Titans will drop their swords and surrender. Everyone finally believed I was worthy of the power Zeus had given me, and it was a lie.'

'It was clever. And brave.' And difficult – how much power does he hold that he can create an illusion so large? A meadow sometimes takes me days.

'It was a stupid risk that I was lucky didn't get me killed. At the time it just felt desperate. I'm not sure you can make a noble choice when you don't have another option. The others were so hungry for war and vengeance that they're still seeking it out with the mortals. I wasn't – I fought because I had no other choice.'

'Kronos did eat you,' I point out, trying to bring some levity to the conversation.

'He did.' Hades manages a weak smile.

'Have you . . . that is, does Styx know this?'

'No,' he says quietly. 'She knows I was rather terrible at all the training but even she believes I won it with brute force. I think she suspects I've never quite recovered – the servants have sworn to keep my secrets, after all. That includes the sleepless nights and, for a few weeks, the empty wine bottles.'

'So . . . you've never spoken about this before?' I ask. I'm honoured, of course, but concerned. If I'm the first person he's told then I need to react properly, to make him feel supported. Rivers of Hell, what if I've already done something wrong?

'I'd really rather not talk about it at all,' he says. 'There's a reason I prefer to be distracted.'

I nod. I can do that. It is such a huge thing to confess – I don't want to push him too far all at once. 'Well, that's good, because someone has spent a lot of time telling me I'm a distraction.'

Hades smiles but his eyes are distant and I wonder what it is he's seeing. Nothing good, if the scowl etched into his forehead is any indication.

'If you don't want to talk about the war can we talk about how atrocious your singing voice is? Because my ears may never recover.'

The glint in his eyes returns as he snaps back to me. 'That's hardly my fault. You were providing appalling backing on the lyre. I don't recall even your mother being able to lie about your instrumental talents and she managed perfectly well with everything else.'

'Bringing my mother into this is below the belt.'

'You turn down my proposal and then wish to discuss what lies below the belt . . .' He shakes his head, then winces. If his headache is anything like mine, I imagine it's not happy with such jarring movement. 'My, my – I never thought you could be so cruel.'

'Are you going to bring your proposal up at every possible second?'

'I'm sorry. It must be difficult to hear so much about my broken heart.'

'That won't be your only broken body part if you continue,' I mumble and Hades roars with laughter.

I could drown myself in that sound. I really could.

No wonder it's so hard to come by. Do I want to think about the horrors he has faced that he can't even talk about? It's enough to make me want to find Tartarus and hunt down every single Titan in the pit, just to make sure they're suffering like they deserve.

And I wonder, too, what it must be like to be born into a war and raised to fight in it. Battle training, agoge, from childhood and forced on to how many battlefields the moment he hit adolescence? Because of what? Because he was born a man? Because Kronos chose him?

An artist raised to slaughter. I want to hurt everyone involved in that decision. I would too, I think, if I could.

Maybe I am too vengeful.

But then I look at him laughing and I don't care. I'd do it in a heartbeat.

*

After breakfast I head straight to the mortals.

I make my way through the souls I have already healed. They're just standing in a field of asphodel and I can feel the boredom aching from those nearest. I need to give them something quick. If I can just work out how – or, rather, if Hades can work out how. I'm more focused on working out *what* they need, while he reads up on how to make it possible.

Damaris, one of the first souls I repaired, wanders over.

'Persephone, darling, why do you look so terrible?'

Her directness startles a laugh from me. 'That's not a very nice thing to say. Also – Persephone?'

'Styx shouted about it last night. I think she was drunk.'

'So much for the secret keeper.'

'Oh dear, is that a secret?'

'No, but she only told you lot, right?'

'Well, I'm not sure but she passed out on her shores shortly after so I don't think she encountered any other gods.'

'Okay.' I nod.

'I assume you were drinking with her?' She gestures at me, like everything from my crumpled dress to my knotted hair says I was drinking last night. Which, to be fair, is not wrong. Although I'm still wearing the sheets I repurposed as gowns and they crease awfully easy, so I don't think I nor my hangover should get all the blame for that.

I nod but, before I can say anything, Larissa comes running over calling my name. We've spoken enough now that I no longer think of that first encounter with her. Instead I think of the dozens of tales she's told me – only good ones. Then again, after seeing her memories, I know most of the bad. But it worked: I healed her soul, and it helped her find her way back to the other parts of herself.

'Persephone,' she says. 'Is it true Hades proposed?'

'What?' Damaris yelps excitedly.

I wince. I'm too hungover for this.

'How many people did Styx tell?' I grumble.

'Oh just me,' Larissa says. 'Well, and Cora, do you remember her? The princess of Thebes?'

'Yes, I recall.'

'Come on,' Damaris says. 'You're in no state to work right now. The afterlife can wait a day. Come sit a while and you can tell us all about it.'

It is awfully loud with all these souls. Getting away sounds nice.

Damaris reaches across me and clasps Larissa's hand. 'Damaris by the way. Farmer, Mycenae and dead ten years. You?'

Larissa blinks. Then she cracks up. 'Is that how we're introducing ourselves now? Larissa, merchant, Argos, dead thirty years. Plague, I think, if we're throwing that out there.'

'Pneumonia.'

'Ah, very fancy.' Larissa turns to me. 'Anyway, so Styx collapsed and Cora – Oh, there she is! Cora!'

A woman with red curls piled so high on her head they seem liable to tip her over turns at her name and rushes to join us.

'Cora and I ran to check she was okay, and that's when she said about Hades,' finishes Larissa. 'So is it true?'

'Is it true?' Cora repeats with more urgency.

'Um.' I'm not really sure what to say. 'We discussed it. It wasn't a proposal.'

'Good.' Damaris nods. 'Never accept the first proposal.'

Cora nods. 'But I'm sure Hades is lovely.'

The others look at her.

'The king of Hell?' Larissa asks. 'I don't think "lovely" is the word I'd use.'

Cora blushes as much as a spirit can blush. They may be whole souls now but they're still vaguely translucent. 'Well, yes, I was going to say I'm sure he's lovely but I don't get the appeal of marriage.'

I nod. 'Pretty much my thoughts on the matter.'

'*Is* he lovely?' Larissa asks as though the thought has just occurred to her.

'Um.' I'm going to blame my hesitation on the hangover. 'No, it's not the word I'd use. But he's . . . not horrible. He's helping me with all this.'

'Well, I for one am looking forward to this paradise you're creating. And if he's helping us get there then I suppose he can't be all that bad,' Damaris says. 'But right now you need water and some food.'

My stomach churns. I nibbled on some bread at breakfast and it hasn't settled well. 'No, not food.'

The women smirk. 'Come on, let's take you somewhere quiet.'

Somewhere quiet is apparently the shores of the Styx and after a while Styx herself comes crawling up to join us. She laughs at her own messy state and makes enough self-deprecating jokes that the mortal women are soon at ease. We spend most of the day talking about nothing in particular, and I know I can't afford to waste a day like this but I feel like I'm getting a better grasp of the humans and their wants and needs this way.

Enhancing this realm feels within my reach more than ever before. And, at the same time, I feel something slipping away. How much longer do I have? A handful of days? Mere hours? I'm half expecting Father's lightning to strike me down at any moment.

All along, I have known I can't stay in the Underworld. But it's starting to feel like I'll be losing something precious if I leave it all behind – perhaps even a part of myself.

CHAPTER TWENTY-ONE

WHEN I RETURN, I FIND Hades in a hidden room, the one filled with easels and the thick smell of paint. He's so focused on the canvas in front of him that he doesn't notice me enter.

I falter, taking a moment or two to stare unabashedly at the concentration on his face, the way his lips purse, his strong hand curled round the point of a brush, making delicate and precise motions. The planes of his face are sharp in profile. I have never longed to paint but suddenly I see the appeal – if I could capture this moment I would.

I can't believe I was terrified of what he was concealing and it was this. I feared hidden cruelty but found gentleness instead.

I could watch him do this for years – the stillness, the intensity is captivating. I feel like a planet locked in orbit.

I stumble closer without even realizing it.

'Hello,' I manage, not sure when speaking became such an effort.

Hades jumps and paint from the brush flicks across his cheek but he doesn't notice.

'Oh, hello,' he says, rushing to put everything down.

'I didn't mean to interrupt,' I say. 'I can leave.'

'No, no, I . . . well, I was about to say I prefer solitude to paint but I'm not actually sure an alternative has ever been possible. It could be nice to share it.' He smiles almost sheepishly and it's too much. I'm so used to his cocky grins. This bashful Hades, the one he becomes talking about things he actually cares about, has my heart doing flips.

Before I'm even sure what I'm doing I'm in front of him and my thumb is wiping his cheek.

Suddenly his hand snatches my wrist, and he glowers down at me. 'Don't tou–' he starts, but cuts himself off from what I realize must have been an instinctual response.

'You have some paint,' I say, waving my fingers to show him the yellow now coating my thumb – and maybe to distract from how flushed I am.

'Oh.' He holds my hand for a second too long before he lets go. 'Sorry.'

Does he want to touch me? Is that why he hesitated?

'I need to ask you something,' I scramble to say before I entirely forget why I came here.

'Yes?' He arches an eyebrow and, by the Fates, I'm still standing so close. I can't think of a way to move that isn't incredibly obvious.

I wipe the paint on my dress and Hades' querying eyebrow turns back into a scowl.

'Is it not bad enough you're wearing my curtains without smearing them with paint?'

The question surprises me so much that I let out a sharp laugh.

'I'll have you know they're actually your bedsheets. And what does it matter, are you a dressmaker now?' I ask.

He considers the question, his eyes running up and down my body. I know he's just looking at the dress but, please, could somebody tell my heart that? It's pounding so fast and *oh* –

No.

Absolutely not.

Surely this is normal. Surely anyone would be struggling to breathe with any man looking at them like this. Especially a man as undeniably attractive as he is. Surely anyone would still feel the ghost of his touch on their wrist. Surely anyone would find him painting like that mesmerizing. This doesn't mean anything. It can't mean anything. This whole situation is complicated enough without adding . . . *that*.

I steel myself. It *doesn't*. Because it can't. So even if it did mean something – which it doesn't! – I'm going to push it down to that dark place inside myself where I squash all my unwanted feelings until they dissipate. I'll numb myself to this man.

'I've never tried it,' Hades says, completely oblivious to the atrocious direction my thoughts have taken. 'No doubt I could do a better job than you have. I've worked with fabrics before – though never bedsheets and linen.'

'I'm sure I'd survive if you used other materials,' I joke and for a moment I think I might succeed at pulling myself from the spiral of my thoughts.

But then he says: 'I'd need to take some measurements.' And I think of his hands running across my body as he gathers such numbers. I feel dizzy, like the room is swooping, like my very legs are unstable. His eyes catch mine, blazing intensity and an edge of desire, and I'm certain he's thinking the same thing.

I jump back, forgetting that there's an easel behind me with wet paint slathered across it. I swear and fumble with the collapsing contraption, trying to balance, and then the same instincts that flung me back have me reaching for Hades, who hasn't stopped laughing. I manage to miss his outstretched hand and go straight for his robes.

He grasps my shoulders and pulls me upright.

'I am so sorry. Is it –'

'Completely ruined? Absolutely. But don't worry – it was entirely worth it for this.' He waves his hand at my dress, now stained with even more paint, and at my flustered appearance.

I let go of his robes. 'You're an arse.'

He still has one hand on my shoulder and I'm far more aware of it than I should be.

'And you're incredibly uncoordinated. Do the suitors know?' he jokes. 'No husband will ever want you like that.'

I manage not to flinch but every cord of my body is suddenly strung so tight the slightest breeze could cause them to snap.

When I meet Hades' eyes again I find him watching me carefully.

'Your mother says similar things, doesn't she?'

'You can't possibly know that.'

'No, but I think I'm starting to.' His jaw is clenched so tightly that I can see his muscles straining down his neck. If I stare at him for a second longer I'm scared about what I'll do.

'I . . .'

'I don't mean to pry.'

I shake my head. 'I'm not sure I understand well enough myself. She's a good mother.'

'Perhaps,' he says. 'So long as you know that you're a good daughter.'

My breath catches. That's it, isn't it? This feeling I keep getting isn't about my mother at all, but about how nothing I do ever feels good enough, that who I am isn't who she wants me to be. No matter how miserable I make myself doing as she asks, it still isn't right.

'If I were a good daughter I wouldn't be here,' I say. And it's less because I mean it – I'm starting to feel like I was always meant to come here – and more because it's the only way I can articulate the guilt that gnaws in my gut, guilt that refuses to listen to logical arguments and feelings of belonging.

'Persephone –'

'Can we not?' I interrupt. I wish we could go back to the confusing muddle of yearnings because it's better than this. 'Later maybe,' I add when he looks like he's about to protest. 'I don't have the energy right now. And I'm covered in paint and need to change.'

'Don't you dare,' he says. 'I worked hard on that painting. If you have to wear it for it to survive then so be it.'

I offer a smile only because I appreciate him letting me change the subject. 'If you don't want to make me clothes you don't have to use me wearing your art as an excuse.'

He laughs. 'Well, was the thought of me designing your gowns really so horrendous that you had to jump into the artwork to escape?'

'Would you actually be interested in making me something?'

'I enjoy a challenge.' When he looks at me I see one in his eyes. 'Would you judge me for it?'

'Of course not,' I say. 'Is it worth it though? You know I'll just ruin them in the garden.' *And I won't be here long to wear them.* The unspoken words linger heavy between us so I rush on: 'But if you'd find it fun then go for it. You're obviously talented.'

'Obviously?' His cocky grin is back in place and I have the sudden urge to press my lips to his to get rid of it.

What in the name of all that is sacred is wrong with me? My moon blood is not due, though it's possible being down here has messed with my cycle. Did I hit my head recently? I might be under a spell, I suppose, but I don't think Hades would do that and I'm pretty sure cursing me would break his vow on the Styx.

My eyes narrow as I examine him, looking for any sign that he knows what thoughts are cycling through my head.

Nothing.

'Why do you keep it all hidden?' I ask instead.

'What do you mean?'

'Why are the halls so bare when you have so much to decorate them with?' I clarify.

'Well.' He scratches the back of his neck and it's such a casual move that I'm almost certain he can't know that it's taking most of my self-restraint not to jump into his arms right now. 'Usually, I have members of the court constantly coming and going. They might ask where it all comes from.'

I realize how little I know of Hades' court. I had so many more immediate concerns when I arrived that as soon as I discovered he'd dismissed them I'd pushed it from my mind. But now I think about it. I cannot imagine Father dismissing his court for a few weeks. It might weaken his hold on them, give them an opportunity to plan a rebellion. But Hades did it without even thinking.

'Where are they? I've only seen the humans and Styx.'

'I'm not the only one with an aversion to human memories,' Hades says. 'Between the mortals and the river Styx, this is considered the less desirable side of the Underworld. They all live on the other side of the Acheron.' The river of pain that flows on the other side of the fields of asphodel. It's the way the souls travel to the Underworld so I've mostly avoided it. 'I imagine they are thoroughly enjoying their time off.'

But that can't last forever. Hades will summon them all back when I'm finally gone.

At least he won't be alone.

'I'm sorry you had to dismiss them all for me.'

'Oh, I'm incredibly sad about it. No more task forces on the latest disease impacting the supply chain or panels on sustainable soul collecting, no more mediating their squabbles ... Several annoying deities traded for the goddess of flowers?' he teases. 'Such a difficult trade.'

I shake my head. 'You're ridiculous.'

'Is another man fawning over you too much for you to handle? Another man begging for your hand in marriage?'

'Oh, not this again.'

'Please be mine. Grace my halls with your presence forever –'

I'm laughing but my heart is galloping. 'Well, maybe if you hadn't been such a dick when I first got here ...'

He places his hand on his heart and attempts to look pained. 'Oh, what a fool I was –'

'You look constipated.'

'I'm trying to seduce you here!'

'Try harder.' I turn from him. I don't think I'm blushing but I want to be sure. 'Gods, I don't remember you ever being in such high spirits.'

He shrugs and it's back to that self-containment that I associate with him becoming serious again. 'Your refusal of my proposal was of course quite the setback but, on the whole, these last few days have been nice.' He hesitates. 'You know, not having to hide parts of myself.'

I nod. I definitely understand that. 'Yes, well, I was certainly never this bossy with my mother.' We're back on dangerous ground, so I race to continue. 'It's actually your painting I wanted to talk to you about.'

'Oh?'

'I'm still working out, well, a lot of all this . . .'

'If crafting Hell were easy I'm sure Zeus would have already made a minor god do it and claimed the credit.'

'True. Well, I've been talking to some of the humans and they describe things I've never seen: mountains so tall they could tear Olympus apart, lakes that stretch further than the eye can see, forests and villages and towns and waterfalls and snow so bright it's blinding.' An edge of longing creeps into my voice and I don't realize until my throat tightens.

'You could look in the Lake of the Five.'

'It's not the same. And anyway, well, I've got the flowers of paradise sorted but everything else? I have no idea. I can't even picture it, really. I'm not artistic and I've been tasked with designing paradise.'

'You tasked yourself, actually,' Hades says pointedly.

Given I am asking him to do something for me, I can't return his snark with more snark so I settle for ignoring that comment.

'Will you do it? Sketch out an idea or paint some concepts?'

'What do I know of human paradise?' he says dismissively.

I won't let him get away that easily. 'I've seen the things you've made. I think you know a lot more about paradise than you let on. Otherwise what's kept you going all these years?'

His shoulders freeze in rigid lines and I worry I've gone too far.

'Very well,' he finally says with a curt nod. 'If you'll excuse me, I shall go and make a start on your paradise.'

CHAPTER TWENTY-TWO

FOR THE NEXT FEW DAYS I flit around Hades like a nervous insect, too fearful of making contact. This longing feels like every bit of what the nymphs discussed so I recognize it for what it is: infatuation and nothing more. One does not fall in love in a few weeks, after all.

But I'm terrified of that infatuation growing.

My own feelings have become the enemy.

And, even though I'm doing my best to stamp it out, occasionally I permit myself to think of him while chewing on my lip, or I get lost in his eyes, or I lose an hour of sleep in anticipation of seeing him the next day. But thinking of softer moments – of what it would feel like to curl into his skin, to feel his breath on my neck, to talk until the small hours of the morning – that is a step too far. I have too much at stake to add emotions to the mix. Similarly, anything beyond the curiosity of his lips on mine is an absurdity. Picturing how we might build a life together – after mere weeks! – is more fantasy than anything the Muses could craft.

I blame his ridiculously well-tailored chiton and whichever god is responsible for cheekbones.

And low voices.

And that damn mocking smile of his.

Oh Fates, this is infuriating.

And yet, regardless of how loath I am to admit it, one thing is undeniable: I don't want to lose him.

At breakfast three days later, Hades hands over a pile of dresses.

'Try not to get paint on these. Mud I will accept as a hazard of your profession.' He grins but then casts an anxious glance at the pile of fabrics. I'm unsure whether he's scared I'll mock them or that I'll simply dislike them.

He needn't have worried.

I take them to my room and try them on, one by one. The silk gown fits me like every movement is a caress against my skin. It's burnt orange with white thread and I glance at the painting hanging above my bed. Asphodel is clearly a flower he likes an awful lot. Another is the pink of styx petals, with gathered material twisted into flowers round the waist. Others aren't inspired by my flowers but feel like they were designed for me nonetheless – navy like the ink of the notes we take, a shifting red like the flames in the fireplace we sit beside, green and beaded like the leaves that float in the tea we share each evening.

They're incredible and I tell him as much.

'Mother buys me dresses the offspring of the Muses have created. They have nothing on this,' I say.

I expect him to dismiss it, like I do with any compliment that comes my way, or to laugh it off with some grandiose statement about his own excellence. But he ducks his head and says a quiet thank you, like he's pocketing the compliment.

Once we've eaten and I've chosen a dress – the navy, something about the way it swirls reminds me of the darkness of his illusory smoke – we head to the lake edge for my daily check-up on my mother. Hades won't let me go alone any more. Or, rather, he begs me not to, tells me to take Styx if I won't take him. I don't mind him coming, though.

And something's different today.

I know it from the moment Mother appears in the waters. There is less desperation in her eyes and more of a determined gleam. I've never seen her like this before. She is in a dark room lit only by the torch in her hand and her eyes dance with the reflection of the flames.

'No,' I whisper.

Hades takes my hand and I think it might be the first time he has chosen to do that. He lifts it to brush his lips.

'You will be fine, Persephone, whatever happens.'

I blink at the lake as a hooded figure appears. The hood lowers to reveal a face so wrinkled and creased it takes me a moment to find her ink-black eyes among the alabaster folds. Hecate, goddess of magic. *No.* She might actually know something and obviously Mother thinks so too.

'I cannot find her,' she says. 'Wherever she is, she is cloaked.'

'But you know *something*, Hecate,' Mother says. 'Or you would not have taken my gift.'

'I know many things,' Hecate croons. She raises a wrinkled finger to gesture Mother closer.

'Magic is a trade,' Mother hisses. She is taller than Hecate but you can't tell. 'I gave you a sacrifice.'

I think of the nymphs she turned to sirens. What would she possibly give as a sacrifice? I have no doubt that, for my safe return, there is no line she would not cross.

Rivers of Hell, what have I done?

'I can see her,' Hecate says. 'This is your trade.'

'Where is she?' Mother's lips peel back to reveal teeth that gleam too white in the darkness. She is tired of asking.

'She is in the mind of another,' Hecate declares almost gleefully.

'Explain.'

'I am not your daughter, Demeter.' Hecate grins like this whole interaction is the best thing to happen to her in years. I have no idea how old she is or where she came from. There are so many rumours about her parentage that there may as well be none. I know I'm not the only god to wonder if she's older than the universe itself. 'You cannot bark orders at me and expect me to comply.'

'Can you *please* explain more?' Mother forces the words through gritted teeth, her knuckles whitening round the torch she clutches.

Hecate cackles. 'As you asked so nicely. I cannot see where she is now. But I can see a version of her, a memory.'

'Someone saw her taken?' Mother's desperation has me clutching to Hades even tighter.

'She disappeared in the middle of the day,' Hecate almost sings. 'On the sunny island of Sicily and only a single soul saw! Just one. Other than the two involved in the act, obviously.'

'Who?'

'I just told you.'

Mother waves the torch threateningly close to Hecate's face. 'I am in no mood for riddles.'

Hecate laughs and the sound is so gravelly the flames shake. She snaps her fingers and the torch flickers out.

'What a good thing your child is smarter than you.' Hecate grins. '*The sun*, Demeter. Helios saw all as he pulled it across the sky.'

'Fates, this is it,' I breathe.

'You are safe,' Hades repeats and I wonder who he is trying to convince. I'm certainly not stupid enough to believe him.

Father must have been watching because, in a lightning flash, Mother is before him. He lounges on his throne like it is the comfiest thing in the world but the fingers on his lightning bolt are taut and his back straightens as Mother approaches.

Mother speaks before he can demand it of her. 'Helios knows,' she says darkly and I pity poor Helios even as he is about to reveal my secrets. Mother will not look kindly on him for keeping this information from her. 'We will have to wait until the sun sets to speak to him but we now have it on Hecate's authority that he knows where she is, or at least what happened to her.'

'Good,' Father growls. He's the angriest I have seen him, lightning sparking in the air around him as he shakes with rage. 'I will kill whoever has taken her for what they have cost me. They have made me the laughing stock of the Heavens.'

'I thought you said no one would –'

'Well, they are!' Father snaps. 'They're all laughing! I will destroy whoever has caused this, whoever dared snatch her away from us. I will tear them limb from limb until the punishment of Prometheus seems a kindness.'

I freeze. I hadn't considered this. I'd assumed that sooner or later my parents would realize I ran away of my own volition. And maybe they will. But, *if* my father mistakenly believes Hades kidnapped me, he'll punish him for it. All those threats, all those promises of pain . . . they're promises for Hades. I've seen Father's rage. I'd never be able to tell him the truth before he enacted his fury and he probably wouldn't believe me if I did. Hades would be hurt. He might even be killed.

And, gods, if Zeus really were to go to war for my honour – and wars have been fought for less – even Poseidon's support might not be enough.

How many humans would die in the slaughter between the three great gods?

I wave the vision away. I take a breath and stare at the inky waters. I can't just stand and watch as they hunt me down, as they turn to Hades, seeking revenge for an imagined slight.

There's only one thing that I can do.

'Marry me,' I say, because it's the only way. If I'm married, they have no reason to be angry. If they believe he did not steal my honour but my hand then he's safe.

He startles. 'Excuse me?'

I can't tell him. If I tell him it's because I'm scared of what they'll do to him, he'll never agree to it. He'll laugh and say that he's fine, even as they level a blade to his throat.

I've put him and every being of this realm in danger. My father will slaughter him, or throw him in the same pit as the Titans, or at the very least snatch the crown from his head and give it to someone else, someone just like himself, and all three courts will be ruled by horrible, awful men. Because of me, Hades could lose everything – even his life.

'You said the offer was still open,' I say. Tears burn into my eyes but I don't let them fall. 'Please, Hades, I have to. They're furious – they might –' But that won't convince him. He won't agree to this because of Zeus's threats. He'll agree to this for me. 'They'll come and take me back and I don't want to leave. I don't want whatever marriage they'll push me into. I can't leave this place.' I drop to one knee because isn't that what you're supposed to do? 'If . . . marrying you is the only definite way to stay then . . . marry me, please.'

It might not be the reason I'm asking, but I'll let him think it is if it's what saves him.

Hades falls to his knees too and then he's looking right at me.

'Persephone.' His hands cup my face, like if I look away for even a second I may not realize what decision I am making. 'Are you sure about this?'

I can't breathe, can't look anywhere but at him. I feel like I could cry, knowing this moment isn't real, not in the way I might want it to be. I don't . . . Even if it were, I . . . In this moment I want him so badly that not having him feels like heartbreak.

'I love this place,' I say, my voice breaking. My throat is swollen with the tears I'm holding at bay. This whole thing is a mess. But I can't cope with the idea of anyone hurting Hades. I'd do anything to save him from the tiniest shred of pain, let alone all my father could bring.

It's not a lie that I adore this world – but, looking into

Hades' eyes, I know it's not what I would mourn the most if I had to leave.

Gods, how am I supposed to marry a man I am on the brink of falling in love with?

He nods, slowly.

'Very well,' he agrees.

I want to scream in delight and crush him in my embrace and break down with heaving sobs. It's too much. I feel like I'm suffocating.

His hands are still on my face and his thumb wipes away a tear that I didn't realize had broken free.

'Persephone,' he says gently. 'I'd do anything you asked of me. But are you sure you're okay with this?'

So I start our marriage off with a lie: I nod. When he doesn't look convinced I force a smile. 'Sorry, sorry. I was just so scared about them taking me back. Thank you, Hades! Thank you so much. Fates, this is perfect! Imagine how angry they'll be when, on the cusp of them finding me, we announce our engagement. We should do it today. Oh, this is going to be so much fun.'

It's one of the best performances of my life. But Hades doesn't look like he believes me.

'All right, I trust you,' he says after a moment. 'But I hope you know what this entails – I'll summon the court and I suppose we'll see how well we can convince them we're wildly in love before we try it with the Olympians.'

I swallow, unable to meet his eyes. When I finally manage to glance up at him, his eyes are lit with a challenge.

'Well, Persephone, I hope you're as good a liar as you claim.'

CHAPTER TWENTY-THREE

HADES HAS THE NYMPHS WORKING on a thousand things at once while I rush to ensure all is well enough with the humans that I can temporarily leave them to plan a wedding. I'm trying to think about anything, really, other than the threat my father has just made. Or that I am, despite a lifetime trying to avoid it, engaged. Even now, just thinking the word 'marriage' has my stomach in knots.

No, I think of anything but those things.

So I repair souls and discuss versions of paradise, and I gather with my regular group of mortal women and tell them I have changed my mind and accepted his proposal. I let their chatter wash over me, relax me, and just being out among these souls I feel calmer.

I can't leave this place. These people are no longer fading to raw husks of memory; they're whole, impossibly alive in the Underworld, and they're wonderful. I can't imagine not seeing them again, talking to them again – I love them and this world, and to stay here I'd give up my freedom, give up any dream of seeing Sicily again. I'd even give up any chance of my mother's approval. And maybe I'm not wholly convinced by the time I return to the palace but I'm ready to lie through my teeth, even to myself.

I'm so distracted that I don't notice Styx until I nearly collide with her in the hallway.

'Would you care to explain why I've been summoned to court this evening?' she asks.

'Well . . . Hades and I might be getting married.'

'Right.' She nods. 'I'm sorry, how drunk was I the other night?'

'Very. But this happened this morning.'

I tell her everything that happened in one breath.

I expect Styx to swear or make some sarcastic comment or insist that marriage isn't the solution.

Instead she asks me how I feel about it all, and I burst into tears. 'I'm scared,' I admit. 'What if this doesn't work? What if the marriage infuriates them more?'

'I don't think they can be more infuriated,' she says. 'You literally have nothing to lose.'

'I have everything to lose.'

'Well, you're losing it anyway. I think it's a great idea – the only way to placate them on the surface while riling them beneath. They *will* be infuriated – is that not entirely the point? You'll have thwarted them at the final step.'

I nod slowly. 'Yes, yes, I suppose so. I also can't think of anything else to do.'

She shrugs. 'Marriage *will* afford you some protection. Being the queen of Hell will afford you more.'

I hadn't even thought of that. Fates, how had I not even thought of that?

Marrying Hades doesn't just mean staying in this realm forever, but becoming a ruler of it, becoming its queen. What does that even mean? Attending the court, watching over the realm – holding power. It's all I ever wanted.

But . . . I can't do that to him. This is his realm. He's already doing so much for me by agreeing to this marriage; he shouldn't lose power in the process. It'll have to be in name only, a tiara on my head and a throne to sit on and my mouth kept shut.

Can I do that? How is that any different from the wife Mother was preparing me to become?

'I can't do this.'

'I thought this was your choice!'

'It is,' I confirm. 'But it doesn't feel like one. How am I supposed to be queen of Hell? I can't actually do anything without usurping Hades, and I can't do nothing for the rest of eternity.'

'Okay, well, you're not usurping Hades – you're marrying him. Besides, since when is that an issue? I seem to recall you saying you didn't care whether he approved of your plans to create an afterlife. You're picking quite the time to worry about taking his power.'

'Yes, well, things change.'

'You're telling me.' She rubs her temples. 'You have met your fiancé, right? He doesn't exactly love ruling this place. He clings to that crown solely because it means no one has the right to question him about who he is or what he does. He'd probably love you to help out so he can spend more time reading or painting or whatever hobby he's favouring that week.'

'Well, I can't do that either,' I yelp as panic surges through me.

'What?'

'I don't know the first thing about ruling a realm.'

She takes my hand and runs soothing circles with her thumb like Cyane always used to. 'You want to make this place better – that's the most important thing. And you've already done that. The flowers –'

I laugh and her grip on my hand tightens.

'No, don't do that,' she scolds. 'The flowers are wonderful. They're life itself – which was lacking before you came here. And you haven't created paradise yet, but you've been restoring souls and keeping them safe. You're already acting as queen. And that's already so much power, Persephone.'

'Yes. More power than I've ever had before. What am I supposed to do with more of it?'

'You're scared of power now? You told your father you wanted the world when you were eight years old. Where's that ruthless, demanding little girl?'

I swallow. If my amphidromia taught me anything it's that my father's world has no place for a girl like that.

'They made it your name, made it an insult, turned it into something it's not. There's nothing wrong with being a little girl, love. Little girls are fearless.'

I consider that. There might be something lurking that I've buried – the side of me that craves power, the longing for something darker that drew me to the Underworld to begin with. The part of me that is thrilled at the thought of a crown.

My hesitation, my reluctance, my fear – is that what I'm supposed to feel?

'It's understandable if this is all a bit much. You haven't had time to process it. And if it helps you to focus on keeping Hades safe then focus on that. But you should know it's not just Hades you're doing this for. And it's not just yourself either. You're doing this for me and every inhabitant of this realm. You've been here three weeks and it's already a changed place – a better one.'

I want to deny it and say that she's wrong, that I'm nothing and no one and powerless and just a stupid girl in over her head.

But I don't think that's my voice talking.

I nod. Styx draws me into her arms. It takes a moment but then I'm hugging her back.

'See,' she says. 'It will all be fine. Now, am I your maid of honour? Or will that be difficult if I'm also Hades' best man?'

'Are we really going to have to fight over you?'

She waves a hand. 'You'll be fine – you have other friends. I'm all he has.'

'Really?'

'No, of course not. But how close can they be when he's keeping so much of himself from them? I, on the other hand, am privy to all his secrets. And that makes us besties whether he wants to be or not. Oh! I just thought – with your proposal and everything, does this mean he knows how you feel?'

'No!' I rush and then she grins a purely evil smile. I immediately realize my mistake.

'I knew it! I knew you had feelings for him!'

I stare at her and, oh gods, *how*? I managed to keep that secret for, what, three days? How long until Hades finds out?

Oh Fates, will he think I've trapped him in a marriage under false pretences?

My palms are clammy and how is this making me panic? My heart is racing like I've run a mile. Incredible. I'll make an excellent queen of Hell if this is enough to scare me.

'You can't say *anything* to him.'

Her shoulders shake, which suggests she's finding this whole thing far too funny. 'Calm down, dear. He likes you too so you're all good.'

'He likes me too?' No – that's even worse. Our marriage is supposed to be a business arrangement. We can't add *that* in; it'll destroy us.

My feelings refuse to bow to my logic. If Hades is feeling anything like this then it's only a matter of time until we make some stupid, reckless decision – and, let's face it, they're my specialty. Then it will all come out that we only married to stop my parents forcing me into another marriage, and to prevent them from realizing I'd run from them voluntarily in the first place. They'll find out that all of this, from the very start, was to stop Zeus getting what he wanted. And we'll be punished accordingly.

'He doesn't like me,' I insist. 'Tell me right now that he doesn't.'

'Well, he hasn't said anything. But I have what's known as eyes.'

'I thought you were serious! Styx! I don't have time for this.'

'You don't have time for feelings for your betrothed?'

'No,' I snap. 'Because that's got nothing to do with us getting married.'

'Other than you not wanting Zeus to eviscerate him.'

'He doesn't know that's why I'm doing this so keep quiet about that too.'

She sighs. 'Trust you to sap all the joy out of a wedding. Your mother really did a fine job with that one.'

Will Mother be happy about this? That I found someone I like, someone who treats me well, someone who would face the wrath of Zeus to protect me?

Or will she be angry that Hades encourages my worst tendencies? That he likes the parts of me she tried to stamp out?

Or will she simply be devastated? I have no way of telling her this is voluntary. She will think I've been kidnapped by the cruel ruler of the Underworld and forced into a marriage.

'She'll be distraught,' I say.

'It's all right,' Styx says gently, perhaps realizing she never should have brought up the subject of my mother. 'You can take her aside at your wedding and talk to her. She might be upset until then but this is better than the lifetime of sadness you'd have had if she'd had her way.' She's unable to stop the wrinkle in her nose. Styx is not a fan of my mother. My thoughts of Mother leave me in circles, battling the conditions of her love, but Styx resolutely decided she was horrible – which only made me feel more guilty. I clearly did a terrible job of talking about my mother if that's what Styx took away.

'She never wanted that. She was trying to make the best of my father's wishes,' I say.

'She should have fought them.'

But that's easy for Styx to say – down here in a realm Hades has kept far away from Zeus.

'You're right,' I say. I don't want to debate this. 'I just have to wait for the wedding.'

Styx smirks as two wind nymphs run past us, arms laden with trays of food. 'Let's get through the court announcement first.'

The nymphs have been rushing around all morning, running food and drink through the halls, crafting decorations and cleaning the walls. I promised them a party of their own after all this, while I try to figure out how to pay wind nymphs who have no want for money.

Now I stare at the empty, shining walls, unable to imagine the palace full of people, full of gods.

But I can see it full of something. And now we have the perfect excuse.

'I need to go,' I tell her. 'I have something to sort.'

'Persephone!' Hades calls when he returns.

I can't tell whether he's furious or happy.

He's standing in the middle of the foyer, staring at the walls around him. My heart beats: *My husband, my husband, my husband.*

'What is this?' he asks.

I can't help but smile. 'Don't you recognize your own work?'

I have plastered every available space in the palace with the tapestries, paintings and statues that Hades has crafted. I found them rolled into stacks in the corners of his art rooms and lying in towers that seemed precarious at best. A whole lifetime of art, of trying to escape thoughts I cannot even imagine.

'Why is it here?' he asks quietly, with a touch of sadness and a hint of longing.

'They're beautiful,' I say firmly. 'Art should be seen and

finally you have an excuse. Everyone who visits can believe I did them, and they won't have to gather dust any more.'

His face shatters into a grin. There are worse beings to marry, so many thousands of worse beings. I hadn't dared to imagine ever making anyone smile like that, so raw and open. I feel accomplished somehow, like every harsh edge I have is softening.

'I did not even consider that,' he says.

'Well, I get the whole realm thinking I'm extraordinarily talented, so it works out well for me too.'

'You don't have to keep complimenting me. I've already agreed to marriage.'

'Besides,' I continue, 'you'll need to pretend to have done all of that.' I nod in the vague direction of the humans. 'Splitting the land and restoring the souls and all the rest of it.'

Hades' smile falters. 'Why?'

'Because Father is much more likely to leave me alone if he believes me harmless,' I say. 'And if I'm plotting to revamp the afterlife, I'm not quite the meek, flower-loving child he thinks I am.'

Hades glowers. Even though he knows what Zeus has threatened, he won't let it stand in his way. 'Who cares if –'

'Darling, I'm already marrying you. I think we've established just how much I care, and just how desperate I am,' I say.

Hades smirks and I realize how much I love this teasing without consequence, where insults are met with smiles and laughs, not icy stares and scolding.

Wait.

Is this all that this is?

Is this infatuation that's been building little more than being

treated like an equal for the first time? It should be promising –
I might not have feelings for the man I am marrying – but it's
not. I feel like I can't trust my own reactions if they can be so
easily warped.

'I always imagined a softly spoken wife who spoke of her
adoration of me so lyrically,' he teases. He lifts my hand to his
lips and as they brush against me I feel like I'm falling to this
realm all over again.

Gods damn you, Hades.

I take a shaky breath and say, 'Fuck you,' like it's the caress
of *I love you*, complete with simpering eyes and the clutching
of his hand.

Hades shakes his head but he can't stop the smile on his
face.

'I always thought you a good performer but, by the Fates, I
hope your acting skills improve by this evening,' he says.

'For the hardest role of my life?' I feign consideration.
'Hades, pretending to love you shall be my magnum opus.'

I just hope I'm right.

CHAPTER TWENTY-FOUR

A KNOCK ON MY BEDROOM DOOR and I see a collection of women: Damaris, Cora, Larissa and Styx.

'I thought you might need a hand getting ready,' Styx says.

She's lying. I know she's only here because she doesn't want me to be alone after I cried in her arms earlier.

'No Tempest?' I ask her.

'She told me to get lost at the mere suggestion she join when she's so busy preparing the palace for the court's arrival. Then she added a few more choice expletives to drive home the point.'

I shake my head as I laugh, feeling a sudden fondness for the nymph and for Styx, and for all these women who surround me and giggle as they dress me like we've all known each other for centuries.

They arrange my hair, spray me with scents and squeeze me into a dress Hades fetched from the mortal realm, having no time to make one himself. Styx sits on the bed, watching with wry amusement. 'Oh no, dear. You would *not* want me doing your hair. That's why I brought the others. Don't worry, I'll provide the entertainment.'

When I first sat in front of the mirror, I could feel walls slamming down and defences being raised. It was too reminiscent of my mother flitting about every time we had visitors – the tug of her fingers in my hair, my breath gasping as she laced me into something impossible so they'd go back to Olympus and spread rumours about my beauty.

But I haven't stopped laughing as I have been painted and dressed. This whole evening is a forgery of a wedding announcement, I will be a forgery of a blushing bride, and everything about my appearance will be a performance. The difference is that I am in control. Mother is not squeezing me into a costume; I am creating one myself.

When I am ready, the perfection of the costume has my shoulders pushed back and my head held high. It is precisely what I needed. My hair is long, pinned out of my face and flowing freely down my back. My black dress sweeps the floor, overlayed in sheer fabric embroidered with black flowers. The sleeves are translucent, my skin glowing beneath the lace. Kohl is smudged on my eyelids and my lips are stained a dark and bloody shade of red.

I look ready to become the queen of Hell. I thank the mortals and promise them updates in the morning. Styx leaves with them, claiming she will feel like a spy when she returns with the other gods. There's a delighted smile on her face, like nothing makes her happier than being privy to secrets.

I look in the mirror one last time and note the steely certainty in my eyes. I can do this. I can pretend I have enough power and potential that a king might want nothing more than to make me his queen. It won't be easy – but it might be fun.

There will be no going back. But my parents will know where I am soon anyway.

I leave my room and descend the marble stairs to meet Hades.

He's straightening a picture and I take advantage of his distraction to unapologetically run my eyes over him. He wears a formal black robe, with twin gold cuffs on his wrists that match the earrings glittering on my lobes.

The robe fits him well, so well that I can't help but think that, if we were really getting married, I might not be able to wait until the wedding before peeling those layers off him.

The thought shocks me and I clutch the banister to keep from stumbling. I have no idea where it came from and part of me wants to run back upstairs. But then he turns and sees me, and his eyes widen like he's spotted enemies on a battlefield.

My own panic dissipates, like just locking eyes with him is enough to make me feel calm.

He mutters something that I can't catch and I smirk as I close the distance between us. I know I look stunning, and I do so very love unnerving him.

'What was that, my dear?' I ask.

Hades cocks an eyebrow. 'I said, you're late.'

'Did you now?'

Hades grins. 'No, I said you look exquisite.'

I smile back, enjoying this one moment of peace, just the two of us before we encounter the masses. 'Now that's more like it. You look rather well yourself.'

'Exquisite and rather well are not on par,' Hades says pointedly.

He's already so close and he's only going to be closer as we pretend to be madly in love. My heart pounds. I can do this. I have been lying for years. I can definitely spin the truth into a lie too.

'Then I suppose you'll have to try harder for the wedding,' I tease. Though honestly if he tries any harder I could faint on my wedding day. I might be dramatic but I don't think that would be beneficial for anyone.

'I've never had any complaints before.' He grins wickedly and heat rushes to my cheeks.

'Before?' I manage. 'Oh, we are discussing "before".'

'Must we?'

'Ever since you ended the war, you've been surrounded by no one but half-corporeal nature spirits and the ghosts of dead humans. We are *definitely* discussing your before.'

His laughter bounces off the walls until I am surrounded by the ringing, glorious noise.

'You forget the court.'

'Well, do you want to fill me in before I meet them all?'

'Oh, I think it will be far more entertaining if I didn't. Now, there's one more thing,' he says and from his pocket he pulls a cloth-wrapped package. He tugs on the cord and it unfurls to reveal, pooled in his palm, a thin gold chain with a large black stone in its centre. A metal frame twists round it like ivy.

'Did you make this?' I gasp, taking it and letting it hang from my fingers. The gem catches the light as it spins.

Hades nods, a little embarrassed. Then that smirk is back. 'Did I not mention I'm also the god of riches? It comes with the territory, apparently, anything under the world, such stones included.'

'Fates, why did I turn down your first proposal?'

He laughs and gestures for me to turn. I hand him the necklace and hold my breath as his fingers brush the back of my neck. Suddenly, I realize that we only agreed to this ruse today. And we've been running around ever since.

Which means he . . . he already made this.

Did he make it for me? Or did he simply decide to give it to me? And, if the former, when? Why?

'There,' he says before holding his arm out for me. 'Are you ready, my love?'

'Oh, "my love". Nice touch,' I say.

'I thought so, and what shall you call me?'

'My lord, I suppose.' The words leave a foul taste in my mouth. They are far too deferential but they are what would be expected. I've only ever called him that in mockery.

Hades apparently feels the same way. He scowls with disgust. 'Absolutely not, not from you. None of this Lord Hades nonsense, either.'

We have two options with this performance: I'm either terrified but acquiescing, or I have quickly fallen in love with Hades and he in love with me. The former would better appease my father, but I'll take the one that suggests I have some choice in the matter – and that positions me better for a crown.

'Then I suppose you shall be "my love" as well,' I say, taking his arm.

He smiles but it's different from usual – smaller, more discreet. Almost hidden but not quite. I'm so attuned to his face by now that I'm not sure he could hide the slightest shift in expression from me.

We are steps from the doors that lead to the megaron when they swing open of their own accord.

There are so many people in the throne hall I can hardly take them all in, so many gods of so many shapes and colours and sizes. Here I spot wings. There I see a tail. I had no idea there were so many gods of the Underworld.

As we cross the threshold, as people see us, whispers spread through the room.

I expected gasps and shocked cries.

But then I remember that no one even knows what I look like. To them, I am just the mysterious girl hanging on to the arm of the king of Hell.

Hades has summoned his illusions once more and we are shrouded in dark fog. It unfurls before us like we are rising from the darkness.

We walk the aisle slowly and I keep my eyes far ahead, on the throne at the end.

I will have my own when we are married.

The thought sends thrills shivering down my spine.

We part round the hearth in the centre of the hall and rejoin on the other side, our hands reaching before we are even close. When we climb the steps of the throne's plinth, I stand beside Hades as he sits, an unsavoury act but a necessary one.

People drop to one knee as we pass and I think of Tempest saying Hades doesn't care for false platitudes. Then I think of how important maintaining Hades' reputation is – it's the only thing giving him the privacy he needs for his art.

I think maybe platitudes are necessary, like the swords that line the palace's exterior. I wonder what else might be necessary too.

Hades looks just as powerful as he did the day I arrived: smoke crawling along his arms, twisted metal crown, black robes harsh against his dark skin, and the obsidian throne towering above the court. I hope that I look just as startling by his side.

I stand to the left of the throne. Hades takes my hand as I move to pull it away.

It is a tender balancing act. I must be hopelessly in love with this man and ludicrously excited for our wedding, yet aloof enough to make it clear that the throne is also my intent. If I'm to be a queen then people will need to see me as one, not a simpering bride in a tiara. Otherwise the position is no protection at all.

'Rise,' Hades commands and the surrounding gods get to their feet. I scan the gods and start when I see a familiar face looking at me with a calculating gleam in his eye.

I saw Hermes just weeks ago, vying for my hand with a caduceus.

He doesn't realize who I am. Not yet at least.

But he is still the cunning god of trickery and that makes him a threat.

'I haven't seen a turnout like this in some time,' Hades says, leaning back to survey the room with a cruel smile unfurling on his face. 'Evidently there is some curiosity as to why court was adjourned rather suddenly a few weeks ago.'

There's some awkward shuffling among the attendees.

'I expect far greater punctuality in the future. I've been

working on something new for the humans and it's given me quite the taste for punishment.'

I bite back my laughter, schooling my expression into one of calm. Hades assured me he's not usually such a sadistic jerk, but, given everyone is going to think he kidnapped me, he has to be more of a dick than usual. I'm glad I'm on the inside of his facade now, but I worry that having seen the real Hades I may struggle to take the fake one seriously.

'We shall start, I suppose, with my wedding.' The silence breaks and whispers storm across the room.

'Silence,' Hades snarls and the assembled gods are quiet once more.

He turns to smile at me but the corners of his lips are twisted enough that the grin suggests mockery more than joy. He is loving this charade as much as I am.

'Court was adjourned because my betrothed arrived in this realm.' His voice is barely louder than a whisper but I know that every single person in this room heard. Those at the back are arching themselves for a better look.

I smile, a small, intimate movement that conveys to everyone here that I don't care for their whispering, just the man beside me.

'I would like to present Persephone. You may know her better as Kore, goddess of flowers and beauty in nature. Soon to be Persephone, Queen of the Underworld.'

Hades does not demand silence again but instead grins greedily as the whispers spread, like nothing is more enjoyable than the sheer chaos that has erupted around us. Everyone is talking, shouting, calling rumours back and forth.

I keep that small smile in place, like I can't hear them at all, and run my thumb over the hand that rests in mine.

'We shall be married,' Hades says and the room falls silent, 'on the solstice.'

My lips part, the only suggestion of the gasp I manage to stifle. We had not discussed this but it's perfect. Mother's powers will be at their weakest during the shortest day. She won't be able to stop us, which will give me time to tell her what's really going on. And it's only a week away.

Clever bastard.

'I invite you all to the ceremony, to bear witness to our union.' He kisses my hand in a manoeuvre so suave and practised that my returning grin is entirely natural. 'We have much to discuss. So drink, be merry and celebrate.'

He stands, dismissing the official proceedings, and tables laden with food and drink appear round the edges of the room. Music starts playing, drowning out the shocked conversations that continue.

'Hades, you sly dog.' Hermes is before us with a grin nothing short of ecstatic plastered across his face. He's shorter than he looked in the lake and he's made some effort to style his slick black hair for court – though it's already sticking up again. He's not bad-looking – I suppose none of the gods are – but I can still barely look at him without thinking about the fact he bartered for my hand.

Hades wraps his arm round my waist, pulling me close to him almost possessively. He too has not forgotten this man was in the running for my hand in marriage.

I'm hyper-alert, pressed close to Hades' side. My back is arched and Mother would be so proud of how I dangle in his arm like the perfect bauble, were it not for the wicked gleam in my eye or the twisted curve of my lips, both mirrored in my suitor's expression.

I try to dispel every reaction my body goes through at the feel of his hip pressing into my waist.

'I had no idea you had it in you. How did you manage it?' Hermes doesn't seem particularly upset to have lost his chance with me. He has nothing but respect for a trick well played, it seems.

Hades huffs in dry amusement. 'Demeter warded against infiltration by sky, land and sea – no one said anything about reaching up from below. I could have taken her any time.' Not technically a lie, I suppose. 'It was like she was a gift waiting just for me,' he adds, bringing his other hand to my chin and tilting it to face him.

I'm torn between the urge to slap him for such a statement and my desire to close any distance between us. He's all I can smell: the salt of his skin, the lingering spices of his evening tea, the peppery smell of his soap. It's like I'm drowning. I could kiss him right now, run my hands across his chest, anything to release some of this burning heat within me.

While I was having my hair twisted atop my head, what the hell was he doing to prepare? He must have worked some magic to have this effect on me.

Then I look up and his eyes meet mine and I see a flicker of recognition there.

He knows.

In that moment, I'm certain he knows the thoughts running through my head. A smile touches his lips and I chafe against it. I refuse to let him take satisfaction in the things he's doing to me.

I laugh into his face. 'You would like to think that, wouldn't you, my love?'

'You disagree?' he asks. The amusement lacing his words is at once provoking in its condescension and startlingly intimate – like he is teasing our charade for all to see.

'What makes you think you chose me?' I ask, trailing a finger down his chest. He shivers, his eyes widening before narrowing ever so slightly. Two can play at this game, Hades. 'Perhaps all this while I was busy choosing you.'

If neither of us can control the effects of being so physically close – a natural reaction that means *nothing* – then we can turn it into entertainment, just another part of the performance.

'Perhaps,' he agrees. He presses his lips to my forehead and it would be so easy to tilt my head up, to catch his lips with my own. I wonder if that's what he wants me to do. I can almost convince myself such ruminations are solely about the facade we are creating but that twinge of longing is undeniable. This isn't a romance, no matter how much I'm beginning to wish it were. His kiss is nothing more than a public claiming of me. It's a lie, as sweet as it is.

I feel every eye in the room on us.

'A gift, Hades?' Hermes asks. 'And, tell me, how was the unwrapping?'

I forget myself and turn my steely glare on the man before me. Hades tightens his grip on me.

'I know you would love details, Hermes, but I'm afraid I must disappoint. Persephone is to be my queen and she has been treated as such,' he says.

Hermes turns that gaze on me, examining every inch of my body until I snap, 'Is there something I can help you with?'

'I presented myself to your mother for your hand, actually,' Hermes says.

My look of surprise might be a little too forced but Hermes doesn't notice, mainly because he is not looking for deceit.

'I did not know,' I say. 'And soon I shall be queen of this court.' His queen. He will bend the knee to me as much as to Hades. I think I'll enjoy being queen after all. 'The Fates do enjoy their games.'

'Indeed. You aren't quite what I expected, girl of purity.'

'I have a new name now,' I say simply.

'Yes, and how did that happen?'

I look to Hades. 'Mutual agreement,' I say.

Hermes chuckles. 'To piss off Zeus then. No, no, don't worry. I certainly won't tell him that. But speaking of . . . you must let me break the news.'

Hades nods. 'You are the only one here who belongs to both courts. It would certainly save me a letter if you were willing –'

'Willing?' Hermes asks and I didn't know a single word could be filled with so much glee. 'I've never been more excited for a conversation in my life. And I'm the literal god of messages!'

'Well, Zeus is meeting with Helios any moment now,' Hades says. 'He will know where Persephone is soon enough, but please do share the news of our engagement.'

Hermes beams. 'With pleasure.'

'Would you . . . would you please let my mother know that I'm happy? I hate the idea of her worrying and –' I lean my head against Hades – 'I couldn't hope for a better match.'

'Very well.'

'Oh, and, Hermes?' Hades says. He flashes a smile at me full of such genuine happiness that, for a moment, even I forget he's faking it. Then he leans forward and whispers something into Hermes' ear.

Hermes grins and nods once before he turns and almost runs to the door.

'Care to explain?'

'You'll see,' he says.

'Fine.' I shake my head before resting it back on Hades' chest.

'I forgot how much I hate all that – the gods clubbing together and trading tales of their conquests. It's disgusting.'

'It doesn't matter.'

'Of course it does,' he whispers. 'It's all part of the reason you're here, isn't it? The way they talk about women is terrible. I know it's not as bad for me as it is for you, but the pressure it puts on men . . . We don't get feelings, we don't get anything but lust – and not even desire, really, just bragging rights. And if you abstain it's because you're weak and unworthy and –'

'Hades, I know. I know it's terrible and we can discuss it later. But we really need to focus,' I say. Though, to be honest, I've never really thought about what tying masculinity up with sexual conquest does to boys. I've only thought about what it meant for me, trapped on an island away from the leering eyes of the gods. I was always told that there was no stopping it, that it's just what boys do and all I can do is try to dissuade them from choosing me. I want to hear more about how this world hurts men too – but not when there are so many gods watching us.

'You're right. Our conversation with Hermes went well at least,' he says.

'But how many of these won't?'

'They will all be fine. We're too good at this.'

He has a point. It's almost too natural to lean on him, to have him turn to me. And there was already enough tension between us, at least as far as I'm concerned. With us both working to create more, there are so many sparks flying I worry something might catch fire.

'Very true. I'm going to get a drink,' I say, pulling away from him. 'Do you want anything?'

He shakes his head. 'Best not to let them see you serving me –'

'I'm not serving you.' I frown.

'Zeus and Ganymede,' Hades says.

And that's the only point needed to have me nodding and moving to fetch just one drink.

Ganymede, that poor boy Zeus dragged to the Heavens and made his cupbearer. Zeus disguised himself as an eagle and paid the boy's father in horses as compensation. Whether he was enslaved, blackmailed or infatuated – as Zeus insisted – Ganymede was made immortal so he could serve the king of the gods forever more, in whichever way Father saw fit.

No, I definitely don't want to be seen as Hades' Ganymede.

I select a chalice of plum wine and am set to return to Hades when a woman appears by my side. She is young but her hair is the silver of the moon and her eyes seem older than the stars. They're eyes I recognize.

'I spoke to your mother,' Hecate says.

I smile blandly. 'I'm so sorry. I don't believe we've met.'

'No, we have not. But we need no introductions,' she says. She's standing close to me and edging closer with every word.

'I –'

'And I need none of this simpering pretence,' she snaps.

I blink at her before scanning the room. It's too busy. 'Perhaps we could talk somewhere more private?'

Hecate nods. 'Very well, Persephone. If that's what you wish.'

I catch Hades' eye and gesture to Hecate and he nods. The last thing I need is him sounding the alarm because I've disappeared.

I take Hecate through to a small antechamber off the megaron, full of plush lounge chairs and dishes with spiced nuts and olives – the perfect place to break away from the main party. I'm sure later it will be filled with gods but for now we're the only ones here.

'You watched me in the Lake of the Five. Do not pretend otherwise,' she says.

'I would not pretend anything with you,' I say. What would be the point? I saw how she played my mother.

'I have been interested in you for a very long time,' she says and I can't help but flinch under the intensity of her stare. What's the point in making herself seem young? No one could ever believe her with those eyes.

'I can't see why,' I say, sipping from the chalice.

She throws her glass on the floor and it shatters. She takes a sudden step towards me and the fragments crunch beneath her.

'This deception of yours . . . when I know precisely what you are . . .' She trails off with the sort of fury that makes me think of a toddler stamping their foot. Something about her is so impossibly old and so impossibly young at the same time.

I take another sip of my wine as I wait for her to calm down, and her fury breaks like it has been snapped neatly in half. Suddenly she's laughing. It's not the cackle of before but a cry of delight. 'Oh, you understand how to play this game.'

'I don't want to play any games,' I say. I'm gripping my wine like it's the only thing holding me together. I enjoy unnerving Hades but I have nothing on this woman and the way she has me on a precipice.

'You *delight* in this game, girl.'

'I could do without the high stakes.'

'Couldn't we all?' She grins and her teeth are stained the red of her wine. I put my own glass down. 'I've wanted to meet you for a long time.'

'What? Why?'

'Your mother never let me on the island. She thought I might corrupt you. Encourage some of your loftier ambitions – and she's right, I would have. Power like yours ripples through the very fabric of the magic coating the world.'

'I'm nothing special.'

'That's your mother's voice.'

I swallow. 'I'm the goddess of flowers.'

'That's your father's decree. Come now, girl, you know you're so much more than that.'

I flounder for words, find none.

Something about her is almost feral as she says, 'The only other child of two great gods has a seat on the council of twelve, has followers flocking to him, has everything you have ever wanted.' Ares. One of my potential suitors, god of battle and child of Zeus and Hera. Born in the middle of a war like I was, but male. He's who I could have been, I suppose, if the Fates had been kinder. 'Zeus must have been terrified if he expected you to settle into the role he assigned you.'

'I love flowers,' I say. And it's true. I might yearn for more but I'd never abandon them, even for the world I asked for. They're my first love, often my only comfort. Of course the rush of power I felt as I swept souls across a ravine with a flick of my hand was enjoyable, rending the ground was fun too, but flowers . . . they're something else.

'I'm sure you do,' she says. 'But your power was never meant to be contained to them. It's been a long time since I had a kindred soul.'

I would cringe if I didn't want to offend her.

'I don't understand,' I say.

'Say what you mean, girl,' she hisses.

'I don't have power outside of creating flowers.'

'Nonsense. It's more than flowers I've felt these last few weeks.'

I shrug. 'I'm sorry, I don't know what to tell you. Everything is flowers when you get down to the root, even shaping the Underworld. And I've been working with healing souls here but that's all. Any god can do that.'

She scoffs. 'I thought you more than this. We will talk once you've come to terms with what you are. Open your eyes, girl.'

I stare at her. I've only just met her and I've already managed to let her down?

'I've forged my own path in this world. You might consider that you are doing the same. It's incredible, your obliviousness.

Youth!' she spits. 'You all think the world snapped into being in Zeus's vision. Like the Earth didn't spin before he sat upon the throne. I'm leaving.'

'Wait – is this all you dragged me here to say?'

'I came to offer advice,' she says. '*Enjoy it.*'

'What do you –' But before I can finish she's gone.

I blink at the space where she stood, feeling my heartbeat slow. Adrenaline is firing round my body, and I slump against the wall.

I . . . have no idea what just happened.

CHAPTER TWENTY-FIVE

RETURN TO THE MEGARON. Even though it's crowded, I see Hades immediately, like a magnet is pulling us together. He meets my eyes the moment I re-enter.

'Ah, my love,' he greets me as I approach. He's talking to three other gods, all of them absurdly tall and ridiculously handsome.

I ignore them for the moment as I cup Hades' face and press a chaste kiss to his cheek in greeting. I'm determined not to feel anything, so I focus on a thousand other things to avoid the sparks that fly when I touch him.

Hades grins smugly and, though he doesn't pull me back to him, his fingers trail down my back. I'm unprepared, and those sparks sneak up on me.

Thank the gods even surprises can't touch my expressions or Hades would be strutting around the palace for weeks.

'Did Hecate say anything interesting?' he asks before I can think of something to rile him up in return.

'Many things,' I say and then I remember the company and rush to continue. 'About you, actually. Things I had no idea about.' There's a look of such panic in Hades' eyes that I push on. 'Fascinating things, truly.' I glance at the gods, who stare at me in unabashed shock as I tease the lord of their realm.

'I see,' Hades says. 'And do I have anything to worry about?'

I laugh. 'Well, I'm not breaking off the wedding but, dear, I have some fantastic ammunition for our first argument.'

Now he finally does take hold of my waist and he stares at me like I'm the centre of his whole world.

It could become addictive, being looked at like that.

'I shall just have to keep you appeased then.' He grins. 'Thankfully I am very, very good at keeping a woman happy.'

'So I hear,' I practically purr.

I can see him swallow and, gods, how right we were earlier that we are far too good at this.

'Darling?' I ask.

'Yes?' He seems lost in my eyes.

'You haven't introduced me to your friends,' I say, flashing the gods an apologetic smile.

Hades nearly starts but he smothers it with a cool smile. He wasn't acting that last part, which means I'm getting to him more than he's getting to me. *Oh, I am never letting him live that down . . .*

And I can almost pretend the little jump of hope lingering behind my glee is non-existent.

'Of course, my love. This is Thanatos, Charon and Tartarus. We . . . fought together,' he says, suddenly formal once more.

'My lady,' they mutter, bowing their heads.

I'm startled but Hades beams at the sight. 'Soon to be my queen,' he says.

I realize not everyone needs to be convinced of our marriage and me taking the throne. Many are already poised to accept it.

Thanatos, the god of death, rises first. His long black hair is swept away from his face. It's the exact same shade as the oil-slick feathers that coat the wings at his back, stark against skin so pale I can see blue veins pulsing beneath. He adjusts his chiton in a way that suggests he is not used to wearing one. A sword rests at his hip, and it is easy to envisage him flying across a battlefield scooping up souls.

Charon ferries the dead across the river Acheron, bringing them to the field they gather in. If he uses anything like the grin he's flashing me now, the dead would follow him anywhere.

And Tartarus could be carved from marble, every inch of him strong in a way that makes it difficult to believe he is flesh.

'Well met.' I nod.

'I saw your paintings in the hall, my lady,' Thanatos says. 'Stunning pieces of work.'

I beam and clench Hades' hand. It is after all a compliment for him. 'You think so?' I ask, lifting my chalice to my lips. Hades has hidden his work for so long that I do not feel guilty trying to pry more compliments from their lips.

Thanatos nods. 'I spend more time among the humans than anyone –'

Charon coughs.

'*Nearly* anyone,' Thanatos corrects. 'And it's astonishing how well you've captured the lights and darks of their world.'

I shrug. 'What can I say, this realm inspired me.'

'This realm?' Hades prompts.

I offer a deep and profound sigh. 'And my love for you, of course. Before I met you my art was bland, colourless, and then

I saw you and suddenly it was like new life had been breathed into me, like never before had I even been able to see. I felt like only now could I paint in colour. I do not know how I –'

Hades covers my mouth with his hand, eyes dancing with amusement. 'Yes, I quite get the picture.'

I lick his hand and he jumps back, more in surprise than anything else. Please, like the nymphs haven't tried the same trick to get me to stop talking for years.

I laugh and, to my surprise, I'm not the only one. The three gods grin and I am instantly wary before realizing they are laughing *with* us, sharing in our joy.

'Perhaps I shall draw you, my love,' I say. 'Sitting on your throne, brooding.'

'I don't brood.' He scowls.

Tartarus mutters something into his drink.

'Something you'd care to repeat, Tartarus?' Hades asks.

Tartarus grins cheekily and I wonder how Hades treads this careful line between lord of Hell and approachable friend. Then I remember what Styx said, about how he keeps them all at arm's length.

'I said it is a pleasure to see you so happy, my king.' He nods.

'Of course you did.'

'I'm not sure how you hid this charming lady from us for so long though,' Charon cuts in, before Hades can push Tartarus further. 'I've been passing flowers for weeks and thought nothing of it.'

'You've just answered your own question,' Hades says. 'It's remarkably easy to keep things from you – you're a very dense person.'

The others chuckle and I note that it does not sound forced or merely polite. Does this happen at Father's court? Some gods there must genuinely respect him, I suppose. Those that are as cruel and self-centred as he is.

'Now that we know your secret,' Tartarus says, 'will you be joining us once more to train?'

'Train?' I search their faces for a clue.

'Worry not, my lady,' Tartarus says. 'We are not anticipating a war but it does not hurt to be prepared.'

Hades' jaw is tight but he nods. 'Yes, of course. Though I hope you've enjoyed the opportunity to win a sparring match in my absence.'

Tartarus's lips twitch. 'I suppose we shall see just how out of practice you are.'

Thanatos smiles at me. 'These two fight more with words than with swords.'

I think of Hades with any sword, in any fight, and my stomach clenches. So he trains? To keep up with appearances? Or something else?

Is it worth it? Dragging those memories back?

'I'm sorry, who guards the Titans and who gathers defenceless human souls?' Tartarus retorts.

Charon groans. 'You know, I hate to give him the point, but you can't play the Titan card. Hades is literally the one who put them in their cage.'

'We all fought in the war,' Thanatos protests.

'The war was years ago. No one is disputing the fact that Hades dealt the final blow.' Tartarus grins. 'But since then someone has been sitting on a throne being waited on hand and foot.'

'Let's save this discussion for when you have a sword in your hand to defend your assertions, shall we?' Hades says with finality.

The gods nod, like they've all suddenly realized the formality of the setting and that they aren't in a training pit.

'My king,' they say as they depart.

'Okay, was that really a discussion of whose sword is biggest?' I whisper.

Hades chuckles. 'You are utterly vulgar.'

I shrug. 'Raised by nymphs, remember?'

'And Demeter.'

'And what child doesn't act differently around a parent?' I reply.

Hades goes to speak but his breath hitches, eyes catching on something that has him ducking his head like he can hide behind me.

'What?' I ask, turning and spotting a couple staring at us. When I look back at Hades he struggles to meet my eye. I realize what is happening rather abruptly and blurt, possibly too loudly, 'Fates, is she an ex-girlfriend?'

'No.' Hades swallows. 'He's an ex-boyfriend.'

'Oh.'

He glances up again, nods politely to them and swears. 'No, no, you're right. I went on a date with her once too.'

'Who are they?'

Hades grimaces. 'Minor gods Ponus and Philotes.'

Laughing at his discomfort is undoubtedly mean but it's so funny I can't help myself. 'So how many people here have you been with?'

'Not many,' he says. 'But it's nice to see they're banding together.'

We spend the rest of the evening making the rounds and I meet so many gods their names flit out of my head as easily as they went in. I meet the gods of the Underworld's other four rivers, none of them what I would have expected. Lethe stands rigid, her eyes quick and ready, like she has absorbed every memory anyone has forgotten in her waters. Phlegethon is calm and subdued, like the river of fire has taken any anger he has to offer. Cocytus beams, more radiant than Helios or Apollo could ever hope to be. Perhaps only someone who has seen such sorrow as that which rushes through his waters can manage a smile like that – someone who has seen the pain this world offers but chooses the positive anyway. The river Acheron runs from the mortal plane into the Underworld so I'd expected its god to enjoy building connections, but Acheron isn't particularly chatty. He solemnly nods at the things we say and excuses himself at the first opportunity.

And then of course Styx is there too.

'My lord.' She bows. 'This is truly a surprise to us all.'

Hades tenses with long-suffering irritation. 'Stop it.'

'So you get to pretend and I don't?' She pouts.

'What are you –' I ask in alarm.

'Oh don't worry,' she says. 'Hades gets his magic smoke and I get an aura of warding. My secrets are kept whether I want to keep them or not – anyone overhearing us right now isn't hearing what we're saying. I doubt they can see us either, actually. It's probably an amiable chat from their stance.'

'Oh, so if I were to punch Hades no one would see it?'

'What? Why do you want to punch me?'

'I don't. It was just an example.'

'Pick a different one!'

'You don't have to keep up the amorous bickering,' Styx says. 'You two make a rather believable couple.'

'Yes, we're very good actors,' I say, trying to give her a death stare that Hades won't catch.

'Is that what it is?' she asks,

'*Yes*. Now, if that's all, we have more gods to meet,' I say.

She laughs. 'Very well. Have fun.'

I lead Hades away, shaking my head. 'She's almost as smug as you are.'

'I am not smug,' he says, unable to stop the smile on his face.

I poke the corner of his lips where that smile still doesn't falter.

'Anyone would be smug with you on their arm,' he says instead, lowering his voice into what I assume is meant to be a sexy drawl.

No one is watching so I let myself gag.

'Come on, Hades, I have a reputation to maintain. If you want people to believe I love you, you're going to have to be a bit cooler than that.'

'Pray tell, why does all of our so-called flirting involve you mocking me and me complimenting you?'

I shrug and take his hand in case anyone glances over. 'We have to keep things realistic.'

'You dramatic, conceited girl,' he moans.

'Yes, and?' I grin.

'Insufferable.'

'Careful, dear husband, compliments like that might go straight to my pretty head.' I realize I'm fluttering my eyelashes as my thumb strokes his hand. It appears flirting with him is becoming instinctive.

He shakes his head with a smile and takes the slightest step closer. I'm not even sure he knows he's doing it. 'I'm not your husband yet and I don't think your insults are enticing me into the union. Aren't you supposed to be convincing everyone I want you so very desperately?'

'I think you're doing a good-enough job of that yourself,' I tease. 'All it takes is one little touch.' I raise a hand to brush along his jaw, tilting his head towards me. 'And you practically forget how to breathe.'

His eyes light with the challenge. 'You're hardly one to talk. One look and you're lost for words.'

'Why don't you just admit that you find me irresistible?'

'And yet here I am, resisting, while you're finding any excuse to touch me.'

I glance down at our entwined fingers. It's a mistake – he has lovely hands. Strong fingers, lines I long to trace and flecks of clay in the creases of his skin.

'Maybe I'm just better at this ruse than you are,' I say.

'Would you care for me to dial it up?' Hades asks. 'Because you dissolving into a quivering mess helps no one.'

'Oh, fuck you.' I laugh.

'Marry me first, then we'll talk,' he quips back, and then we're both laughing, clutching on to one another to keep from doubling over.

Breathlessly, I shake my head. 'This is so ridiculous. We can tone down the flirting after we're married, right?'

'I should hope so,' Hades says. 'Although I must say you're awfully good at it. I suppose it's easier when it's meaningless, but I nearly bought it sometimes – even knowing you're lying.'

Meaningless.

I don't want to talk to him in private any more. I want to go back to the public performances – to hide whatever mess I'm feeling behind our projected adoration for each other. 'Do you want to dance?' I ask.

Hades' nose wrinkles. 'I don't dance.'

I feign shock. 'What? You? Never . . .'

'Then why ask?'

'Because you're marrying me so I've decided you dance now.'

'No.'

'Urgh, fine, but I am so getting you on the dance floor for our wedding.'

Which is when Achlys appears before us and we are wrapped back up in each other's arms, anything real slipping neatly away.

Then Hypnos.

Then the Erinyes.

Then Nyx.

The gods continue, one after the next, all congratulating us and wishing us well, and it's enough, almost, to believe everyone wants this to happen. To forget that the king of the gods himself will soon be furious to discover our union.

CHAPTER TWENTY-SIX

'M EXHAUSTED BY THE TIME we retire. Hades flashes all who remain at the party one final, satisfied smile and says that he will see them at the solstice, before he takes my hand and leads me from the hall.

The doors shut behind us and finally we are alone in the comfort of our palace.

'Do you think it was enough?' he asks.

I nod. How could it not be?

I lean against the cold marble wall as it settles upon me that my parents know where I am. All that time by the banks of the Lake of the Five Rivers, trying to catch the moment it happened, and it passed by while I swanned around the gods of the Underworld.

I glance towards the door to the lake for just a moment but it's long enough for Hades to catch.

'Care for company?' he asks.

He would let me go alone this time, if I asked him to. I can tell in the careful way he balances his words.

I surprise him by offering a small smile and revealing the bottle of wine I swiped.

'Of course, something this entertaining should be shared.'

He meets my grin with his own before nodding at the bottle. 'You know, it's my wine. You don't have to steal it.'

'Ahh, but a covert operation is so much more fun.'

'And if someone saw you?' he asks. 'What then? They might think drink the only way you can tolerate me.'

'They might wonder what else I've stolen ... your hand, your heart, your innocence ... your throne?' I tease.

Hades brings a hand over his heart and says mournfully, 'And they would be right.'

'The throne perhaps, but innocent is not the word that comes to mind when I think of you.' I shoot a sidelong glance at him. 'Speaking of, tell me more of these *befores* of which you speak.'

'Persephone, why are you so obsessed with my sexual history?' he mocks, but my face flushes anyway. I'm glad I'm walking down the steps in front of him so that he can't see. It's incredibly annoying when he thinks he's won a point.

'I just don't want any surprises when we're married. Like an illegitimate child on our doorstep or some youth pining for you.'

'So, in your imagination, I'm so talented that old lovers begging at my feet is a possibility?' he clarifies.

'Well, if certain body parts are as big as your head then ...'

His laughter echoes as we emerge in the lake's cavern. I spent years around nymphs making such jokes, never daring to make them myself, but now they come so naturally.

'Is this because we saw Ponus and Philotes earlier?' he asks.

'No, that was hilarious,' I say. 'This is because I've heard far too many stories. Not about you, granted, but the things the other gods have been up to have scarred me for life.'

'There have been girls and there have been boys. Not many of either. No illegitimate children. Is any of that a problem?'

'Well, I didn't think you were a virgin,' I say. I'm somewhat relieved, though I don't care to admit it, that he likes women and I theoretically have a chance. Not that I would ever go there, of course. But my concern was not about gender preferences. The gods can be ... creative. 'Any animals, inanimate objects or chaos-created monsters?'

'No,' he sputters.

'Ever appeared as a golden shower? Or a swan? Or a cloud? Or –'

'I'm going to stop you right there and say a very firm no.'

'Then I'll cope.'

I sit on the rough rock at the edge of the cavern in this room that is more natural than the rest of the palace and so much older.

'I could summon chairs?' Hades suggests.

I begin pulling pins out of my hair. 'Just sit down.'

He grumbles but finally sits beside me on the floor.

He laughs as I shake my hair out. I wipe the colour staining my lips on to the back of my hand. 'Only you could go from so glamorous to so messy in a matter of seconds.'

I think he has a thorough misunderstanding of how glamour works, but I just grin a lipstick-smeared smile at him instead. 'You're marrying this mess.'

He takes the wine and pours out two cups. 'Yes, yes, I am.'

'Did tonight feel too easy to you?' I ask.

'How do you mean?'

'Just ... the way we were acting. I've been putting on performances my entire life and not much of that felt like pretending.'

'Well, yes,' he says. 'We're not pretending to like each other, are we? We just layered a romantic performance on top of our friendship.'

'Right.'

But friends don't touch each other as much as we do.

Or talk about the things we do.

Or long for something more than this – whatever *this* is.

I run through the seven types of love, quickly disregarding agape, philautia and storge because I'm fairly certain that 'this' is not love for humanity, the self or your children.

I can postpone ruminations of pragma. It is the bond forged by years, not by days.

And eros I refuse to think of. Eros is what has me staring at the muscles stretching beneath Hades' robes and had me shivering in his arms only this evening. Eros is that longing that draws me to him, like an invisible thread tied round my insides. Eros is madness and lust and desire and I refuse, absolutely refuse, to consider it. Eros could ruin you.

But philia and ludus? They worry me.

I do not love Hades on the level of the soul – philia – but sometimes, when I let that vice I keep on my emotions slip, I feel like I could. Surely love is not a choice, but I feel so often that I'm standing on a precipice, and the only thing keeping me from falling is choosing not to. I sometimes fear that philia would be very easy to fall into.

And ludus, that playful love . . . what is our teasing and our jokes if not ludus? It is that light-as-air feeling I get when our smiles meet.

It's easy to admit I love him.

Harder to figure out in which way.

'What are you thinking?' he asks.

I desperately scramble for anything that's not my actual thoughts and land not too far away. 'Thank you. For doing this, I mean. It's a lot, giving up your one shot at a happy marriage for me.'

'Believe me, I was never going to wind up in a happy marriage.'

'You don't know that. This is a sacrifice and I'm grateful.'

'Well, I'm not doing this for your gratitude,' he says. 'I'm doing this because it's the right thing to do. As far as I'm concerned, it's not even a choice.'

'Romantic.' I laugh.

He doesn't.

'Oh, you're not going to brood over me saying thank you, are you?' I ask and then drain my cup. 'Refill my wine, would you?'

I clamber to my feet and move to the lake. Mother appears as I run my fingers through the water. She is making the journey to Olympus.

'I'm not brooding,' he grumbles but there's a lightness to his words that's been missing.

'Sure you're not, darling.'

'That's what sold it.' He points to me as I turn and I'm almost too distracted by the sight of him, sprawled on that rocky floor. I don't think I've ever seen him look so relaxed.

I flush as thoughts of what could be done on this rocky floor fill my mind.

'My face?' I ask, managing a look of disbelief.

'That smirk.' Hades smiles lazily and I wonder if it is only the wine putting him at such ease. 'That amused, satisfied smirk – like you have everything you want and you're revelling in the fact no one can take it from you.'

'I wasn't always faking it.' There were moments tonight when I felt like maybe I did have some power, and maybe I did have everything I wanted.

'I know. That's what makes you so difficult – and so convincing. You do the same things in a lie that you do in truth,' he says.

I'm not sure how I feel about being called difficult, but I suppose as long as it's working I don't care too much.

'Can you stop analysing me and give me my wine so we can enjoy watching my parents' plans collapse?' I ask.

He waves to the full cup beside him and I join him on the rocky floor just as my mother reaches Zeus.

It's always a shock to see my father on his throne. I have seen him on it in person only once. The megaron looks just like Hades' – just like *mine*. There's something so repulsive about seeing Zeus sitting there, his beard uncut and hair ragged beneath the confines of his crown. He is simultaneously trying too hard and not at all. He has nothing like the raw power Hades commands.

'Take a sip every time Mother calls me "my daughter",' I mutter.

'And every time Zeus threatens someone,' Hades adds.

'Down your cup every time the person he threatens is you,' I say, and I'm met by that rich laugh of his.

The rough wall is digging into my back and gods I wish it were Hades' side I was leaning into instead.

'The sun has set,' Zeus says.

'Yes, I noticed as much,' Mother says, temper burning like a smothered fire, just inches from the surface.

'Helios will be back,' Father continues.

'Then what are we waiting for. Let's talk to him.'

'I want this over as much as you do, Demeter,' he says, his voice so low it grumbles like thunder. I wouldn't be surprised if some mortal island just experienced a very unexpected storm.

'And I want my daughter back,' Mother snarls.

Hades and I chink glasses. The wine is delicious.

'Whoever took her has made fools of us both, as well as what this throne means – and the entire institution of marriage,' Zeus says.

'So Hera is growling down your throat,' Mother snaps. 'I want my daughter back, not a monologue.'

Lightning strikes terrifyingly close to my mother, so close that I gape at the fact she does not flinch, even if her hands bunch in the folds of her dress, the tendons in her arms tight.

I swallow round a lump that has appeared in my throat. *He won't hurt her. He wouldn't.*

'When we are done with this I don't want to see you on Olympus before the next Panathenaea,' he growls.

'I'm on the council. You can't hold court without me,' Mother protests.

'Take a holiday,' Zeus says. His unspoken threat lingers in the air.

Mother hesitates before nodding. 'Can we please go and find out who took her?'

'Yes.' Zeus storms from the room and Mother hurries to

catch up. 'When we find out who it is I'm going to drag them to Tartarus myself, and when I'm done no one will remember them for what they did, they'll just remember their screams for mercy until their very name comes to mean horror itself.'

'Zeus is becoming poetic in his old age,' Hades comments dryly.

'Do we count that as a threat for you?' I ask.

'He doesn't know it's me yet so I vote no, or we'll be on the floor,' he says. 'Well, more on the floor than we already are.'

'Just the one sip then.' I've been drinking the whole time, so I set to work refilling our glasses as Father reaches his chariot.

Mother climbs in hurriedly.

They reach Helios in seconds. His chariot gleams so brightly that even my immortal eyes need a moment to adjust.

Apollo is sitting on its edge, tuning some stringed instrument or other.

'What –'

'Be gone,' Zeus says to him.

Apollo nods and disappears with a strum of those strings.

I'm reluctant to admit it, but I'm impressed that he's tied transport to his magic somehow. I wonder if I could do the same with flowers.

Helios had been cleaning the wheels of the chariot, but now he looks up nervously.

'Your Majesty.' He stumbles to his feet to bow. 'I –'

'Where is my daughter?' Mother demands.

'Drink!' I sing.

'Umm, well.' Helios runs the cloth through his fingers. 'I can't be certain –'

'Answer the question,' Mother says. I've never seen her angry like this – her anger normally comes with clipped words and a cold edge, not this acid that sticks to the very air around her.

'The earth opened beneath her. She fell through,' he says, flinching.

'And you thought you ought not mention this?' Zeus booms with none of Mother's ice-cold fury.

'I thought myself mistaken, my lord,' Helios says. 'I did not hear of her missing.'

He's lying, obviously, but they can't prove it when they never publicized my disappearance.

'Who took her? Gaia?' Mother asks, a frown on her face.

'The pit was, ah, deeper than Gaia's reach,' Helios mutters.

'*Hades?*' she breathes, shocked and disgusted at once.

'I . . . I think so, my lady, but he is a . . . a king. I congratulate you on such a match –'

'Silence,' Mother snarls. 'He is *nothing*.'

'I can see where you get your charm,' Hades says tonelessly.

'How dare he . . .' Lightning flashes around Zeus. The Heavens shake. 'I will make him regret his very existence.'

'And we have it!' Hades proclaims. 'Our first direct threat of the eve.'

The wine tastes less delicious when I'm downing it like this.

'What do we do?' Mother demands.

Zeus blinks. 'We get her back.'

'You can't,' Mother says, level-headed as always. 'It's *Hades*. You can't betray the rules of your peace –'

'That's right, you can't!' I cry, terribly close to poking my tongue out. By the rules of the Fates, any child snatched by Kronos has a right to rule. And Hades and Poseidon allow

Zeus to do so with a pact so fragile it could be shattered by –
well, me.

'Hades betrayed that peace when he snatched Kore,' Zeus
snaps.

'Keep your voice down,' Mother says. 'We need to handle
this quietly and sensibly or it will ruin her.'

'Drown in the Tiber, Demeter,' Hades says almost pleasantly.

I sigh. 'She's not wrong, is she?'

'She should be more concerned for your well-being than
your marriage prospects,' he says. I don't really know how to
tell him that, in the world of the Olympian court, they're one
and the same.

'Kore's reputation won't be what anyone is discussing when
I'm through with Hades,' Zeus growls.

Hades and I groan as we down another glass.

'Is this bottle refilling itself?'

'Of course. They're all connected to the stores in the cellar.'

My eyes widen. 'Well, if I didn't want to marry you before . . .'

'My liege,' Helios stutters, pointing at a speck in the sky.

As that speck nears, I realize that, of course, while all this
was happening, Hades and I were announcing our engagement
to the court.

And here comes Hermes, delightfully well timed – as I'm
sure he knew.

Hermes flies upright, and the wings that have sprouted from
his sandals gently lower him to the surface of the cloud where
they stand.

'Now is not the time –' Zeus starts but Mother, at least,
understands what his presence means.

'Is she there?' Mother demands. 'Hades?'

Hermes nods, a sharp, short movement which is as contained as the smile that doesn't touch his lips but glistens in his eyes.

'Oh, thank the Fates,' Mother says, her pragmatism vanishing. 'Is . . . She's . . . That is to say . . .'

'Hades,' Zeus spits, 'will –'

'Even your lightning cannot strike down there,' Hermes cuts him off before we have to drink another cup.

'Perhaps not, but my sword can,' Zeus snarls.

'Is that a euphemism?' Hermes quips. 'Helios, go and busy yourself elsewhere.'

Helios doesn't have to be told twice, even as Zeus rounds on his messenger.

'You have no right to dismiss my subjects.'

'Trust me, Father, you will want a more private audience for this.'

Mother gasps. 'Is she okay? What's he done to her?'

Hermes snickers. 'Oh, she is quite all right. I'm not entirely sure you were honest with us, Demeter; beautiful though she undoubtedly is, bashful and demure is not quite what I got from her.'

'What?' Mother breathes and, for the first time in all this, a more familiar kind of concern touches my mother's eyes. 'What has she done?'

'She asked me to tell you that she is happy,' he says.

'Is that all?' Mother snarls. 'He could have forced her to say that.'

Hermes smiles. 'Not quite.'

His smile rapidly disappears as Zeus grabs the collar of his robe and lifts him from his feet. His sandals flap their wings and his panicked look of strangulation disappears in seconds. The wariness lingers.

'Enough of this,' Zeus snarls. 'What do you know of Kore?'

'Well, for one, she goes by Persephone now,' Hermes says.

Zeus drops him and after a second Hermes lands softly back on the surface.

Hades and I burst into laughter at the expressions on my parents' faces. The bewilderment, the anger and, finally, the suspicion.

'Chaos bringer?' Zeus mutters. 'Isn't that what I –'

'Is that truly what matters to you?' Mother cuts him off.

Zeus considers it and a new wave of rage crashes over him. 'Hades thinks he can kidnap my daughter, keep her prisoner and *rename* her?'

'Your father really does have a very low opinion of me, and of your agency,' Hades says.

I shrug. 'I'm an innocent party here.'

And then we're laughing again, so much that we nearly miss Hermes' response.

'I believe it was mutual.'

'This is ridiculous,' Zeus snarls. 'I'm not wasting another second discussing this when I could be taking *Kore* back and wringing Hades' neck.'

'My wine store was not made for Zeus drinking games,' Hades says as he refills our glasses.

'Did you see how drunk the Erinyes were? This is hardly a dent,' I protest.

'If they continue like this we might drain the whole cellar.'

'Then I'll grow some grapes. Now shush, we're missing the show.'

There's another quick-fire argument between my parents: Father screaming that he will wrench me from the Underworld and Mother saying that no one wants me back more than she does but they have to be more subtle than that or it will be war.

'There's no need for all that,' Hermes says calmly.

'He took my daughter,' Mother says, eliciting another sip from both of us. 'He has done unspeakable things to her –'

'If it helps, I truly do not believe he has.' Hermes wrinkles his nose. 'Honestly, this is the first thing he's ever done to suggest he's anything but a law-abiding, boring prick.'

Hades arches an eyebrow. 'It seems words are to be had with my court messenger.'

I'm too busy laughing to reply. After all, it was that very reputation that had me risking the leap to Hell.

'And did he say that?' Mother asks. 'Why else would he take her?'

'Her artistic talents?' Hermes suggests.

'Zeus, do feel free to wipe your son from this realm at your earliest opportunity,' Mother says calmly.

Hermes gives her a withering look. 'Surely it's not been so long since the war that you're incapable of doing it yourself?'

'Boy.' Zeus's voice is deadly as he lifts his lightning bolt.

Hermes raises his hands in surrender.

'They announced their engagement tonight,' he says.

'What?' Mother asks, hand on her heart. 'She can't marry him. She . . .'

'Has lost all other prospects.' Hermes shrugs. 'And she asked me to tell you that she could not hope for a better match.'

'She doesn't know what she's talking about. She's just a girl,' Mother says.

'She was,' Hermes says. 'As I say, she is "little girl" no longer.'

'That bastard,' Zeus growls. 'He did not even have the decency to vie for her hand with the others.'

'Perhaps he knew you'd never give it,' Hermes suggests.

'If he thinks this will stop me from throttling him then he is very much mistaken.'

'He actually made a suggestion,' Hermes says as we down yet another drink. 'He offered you the opportunity to claim ownership for what happened.'

Zeus sputters and I struggle not to choke on the wine.

'I'm sorry, what?'

Hades grins like nothing in the world could amuse him more.

'He told me to offer you the idea of claiming you helped orchestrate it. I presume he means that you imply you wanted this match and needed to go behind Demeter's back,' Hermes explains.

'That's what you whispered to Hermes?' I ask.

Hades nods.

'You evil genius.'

'Evil?'

I shrug. 'It's relative.'

This time Zeus's anger is too explosive for cleverly worded threats. Hades smirks proudly.

'How dare he?' Father seethes.

'I'd urge you to consider it,' Hermes says. 'It would save face with many gods.'

'And let him believe he can do something like this to his king again?' Zeus demands.

'Well, he only gets one wife,' Hermes says. 'And she did seem truly happy. And he is a king in his own right – I know, I know, you're the king of all of us gods, that's not what I'm saying. I'm saying it's a fine match for Persephone.'

'Stop calling her that,' Mother snaps. 'She can't marry the king of Hell. The Underworld is no place for her – she's too delicate. She needs flowers and nature and her mother. She needs to stay at this court.'

'She's wasted no time in redecorating, if it helps,' Hermes interjects. 'She hardly seemed delicate either. Actually, if I had to say anything, she seemed right at home.'

Mother's eyes flash. 'What would you know of my daughter, Hermes?'

'Very little and I assume it would have stayed that way,' he says, smiling in that uniquely provoking way of his. 'I take it I was not successful in vying for her hand?'

'We were still considering our options,' Father says grimly. 'But now it appears there's only one.'

'What?' Mother turns to him, suddenly alarmed. 'You can't seriously be considering this. I know I said you can't just barge down there and take her back, but, just because we haven't figured out how to get her back *yet*, doesn't mean we stop trying to work that out.'

'And what do we do with her when we do get her back?' Zeus asks. 'No one else will have her. And they have announced their engagement publicly.'

'No,' Mother says quietly.

Father's anger still bristles in the tense, resigned nod he

gives before turning his steely glare on Hermes. 'You tell Hades that he only gets one chance to humiliate me. This is it.'

'I get many chances, Zeus dear, I just don't take you up on them,' Hades says.

'I think that's enough of that,' I say, rising to trail my fingers through the water. The journey is a lot more dizzying than I recall.

The image disappears.

I stumble on my way back, collapsing half on to Hades' lap.

'There's that grace I know so well.' Hades smirks as I slide next to him.

'I didn't knock the wine over and that's all that matters,' I say. I'm not sure if Helios's chariot's power has reached through these waters, but the whole cavern feels lit by sunlight.

He's closer than before and I inhale that scent, the irresistible smell of him now tinged with wine. It's stained his lips. It must have stained mine too.

If I kissed him, would that be all I could taste?

I'm too drunk to chase the thoughts away. The alcohol almost feels like the perfect cover – I could blame it on the drink if he doesn't feel the same way.

And I'm far, far too drunk to consider the consequences if he does feel the same way, the two of us trapped together without the space to explore whatever this could be.

He's looking at me, laughter still ringing, and there's something about the expression on his face. I'm lying on the floor in an evening gown Aphrodite would rip right off my back. My hair is a mess, my lipstick smudged and my cheeks flushed with amusement. No one has ever seen me like this before and, for the first time in what feels like so long, I'm glad

I feel vulnerable. What if my walls, in failing to keep something out, have let something wonderful in?

'I can't tell you how good it is to see you so happy.' Hades' voice is suddenly serious, his eyes focused intently on mine. They're so close, so captivating. I could waste an eternity looking into them. 'I'd marry you a thousand times if it let you, the *real* you, find happiness like that.'

Indeed, I taste the wine first before the feel of his lips registers. My kiss is hungry and desperate and so full of things that I can't say that it feels like a gasp for air. His lips are firm and his skin soft as my hands cup his face, pulling him towards me, and I'm not even sure if my heart is beating. My whole body is hyper-alert and numb at the same time and –

Hades pulls away, eyes frosty, body tense.

'Don't do that,' he says softly, blinking with dazed confusion, like he can't believe what I've done, like I've hurt him somehow.

He hastens to his feet as if his only purpose is to put distance between us.

'There's no one here. No one is watching,' he says, anger building with each word. 'I don't need a damn performance.'

I jump to my feet too because I can't stand his anger while I'm staring up at him. 'Hades, I –' But the words get stuck in my throat as something slams shut inside me, and I don't know what I'd say anyway.

'I don't want this,' he fumes. 'I don't want this from you at all. Why do you keep thinking I do?'

My eyes sting but I nod. 'Okay, okay, I'm sorry.'

He shakes his head. 'I can't keep doing this. Every time I think you understand me, you go and . . . It doesn't matter. I'm going to bed.' His lips twist. 'And, just to be clear, I don't want you there either so don't come and find me.'

I bite my tongue to hold back my tears. Is the rejection not bad enough without his anger? His rage? I thought ... I thought ... Fates, I wasn't thinking at all, but if I were I might have expected a gentle refusal, not this apparent disgust, repulsion so strong it has the kindest man I know on the verge of shouting.

Go! I want to scream. *Get out of here!* I don't want him to see how much his words have hurt me. Worse, I don't want him to see how angry I am at myself for ever risking this and managing to fuck it up quite so badly. But if I open my mouth I'll start sobbing, so I just nod instead.

He gives me one last look that I can't decipher, something raw and angry and hurt.

And then he's gone.

CHAPTER TWENTY-SEVEN

I SPEND MOST OF THE NIGHT crying into my pillow, snotty and choking on my own tears, wishing I had Cyane or even my mother to comfort me. But then I think of what my mother might say: '*Oh my darling. Young hearts are so easily swayed – and so easily broken. That's why I'm choosing your match – to save you from all this. Chin up, and next time you'll know to leave it all to me.*'

And then I'm crying harder because maybe she would be right. Maybe I never should have trusted the way I was feeling. In the sways of my hurt and the effects of the wine, I even start to feel that, if I'd never come to the Underworld, I wouldn't be in so much pain right now.

By morning, my throat is raw and my eyes are bleary.

I contemplate staying in bed, but my mouth is the driest it's ever been and the need to inhale a bucket of water drags me towards the dining room.

Hades is sitting waiting.

Right. Of course he is.

Just the sight of him has my heart thundering again, mostly

from embarrassment and fear of his rage lingering, but – and I hate to admit it – partly from the excited memory of his lips.

Did he kiss me back at all? I can't remember. Would I have been able to feel it? It's not like I have much experience to go on.

'Good morning,' he greets me. 'How are you feeling?'

I stare. Is that it? A night spent sobbing, thinking I ruined our friendship, replaying his angry rejection a thousand times, and he greets me with something so mundane?

'We drank a lot of wine,' he clarifies.

'Yes,' I say, fumbling for my chair. 'I think I'm fine. You?'

'I've been better,' he says, picking up his glass of water. 'Persephone, we need to talk about last night.'

'No, we don't,' I say, grabbing for any food on the table and ending up with pomegranates again. Bloody pomegranates. 'I'm sorry. It won't happen again. There's nothing more to discuss.'

'All right.'

I glance up at the quiet gentleness in his voice. There's something off about him. He's speaking like he's rehearsed it. I wonder if I wasn't the only one awake for half the night.

'When we decided we would marry and rushed the announcement, we never really spoke about what that might mean in reality. I know we are pretending in public and I know you think I am doing you a favour, but I'm not. I don't need something in return for this arrangement. You don't need to . . . to try to please me or anything like that. You don't owe me. Irritating the Olympians and keeping you safe is reward enough.'

I hesitate, completely lost for words. Well, not *completely*. It's more that 'You're an idiot – that's not why I kissed you' doesn't seem the best response right now.

I can still see the way he pulled away – no, cringed back – from me.

The way he frantically got to his feet.

He couldn't get his angry words out fast enough.

He doesn't want me that way.

That's fine.

And now he's giving me an out, a way to stop this being awkward.

I nod. 'I understand.'

Hades sighs. 'Good.'

He reaches for his food and we lapse into silence for a few moments.

'Well?' he asks.

'Well, what?'

'Insult me or something. This silence is weird,' he says.

I grin, although I still feel shaky. 'Well, we established yesterday that me insulting you counts as flirting, so under the circumstances I don't think it would be appropriate.'

His shoulders fall as he finally relaxes, a hesitant smile on his lips. 'I think insulting each other is just us being us.'

I'm not sure what I expected from the day but it's not the relentless wedding planning I encounter.

'Isn't this what your mother has been training you for since birth?' Hades groans, head in his hands, as Tempest asks us to pick between yet another two pieces of identical-looking fabric.

'Isn't this what you spend all day doing?' I retort.

'This isn't art.' He looks at me like his will to live has disappeared. 'This is admin.'

'Okay,' I say, standing up. 'That's enough of this.'

'Persephone, we're getting married in five days.'

'Yes, and I have flowers to organize,' I say. I turn to Tempest. 'Do you enjoy this?'

'Take one guess.' She glowers, the fabric swatches clutched tight in her intangible hands.

'I thought not. You're dismissed.'

I can almost feel her relief. She runs before I can change my mind.

'Persephone,' Hades protests.

I shake my head. 'Believe me, most of the people I grew up with would love this. I'm sure some of the mortals would jump at the opportunity. I'll let them organize it.'

Hades hesitates. 'I'm not sure that's best.'

'We'll review it all,' I say. 'And you'll be given a chance to add your own overly dramatic flair.'

He scoffs. 'I'm terribly sorry, did you just have the nerve to call *me* dramatic?'

'Darling,' I say, 'there is a literal deity of drama and I'm fairly certain he doesn't come close to our level. I'm dramatic, yes, but so are you.'

He suppresses a smile. 'Perhaps.'

'So . . . I'm going to go outside because I can't stand this, and I can do something useful by sorting out the flowers. And you can go make the crockery for the feast or whatever it is you want to do,' I propose.

Hades smiles in that small, self-conscious way he does

whenever we discuss his art. All those hobbies he swore to keep secret, the ones he isolated himself to defend.

'I wanted to ask you, actually,' I say, 'whether you were planning on making my wedding dress?'

'No,' he says quickly. 'I don't think that's a good idea.'

'I thought you liked a challenge?' I tease.

He picks up the scraps of fabric we were comparing and rubs the fibres together like he's trying to gauge their quality. 'I just think,' he says without looking at me. 'That . . . it might be odd. It would be like I'm dressing you for how I want to see you. Like I'm selecting how you appear to me.'

My heart pounds at the thought, the idea he might have opinions on that. He might fantasize about how I might look . . .

I manage that smirk again, the one he pointed out only yesterday. 'Just how wild do your wedding thoughts run? If I'm standing before you in either a battle tunic or lingerie you might have gone too far.'

He laughs. 'I hadn't considered it.' He looks at me, his lopsided smile back again. 'Although . . .'

I swat his arm. 'Behave. It's a dress, Hades. You've made them before.'

'It's a *wedding* dress.'

'Make it, please,' I say, hugging my arms to my chest. I'm not sure why it matters to me but it does. 'I . . . don't want to wear something made by anyone else when I marry you.'

His brow furrows but he nods anyway. 'Very well.'

'Thank you,' I say. 'Now, if you'll excuse me, I have bouquets to plan.'

I leave before he can back out.

*

My mortal friends are reasonably excited by the prospect of my wedding, though more for the drama of the gods descending on the Underworld – and the opportunity to tease me about any feelings I *might* have for Hades – than any genuine love of such events. Larissa says that in her hometown the focus at a wedding was entirely on the feast, and she'd be happy to help with the menu. Damaris, the farmer, grins slyly and says the most important thing is the guest list as it dictates how good the gifts will be. And Cora, the former princess of Thebes, wrinkles her nose in disgust before changing the subject and asking if I am able to search for spirits because there's a poet from Lesbos she is looking for.

So I leave them to look for some spirits who are willing to help, but instead I find myself at the Styx.

'Hello?' I call, unsure how to find her. It's a long river.

'What?' Styx whines, instantly appearing before me. She has dark shadows beneath her eyes – though really all of her is shadow. Her high cheekbones and long eyelashes cast dark lines down her face. Her skin is less white than grey, and her eyes are so dark the pupil is lost.

'What's wrong?' I ask her.

'My blood alcohol content, I imagine,' she groans. 'Did I kiss Pallas last night?'

'Not that I saw,' I say, freezing up. That's too close to what I want to discuss.

'Must have been at the after-party. Or maybe it was Thanatos.' She presses her palm to her forehead.

'You don't remember whether the guy you kissed had wings?'

'You're not helping.'

'Well . . . I did kiss Hades.'

'What?' She snaps up, eyes wide.

'Yeah, don't get too excited though. He didn't exactly enjoy it.' I tell her everything.

'Okay, first of all, Hades kept his wine store secret from me for years, and then *still* kept secret its magic refilling capabilities? That dick.' She winces. 'Though remind me to come back to that when saying the word "wine" doesn't make me want to vomit. Secondly, his reaction doesn't mean anything. You can't just kiss him while you're both drunk and expect him to declare his love for you.'

'It does mean something. It means he only likes me as a friend,' I say firmly. 'That's fine. That's more than fine. I don't have time to get upset over this.'

'It's okay to be upset about unrequited feelings,' she says.

'Not when you're marrying the person involved in said feelings in five days and you need to search the mortals for a wedding planner.'

'I really don't like the way you just ignore your emotions because you're busy.'

I shrug. 'Yeah, well, I promise I'll break down properly once I'm married.'

She pulls me into her arms. 'Point me to the mortals. Maid of honour duties and whatnot – I suppose I should help.'

Together we find some people. A woman from Crete tells me she saw her five daughters all wed and every single one had a wedding that made the town talk for years. She's organized beyond my wildest expectations and corrals everyone into various tasks. There's a young man from Kos with a fantastic eye for lighting and an older woman with a sense for glamour.

But in the end it's still not enough.

Hades and I don't need a wedding. We need *the* wedding.

This isn't just a ruse to spite Zeus. Hades was chosen by Kronos. In accepting him, I rejected the proposals of four of the twelve council members. Zeus, king of the gods and ruler of Olympus, and Poseidon, king of the sea, are married. This is the last royal wedding anyone will ever see among the gods.

I came into this knowing we were both dramatic, but it turns out we're far more dramatic than I thought. Hades barks orders to emboss everything with skulls and Cerberus and other symbols of his realm.

'What was it you said to me about a dog marking its territory, dear?' I ask wryly.

'Would you care to wear a burlap sack?' he retorts, agitated as he surveys the courtyard where we will be married.

I make up bouquets in some of my best work. From a distance, the asphodel and styx stand prominent in the bunches but up close thousands of tiny blossoms in a rainbow of colours glisten like oil spills among the petals. I make the whole courtyard bloom, coat the walls in ivy, grow trees to provide shade.

Hades makes glass candle holders, elaborate centrepieces and huge marble statues. I hang garlands on the latter.

And in the flurry of running from one task to the next, the first day of the wedding is suddenly upon us.

CHAPTER TWENTY-EIGHT

THE MORNING OF OUR PROAULIA, I sit in front of the mirror staring far beyond my reflection. Scissors hang limply in my hand and I'm more aware of being alone than ever before.

I never wanted to get married – even when I was little and that was the only dream poured into my head. But I knew it would happen. And I thought I would be surrounded by my friends when it did.

I thought that when my proaulia came it would be Cyane handing my mother the scissors. I thought Eudokia and Myrrha would help dress me and that Amalthea would hang beads round my throat.

Styx is great, and I might venture so far as to call some of the mortals my friends too, but they aren't the people who have known me my whole life. I am alone. And that's fine. But on a day like today it really isn't.

I pull my hair free of its braid, sighing to myself to just get it over with.

I watch myself in the mirror, see the waist-length hair that made me 'little girl'. I grate at the mere thought of cutting my hair off and suddenly I'm on my feet, flinging the scissors across the room.

Why is every single *bloody* part of me dictated by what men want? Long hair for virgins, short for married women. Even the style: loose hair says you're a slut, too tight and you're frigid. Your dress is too short – you look too easy. Your dress is too long – you're not easy enough. Not enough make-up and men won't desire you, and what value do you hold if they don't? Fully made-up and they'll desire you too much and whatever happens, whatever they do to you, it's your fault. Gods, everything – right down to my old name – has been decided by men.

And what's worse is that no man has ever told me these rules. They've thought them, of course, but it's my mother's voice I hear. It's the voice of the nymphs saying that Daphne wanted Apollo's attention – she flirted too much. It's me clutching a sickle and nodding mutely in the hope it keeps me safe.

Gods, I could scream because there's no way out. Literally every decision I make is because of men, one way or another.

There were no men on my island and yet I was there because of them.

It's nothing I haven't thought before. But I'm tired of dancing within the confines of a prison, particularly when I've reinforced the locks within my own mind.

I'm not even sure if I don't want to cut my hair because I like my hair long, or because I resent the implications of short hair.

There's a knock on the door and I yell for whoever it is to

come in. I don't think I should be alone to continue this breakdown.

Hades steps through the door and his eyes flit around the room.

'What did the scissors do to you?' he asks.

'Symbol of the patriarchy,' I mutter.

He scowls. 'I've never heard that one before.'

'I'm having a bad day.'

'What every man wants to hear on his wedding day,' Hades says, leaning against the wall. 'Anything I can help you with?'

I shake my head. 'It's a "damned if I do, damned if I don't" situation.'

'Is there a third option?'

I shrug. 'Shoulder-length?'

'You're going to have to explain a bit more, love,' he says and my heart lurches.

'Okay, first of all, I thought we agreed none of that in private.' I point my finger angrily.

'But "dear" and "darling" are fine?' he asks sceptically.

My friends and I call each other 'dear' and 'darling' so often I had almost forgotten they have alternative meanings. But hearing him say them now has me stuttering for a reply.

I turn back to the mirror. 'I don't see why my appearance has to indicate whether I'm a virgin or not,' I say. 'Yours doesn't.'

'My appearance very clearly says I'm not.' He grins slyly.

I glare at him.

He raises his hands in apology. 'Not the time.'

'No. But I don't know what to do,' I admit.

'Well, do you want to cut your hair?' Hades asks. 'Personally, I'm not particularly hopeful about your ability to do it well.'

'It's not exactly like there's another choice,' I snap. 'If you haven't noticed, nearly everyone I love has a life force rooted to an island thousands of miles above us.'

'Persephone,' Hades says so gently it brings tears to my eyes but, no, I'm not crying.

'It's fine,' I say quickly. 'I want to stay here. I love this place. And when we're married and we're both safe I'll be able to visit Sicily. But it does make all this harder. I've spent my whole life dreading my wedding, and now the people I thought might make it bearable aren't even here.'

Hades fidgets uncomfortably. 'And we come back to things a man wants to hear on his wedding day.'

'*Hades*,' I growl.

'Sorry, I'm trying, truly. But comfort was never my forte.'

'I've never bloody noticed.'

'What do you mean by "both safe" anyway? I'm perfectly safe,' he says.

'Zeus threatened you at least once.'

He waves the comment away. 'Just words.'

I think it's been a very long time since Hades saw my father. And right now I don't have the energy to correct him. Not when as of tomorrow, on the day of our gamos, we will be properly wed and it won't matter anyway.

'Let me try this one again,' Hades says. 'Do you want to cut your hair?'

'It's not that simple,' I say. 'Any decision I make is more to do with everyone else than me.'

'Very well, forget cutting it then. What else would you do with it?' he asks.

'Thread it with flowers,' I answer instantly. I could braid them in or form some sort of crown — like a shadow of the one I will receive on the third and final wedding day, my epaulia.

'Then don't cut it,' he says.

'But it's supposed to be cut short to honour Artemis.'

'Who cares?'

'I do! And she will. We don't need more enemies among the council,' I say. 'There's still every chance Zeus will decide a marriage isn't enough to soothe his ego, and then we really will need all the allies we can get.'

'One step at a time,' Hades says, coming to join me by the mirror. 'We'll tackle this together.'

'No, we won't. It's different for me and you know it.'

'Fine, then I'll hold your flowers while you tear the world apart,' he says.

It's ridiculous, but somehow, despite everything, he's made me laugh. 'Do you have any suggestions that aren't world destruction?'

'Yes. If honouring Artemis is so important to you then find another way to do it.'

There's an idea. I have done that before.

'I know that look,' he says.

I smile. 'It's the one I wore before making the asphodel.'

He glowers. 'And the styx. You know, with each new deity you make flowers for, the less special I feel.'

'Aww, poor king of Hell.' I pat him on the shoulder. 'You'll survive.'

'Darling?' he adds before I can go and create something for Artemis. 'Let's just focus on getting you on the throne first, yes? Then you can raise Hell.'

'I create you in honour of the goddess Artemis,' I whisper to the dirt before summoning a flower. It's only a small creation, and similar to others I have made. But it is a little harder than I expected. I've healed so many souls now that it's almost second nature to connect myself to this realm. I suppose that I'm just letting divinity revive their souls, whereas flowers are a power unique to me and require more conscious effort. It's been a while since I connected to this part of myself.

I feel tired by the time I've pulled a small flower patch into existence. I might be forgoing the traditional haircut, but I'm excited for the proaulia's soothing bath and cleansing ceremonies. But first I stare with resolute satisfaction at the little white petals and their yellow centres. I think Artemis will like them – and, better, I think she'll recognize the act of rebellion contained within them.

When I was younger, I wanted to be just like her: a guardian of young girls, running wild through the forests with her friends – if that's all they are – hunting wherever she goes. But she never protected me, and she's never protected hundreds of young girls just like me. Aloof and intimidating, Artemis has always felt a little too distant from the world she inhabits. If she thinks my long hair an offence, her fury could be a terrifying thing.

But Hades was right: this is a good way to push back.

I'm becoming quite used to rebelling against the traditions of my father's world.

I merely hope the wedding works and isn't the rebellion that gets me in trouble. Staring at the flowers that stretch across this land uniting gods, mortal souls and every creature in between, I know it's not just me at risk if this goes wrong.

CHAPTER TWENTY-NINE

T HE SECOND DAY OF THE wedding, the gamos, is the most important. For one, it's the day of the actual wedding ceremony. But, far more importantly, it's the day gods of the other courts arrive.

The morning begins with Tempest delivering a steaming pot of mint tea to my room. My fast will continue until the moment of the ceremony, when Hades and I bite into the ceremonial apple.

It's a good thing too because I feel sick enough without food.

It's not quite that today I will be married.

And more that today I will see my parents.

Hermes says Zeus has agreed to claim this was his idea. Apparently he has been parading around Olympus chuckling at how he manipulated Demeter to secure my hand for Hades. And, if he wants everyone to believe him, he will be among the gods today.

And Mother . . . I have no idea what she will do. Stand there plotting Hades' murder? Cause a scene in her displeasure? Her magic restricted by the solstice, will she turn instead to screams and shouts? It doesn't sound like something she'd do. But I wouldn't put it past her.

When there is nothing but dregs at the bottom of my cup, I wonder if curling mint leaves can be read by the oracles the same way black tea might. If so, I'm not hopeful for my future.

I'm still staring into their depths when my mortal companions burst unexpectedly into my room.

Larissa pulls me close and asks how I am feeling, coiling a finger round my still-long hair and nodding approvingly. Damaris asks where my dress is and floods with relief when I tell her Hades has it arranged. And as I'm feeling overcome by the fear of all that is ahead – more people and gods than I have seen in my life – Cora distracts me with a giddy story about the poet she was finally able to find. We all smile knowingly at the blush across her cheeks whenever she mentions her name.

Styx arrives an hour later, clutching a cup of nectar and glaring in the mortals' direction as they babble. I love the chatter; it feels like home, where I was never among just one or two nymphs but twenty, maybe thirty. But Styx says it's not something she can stand before midday.

Tempest appears with cosmetics and scowls at the array of toiletries already scattered across the bed. I expect her to disappear the moment she hands everything over – she never stays long – but she hovers by the wall. Soon, she and Styx are making disparaging comments about the whole affair and the fact Hades won't be going to such lengths to appear palatable to the gods. They don't get how it feels more like armour, or a disguise.

But the mortals do. They pull me to the bathing rooms and pour rose water over my skin, layer my hair in hibiscus foams and freesia soaps. Once the cleansing water has worked its magic and I am as pure as the creators of this ceremony intended, Damaris rubs olive oil into my hair to make it shine while Larissa dusts my skin in crushed-shell powder to make it shimmer, and Cora sprays a mist of lily and gardenia. Next, Tempest hands Styx flowers to tuck into my curls, though Styx tries to sneak in far too many styx blossoms and pouts every time I tell her to add some of the others.

It's not the same as Cyane and the nymphs, but it's something.

And then, back in my room, a gown is waiting for me.

My companions freeze at the sight.

I had no idea that anything could be so soft, that lace could look so light, that fabric could drape like frost on grass even when bundled on the bed. I hold it up and the material unfurls like pouring water – liquid silver that gleams where it catches the light.

'Persephone,' Cora breathes. 'I'm a literal princess and even I . . . By the Fates.'

'Wherever did he get this?' Damaris asks. Tempest stares at her warily, like she's ready to whisk her away to some corner of the realm if she figures it out. 'Is there a goddess of fashion that no one told us mortals about? I would have sacrificed anything to her for a work like this.'

Even Styx's eyes are wide. It is one thing to know of his talent, I suppose, and another to see it.

If it was beautiful before, it's nothing compared to the way it sits on my skin like the soft kiss of a summer breeze. Hades has used a material I've never seen before – a loose weave that would be transparent if he hadn't layered it with lace. The skirt floats around me. The draping is artful; it clings to my body and swirls to my feet. So much movement that Mother never would have given me. Instead of sleeves, Hades has stitched beads so tight they form caps across my shoulders, and the hem is embroidered with spiralling patterns.

I think of Hades saying that embroidery was a craft he never particularly enjoyed and I flush.

I thank the mortals and tell them I will see them later. I invited them to the ceremony, but they blanched at the thought of all the gods and politely excused themselves.

Styx says she should go get ready herself as she wants to look hot for Pallas or Thanatos or whoever it was she kissed.

'Tempest,' I ask when they're gone, 'where is Hades?'

She shakes her head. 'I saw him last hours ago, when he asked me to fetch your mortals and the river goddess.'

'He asked you to do that?' A smile creeps across my face and I let it – anything that screams 'blushing bride' is permissible today.

'Yes, he trusts me with a great number of important tasks.' She stays for one more eye roll before leaving to check on the place settings. I set about finding Hades.

He's in one of his workrooms, surrounded by swatches of metallic fabrics. I see all the effort he put into this gown that I commanded him to make.

'Thank you,' I say. 'It's perfect.'

He turns and I'm not sure what I was expecting – perhaps more of the shock he showed when he first saw me on the stairs the evening our engagement was announced.

Instead his features freeze and after a moment he swallows.

'I thought I wasn't supposed to see you before the ceremony,' he says.

I scowl. 'Why?'

'It's tradition.'

I shrug. 'Not one I've heard of. Anyway, you always say that I don't compliment you enough so you should probably write all this down. This is the most amazing dress, Hades. My friends could barely contain themselves. How are you so talented?'

Hades shrugs but his eyes shine – deep brown pools shimmering like water beneath the sun.

'It's rather easy when you have the right muse.'

'Ahh, practising already, are we?' I tease.

He blinks and a second later a lazy grin falls into place. 'Are you suggesting I need practice?'

'To get to my level? Definitely,' I say but my grin falls as I spot what he's working on. 'Is that . . .'

I'm not sure how it evaded me so long. The flowers are pulling at me, all but screaming in my head to pay attention.

'Your veil, yes,' he says.

The anakalypteria, the lifting of the veil, is the most crucial part of the wedding ceremony.

Hades has filled every single gap in the lace of the veil with flowers, so that only flashes of fabric peek through. I will be covered head to toe in flowers, and I laugh when I see which ones: daisies, freesia and gardenia. *Purity*. The flowers I told Cyane I was going to collect before I leapt to the Underworld. What a delightful coincidence, and how gloriously defiant: a secret nod to the fact I chose to be here all along.

'They're from home,' I say quietly, lifting a corner of the veil gently. The flowers hum with the feeling of Sicily, the meadows I have run through and the dirt I have dug.

'Yes, well.' Hades scratches the back of his neck, staring at something on the other side of the room. 'I couldn't bring your friends to you. So I got a message to them and they made you this.'

'You . . . the nymphs made this?' I'm staring at him like I'm seeing him for the first time as he stands awkwardly, doing anything but acknowledging the thought he put into this. My heart breaks for the fact I cannot pull him to me, cannot show him what this means to me.

He doesn't love me that way and in moments like this I wish he'd stop acting like it.

I focus on my friends instead, the love they have stitched into this veil.

'They took some convincing,' Hades says. 'I sent a message to Cyane. Obviously she thought I'd kidnapped you, so she wasn't happy at first.'

'How did you persuade her?'

Hades grins. 'By being my regular charming self.' At my sceptical eyebrow he laughs. 'My dear, they may have got me wrong, but they know you quite well. I regaled them with a tale or two of how you stormed into my realm, covered it in flowers and demanded changes. They knew I wasn't making it up by the end.'

I'm not sure my smile has ever been so wide. 'I can't believe this. Thank you so much.'

'Yes, well, your wedding is supposed to be the happiest day of your life,' he says. 'If you can't have the suitor you deserve, you can at least have the outfit.'

'You're fishing for more compliments and I won't have it.

You know I find your company quite tolerable,' I joke and Hades feigns a wounded look.

'There was one thing. Cyane demanded that, the moment you're able, you visit.'

'Perfect. That was my plan anyway.'

Hades nods. 'I had better go get ready. The guests will already be crossing the Acheron.'

'Okay,' I say. 'I guess I'll see you when I marry you.'

Hades beams. 'Farewell, my future queen.'

The veil is heavy with the weight of the flowers but I feel swathed in the love that threaded them. Cyane is here with me and I know somewhere by her river she is thinking of me. The nymphs are probably discussing me right now, speculating and giggling at my happiness.

It's almost enough to make me step forward but I can sense the gods on the other side of the doors, and a tingle on my neck tells me to run.

Then something cuts through, like a sense of calm.

I am fine. I am safe.

But Hades isn't. He's in that room and so is my father.

And, if I don't marry Hades, Father will do unspeakable things to him. Father's threats to tear him limb from limb are not exaggeration. He has done far worse before. I would not be surprised to learn of pits in the four corners of the world prepared for Father to scatter Hades in.

My nails tighten on the bouquet in my hand and with fury in my veins I step forward.

This should be about desire. It should be about love. It should be about choice.

But weddings are sales transactions. They are about control. I cannot be the only one for whom the thought has always been a nightmare.

So I'm going to marry this man.

I desire him. I love him. I choose him.

I love this realm. And I choose these people.

But it doesn't matter.

Because what I desire most is power.

So I step forward.

I'm going to marry Hades and claim what is mine. I am going to reward and punish the dead, but, more than that, I will inspire and I will strike fear until the mortals above pay attention. It might take generations, but the humans will no longer love or fear my father – they will laugh at him, scorn him for his lack of self-control. They will turn from the gods and they will forge their own paths.

And it will be because of *me*.

I step forward.

In time my name will be more revered than my father's, and the mortals shall value freedom above all else.

And maybe there will always be people who make life worse for others.

But I will always be here to give those others sanctuary and apologize that I could not do it sooner.

I step forward.

I snap my fingers and the doors fling open.

The courtyard has been transformed into a paradise. I feel like I should take notes for the human afterlife I'm creating. My flowers glow like torches, their power pulsing, swarming round the guests to remind them just who I am. And soon they will discover that I am so much more.

I can see perfectly, despite the flowers in my veil. But the crowd can't see me.

So I stare unapologetically as I walk down the aisle, surrounded by gods I have not seen in years. The members of my court are so easy to spot among the gods of Olympus. They smile proudly, basking in having the upper hand and glancing at the Olympians, who stand uncertainly with wry smiles.

I pass Aphrodite, who runs her eyes up and down my dress with fury. She whispers to Hephaestus, no doubt demanding he find the source.

Ares glowers sullenly – exactly the kind of husband I was trying to avoid. If I needed one more sign I am making the right choice, the god of war is providing it.

Hestia and Hermes grin beside each other, Hestia warmly and Hermes with the impish delight of being in on a joke.

Dionysus holds his spectacles to his eyes like he is at the theatre. I wonder if the god of drama senses all the performances I have given so far – and whether he is judging the greatest one of my life.

Apollo is gazing around the guests, probably searching for nymphs in lieu of bridesmaids. Artemis stands to his side, awkwardly toying with a silver leaf-shaped hair clip, which would be more sophisticated if there wasn't a real leaf tangled beside it.

Athena's look is as iron cold as the shield that hangs from her side.

Now my steps become more purposeful.

Because there is Poseidon, his eyes a raging ocean and utterly indecipherable. Is he angry that Hades took what he could not have? Or is he delighted that Zeus has lost control?

Hera smiles serenely, embodying the graceful harmony she expects of a wedding.

And Father . . .

Zeus is doing a pretty good job of looking pleased. His hands rest behind his back as he surveys the scene before him. But his jaw is too tight, the muscles of his arms too tensed.

I grin, not even trying to suppress it because the veil does such a brilliant job.

This whole marriage would be worth it just to anger Zeus.

Beside him there is only empty space. My heart jumps. Where is she? It takes all my self-restraint not to search the crowd. I feel panicked like I'm a child again, lost in the woods and screaming for my mother.

Because she is not here.

She's not here.

I imagined so many things, so many horrific confrontations – her screaming at Hades or dragging me away without listening to my protests. But no confrontation at all is so much worse. How could she not be here? I want to tell her the truth, show her what I've done with this world, introduce her to Hades and tell her all the things he's done for me. But she hasn't come. My mother hasn't come to my wedding.

I keep going. The last thing I turn to see is Hades.

I nearly stumble.

It's not that he's gorgeous, because of course he is, his dark skin radiant, eyes bright, cheekbones and jawline carved from something harder than marble. It's not that his white robe is perfectly cut to enhance all my favourite parts of him – his strong shoulders, muscled thighs and narrow hips. It's not even the crown that rests upon his head, catching the light and pulling me closer, or the smoke that falls off him in waves, or the darkness clinging to his skin, more exaggerated than I've ever seen it so that he resembles a creature from a nightmare.

It's the way he looks at me, the smile that isn't visible but plays across his face nonetheless. It's the way he is almost entranced. It's the way I feel caught in his gaze.

My heart is beating hard and strong. From the corner of my eye I see Aphrodite, goddess of love, snap her head up, her eyes widening, and I wonder if she can sense every feeling thrumming through me.

Three women rise behind Hades, all unassuming in appearance, different only in their age. The Fates. The youngest's hair is long and uncut. She is barely out of adolescence but something about her feels ancient. The middle reminds me of Mother, though they don't look a thing alike. I remember that my mother is not here to see this. The final Fate makes Hecate look young. Her eyes, white with cataracts, stare straight at me.

I can feel their power. Every eye draws towards them. Hades and I bow our heads and the attendees drop to one knee.

Zeus bows – a stiff, jerky movement.

Even kings must bow to Fate, but the sight is delightful nonetheless.

I take my place beside Hades and the gods around me melt away. They are no longer individuals but a distant audience. All I can see is him.

The desire for this wedding to be real hits me so strongly that it feels more like pain than longing. The thought doesn't shock me like it should; it's just another wave of sadness pulsing through me. I knew I liked him, and I knew I wanted more. But it would be so like me not to realize quite how much until the moment I'm standing beside him, about to marry him.

Hades smiles slightly, the demure nod of a pleased monarch. But his eyes? Oh, his eyes are positively radiating happiness. Everyone can see how truly happy he is.

I have to concede defeat. My ability to lie has nothing on his. His performance is truly something else.

Clotho, the youngest Fate, steps forward. She wears a white dress of the kind it will no longer be deemed suitable for me to wear.

I don't care too much about that. I only ever got them dirty anyway.

'Lord Hades.' Her voice is clear as it rings through the room like a tinkling bell. 'You may lift the veil of your betrothed.'

My breath catches and this is it. I thought there would be more preamble, more ceremony.

Hades reaches for the lacy edge of the veil. His fingers brush mine and a thousand jolts shake my skin. There is something about being surrounded by this many people that makes every look and every movement mean so much.

His hands shake as he raises the veil.

I plaster an adoring look on my face, determined not to show any of the anxiousness or heartbreak that I'm feeling.

The veil falls back and gasps ring through the room.

'She's beautiful . . .'

'By the Fates . . .'

'Her hair, though – it's not cut . . .'

Whispers catch at me but I ignore them. My eyes meet Hades' before I lean up to him and he down to me, just as we planned – the perfect second of hesitation, the charged air crackling, and then the moment our lips touch. All of it timed to cause the exclamations that sound around us.

I move my lips against his methodically. Yes, his lips are soft, and all I want is to give myself over to what we are doing. But I can't.

I couldn't do that to him – take advantage of the kiss necessitated by this ceremony to imagine a kiss that means something. I think of our kiss at the lake, and how I put everything into it. Now I focus on deceit, the muttering gods and angling my head so everyone can see. There's nothing in it at all.

But then his breath fills my lungs and I pull back, the unexpected intimacy catching at the iron I had wrapped my feelings in.

Hades blinks like he's disoriented and I force a smile, ducking my head as though embarrassed while the crowd cheer.

I didn't think faking this would be so difficult. Surely it should be easy to pretend if you're not really pretending? But I've layered myself in so many pretences that anything true has been strangled.

The middle Fate, Lachesis, steps forward, as Clotho fades back. Lachesis holds an apple in her outstretched hands. There's something wicked about its red gleam in the palms of Fate.

Something that makes me reluctant to pluck it from her fingers. It is something the man would normally do first – Hades and I agreed it would be an easy act of rebellion.

I snatch the apple before I can think better of it, and my teeth tear into the crisp skin, its tang coating my tongue before the first murmurs.

I hold the apple out to Hades. He smiles that amused, teasing smile of his and then bites not the other side, as would be custom, but next to my own bite. His lips meet the skin where mine just were.

My knees go weak.

I'm not sure why this one small act has butterflies fluttering in my stomach when our actual kiss did, well, not nothing but close to it. But here we are.

And I'm not the only one. The Muses are fanning themselves in the crowd.

I suppose if I must have a fake husband, having one so attractive is definitely a plus.

The crown doesn't hurt either.

He hands the apple back to Lachesis and she buries it in a pocket. I dread to think what spells that apple will be used for.

Atropos, the third Fate, steps forward, a loutrophoros in her wrinkled hands. Water sloshes in the vase with each step.

Hades takes my hand and we kneel before her. The cold stone presses through the thin layers of my dress until my knees ache.

I startle as the water hits me. My veil dampens and water clings to my hair, but not much is poured before the thin stream moves to Hades. His white robes turn translucent where the water hits – a flash of collarbone presses through, muscular grooves across his abdomen I ache to trace.

All at once the water stops and we rise to our feet.

Atropos steps back to join her sisters.

My heart pounds and I look at Hades, our hands still entwined, my other hand clutching my bouquet like it's the only thing in all this that makes sense.

It's over. We're married.

I recover quickly. 'Husband.' I grin, unable to tear my eyes from the drops of water that cling to his eyelashes.

Hades pulls me closer. 'Wife.' The one word spills with such joy that I suddenly can't imagine it being said any other way.

Around us, cheers erupt.

CHAPTER THIRTY

THE CHEERS ARE OVERWHELMING AND we only have a moment of being crushed by the noise before the people swarm us too. They shunt us towards the palace and it's chaos, but Hades clings to my hand and I'm shocked to find myself not just smiling but laughing ecstatically. In all of our planning, I didn't prepare myself for how happy an event it would be. I was so focused on convincing everyone we love each other that I didn't think about how joyful a wedding might be if you believed in that love.

When we finally cross the threshold the excited shouts get even louder.

Ares claps Hades on the back.

'Very nicely done,' he says.

'Tell me the food in the Underworld is decent,' Dionysus whines. 'I'm starving.'

I look round the room for my parents – as though I might have missed my mother and she's here after all, or my father might be storming through the crowd, lightning bolt clenched tight in his fist. But there are too many people. The women are already gathering together, waiting for me to take them through to our separate feast.

'I will see you soon?' Hades asks as the men gather on his side. His robes are still splattered with the water that joined us, the same water that's clinging to the petals of my veil. I don't want to go separate ways; I want to be alone with Hades, to strip out of our damp clothes into cosier robes, to drink tea by the fireplace and chat for hours.

But the wedding is so much more than the ceremony, and there are other traditions to get through.

'Of course,' I say chirpily, hoping that if I sound excited I might become it. 'You aren't getting rid of me that quickly.'

People around us titter at the idea Hades, who has masterminded my abduction, has become bored of me already.

Maybe they don't believe our love after all. Maybe they're just excited for Hades to have won in such a way. Or maybe they believe he took me and I've fallen for him, held prisoner until I grew fond of him.

I remind myself that, to be my true self, I must be safe, and to get there I must conform until the moment this wedding is over. The moment the crown is on my head. So I smile, lips thin as a knife edge, and tell myself that everything that has my stomach in knots and my head swimming is ammunition. It will be a joy to bring these cruel beings to ruin.

'Ladies.' I nod to the goddesses. 'Shall we?'

As we start walking, Hestia comes to my side and slings her arm round my neck.

'You look beautiful,' she says excitedly.

'As do you.' It's true – Hestia doesn't need all the extravagance I have reached for in my outfit. She has a way of making plain items graceful. With her simple umber dress, held at her throat by a chain of wooden beads a few shades lighter than her skin, and her intricate braids bound together in a twisting knot, she's lovely – and then she smiles. Hestia's smiles contain the warmth of a dozen hearths and I'm so glad she's here.

She lowers her voice and asks, 'Are you all right?'

I'm not prepared for the sting of tears. She's the first person to ask me that.

'Yes,' I say firmly, offering a smile. 'Thank you.' I put so much sincerity into my thanks that Hestia nods, seemingly convinced.

'Xenia gets used a lot,' she says. 'I can't really keep track of it all – but you used it, didn't you? And he didn't break it?'

'Hestia, I . . .' I don't really want to discuss this here, even with the other goddesses chattering among themselves. Someone might hear.

'I was just going to say,' she continues, 'as goddess of home, I can feel that this is yours. And I'm glad you found it.'

She lets go with a final squeeze and slips back into the crowd of goddesses. I blink, my heart a little warmer.

I take them all to the east wing. On Olympus, it is rumoured to be Zeus's favourite wing, where he can watch the sun rise and view his world in glorious splendour. Down here, the wing is mine. The huge arched windows look out on to fields of flowers, the edges of the human lands traceable on the horizon. Bouquets hang from the torches in the corridor, guiding us to the hall at the end. The white marble no longer feels like a mausoleum, not now it's hung with tapestries and art.

When we reach the hall, a long golden table stretches down its length. Chandeliers shine with twinkling lights, the ceiling so high you could blink and believe the lights were the stars themselves.

'We're eating?' Hestia asks gleefully as she sees the spread before her.

I have been working with the nymphs and mortals for days to prepare. With access to myriad ingredients, they have created dishes I've never even heard of. The long table groans under plates piled with juicy meat cooked in garlic and parsley, twists of bread studded with olives, vegetables roasted in olive oil and coated in flakes of salt, rice fragrant with jasmine, curried dishes with their scents that spiral into the air, and other plates with names in languages I am yet to learn.

'Yes,' I confirm, heading to my seat at the head of the table.

'Now?' Hera asks sharply.

I nod, feigning innocence. 'Yes, I'm so hungry. Aren't you? I've been so excited that I haven't been able to eat for days.'

Wind spirits gust in and chalices of wine appear to fill themselves.

'It's customary to –'

'Oh, the waiting?' I ask. 'I know, but Hades and I both felt we couldn't keep such important women as yourselves waiting.'

Hera freezes, jaw tensing.

I can scarcely breathe as I wait for her response.

Technically, the women are supposed to eat only after the men have finished. Hades and I decided that was completely sexist nonsense, but it was Hera who dictated these marriage customs – no doubt in some effort to appease her husband.

Hera is probably the goddess I'm most nervous around. I don't want to insult her by subverting her traditions. She's powerful – the queen of the gods and my father's wife – and there are plenty of stories of her vindictiveness and cruelty. She was also forced into marriage with my father and even tried to overthrow him once. He hung her from the sky in chains until she was in so much pain that she swore on the Styx never to rise against him again. But that doesn't mean there aren't loopholes. If I can get her on my side, she could be an invaluable ally.

Of course for now my focus is on surviving my father, but I have an eternity ahead and I'm idly thinking about the long-term.

'Wonderful,' Athena says, taking a seat at my side and it's like she's given the others permission to sit too. Hera hesitates only a moment longer before she joins us at the table, burying her expression in her wine glass.

There is no seating chart but the deities arrange themselves in a certain order anyway. Members of the council surround me: Athena to my left, Artemis to my right, and Hera, Aphrodite and Hestia – who rumour has it might be joining the council any day now – joining next to them. Other Olympians fill the tables after them, from the Muses to minor gods: Melpomene, the muse of tragedy, next to Selene, goddess of the moon. The three Graces line up next to Tyche, goddess of fortune. They sprawl on and on until they run into the deities of Poseidon's realm, Oceanus, bookended by his wife, Amphitrite, and Thetis, a goddess of some sea I've never seen. The goddesses of my realm cluster at the other end, Mania chatting amicably with Enyo and the Fates bent together at the furthest edge.

'To this union,' Hera says, her voice ringing through the room and cutting short any conversation.

Everyone raises a glass, even Athena and Cybele who pointedly place them straight back down. It appears some deities are loyal to my mother. I don't know whether that's a relief or not. At least no one left a seat for her. I couldn't cope with an empty space where she should be.

As I place my bouquet of flowers in an empty vase on the table it catches Artemis's attention.

'What is that?' She nods. 'It feels . . . odd.'

'Ah.' I smile. 'Well, I wished to make an aparche but I'm rather attached to my hair.'

'Yes, I had noticed,' Artemis says, suddenly cold.

'I thought I would honour you in a way only I can instead.' I nod to the flower that caught her attention, clusters of white petals round a bud so yellow it makes the sun look pale. 'I call it chamomile.' The name feels like a secret joke: *earth apple*. It is the first thing I have created in this realm intended for consumption. 'It is designed to survive many climates, it has many medicinal qualities, and it is quite delicious in tea. I thought it would be useful for you and your hunters when foraging.'

Artemis – no, the whole table – is quiet, staring at me.

Athena breaks first and taps a sharp nail absent-mindedly against a wine glass. 'You have certainly made the most of your gift,' she says, her gaze all the more intense for the stark contrast of her slate-grey eyes against her porcelain skin.

My smile is perfect: demure, bashful and pleased all at once. 'It's a delight to bring beauty to the world – but to bring use too is a brand of magic I feel honoured to have.' My eyes meet Hecate's and I expect her to return the spark of joy. She told me I was more than flowers. Is this not what she meant, the way I spin flowers beyond themselves?

But she's not happy. Her dark eyes burn like wildfire.

'Thank you . . . *Persephone*.' Artemis's clumsy tongue struggles with my name but I flush at her using it. No other Olympian has yet acknowledged that I have refused the name they all witnessed Zeus give me. I'm not sure if it's loyalty to my mother or him. 'It's a gift I did not expect and far superior to a lock of hair.'

'Yes, well,' I say. 'A thank you for protecting young girls.' I raise my glass to her, biting my tongue.

I wonder if she can feel the challenge, see the glint of anger in my eyes.

Because *she* didn't protect *me*. I protected myself. Where was she when Mother was trying to marry me off? Doing whatever our father told her. Everyone in this room thinks I was kidnapped, forced into marriage and gods know what else, and not a single one of them has done anything to stop it.

And maybe it didn't happen to me but I've spent enough time with the mortals to know such stories are far from rare.

All those young girls, forced to cut their hair in honour of a goddess who can't protect them because she's too busy pacing the cell her father created for her. He lets her run through the wilds but stops her from interfering with anything but the outskirts of this world. And she has embraced that. She clutches her limited freedom, too scared of stepping across the line he set.

She knows that.

As if hearing my thoughts, Artemis flushes but nods.

She's no protector. Not yet.

But maybe it will only take one of us to successfully defy my father before the others follow suit. The icy glare in Artemis's eyes, ducked to the table, suggests she'd love to take on everyone that ever put a girl in danger, preferably with an arrow through the eye.

'Please, do eat,' I insist. The men certainly wouldn't be hesitating. The women of my court have already piled their plates high.

'None of this food was grown here?' Hera checks.

I assure her it was not, shuddering at the thought of any Olympian here for eternity.

I perform for the next hour, glittering like a crystal ornament for them to admire. I feign interest in the gossip they share, giggle at their tiresome jokes and bow my head with a blush at any questions about Hades. They will get nothing from me.

I scan the faces around me, wondering who else is performing a role. I'm a little concerned – though perhaps not surprised – to find that I think all of them are.

Nymphs return with cakes that shimmer with sugar, whips of cream and torrents of honey. Fruit is piled so high in the baskets they carry that it makes Mount Olympus look small. I pull Tempest aside before she leaves, whispering to her to refill the wine of the goddesses.

I wonder if Hades' party is this dull. Perhaps they're all playing their roles too – bawdy men with riotous feasting and vile questions. I wonder if Hades answers them as I reach for my own goblet. He could barely manage Hermes at our engagement announcement. How will he cope with a roomful of gods wanting lewd details about our non-existent relationship?

By the time the cakes are cleared, the chattering has reached fever pitch, thanks no doubt to the swiftly filled glasses. Two minor ocean deities are heatedly arguing, and those round them turn their heads from side to side like they are watching a pentathlon.

Astraea, another of my father's bastards and technically, I suppose, my sister, leans into Peitho, goddess of seduction. Peitho rests her hand on Astraea's thigh and Astraea blushes a shade of red I've only seen on flowers.

People are pushing their plates away and moving to talk to those sitting further away, forming small huddles of goddesses trading gossip. Just as I'm about to join one, Hera's hand grasps my arm.

'Your mother is distraught, you know,' she says. Her eyes are more alert than her clumsy movements suggest. She's not too drunk then; this is something she would callously say sober.

'Have you spoken to her?' I ask. 'Is she okay?'

'How could she be?' Hera says but she doesn't sound compassionate. She sounds cruel, a sneering lilt to her voice. 'She thinks he's forcing you to act this happy but you really are delighted, aren't you? How could you do that to your poor mother?'

Well, if she were here, if I could speak to her, maybe she'd understand.

'I love Hades,' I confirm. 'And I hope that in time she may see that. She'll be pleased with how happy I am with my husband.'

Hera snorts derisively. 'You've been married less than a day and you're expecting happiness? You truly are naive.'

'I am demanding happiness,' I correct and pull my arm from her so abruptly she jolts. I stand just as abruptly. 'Excuse me.'

Perhaps any plan to ally myself with Hera will have to wait. Before I can choose a group to converse with, Hecate appears beside me.

'May I speak to you privately?' she asks.

I suppress a sigh. I get the feeling protesting will not end particularly well.

I take her to a small room so close to the banquet hall that I can still hear the chatter of the goddesses.

'What is this?' she asks, waving her wrinkled hand at me.

'Could you elaborate?'

'Your web of deceit is a disgrace.'

I close my arms across my chest. 'I'm sorry you feel that way.'

I turn to go but she steps in front of me, pushing me back.

'What are you doing, playing at the blushing bride when you could be doing so much more?'

I swallow. 'If I want to help the mortals then I need –'

Hecate winces. 'You're still thinking so small.'

'Stop talking in riddles then. If you think I'm so much more than this then tell me. Tell me what it is you think I am.'

She cackles. 'But that's no fun. No fun at all.'

'I don't have time for fun. I'm a girl trying her best to survive in this world. This marriage is how.'

'You shouldn't be trying to survive this world; you should be trying to destroy it.'

'That's not quite something I can achieve in an afternoon,' I say dryly, hoping indifference might cover my panic. I don't need Hecate knowing that's exactly what I'm trying to do: bring down the Olympians and the world they've shaped. If I can actually do this, then my afterlife will alter mortal morality so fundamentally that the world will never be the same again – and nor will the gods. I don't know what she'd do with that information. The only person I trust with any secret right now is Hades. 'Now if you'll excuse me.'

She hisses. 'That boy is a distraction.'

'Hades –' I start.

'Is incidental.'

'He's my husband.'

'He's an addition,' she growls. 'You love him? You're lucky. But you hide your power behind his as though you could only be queen of this realm with his help, like the power running through your veins doesn't mean you couldn't just take it from him. Like it wasn't always destined for you.'

Her words catch me off guard. 'This realm? You think my power has something to do with this realm?'

'Ask your husband if you care so much about him. He knows.'

She walks away and I stare at the wall. *Is* Hades keeping secrets from me? Secrets about me and this realm? I haven't done anything somebody else couldn't do – a brush with divine energy to restore some simple mortal souls and a rift in the land that I managed to connect to the flowers my father gave me.

But . . . what if I didn't?

What if she's right? What if it's something else?

Maybe Hecate says all this to throw me. She doesn't like Hades – she's made that clear. Or, rather, she thinks I don't need him. Maybe she's trying to distract me. Maybe it's just another game. At any rate, I can't afford to think about it in the middle of my wedding.

I am returning to the party when I hear voices rumbling down the hallway.

'You think because I am here that you are forgiven?' Father demands.

'Of course not,' Hades says, his voice placating in a way that reminds me too much of when he was begging me not to hate him.

'You step the slightest millimetre out of line and you –'

'I know you're not threatening me in my own realm, Zeus,' Hades says. 'Not when you are a guest of my hospitality.'

'If you think I fear Hestia and her forsaken xenia after all this then you –'

'Father?' I ask as I turn the corner. I flutter my eyelashes in confusion, widening my eyes ever so slightly in the hope it conveys something innocent. Hades visibly bites back a laugh. 'Is everything okay?'

My father leans away from Hades, who he'd had pressed against the wall with snarls and fists.

'Of course, Kore,' he says.

'Persephone, now,' I rush before he can correct me. 'I have been meaning to talk to you, to thank you for arranging such a fine match for me.'

Hades for his part has swapped terror for admiration, though I do not believe either emotion is real.

'Well,' Father says, adjusting his robes, which are skewed across his shoulders – they are not designed for manhandling gods. 'It's all any father would do for his daughter.'

'Indeed,' I say instead of the tirade I long to give about him treating me as his property.

'I'm just glad to see you finally accepting your role, Kore,' he says, his anger with Hades subsiding into grim satisfaction, as I knew it would. By the end of the night he might be so pleased at my subservience that he will really believe he wanted this. 'You've impressed me, doing all that you have to make your husband happy.'

'Well, I knew there was no way Hades could have taken me if you didn't want him to,' I say, slipping beside Hades, my arm twisting round his waist. 'And if you want this match then I want it too.'

'I hope some of the other goddesses of the court can learn from you, Kore,' Father says.

For the first time, I see that this has never been about me. I could laugh or scream or run at my father, nails reaching. He's spent my whole life making me miserable because I wanted too much, too publicly. If unchecked, I might have inspired other girls to do the same.

Hera given power and bound to his side. Mother a seat on the council and a daughter to protect. Artemis freedom so long as she is outcast. Aphrodite something as enormous as love and a forced marriage to a man she hates. Athena his ear so long as she sides with him. Hestia eternal virginhood if she sticks to the home. Always stipulations – things to temper what we could do, the women we could be.

Hades stiffens at my side, his hand at my back running in soothing circles like he senses my anger and knows it would be a dangerous thing not to temper it.

'I hope so too,' I hiss. 'Are the parties back together?' I ask Hades before I say anything I might regret.

'I believe so.'

'Then it's time to dance.'

Despite everything, despite his powers of acting far surpassing mine, annoyance flashes in his eyes.

My grin widens.

Just try to say no to dancing now, Hades.

'Very well,' he manages, words escaping from his clenched teeth.

'We shall continue this conversation later,' Zeus promises, eyeing Hades with a hatred I doubt he's shown since he strapped Prometheus to a rock.

'Oh, there's no need for that.' Hades' happiness is the same mischievous kind that led him to suggest to Hermes that he present the match as Zeus's idea. 'I believe we both know precisely where it was going.'

Drunken deities cheer us the moment we return and, though I couldn't have been gone for more than fifteen minutes, but it's clear that wine flowed swiftly for every single one of them. I spot Dionysus in the crowd and he raises his glass with a smile not dissimilar to the one Hades just wore. I wonder whether he is responsible for the stumbling gods and hiccupping goddesses.

'I hate you,' Hades whispers in my ear.

'Well, that didn't take long,' I say. 'The wedding isn't even over yet.'

One of his hands grasps my waist, pulling me close, while the other takes my hand. 'I shall add it to my list of regrets.'

'Perhaps the Muses will inspire you,' I propose. 'In fact, they were just at my table.'

His eyes are particularly captivating today.

'It's unlikely,' Hades says. 'I am not a creative person.' His fingers brush the dress he made.

'And a terrible dancer, from what I hear,' I say.

Hades' returning smile is wolfish. 'Oh no, not at all.'

The music starts and he whisks me off my feet.

I've danced so many times but the music of the nymphs is wilder, less rhythmic and more intuitive. I would twist and shape my body until its movements felt like a natural extension of the notes.

Nothing about this is easy.

I dart and turn, guided by Hades, and while I'm stumbling to keep up he moves like he invented dance itself.

No, he's definitely not a terrible dancer.

He smiles at me the entire time, never looking away once, his strong hand in mine the only thing keeping me upright.

'You're awful at this,' he whispers in my ear.

'Where did you even learn to dance like this?' I demand.

'It helps with footwork, you know. Swing a woman round a dancefloor and you can swing a sword on a battlefield. Here.' His hand presses against the small of my back, drawing me closer to him, and with his breath hot against the side of my cheek I can't help the shiver that runs through me. 'Let me help.'

Suddenly he's the only thing keeping me moving, holding me close and lifting me, one hand on my back and the other clasped firmly in mine. I feel so dizzy as we spin round the room. I'm glad he's holding me or I'd stumble to the floor.

'Keep your eyes on me,' he says and I turn from the blurred room to his eyes, steady, unwavering, a brown so dark it could pass for black. I don't think he's doing it on purpose – playing that game where we try to make the other's desire burn. I don't think he's *trying* to make me come undone. But I don't believe my dizziness is solely from spinning on a dance floor.

He releases me suddenly only to use the momentum to spin round me and catch me again. I twirl and he dips me so low his arm really is the only thing holding me up. I'm out of breath and gazing up at him. When he guides me up I collapse against him with delighted laughter.

'Well, aren't you full of surprises,' I gasp.

Hades raises an eyebrow. 'I aim to please.'

Apparently. The gods break into thunderous applause before joining us on the dance floor. I dance, with much less vigour, with other deities.

Hades returns with my wine glass and other gods pull me into conversations with them that are at turns fascinating and tedious. Nymphs appear with yet more food and, as the evening progresses, Apollo, Hemera and Helios begin to fade until they resemble regular immortals and Selene, Nyx and Artemis begin to glow in their stead. When the star gods too begin to glisten, Ares climbs on to a table and begins bashing his dagger against his glass.

'Come now, it must be time!' he roars.

The assembled deities give resounding cheers of agreement.

'Get them!'

I had been talking to Aether, Pan and Eros but now they all grasp me, laughing at my startled expression.

This is the part of the wedding Mother always skirted past – when the bride and groom are marched to the bed chamber.

Other gods rush to join in. Antheia grabs my left arm while Morpheus takes my right. Across the room I see Hades facing a similar crowd: Pontus pulling his arms behind his back while others grasp his robes to pull him forward, Pheme and Peitho giggling as his sleeve rips in their hands.

I'm not sure how they know where they're going, but they drag us – not that we're resisting – to Hades' bedroom and fling us inside. The door slams shut but it's not thick enough to keep us from hearing the uproarious laughter of the gods on the other side.

And, finally, I turn to face my husband.

Alone.

CHAPTER THIRTY-ONE

HADES' AURA DISAPPEARS THE SECOND the door shuts. He brings his finger to his lips as I open my own to speak. He draws close to me and the moments seem to take forever.

Wine pulses through me and I lean into him.

'They're still outside,' he whispers, breath hot on my skin.

'Why?' I ask.

'Because they have nothing better to do,' he says quietly. 'And to ensure the marriage is consummated.'

I blink at him, wondering if he's about to exclaim that he's joking.

He doesn't.

'Oh,' I say.

Then without warning I moan against his finger on my pressed lips, not taking my eyes off Hades and revelling in the horrified shock that flashes across his face.

The faint sound of snickering gods filters beneath the door and I smile my most innocent of grins.

'What are you doing?' Hades hisses.

'Remember that reputation of yours?'

'I'm familiar with it.'

'It just got *so* much better,' I say before whimpering so loudly I can't even hear the gods respond.

'Where did you even learn this? When I met you, your name meant pure,' Hades whispers, pulling me away from the door and into the room.

'How many times must I tell you that the only company I've had for my entire life are nymphs?' I ask, though, to be fair, I'm a little surprised at myself.

'I'm surrounded by nymphs and I've never found the whole "nymphomania" thing to be true –'

'It's hardly something they'd talk about with you.'

I kick his shin and he grunts.

'What was that for?' he demands.

I shrug. 'I have a reputation to maintain too.'

'No, you don't,' he says.

'Well, I do now.'

'What if I'd said "ow" instead?'

'Then I would have made fun of the almighty king of the Underworld for saying "ow".'

'*Persephone.*'

'I would have made it work. They're gods – they've definitely heard weirder things than "ow" during sex.'

'And now what? We jump up and down on the bed?' he asks.

'Oh, good idea,' I say. 'Although let's give it a bit – we don't want them thinking you skip foreplay.'

Hades mutters something I don't quite catch but I don't think it's complimentary.

I finally look at the room we're standing in, and I'm surprised to find it full of colour and also, shockingly, flowers. My flowers.

Not that them being mine is a surprise. All flowers are mine.

But these are the blossoms I have grown in this realm, dried into frames and blooming in vases.

More scrolls line the walls, which seems excessive for a god with several libraries. The fabrics have been marbled with dyes to form rich patterns that soften the harsh stone walls. There are no canvases but he has painted the furniture, tiny details that I never would have noticed before I met him: swirls and ridges and patterns I've only seen in nature.

It's like this room is the only part of the palace he has decorated to his tastes. No one else must venture here.

He's no virgin, but I do wonder how long it's been.

I pour Hades a drink while erratically moaning and at last he breaks into peals of laughter even as he shakes his head with despair. He finally joins in and we have to bury our faces into each other's shoulders to stop our laughter being heard. Hades jumping up and down on the bed in his formal wedding robes is a moment I hope will never end. I don't think I could be more entertained and then he starts shaking the headboard and I have to clap my hands to my mouth to stifle my laughter.

I manage to ignore the sobering fact that what we're pretending would actually be happening if my father's plans had come to fruition. I always thought sex was funny in an abstract way, terrifying if applied to reality. But this feels nothing more than giggling at the word 'penis' with the nymphs.

I glance at Hades. They think I'm having sex with him. What

do they imagine is happening? Do they think he's running his hands across my body? Or . . .

I can't. I genuinely can't imagine it. It's like a block falls in my mind. I want him – in a way that feels almost tangible, in a way I never imagined I could. All those stories about waiting for marriage and only sleeping with your husband – it never felt a hard thing to do. I don't think I ever really understood desire. Until now.

But it's still too much to imagine more than his lips on mine, his hands on my waist, perhaps elsewhere . . . not clothes coming off, not skin against skin.

Finally we collapse on to his bed, our faces flushed from jumping on his mattress. I lie facing him, breathless, our heads propped on the pillows. Is this how we'd look at each other after?

I can't imagine it, but maybe I'd like to. Maybe I'd like to discover it with him.

I suppose it doesn't matter anyway, not when it will never happen.

We lie quiet until even the most suspicious gods must have returned to the party or else retired to a suite – most likely with others.

'So we're married,' I say after what feels like forever.

'I'd say the wedding went astonishingly well,' Hades says. His ceiling is painted with gentle swirls of colour and we stare at it like they are the stars in the sky. 'A room full of Greek gods and no one killed anyone? No one started an orgy? No one accused anyone of crimes or infidelities? It was almost boring.'

'Ha, I think they knew nothing they did could be as dramatic as the marriage itself.'

'I suppose there's always tomorrow,' Hades says.

Tomorrow is the last day of the wedding. And my coronation.

'No one will upstage me on my special day,' I joke. It seems ridiculous that I will be front and centre in a ceremony, receiving a crown. The only way I can get through it is to pretend I am some cruel villainess and this is all part of my evil plot to steal the throne.

Hades smiles as he turns to me. 'No one could, no matter how hard they try.'

'Careful, husband, that was almost nice,' I say.

'I meant that you are far more dramatic than they could ever hope to be.'

'Precisely.'

'"Dramatic" isn't the compliment you seem to think it is.'

'Then do feel free to shower me with others. It is my wedding night after all.'

Hades' lazy smile fades. 'I'm sorry this is what your wedding has become – a ruse for your safety.'

'You know it's better than anything else I had expected.'

'I do know. But that shouldn't have been what you expected. It should have been a happy celebration. It should have involved love and –'

'Have you spent too much time tonight with Aphrodite, dear?' I ask. I can't bear the way he echoes my thoughts back at me. 'You're sounding awfully sentimental and it's concerning.'

'Indulge me a moment of sentimentality on a night like this,' Hades says. His eyes meet mine and they're warmer and happier than any that have ever looked at me. 'Please.'

'It's your wedding too,' I say quietly. 'Your marriage. You deserve more than a ruse as well.'

'Persephone, I'm happy,' he says. 'Truly. It would be an honour to spend eternity with you. Which is also more than I had ever expected from a marriage.'

I swallow, resisting every urge to close the distance between us.

Is this what eternity will be like? Hopelessly pining for a husband who has made it clear several times over that all he sees between us is friendship?

'You know, you're more than I ever expected and more than I ever hoped,' I say instead. 'Thank you, for all of this. It was the perfect day with the perfect person. The start to a perfect eternity.'

Hades wrinkles his nose. 'Okay, you're mocking me now, right?'

'Yes . . . but I do sort of mean it too.' I grin. 'I'm just not very used to this. I love you, Hades. Not . . . not of the sort that might be expected within a marriage,' I half lie because eros – that lustful love that Mother said should *only* be found in marriage – is all I can think about. 'But I love you nonetheless. And that's not something I've ever found easy.'

Whatever it is he's feeling, he hides it well.

'I love you too,' he says but he's addressing the ceiling. 'Which is not something I've ever – well, you know.'

Of course I don't know. But then, I sort of do. And, oh gods, sometimes I long for the forgetful waters of the Lethe just so I don't have to think at moments like this.

'Are you –'

'You take the bed tonight,' Hades says abruptly and whatever moment might have been forming between us shatters. 'I'll sleep on the floor.'

'Don't be ridiculous,' I say. 'This bed is nearly as big as Sicily.'

Hades laughs, a short, sharp exhale that takes him by surprise. 'I think you might be exaggerating.'

'You're my husband and my friend,' I say. 'You're sleeping in the bed with me.'

'I truly don't mind the floor. It's far nicer than most places I slept during the war,' he says.

'"Better than the war" isn't actually something most girls want to hear on their wedding day, darling,' I say. 'Get in the bed please.'

He pauses a moment before finally nodding. 'Fine, but turn round while I change into my nightclothes.'

'Really?'

'Yes,' he says and I can almost feel the heat rushing to his cheeks from here.

I do as he asks and pick the flowers from my hair while I wait, letting them fall into a neat pile on a nearby table. Finally he calls that he's done.

'I couldn't ask the nymphs to bring you anything,' Hades says. 'It might have suggested that we weren't planning on . . . you know. Most newlyweds don't sleep in clothes on their wedding night. But you can borrow something of mine, if you like?'

I nod and he passes me a soft silk robe. I gesture for him to turn round and, even though I trust him completely not to look, my skin still races with goosebumps as I take my clothes off. I nearly break something trying to unbutton the dress myself but I don't think I could cope if I asked for his help.

Him peeling the buttons open one by one, his fingers brushing my spine . . .

I get the dress off and it feels ruinous, all that carefully crafted tulle and lace falling in a heap on the floor. I pick it up and fold it before I even reach for the robe to cover myself.

'I'm done,' I say and his face is impassive as he turns round from very determinedly staring at the ocean waves painted on his wardrobe. My heart is thumping erratically, like I had hoped he would not be able to keep his eyes from me, just like earlier at the altar.

If his pretence is capable of tricking my feelings, maybe mine can be too. So I do what I do best, what I have done for years around my mother: I plaster a smile I don't mean across my face.

'Well, then,' I say, crawling on to the bed and pulling the blankets up when a shiver crosses my skin. 'Tell me everything.'

'What do you mean?' he asks, standing still by the edge of the bed.

'How were the gods when you were alone with them? Do you think they were convinced?'

'Of course they were convinced,' he says. 'Our deceit works so well precisely because no one is looking for it.'

'Everyone was looking for it,' I say, voice dropping. 'Everyone wanted some clue that I wasn't nearly as happy as I was pretending. Everyone was looking for a tragedy.'

'And did they find one?'

'Of course not.' I'm offended by his lack of belief.

'Zeus was predictably furious, as you heard,' Hades says. 'Ares wasn't happy to have been – what was it he said – "usurped by trickery". That was it, mostly. Dionysus was as delighted as Hermes. It seems neither is particularly fond of their father. Poseidon was so overjoyed it almost overshadowed my own excitement for the wedding.'

'Did it?'

'No,' he says without hesitating. 'But between attendees from my court and his, any disgruntled Olympians were clearly outnumbered. By the end, I'm sure most probably couldn't remember why they were hesitant in the first place.'

'So it went as well as could be hoped for?'

Hades pauses and I wonder if something else happened that he's not telling me. But all he does is look at me. 'It was perfect.'

He takes a pillow from the bed and places it on the floor.

'What are you doing? I told you to get in the bed,' I say.

He smiles but I'm not sure I've seen a sadder expression cross his face.

'I hate to disobey my queen,' he says. 'But I'm afraid I must – just this once.'

He takes the thinnest of blankets from the foot of the bed and lies on the floor.

'Sleep well, wife.'

I'm not sure what just happened or what to say but at last I manage, 'Goodnight, husband.'

The lanterns flicker out and I lie with my eyes open, staring at the darkness while echoes of still-partying gods filter down the hall.

After an hour, Hades' deep breathing fills the room, but I still can't sleep.

This is ridiculous.

And after another sleepless few hours, I haul the rest of the blankets over to the floor and join him. I can't relax, knowing he's down here just so I can have the bed.

And it seems almost the moment I lie on the rug beside him, I fall asleep.

CHAPTER THIRTY-TWO

WAKE IN A TANGLE OF arms and flinch almost out of my skin.

Hades is still sleeping, thank the gods.

I don't know who was holding whom, and my heart races to think that all it would have taken was Hades to wake first and ... then what? He would have known how I feel? Or worse, he would have suspected. And I would have been on eggshells forever more.

I sneak from the room before I can even glance at him as he sleeps. He's all I can smell, all I can feel – the press of his leg against mine, his fingers on my waist ... Looking at him is something I cannot risk doing if I ever want to put these ridiculous feelings to rest.

I return to my room, seeing only one god on my way – Apollo, who quickly clocks Hades' robe and offers me a thumbs up. He is draped in a robe lined with embroidered shells, clearly gained from a member of Poseidon's court.

It takes me hours to get ready. I have no mortal companions this time but I am determined to look stunning on my own. I want to look powerful and frightening and somewhat ethereal. I must dress for the role, after all.

Beauty belongs to yesterday. The coronation today is the time for something harsher, something more threatening.

I shade the hollows of my cheeks, the creases of my eyes. I exaggerate what can be exaggerated. I curl my hair so that it takes up as much space as possible, pinning it out of my face almost severely. It looks good. With a crown, it will look incredible.

I pull gloves on and ask Tempest to help lace the back of my dress. I don't look like the queen of Hell; I look like death itself.

I might not deserve this crown but if it's what I need to stay here then I'll tear it away from whoever holds it. I'll take it like I took charge of this realm, like I took my opportunity to escape that island. This isn't about Hades. This is about me, and this world. I think of the flowers I have planted here and the rivers and the lake, I think of the mortals and the creatures and how much I adore this place. It's not just Hades or Styx or the mortals I have done all this for, that I am staying for, but myself.

When I look in the mirror, there's something almost insubstantial about me, like I have pulled the aura of this world about me like a cape. It reminds me of the sheer black fabric I need to attach to the lace across my shoulders – a veil nothing like the one I wore yesterday.

I think about what Hecate said. About me and this realm. About the power I might hold.

If I had looked like this yesterday I might have been more inclined to believe her.

There's a knock on my door and I call for whoever it is to enter, knowing that no one who isn't supposed to be there would dare.

It's Hades, of course.

His robes are encrusted with jewels, all of them crushed so fine it's like they've been woven into the fabric. Ceremonial, I suppose. But he looks rich, decadent – like an embodiment of all this world has to offer. He's the most beautiful man I've ever seen, and in such formal robes he stands a little taller, the gems sparkling so bright that every eye in the room will be drawn to him.

'You look deadly,' he says.

'Thank you.'

'And we come back to you having an odd sense of what a compliment is.'

'Did you mean it as a compliment?'

'Well, yes, but only because I know you.'

'Then my thank you stands.'

'Are you ready?' he asks.

'One moment,' I say, tucking a sprig of asphodel behind my ear.

Hades grins. 'Well isn't that just waving it in their faces?'

'Of course,' I say. 'But they have no idea that's what I'm doing.'

It is what brought me here. This is me screaming that it was my decision all along.

I think of other decisions I have made as we walk to the megaron – the human afterlife and everything it is shaping up to be. I think of Zeus on his throne and the other gods of Olympus and the wars they start and the people they hurt.

I tell myself that even though it might take generations of humans, one day the gods will be lucky if they are even remembered. And maybe I'll go down with them, but I'll be smiling the whole damn way.

Maybe I do hold power, simply by choosing to act when others don't.

Hades slips in first and I wait for my entrance.

With such thoughts swirling in my head, I don't have to feign regal disdain as I push the doors open and traipse down the aisle.

The Muses and their offspring sing and minor deities play instruments, all of it eerie and echoing in a way that music can only be in the Underworld. It sends shivers down my spine and goosebumps prickling across my skin. Hades manipulates illusions without batting an eyelid: the whispers beneath the songs, the shadows creeping along his skin and sticking to every hollow and crevice of the hall. He even adorns me with them, tendrils beneath my feet as I walk, stretching in the reflections of the golden floor.

Hades waits at the end of the aisle, only it's not an altar he stands by – it's two thrones. A canopy of sheer fabric is draped above, floating on a non-existent, haunting breeze.

I ignore the gods, my sight set dead ahead on the throne that will be mine. When I reach Hades he turns with a pillow, upon which lies the most intricately designed crown I've ever seen – not that I've seen many. Metal twists like ivy, fragile and dangerous at the same time, like thorns on a rose. The gems are deep within, most of them black but dark reds and purples twinkle too.

Hades must have made it, I realize, feeling his signature. Like the cadence of his words or the tap of his footsteps, I recognize it.

The tip of each spike curls like smoke from a flame, his illusions made metal.

I remove my gloves delicately and slowly, tossing them aside without apparent reverence but very deliberate ease. My fingernails are long, blood red and pointed. Dark iron rings twist the length of my fingers.

Traditionally, the king would crown his queen. I snatch the crown myself and raise it to my head. There are gasps from the assembled gods but no one dares utter a word as a careful smile unfurls on my lips.

No one breathes as I clasp the collar of Hades' ceremonial cloth. It must cost more than all the riches of the mortal realm. I pull him close. He wastes no time in clutching my waist to him and our lips meet like a collision.

In all honesty it's messy and clumsy, both of us trying to move the same way at once, our teeth clashing. It's still a performance – but a clunkier one than yesterday's.

But no one can tell and as we pull away the whispers have already started. My focus lingers on my waist, Hades' fingertips iron hot through the fabric – like my body remembers how he held me there last night, like it never wants to forget.

We are young. We are powerful. We are beautiful. And who knows what we could do together.

Zeus may be the god of lightning, but he looks thunderous. And so it begins.

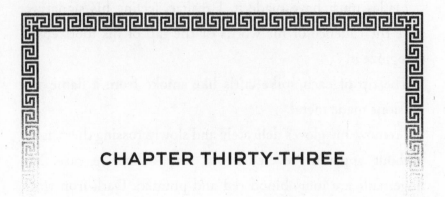

CHAPTER THIRTY-THREE

THE GODS LEAVE RATHER QUICKLY, smiles on their faces and whispers in the air. They're gone hardly an hour before Hermes requests a drink with Hades, who later reports that the rumours are already flying. That Aphrodite had never sensed love like ours, powerful and alluring. That there was something about both of us that seemed more defined. That Hades tricked me into loving him. That I tricked him. That something is different, something is stronger, something –

'Stop,' I interrupt. 'I need to talk to you about something.'

'Divorce on your mind already?' He grins. He's been awfully smiley all day, clearly pleased with himself. Now we're sitting before a fire in the study, a cosy little room with plush chairs and soft candlelight, supposedly toasting our success, and all I can hear is Hecate, like wherever she is she's whispering at me. I dismissed her words yesterday, have barely thought about them since, but now they're drowning out everything.

'I didn't want to ruin the wedding,' I say. 'Or the coronation.'

'But now you've got your crown you're –'

'Hecate isn't your biggest fan.'

He arches an eyebrow in moderate interest but his eyes are sharp and piercing. 'Is that so?'

'She thinks I'm powerful. More powerful than the goddess of flowers has any right to be. And she thinks you know that.'

It's almost imperceptible, the way he tenses, his jaw clenched, his fingers tightening on his glass. But I catch it all like I have been training for nothing else these last few weeks than reading him.

Which of course I have.

'Is she right?' I prompt when he doesn't answer.

He turns his stare from me to the flames and drains what's left in his glass. 'Yes.'

I expected it and it still hurts. That 'yes' cuts right through me.

'Right . . . so you were going to tell me this . . . when?'

'When I knew for sure.'

I'm cold despite the fire. I feel the threads of everything we've built falling away. I search for the moment he saw me, or at least the potential in me, to be as powerful as Hecate suggested. How long from then until he proposed marriage?

'Or when I had more of an idea of what I knew,' he adds.

'So you didn't, for instance, marry me because you were scared I had some power in this realm. And this way you can control it.'

Hades flinches. 'Fates, no. Is that what you've been thinking?'

'Not really,' I say, coldness seeping into my words. 'I have been trying not to think of what she said at all. But now it's all I can think about. She said I could rule this place without you.'

He considers it, that thoughtful crease etching itself into his forehead. 'Well, of course you could rule this place without me. You've got far better ideas than anything I've managed to come up with in the years it's been mine.'

'Don't put yourself down to lift me up, especially not when I'm mad at you,' I scold. 'Besides, I don't think she was talking about my diplomacy skills.'

'Persephone,' he says, adding a weight to the name that makes it hurt every bit as much as *'yes'* did.

You lied to me, Hades. You don't get to say my name like it means something to you.

'You're one of the most powerful goddesses I've ever met. You created a rift in Hell.'

'*I* didn't do that. *We* did.'

'No, you tore through the ground and you used my power and Styx's to do it.'

'You gave your power to me.'

'No, we didn't. I wasn't sure what was happening, but it certainly wasn't an active choice of mine. I haven't spoken to her, but it didn't seem that way to Styx either. And afterwards we were exhausted, ready to collapse. But you just straightened up and swept the souls across the divide. Besides, even if your theory is correct and you managed that incredible feat with nothing more than your power over flowers and their connection to the land, there's still the fact you've been restoring souls and stopping their decay.'

'Any god could do that.'

'I don't think they could,' he says. 'I couldn't.'

'Of course you could if you went near them! I didn't do anything to make their souls start repairing. I just walked through them or stood near them and they started leeching divine energy from me.'

'Which I think is a sign of how incredibly powerful you are. You didn't even need to think for your power to take hold. You shouldn't be able to do any of this.'

I stare at the flames. I'm not sure I can look at him right now.

'So if I had to guess – and before Hecate confirmed it guessing is all I was doing – I'd say something here is claiming you, the same way illusions did me. Like the domains chose the gods before Zeus assigned them.'

It would explain a lot: why I've felt so at home here, why the thought of Hell never scared me the way it seemed to horrify everyone else, why the land has yielded to me so readily.

'You still hold sway over flowers. Zeus gave them to you,' Hades continues. 'But this power is primal, not something you *have* but something you *are*.'

I put my glass down and stand. 'So let me just get this straight for one moment. I have some magical power, which you've known about for weeks, some power that would arguably give me a claim to part of this realm *without* having to marry you to get it, and you said nothing.'

'I didn't know what I knew,' Hades says. 'After the rift, I suspected something was happening, that you had some power unrelated to what Zeus gave you. But I didn't know it was connected to this world. We still don't know that for sure – we only have Hecate's word for it. But . . . yes, I suspected you were more powerful than you believed.'

'So you just married me anyway. And not because this power might make me a threat and if I'm your wife you can control that?'

'Persephone.' He reaches for my hand and I flinch away. Hurt cracks across his face. *Good.* 'Please, I can honestly say that never crossed my mind. I had my suspicions about your power, yes, but we had more important, more urgent things to consider. I married you for you, to help you get away from your parents, to stop the control they have over your life.'

'No,' I say. 'You're too clever not to have considered it.'

'Yes, I would have thought so too. But I really, *truly* didn't.'

I can't believe this. Fates, I am such an idiot. For a moment I really believed we were doing this together, fooling everyone together, but, no, it was just me being fooled. And now I'm stuck. I'm married, somehow, despite fighting against this very thing for so long.

I'm so angry, so furiously angry that if I were my parents the ground would be shaking and lightning would be flying, and I long for some visible manifestation of my rage because my clenched jaw and curled fists don't mean anything. And worse still, however angry I am, a bigger part of me is cracking. I'm one caught breath away from tears and I can't stand it.

'Even if I believed that our marriage had nothing to do with this, you still kept it from me.' I hate the way my voice shakes.

'I . . . I'm not the type to think out loud. You know that. I just wanted to work out what it was before I voiced anything. You were under enough pressure and stress –'

'Well, which is it: you kept it from me because you didn't know what power I held or because I was too fragile to handle another worry?'

He fumbles for words. 'The former, I swear. Sorry, I don't know why I said that. It's not true.'

I shake my head, clutching the back of my chair just to stay standing.

I have power.

And, in marrying me, Hades has taken it for himself.

'I'm sorry,' he says quietly.

'There we go,' I hiss. 'How long did it take to get there?'

'I should have told you the moment I realized, but I just didn't – still don't – know exactly what we're dealing with here.'

I glare at him, waiting for him to go on.

'I'm sorry,' he repeats.

'No "but" this time?'

'Persephone . . .' He has nothing to add this time, it appears.

'I'm going to bed. In my own room.'

'But the court is back. They'll –'

'Well, if they ask, tell them you lied to me and I'm trying to work out how to forgive you.'

He goes to say something but stops himself and simply nods. He does really seem upset to have caused me such distress. But right now I don't care. I rushed into a marriage to protect myself. Now it seems I might have been able to do that without one all along.

The next day there's a note with my breakfast.

I know you need time. And space. I'm doing my best to give it to you but if there's anything you need from me, anything I can do, please let me know. Hades.

I crumple it up and throw it in the fire.

I don't see Hades for days.

Court is open once more and, while I'm dying to take part, I know it's where Hades is. I also know that he hates it. He'd much rather be researching the mortals like I am. Instead he's chairing meetings, sparring with the other gods and mediating disputes.

Meanwhile, I alternate between the library and talking to the mortals. It seems I needed a break to work out exactly what I wanted to do – even if the wedding was far from relaxing – because, coming back to it, everything seems so clear. In just a few days I finish my concept for the afterlife. Not just the big picture but all its little working parts, the things that have occurred to me in the middle of the night, solutions to problems that have tripped me up for weeks.

His research is instrumental. His paintings of paradise are inspirational.

All I want is to share this with him.

And, gods, it's the last thing I want to admit, but I miss him.

I start, several times, to write a letter to my mother, only to end up screwing it up and throwing it into the fireplace. I thought it would be a simple matter, contacting her after the wedding to plead with her to meet me so I can explain.

But what do I say?

Mother, I wanted this. I know I put you through so much and I'm sorry. But I love you and I miss you and I think there's a way we can all be happy.

Please meet Hades. I think you'll like him. I'm not actually talking to him at the moment but I'm sure it will be fine. You see, our marriage is a ruse. Only maybe it's not. Because it turns out I have power – massive, seemingly life-changing power – and there's a slight chance Hades married me for it.

I don't think he did. But he might have.

And the only reason I don't think he did is because it would go against everything I know about him. But maybe I'm wrong. Maybe you were right – maybe I really don't know much of this world and I should have listened to you rather than be manipulated like this and I –

The worst part is, if he did marry me for power, then he used my greatest fear to trap me.

Sorry, I know a marriage for my power isn't really all that different from a marriage for my skills in weaving or sewing – but I tried telling you so many times that I couldn't do that. I never wanted to run away but I felt like the other option – marriage – was no option at all.

I wish you'd fought Father. I know that's not fair – how could you fight the king of the gods? But I think I'm angry with you that you didn't. I found another option – why couldn't you? I would have stayed with you on that island forever, even though all I wanted was to see the world. I could have suffered giving that dream up, but I couldn't suffer marriage to an Olympian. I never wanted to hurt you, though, and I'm so sorry. Please forgive me. I hope you can find a way to love who I've become. My friends here make me feel like that's possible: Styx and these mortals you'd love and Hades –

Maybe I just want to believe him because I like him. I really do, Mother, and I'm worried about it. I love him – and I don't know in what way. Eros? Well, Mother, I'm not talking to you about that one. Philia? Love on the level of the soul? How would I even know what that feels like? Ludus? Yes, I think so – playful love is all we have. Unless he lied to me.

And what does it matter how I love him, when he's made it very clear he only loves me as a friend? A friend he lied to . . .

Yeah, I'm not telling my mother anything until I work this out.

Styx is no help. Though I'm not sure why I thought she would be when her usual advice about anything relating to Hades is that we just hurry up and kiss already.

I finally venture to where the other gods live, a sprawling collection of homes made of deep red stone and black slate roofs. The river of fire crackles round the town's edges and my flowers gather in ragged patches. In a field on the other side of the river, Cerberus charges past, chasing one of the flapping Erinyes. The whole thing is cosy and warm and fun – drinking halls and parks, long sloping gardens attached to each home, though what they were before I brought flowers I have no idea. One garden appears to have a pool of lava, as though the Phlegethon were not right there, offering its flames.

Styx walks alongside me, pointing out who lives where until I blurt out that Hades and I aren't talking.

'Already? Shouldn't you be in your honeymoon phase?'

I explain why and her brow furrows.

'That dick . . .' She folds her arms and glares in the direction of the palace, playing up her displeasure a bit too much.

'But?'

'But?'

'There's a but, I assume.'

'Well.' She pauses. 'Okay, he should have told you. But I thought you knew.'

'And how would I know?'

'You *were* there when you caused all those things, right? And you knew you were supposed to be a goddess of flowers and natural beauty. What do you think repairing souls has to do with flowers?'

'I assumed all gods could do that!'

'Well, that's not Hades' fault,' Styx says. 'And I also suspected something so you might as well be angry with me too.'

I glare at her.

'Okay, don't actually be angry with me though. I'm too cute to be upset with.' Cute is not the word I would use for a woman who looks one genetic line away from a banshee. 'I'm just saying . . . I kind of see his point.'

'Well, I didn't marry you.'

'More's the pity. I'm just saying he –'

'I can't believe you're taking his side on this.'

'What? I love you, darling, but I love him too.' She smiles serenely. 'I am the calm centre, refusing to take sides.'

'You're literally a raging torrent of pure hatred. Pick a side,' I grumble.

She grimaces. 'I know it can't be fun being accosted like that at your own wedding. And, even if you did suspect something, Hades clearly thought he knew something you didn't, which, as I say, dick move. But I don't think he thought marrying you would be a way to control your power. Firstly, that would be a stupid thing to do when he doesn't even know what that power is. Secondly, he has enough power of his own – what does he need yours for? And, finally, I think you know he didn't do that, because you know he would never do something like that.'

I shrug. 'I can't exactly be unbiased though. I care about him.'

'Well, there's your answer. Get over it.'

'Caring about him doesn't give him a free pass for shitty behaviour.'

'No, but it doesn't sound like he's asking for a free pass – he's asking for forgiveness. He apologized, you miss him, go kiss and make up.'

Ah, there we go.

'I'm going to kill you.'

'Can't wait to die and go to Hell!' She flings her arms round me, clinging even harder when I try to push her off.

I understand what she's saying, I do. But every time I think that he may have had an ulterior motive for marrying me, no matter how unlikely that is, no matter that ninety per cent of me believes he didn't, my heart pounds and my throat seizes up and I'm so dizzy I could faint.

And I don't know how we move past this.

CHAPTER THIRTY-FOUR

THROW MYSELF INTO CREATING the afterlife, refining my plan, talking to the mortals, discussing it with the gods who will be involved and doing whatever I can to make it possible. Except, of course, working out *how* to make it possible. There's nothing in the books, no knowledge collected by other deities, no bright spark of an idea that comes to me when I least expect it.

I don't want to admit that I know exactly who to go to for answers, but I'm too scared to actually talk to her. Even the thought of Hecate makes me nervous. There's something about her that reminds me of Mother, though they couldn't be more different. Whatever anxieties I have about Mother, a shadow of them lies within Hecate too.

I so desperately want to talk to Hades about it. I need more time but I miss him too much to take it. Just when I feel like I might crack — when I come closest to saying that I forgive him when I know I don't — I request a meeting with Hecate.

'You believe me now, then?' she says, still in wizened-crone form. We're in a reception room overlooking the courtyard in the centre of the palace, where Hades and I were married. There's a bowl of apples on the side table, fruit from the trees I planted finally grown, and she gravitates towards it. She picks one up, examines it and tosses it back before I can warn her not to eat it. It was grown here and she'd be trapped.

'I have questions,' I say.

'I'm sure you do.'

'What are my powers?'

She cackles. 'If you don't even know that then I can't help you with anything.'

'Then how do I find out?'

'You do it.'

I consider. 'I want to create an actual afterlife for the souls here. Do you think I can?'

'If you can't, I'm not sure who can.'

'Why?' I ask. 'Why me, why this power?'

'Why not you? You're nothing special in that regard. Was Apollo special when he touched a lyre and music threaded through his soul? Was Dionysus special when that first cup of wine touched his lips and clung long after the drops were wiped away? Domains choose gods all the time.'

'Well, if my power is nothing special then why are you so obsessed with it?'

Hecate turns, walks the length of the room and stops at the window when something catches her eye. When she speaks her voice sounds distant, like she's only half here.

'They never asked you the important question, girl. You wanted the world – but what would you give for it?' I say nothing and a feral smile flashes on her face. 'Precisely. Why would you sacrifice something for power when you could just take it?'

'That's not what's happening here.'

'Isn't it?' Her grin is a snarl of teeth. She stalks towards me until she's so close I long to step back – though I refuse to move.

'This power claimed *me*. Not the other way round. You just said so yourself.'

'After you leapt to it. If you hadn't stepped foot in the Underworld, as they never intended you to, it wouldn't have found you. That's what makes you special. This power chose you and you chose it. You ran to each other. And frankly, my dear, I'm fascinated.' She reaches out her wrinkled hand to stroke my cheek. 'Why do you deny the truth?'

I let out a shaky breath. 'Maybe this would be easier if I knew exactly what power I hold.'

'Well, what are you talking to me for, girl? Go and find out.'

'Will you help me?'

'You don't need help.'

'But I'd like it.'

She examines me closely and then laughs once more. 'You have other gods to ask for help, no? Or is he only a screen to mask your power?'

'Hades is more than that.'

'But he is a screen, you acknowledge.'

'I never knew I had power to hide.'

'And now?'

'Perhaps one day I'll never hide again,' I say. 'But if what you're saying is true then . . .'

I imagine it. What if I not only manage to create the afterlife

I envision but actually take credit for it? Father would know I have power, but what could he do when I have the crown of Hell on my head? Unless I threaten his power directly – and I plan on doing that so subtly he won't even realize it's me – I'll be safe.

'No. I don't need to hide behind Hades any more.'

'So you admit you don't need him.'

'I want him,' I snap. Maybe I've already forgiven him more than I thought if Hecate speaking ill of him bothers me this much. 'And if I really do have this power then I'm not giving up what I want ever again. If he matters as little as you claim then why do you keep mentioning him? This has nothing to do with him. Can you please tell me what it is I'm supposedly able to do?'

She glares at me suspiciously, like this is a trick. 'Very well. I grow weary of these circular conversations. If we can move past them then you and I could achieve great things. Three moons in the sky and the whole world under our control.'

'What?'

She gives a disappointed, reluctant sigh. 'You are a child learning to walk, my dear. Let's not race you to Olympus before your time.'

'Come,' I say before she can spin another riddle. 'I'll take you to the mortals.'

I bring Hecate to the same ledge that I stood on with Styx and Hades. No other flowers have joined with the asphodel. It has claimed the field as its own and left no space for other roots to grow. The land is a sea of ivory petals. Some of the souls are whole now, a little more solid – grey mist against the white flowers and the black sky. Hades is intent on filling the afterlife with colour – every painting he's drawn of paradise practically bursts with it – and looking out now I miss him more strongly still. This will be ours. I want to create it together.

The healed souls sit talking in groups. I can't keep them like this much longer – they'll get bored and restless. But if my plan works I won't have to worry about that. On the other side of the Styx is a second field, and all the souls there are hazy and insubstantial. I'm not healing more until something can be done about them.

In the very distance I can see Charon and a boat full of new souls on the Acheron. I swear more come through every day.

'This is a petty use of your power,' Hecate says, 'sorting through a handful of souls.'

She's right. Hazy, fading souls outnumber the repaired ones even on the side of the Styx I'm prioritizing. I could spend all day healing and I still wouldn't get through them as quickly as more arrive.

'I don't want it to be a mere handful. I want it to be all of them.'

'Then will it so.'

'It's not that simple.'

'Is it not?' She turns on me, a challenging gleam to her eye.

'I tried – when I split this place. And it didn't work.'

'Did you believe you could do it?'

I roll my eyes. 'Believe in yourself? Really? That's your grand advice?'

'Heal them if you want to. Or don't. I don't care.'

If trying and failing is what will convince her I can't do this, then very well. I think about how I have repaired the souls before. I suppose I haven't really acknowledged it as an active thing – the souls heal around me, so I focus on that and force the process to quicken. It doesn't seem like much, but if Hades and Hecate are correct it's an enormous thing that I've been doing.

I have been turning them one at a time. Could I truly turn thousands at once?

I close my eyes and, because he's on my mind, I think of Hades. He said I'd swept the souls across the divide like it was nothing. And I did, didn't I? It was instinctive. I reached out . . . and then there they were.

All right then.

I do not *search* for connection to the realm, like a hesitant girl desperate to make this work, listening for distant footsteps. I summon it to me, call it here, demand its attention like I know it will give it, like we are one, this power and me.

You ran to each other.

It snaps like a band, pulsing beneath my touch. I feel charged, crackling with energy, and I wonder if I'll be able to contain power so momentous or if it will spark from me, hotter and more fervent than even my father's lightning.

The souls flicker in front of me like candles in the dark. I hear whispers of memories and feel their emotions reaching out, desperate for connection. I gather the energy swirling within me and pull at its core like wool, separating the strands. Just as I'm on the verge of wrapping the souls in its cocoon, I feel something else pulsing at the edge of my vision: a small golden beam, closer than the humans, and familiar.

Hecate.

I sense her in the way I sensed Hades and Styx. I thought I was feeling them connect to the world but I wasn't. It is a magnification of what I feel with the humans because as gods they *are* a magnification of the humans – their souls, their auras, their very lives.

Goddess of life.

As the thought flickers it cements itself, solidifies, declares itself true.

I take those human souls, and I twist the energy thrumming through me and surge it towards them, make them burn brighter, make them burn like they are almost alive. And they are whole again.

My eyes snap open.

'I don't see the need for the dramatics,' Hecate says like something incredible did not just occur. 'But if closing your eyes helps then very well.'

My heart is pounding but I feel . . . like a flower, roots dug deep, petals open to the sky. I feel centred, certain in who I am for the first time in my life.

'I'm the goddess of life.'

'Yes.'

'And I'm the queen of Hell.'

'Yes.'

I nod, slowly, because I can't find anything else to say and breathing is difficult enough right now. I did this. I turned them all. And it was so easy. All this time searching for ways to make it possible, late nights with Hades poring over texts by candlelight, and I could simply do it all along.

'I want to create an afterlife,' I say. 'I have plans, blueprints and all the rest of it.'

'Do it. Then dream bigger.'

I am tired of her lectures. I am tired of being told I could be more – I just restored thousands of souls. I am clearly enough. 'What is it you want?'

She takes a breath. 'I want power.'

'That's it? You don't need me for that.'

'Yes, I do. And I need your mother too.'

'What?'

'There's something about three goddesses together. Some ancient power. Three Fates. Three Graces. Three Graeae. We're more powerful together, and they can't stand it. That's why they try to tear us apart. You are powerful but you are weak – distracted by things like mortals and friendships and that boy of yours. There's a place called Eleusis that calls to me. It will take centuries, aeons maybe, but we could create something beautiful. Remove ourselves, grow greater than the Olympians, become something other.'

'No,' I say instantly. 'They aren't distractions, they're *it*.'

She bares her teeth then shuts her eyes, shaking her head. 'Small steps. We have all the time in the world. But when you are ready to seek all that you could be, to discover who you are without all this, find me.'

She disappears and I stare at the mortals. She's wrong. This is important. It's essential.

Why wouldn't you try to minimize the pain in this world?

Mother told me to focus on the small things, the things I might stand a chance at controlling. Hecate wants me to focus on things so large they eclipse me.

But it's all important. It all matters.

The power humming through me, the certainty in who I am for the first time in my life – I've never felt so sure of anything. I'm right in this.

I can do what I set out to do. I could do it right now.

I turn instead and run back to the palace.

Hades is in one of his libraries, glaring at a document.

'Oh, hi.' He stumbles up from his seat when he sees me. He looks tired, with lines under his eyes, and he pushes his shoulders back like it's the first time he's straightened his spine in days. He blinks at me nervously while fumbling the quill in his fingers and staining his hands with ink.

'Hi.' I shut the door behind me.

'Is everything okay? Are you all right?'

My heart squeezes. Urgh, these stupid feelings shouldn't make me yearn for him through my anger. I was right to be annoyed. I should be annoyed still. The nymphs used to joke about how long I could hold a grudge for.

And yet . . .

'I'm the goddess of life,' I say. Without the thrum of power still echoing inside me it's a little harder to assert with any kind of authority.

His eyes widen and he just stares at me. 'I beg your pardon.'

'Sit down,' I say. 'Tempest!'

Hades eyes me warily but sits down again and Tempest appears before us.

She crosses her arms, her weight on one hip, and glares at me. She's so hazy, more solid than the humans but also even greyer.

'You rang, my lady,' she mocks.

'I think I can send you back to the mortal world,' I say before I can get too lost in whether it's something I really can do. I need to feel that rush again and I need Hades to witness it.

He's seen me in ways no one else has, deeper even than Styx or the nymphs or my mortal friends. If he sees me like this too, maybe it will truly feel like reality.

'What?' she breathes, eyes snapping to Hades. 'Is this true?'

Hades shakes his head like he doesn't know how to answer. 'I'm not sure but apparently so.'

I shrug. 'No guarantees, but it's worth a shot.'

She nods eagerly. She already seems more alive than before.

I offer my hand and she takes it. All I feel is a sudden drop in temperature, maybe the distant echo of wind, like a seashell to my ear.

I focus. This should be easy, given all I have done. Hades says it takes years but I don't think that's true – it just takes *him* years.

I don't close my eyes this time but stare deep into Tempest's until something tugs at my core. I pull that thread until it becomes taut. *Life*, I think. That one word is so glorious, so impossibly incomparable.

Tempest gasps as colour rushes into her. 'You did –'

And then she's gone.

I stare at the empty space where she once stood.

'By the Styx, I didn't even think.' I bring a shaky hand to my mouth. 'I should have said goodbye, should have forced a hug on her, I just . . . Fates, it worked.'

Hades nods slowly. 'Um, yes. It appears to have worked.' He's staring, unblinking, at the space where Tempest was standing and the words seem to have tumbled from his lips without thought.

'Hey.' I wave my hands to get his attention. 'Are you okay?'

He startles. 'It would have taken me years to channel that power.'

'You aren't the goddess of life.'

He stands, walks round to the front of his desk uncertainly and leans against it. 'And this . . . you say this is something you can do more of?'

'I made all the human souls whole,' I tell him.

'*All* of them?'

I'd love to tease it out but I'm too excited to linger on dramatics. 'Yes. And I think I can create the afterlife. It's easy, Hades. I've connected to it or embraced it and Hecate thinks I can do enormous things.'

'Hold on,' he says. 'Let me wrap my head round this.' I give him a moment to lose himself in his thoughts and, when he looks up, it's as though he's seeing me for the first time. 'I knew you were powerful. This is something else.'

'I know.'

'And you can create the afterlife? You know how to do it?'

'Yes,' I say, a little quieter, a little less confident. 'I just didn't want to do it without you.'

'Oh,' he breathes.

I thought this would be easier. I'd felt so settled, so sure of what I wanted, but in front of Hades I realize I still feel lost. But I want him in my life again. I know that.

'Don't keep things from me,' I say. 'Ever again. Especially things about me.'

'I won't,' he says. 'Do you need me to swear it?'

'You don't need to swear everything, Hades. I'd like to be able to trust you without binding you to your word.' I sigh. 'You have to understand how difficult it was for me to agree to marriage – the things I needed to get over to ask you to marry me. If you had an ulterior motive then I wasn't taking back control at all – marriage was exactly the trap I'd always feared. I was right to be angry but I think that's why it hit me as hard as it did.'

'I'm so sorry, Persephone. I never wanted to make you feel that way but I can certainly see how I did. I apologize. I should have told you my suspicions right away.'

'Thank you.' I nod. 'And thank you for giving me the time to move past it. I suppose it doesn't change anything. Even if I'd known I was capable of this, I still would have married you. No power would have allowed me to stay if Zeus had decided I needed to leave. He ripped the domains from the Titans and handed them to the gods. He might not have been able to take my power, but he still could have torn me from Hell and married me off elsewhere if he'd wanted to.'

And he could have hurt Hades. Which I would have done anything to prevent. Goddess of life or not, I might have gone with Zeus gladly if he promised to leave Hades alone – marriage is an easy thing compared to that.

'Honestly,' I say, sighing, 'marriage is probably the perfect answer.'

His eyebrows shoot up. 'It is?'

'Yes,' I say, struggling around words that feel heavy, laden with the confessions I wish I could put into them, all the care and love – whatever kind of love it is. 'If I knew I had this power that connected me to this realm? I . . . I don't want *your* power, Hades. I don't want *your* crown or *your* throne. I want to find my own that lets me sit by your side. I want to rule this realm *with* you. Frankly, I think we're better together. We balance each other out. So, yes, marriage seems to be the answer whichever way you look at it.'

'Well, I'm glad to hear I haven't trapped you in a marriage you don't want,' he says. From the look on his face, that's what he's been worrying about for days. 'I didn't want to be the reason you were unhappy.'

'You're not. I . . . Listen, this marriage might be a ruse, but it's an enjoyable one.'

He smiles, not his regular mocking smile but something slighter, more intimate, like there's a joke only he gets.

'No more stupid arguments, okay?' I say.

'Stupid argument? So you acknowledge it?' The mocking grin is back.

'Shut up.'

'Witty retort. You should challenge Thalia to be the Muse of comedy.'

'One more word and I'll be challenging Melpomene for Muse of tragedy.'

'Oh, wife, how I've missed you.'

A blush starts creeping up my skin. Oh Fates, not this again.

'Don't lie to me again and you won't have to miss me.'

'I wouldn't dream of it.' He raises his hands in fake surrender.

'Good. Come with me. We have work to do.'

Back on the ledge overlooking the humans, I tell Hades my plans. We scan the plains and I'm unable to really believe what I'm seeing. So many souls and none of them ambling around as their memories decay.

'So I'm thinking we divide the afterlife into three separate parts,' I say. 'We have one part that's paradise. I'll create all the things you've painted and make them real, and we can keep building as we think of more things, an ever-expanding world of promise and hope. One that might entice a human to make moral choices, unlike what the gods of Olympus encourage. The paradise can have different parts for different people, so those who long for mountain ranges can have those and people who want to play petteia all day can do that.'

'What if they want to play petteia up a mountain?'

I pinch the bridge of my nose. 'Maybe I haven't forgiven you for lying to me. There were actually quite nice parts about you not talking to me.'

'I'm terribly sorry. Continue.'

I can see from his smirk that he's not sorry at all. And I'm even more annoyed to find I've somehow moved closer to him during our discussion. Our sleeves are brushing. Now that I'm aware of it, it's the only thing I can think about.

'And then . . . you know, um . . . most humans aren't really all good or all bad, so we can create a place that isn't terrible but isn't exactly exciting either. It's like . . . I don't know, just being fine for all eternity. Like this, actually. I'm thinking it could just be this field of asphodel – peaceful but not really much of anything. And then there's a place for the worst humans.'

He hasn't moved away from me. Is he aware of how close we're standing?

'After speaking to some of the humans,' I continue, 'I have decided you're right.'

'As I am about so many things, yes.'

'My experiences are limited and I don't know enough to judge them. Human life is hard and mine is easy.'

'I don't think I ever went that far.'

I ignore him and carry on. 'I've decided to create a council of humans so they can judge each other. All hand-selected, plenty of them, and they all want to do it. They'll decide who goes where.'

'It's a good idea.' He nods. 'Not perfect, though – it could easily be corrupted.'

I nod. 'Yeah, we'll have to regulate it – maybe talk to some of the gods and goddesses of justice and things like that.'

I don't suggest my mother. Her primary domain might be agriculture but she's also goddess of sacred law. She oversees the very cycles of the world. Maybe once everything's settled she can visit and I can hear her thoughts. I could bring some small part of her here with me forever.

'Great.' He nods again. 'And the punishments? Will they decide those too?'

'I think so, though I have a few ideas myself. I, uh, spoke to Tartarus and he's fine with us putting the worst humans into the pit he guards. Not as deep as the Titans, obviously, but on a tier above.'

He flinches – though I'm not sure if it's a response to my plan for the humans or the mention of the Titans. 'That seems cruel.'

'These humans have done things every bit as bad as the Titans ever did,' I say and rush on before we can linger on it. 'And no punishment is forever. It'll be over the moment they truly feel remorse for what they've done. We can re-evaluate if it's not working – but if we want to scare the humans away from mimicking the gods' awful behaviour, then we need something to threaten them with. Paradise and punishment – carrot and stick.'

'Okay, yes, you're right. And you can create this?'

'I think so.'

We've brought Hades' paintings with us and now we lay them out on the ground. Could it be possible? To translate something so beautiful into something real?

'No time like the present,' he says, staring at his pictures.

'I expected something more ceremonial.'

'Oh great goddess Persephone,' he intones, sweeping his arm across his body in a dramatic bow. 'Today heralds a new era for the realm of the dead, one of judgement and reward. It shall have justice for sinners and those sinned against. Let us rejoice as the realm is split and the spirits of the dead are returned to fruition.'

'Very nice,' I say, knowing him well enough by now to cut him off lest he continue forever.

'Why thank you.' He sobers and when he speaks again his words are suddenly heavy, intentional – like he needs me to believe them. 'You can do this.'

It seems extraordinary that, only a few weeks ago, any belief in myself felt like a delusion, fiercely clutched to despite the realities of the world.

But now that belief seems undeniable – and the world will take notice.

This is what I was meant to do. It's who I am.

Of course I can do this.

I look to the paintings and then to the land in front of me. I don't crouch to touch the land this time. I don't need to do much at all to reach out and feel the Underworld's pulse. It is static and it is warmth and it is the thundering heart at the centre of this realm, calling out to me. Energy rushes down my spine and glows in my fingertips. I wouldn't be surprised if my eyes are glowing too – a god's true immortal form, lying beneath the surface and only ever a brush of our power away. Everything else fades: the quiet whisper of doubt at the edge of my mind, the urgent rush of my thoughts, even Hades standing beside me. I can't even feel the clothes on my skin – just this power and just this world.

And I could laugh, even in this state, because my mother springs to mind.

Her delicate fingers plucking at the threads of a loom.

It's the closest thing to what I need to do that I could describe, and I understand now why Athena, goddess of war and knowledge, is also the goddess of weaving.

That's what I do now. My hands reach out for threads only I can see, the golden strands that make up this realm. They flex under my touch as I rearrange them, shifting whole cords of this world.

I raise mountains and carve valleys.

I spin forests and weave oceans.

I build cities of coloured marble in every shade Hades has ever painted.

I think of the people, the lives I have jurisdiction over; this world was always meant for them. I think of them filling these spaces, their joy and their laughter and their love, and the strands burn beneath my fingertips. The world wants it too, I can feel that, but this is so much. Every little thing I create tugs at me, draws me down, begs me to rest.

I feel incredible. I feel exhausted.

I grit my teeth, some instinct telling me that if I don't finish this now while the strands are malleable they will settle into their new shapes. I either do it all at once or I don't do it at all.

I warp grains of sand into being until beaches stretch for miles, complete with lapping waves and seaweed clinging to the banks. I press in the footprints Hades added to his painting and make sure everything moves the way it should, specks of sand shifting under foot, moulding together, ebbing and flowing with the breeze.

I stagger.

I draw birds in the trees, open their mouths and fill them with music, until all I can hear is their singing, a cacophonous shriek of euphoria.

My knees hit the ground beneath me.

I trail clouds in the sky, every shape I've ever watched drift past while dreaming of a better life, every shade between eggshell white and iron grey. I let them waft in a soft whisper across the sky.

I can't breathe.

Snow floats down on the mountaintops, big and fluffy pieces that cling together on the slopes, icy cold and I –

I'm so cold.

A blaze of warmth – pressure, a hand in mine. A beacon – glowing and pulsing, molten gold begging to be poured.

Hades is giving me his strength, allowing me access to the power I accidentally took once before.

I take it and a jolting rush threads through me. I draw myself back up and blaze a round sun into the sky, let its heat revive me and finish crafting this land: seashells, rainbows, dew, coral reefs, butterflies. *Flowers.*

I let go of Hades' hand and thrust the power away before it can overwhelm me. The burn is replaced by a warmth that floods through me – a comfort, a muscle that has enjoyed being stretched. I blink golden light from my eyes and, even though I just created it, I gasp when I see paradise before me.

The sky is blue – the kind of blue I only saw in Sicily if I woke at dawn and watched the sunrise fade. An oasis glistens in the distance. Trees are scattered everywhere and flowers spread free in meadows, across buildings and down streets, their scent mixing with the salty sea breeze. Flowers are everywhere. And all I see is colour.

Hades comes to my side, stretching his arms, and I wonder if he feels as exhilarated as I do or if he just feels the tiredness making my bones heavy.

On the other side of the Styx, the field of asphodel remains untouched. There, souls await judgement to determine whether asphodel is all they can hope for or if they have something brighter – or darker – in their futures.

'Fates,' Hades breathes, staring wide-eyed. This is his creation as much as it is mine. These are the things he painted: the city that crawls towards an ocean, waves lapping at the shore, boats floating on the horizon. He created every tip of those mountain ranges. He made that forest with its hidden lakes and meadows, the deer rustling through it. He painted this. And I drew it to life.

The sight of paradise is nothing compared to the sound of joy. The souls are screaming and cheering and running to see their new world. In moments music fills the streets as instruments are taken up. Fires burn and the smell of roasting garlic carries on the air while platters are hauled out, carrying bright drops of fruit and honeyed cakes. The cheers and jubilation reach a crescendo. The souls are singing. And dancing. They're so happy.

I turn to Hades, tiredness vanishing in the heat of my excitement.

'It worked!' I screech, and I reach for him, throw my arms round him.

'It did,' he confirms. He designed this paradise but he's not even looking at it any more. He's staring right at me, tired eyes alight with wonder. He wraps his arms beneath my own, his hands on my waist, and I jump up and down and he spins me and I hold on tight. He smells like pine needles and paint.

'It will need work, some refining as issues come up, but . . . Hades, it worked!'

He puts me down but I don't let go. He tucks my hair behind my ears. I don't think he even notices he does it, but I'm rooted to the spot, heart pounding. Then his hand is on my shoulder, warm and heavy, and I can't stop staring at him, every plane of his face, every eyelash, every tiny movement. I just created something incredible but, right now, this ledge with him feels like the real paradise.

'It did,' he confirms. 'And the whole court shall know about it, will know it was you. No more hiding.'

How does he do that? Always know the things I want without me even having to say.

His hand squeezes my shoulder. 'You once asked for the world, Persephone. Congratulations, you just created one.'

When we're back in the palace I assume we're going to celebrate, just the two of us.

But Hades disappears for a few minutes, leaving me in the courtyard, and when he returns the whole court begins trickling in. Just on the edge of the horizon, you can see the humans – you can see paradise.

'Your queen has an announcement,' he declares.

I'm not even nervous about speaking in front of them all, revealing myself to them. I don't know where to start so I just say it. I look at the crowd of faces – Styx grinning and Charon confused and Hermes intrigued and more gods I'm yet to know casting uncertain glances towards one another – and I say: 'I'm the goddess of life. And I just moulded the afterlife. I created paradise for the mortals.'

A beat of silence is broken by Styx screaming: 'Rivers of Hell, you did it!'

Which is followed by a stampede to porticoes and a dozen different exclamations.

I jolt as Hades comes up behind me and wraps his arms round my waist. He brings his head close to mine and whispers in my ear, 'I imagine the whole court is wondering how I got so lucky.'

I press back into him almost instinctively, his firm body against mine, and I'm arching my head to find him when I suddenly remember our performance – the romance before the court. This is an act. He'd never hold me like this if it weren't for the audience.

In the rush of everything, I was swept away from the pretence.

I don't want to feel the weight of my disappointment. I don't want to reckon with all those feelings right now, not when I should be so excited.

'Oh,' I call in a desperate attempt at distraction. 'Also Hades never kidnapped me. I ran here. There was a power in this land that was calling to me and I'm so pleased to have found it.'

No more hiding.

But I won't destroy the illusion of our love – that would get back to my father. This hint of the truth we might survive. So I clutch my hands over Hades', keeping his hold on me – an attempt to tell him not to give the full game away.

The court fall silent as they reckon with this new information.

'Ah, that makes so much more sense.' Thanatos shakes his head.

'To Queen Persephone!' Styx calls, raising a bottle of wine.

Hades curses beside me. 'I knew I never should have shown her where I kept that stuff,' he mutters, but he's swiftly drowned out by cheers.

It's like watching the humans again – the gods grab instruments, food and drink. Some rush off to see paradise and return so elated that others run to see it too. I spend the whole night dancing, talking to subjects who seem genuinely happy I am here. I feel more at home having removed one facade. My love for this realm has never been more potent.

I pull Hades aside. 'Thank you for giving me a way to stay here.'

He hasn't been able to stop smiling, has been wandering around the party in constant conversation, his smile not wavering once, even as he sways on exhausted feet, his power drained from him. He has shaken off any suggestion he might rest, too busy revelling in the celebration, always beaming with delight. But now his smile falls and he looks at me, serious and sincere. When he speaks, it's with a gravity beyond mere words. 'Thank you for staying.'

My knees feel weak and I want to grab his robes and pull him down to me. I could kiss him – we're in public after all – and he'd kiss me back. But I don't want this to be fake too. So I settle for hugging him. My head pressed against his chest, I could almost convince myself I hear his heart beat faster.

Rumours of my new-found power will undoubtedly spread and I think of my father finding out. A few days ago that would have terrified me. If he thought me a thing to be managed before, me being truly powerful can only make that thought worse. But now that I am queen of an entire realm? There's nothing he can do about it, which is pleasing enough by itself but I have never imagined anything outside Father's remit. He is all-powerful. And yet here I am, perfectly safe in a home I have built for myself with people I am growing to love.

There are gaps in Zeus's power.

And I am one of them.

CHAPTER THIRTY-FIVE

I WAS PREPARED TO FOOL EVERYONE with a wedding, less so with married life.

Now that court is officially open there is nowhere Hades and I can go without having to pretend, except the topmost floors of our home. In court I hold Hades' hand and he kisses my cheek and there are so many careless glances it feels more of an effort not to pretend when we cross the thresholds of our rooms. It's all pretence. It all hurts. But letting go of his hand when we walk upstairs aches more than I thought it could.

It's only been a few weeks and the loneliness of all this distance from him is cutting. I have no idea how I'll survive a lifetime of it.

I can't even take solace with Styx or the mortals, or even finally visit my mother, because the demands of the new afterlife and court are so pressing. There are so many disputes, so many things to arrange, and, while I'm confident things will settle down eventually, right now it's thrown everything into disarray.

'So if I'm ferrying the dead souls, do I take them to Elysium, Asphodel or Tartarus? Elysium *is* what we're calling paradise, right? And, wait, did we settle on just calling it Tartarus or did we go for the Dungeons of the Damned?' Charon asks. 'My vote is still for the latter.'

'Kind of unfair that the mortals get all this paradise. Don't we deserve one too?' This from the Furies, and I promise that as soon as the mortal afterlife is fully functioning, I'll create more beauty in this realm for them to enjoy too.

'More people are dying lately,' Thanatos says. And when I look at him with shock he continues with a shake of his head. 'I don't know why, but there are certainly more than usual. I can manage for now but soon I'm not sure I'll be able to fetch all the souls. Can we get some sort of contingency in place?'

'Which god is having a tantrum this time?' Hermes calls. 'And do we think it's plague or war? Shall we place bets?'

'Bets?' I ask. 'Shouldn't we investigate? If people are dying from unnatural causes we should –'

'Oh, it happens,' Thanatos says dismissively. 'Human lives fall to the whims of the gods and we tidy up the mess – give it a few weeks and it'll blow over. I just might need some help if the numbers keep swelling. I'd put my money on natural disaster – those gods love an earthquake.'

I'm not exactly reassured, but the court know better than me and they're already on to the next point. I'll have to take their word for it.

In court, Hades is incredible. He can settle disputes in seconds, juggle a thousand tasks, soothe anxieties before they're even voiced. But when they leave he groans and buries his head in his hands and asks how much longer we must stay here. He is a brilliant king – though he clearly hates it. I might be tired of the long hours, but I do not despise ruling the way he seems to. When I catch his eye he forces a smile, kisses my hand and performs a love he does not hold. Even that seems to tire him. In the mornings we eat breakfast in comfortable silence as he reads and I plan the day ahead. In the evenings we talk until the last stars appear in a sky we can't see. It's tiring and complicated and stressful, but for the most part I'm happy.

The only problem is that he's clearly not.

It would be one thing if Hades were only sullen during the day, when we're in front of everyone, but it's when we're alone too. For the first few weeks after we reunited it was bliss. We chatted and joked and spent all our time together, we moved back into the same room so the court wouldn't ask questions, and we barely slept because we couldn't stop talking.

But now more time has passed, he drops my hand like it burns him the moment we cross the threshold of our private rooms. He hardly looks at me. When he speaks it's with forced politeness. It took him a week to finally relent and sleep in the same bed as me, and even then he rolled as close to the edge as possible. Now, as I begin the usual chatter that would take us to the early hours, he turns away.

'Not tonight,' he says.

'Is something wrong?' I sound affronted but I don't mean to. I'm concerned more than I'm hurt.

'It's getting to me, that's all,' he says. 'All this pretending . . . I'm not . . . I'm not like you. I don't enjoy lying with my every expression or manipulating people with my every word. It's draining.'

The silence drags between us in the pitch-black room. I can't see him but I know his eyes are open, staring vacantly anywhere but towards me. His breathing draws out the seconds until I finally break.

'You think this is easy for me?' I ask. My voice is steely but somehow catches still. 'Pretending to love you?'

'Isn't it?'

Is it? It's satisfying, yes, to see the gods who don't question us, the goddesses who stare on with jealousy, and to know that it's working. They're convinced. But losing those intimate grins and careless touches the moment a door shuts? To second-guess everything . . . it's hard.

I can't tell him that for the first time in my life I'm being myself. I'm not worrying about fitting the mould of a perfect daughter or a good girl. I rule. I say what I want. I don't apologize for my power. I'm so tantalizingly close to enjoying that freedom, and I would be if I weren't pretending not to desire the person I'm pretending to desire. It's destroying me, one tiny gesture at a time. And I'm ignoring the way it hurts because I have so many other things to do, a whole turbulent realm to run. I don't have time to think about how much these unrequited feelings are harming me. And I thought that couldn't get worse but the fact it's hurting him too is unbearable.

But I can't tell him that.

'I thought not,' he says to my silence.

As I toss and turn that night, I know he's not asleep either. But I can't think of anything to say so I pretend he is. When it comes to Hades, it seems pretending is all I can do.

*

A few days later I wake him earlier than I usually would.

'What are you –'

'Come with me,' I say, tying a ribbon round my green gown, the sheer fabric made opaque with layers that rustle like crunching leaves when I move.

'Do you have any idea –'

'Trust, dear husband,' I insist.

He mutters something but acquiesces.

He dresses and, a few minutes later, we're walking across our world. On the horizon are the human lands and the blue sky above it melts into the black hanging over us like an ink spill. We walk through the garden I planted only a few months ago, trees sprung high and bursting with fruit we can't actually eat if we want the freedom to leave the Underworld as and when we please. The leaves flutter overhead, the soft grass crunches underfoot, and the sweet smell of apples, pomegranates and nectarines follows us long after we have left the garden and begun traipsing through meadows.

'Why are we doing this?' he asks. 'We could shorten the distance with one of Hermes' doors.'

'Just because we can doesn't mean we should,' I say, surprised. How can he not love this? Every step I take seems to pulse through me. 'Have you ever just taken the time to look and enjoy this world?'

Hades glances around and shrugs. 'It's certainly nicer than it was,' he says. 'But it is still just soil and air.'

Is he serious? I can think of few things more wonderful than soil and air.

'I want you to love this realm as much as I do. Where would you rather be? I assume not at court.'

Hades shakes his head. 'There's nowhere I'd rather be – that's the irony.'

'I always wanted to see Cyprus,' I confess.

Hades snorts. 'Aphrodite? How cliché.'

'It's a cliché for a reason,' I say. 'She's the goddess of beauty and Cyprus is her island. It's supposed to be just as stunning as she is. I've always imagined that the life that blooms there must be something ethereal. I feel it sometimes, calling to me – all those flowers. I want to explore further edges too, to visit islands like mine and islands the complete opposite, to see flowers blooming in snow and in desert, to see life on the shores and on the mountains.'

Hades stares into the distance.

'Are you all right?' I ask.

'Your mother keeping you locked on that island was such an act of cruelty.'

I bite my lip. 'Maybe. But . . . Mother is a lot of things, but the dangers she spoke of? They're very real.'

He nods. 'Yes, that's true.'

I need to write to her but, every second I don't, the idea of doing so becomes harder, the consequences greater. I don't know how to say all I need to say. I keep thinking of the many ways she might react – and lingering on rejection.

'Sorry,' Hades says. 'I shouldn't have mentioned your mother.'

'I just . . .' I shake my head. I can't even tell Hades how I feel because I'm not sure I really know. And, if I can't tell him, how am I supposed to tell her? 'I love my mother so much,' I finally manage. 'But sometimes I think I might hate her too. I think I blame her for things that aren't even her fault and I don't know how to reckon with that. You're right – I am angry at the fact she kept me on that island. But what else was she supposed to do? It's so confusing.'

'I can only imagine.'

'Do you think she's a bad mother? Am I a bad person for thinking all this?'

'You're not a bad person, Persephone,' he says without hesitation, but he takes a moment to consider the rest. He stops walking and turns to face me. 'From what you've told me, I think your mother raised a daughter who would survive this world. I think she tried to force you into a box you didn't belong in, and she did it with enough scolding and praise that she convinced you her love was conditional on your behaviour. I think your self-worth is too bound up with your mother's approval. And I think you're allowed to feel however you want about it all.'

He's right. Here I am, having gone against her, and I'm terrified she might never forgive me, might never love me again.

And still I can't think of one concrete thing I wish she'd done instead.

'I think maybe it's impossible to be a good mother in the world my father created,' I say. My voice catches on how devastatingly sad that truth is. Was I destined to feel this pain? Everything my mother did, all the difficult choices she made, she was always going to fail because this is not a world where you can succeed in a thing like having a daughter.

'That's probably true,' Hades says. 'But people can have good intentions and still hurt other people, and you don't need to feel guilty for feeling upset about it.'

'I don't think I am upset. Or I'm not *just* upset – I'm angry too and I can't really work out where the line separating those things is. I just . . . keep thinking of all the things she was trying to keep me safe from. Even you. All those barriers round the island, and I realized she'd never warded against the Underworld. If you were a different kind of person, the kind who would have exploited that, then she would have done everything right and still lost.'

'I know,' he says. 'I think about that a lot. And then, on top of that, you chose to come here anyway. Sometimes I find myself . . . furious knowing you took such a risk, put yourself in such danger. I could have been anyone.'

'It didn't feel as big a risk as my parents' plans. In the only stories I'd ever heard about you, you wouldn't wield a sword, and I kind of . . . well, fixated on the thought that somewhere out there was someone – some boy – who didn't want violence. Then I heard about the army of the undead. I couldn't understand how a man could have that much power and Mother wouldn't have a single story about him abusing it. That's all I knew and it was a risk I was willing to take because I was desperate. Maybe you would hurt me but you'd at least be breaking xenia and there would be consequences – whoever Mother married me off to would've had the right to do all that.'

He is devoid of expression but tension creeps along his shoulder blades.

'Come on,' I say. 'We know the world is terrible. That's why we're making all these changes to the afterlife. I don't want any more girls to be raised on islands and told to dress a certain way, act a certain way and take precautions so that they don't "provoke" men into violence. We're creating our own consequences. We're changing everything.'

'With an iron fist,' he says grimly.

'Gentility will get you nowhere in a world where my father sits on a throne,' I say firmly, as though daring him to disagree. 'Do my methods bother you?'

'I couldn't do it. I'm not . . . ruthless like you are.' I think he's insulting me but when I look at him he almost seems admiring, his eyes sparkling when they turn to me. 'But I don't think it's a bad thing that you are. It's why you're better at ruling this realm than I am.'

I don't know if it's good or bad to be so unrelenting. I could only survive, only avoid sliding into an awful place, with someone as peaceful as Hades by my side.

The only way to fight my father is to lean into the darker side of myself. And maybe I'm not apologetic that side exists.

'I always assumed . . .' Hades starts, before looking around. 'Sorry, what is it we're doing here?'

'We're having breakfast,' I say. 'Here should do as well as any other place.'

I unfold a blanket and begin to unpack the pouch slung across my back.

'Sitting on the ground once more?' he asks. 'Why do you detest furniture so much?'

'Stop whining and sit,' I say, planting myself on the blanket. 'Now what were you saying? You were using your profound, melancholy voice.'

He shakes his head. 'It doesn't matter.'

'It does,' I insist. 'You've been so . . . down lately.'

'I have not.'

'You have – and I know why.'

His head snaps up and his back tenses.

'If you hate court so much, why do you come?'

His shoulders relax slightly but he scowls at me. 'Because I am the king of Hell and I must?'

'You're the king of Hell. Do whatever you want. But . . .'

'But?'

'You keep saying I'm better at ruling this realm than you. It's not true. You're brilliant. But you clearly don't like court very much. So why don't you do the parts of ruling that interest you and leave court to me?' I say, piling pastries on to a plate.

'I can't ask you to do that,' he says. 'It's tedious and –'

'It's wonderful.'

He scoffs. 'Oh, of course.'

'I'm serious.'

He narrows his eyes. 'You *are* serious. How could you possibly find all that interesting?'

'Because it is. Everything to do with running the realm, all the disputes between the gods, all of it. It's fascinating.'

'You're very strange, Persephone.'

'It would seem I'm a politician,' I say. 'And you're an artist. And a scholar. We don't both need to do everything, do we? Why don't we split it up and make our lives easier?'

'What, you mediate the gods and manage the human courts, and I sit with scrolls, ironing out the kinks in your afterlife?'

'If you want to.'

'I do love research.'

'I know.'

'Not that it would be the same without you getting bored after mere moments and trying to distract me with a dozen questions,' he says. He smirks but his eyes glaze, distracted, as though genuinely reminiscing on our time locked in the library together and his smile softens with fondness.

'And court won't be the same without you scowling,' I joke.

'I don't want to leave it all to you,' he says, already lighting up at the idea. 'But I can work on treaties, liaise with Olympus and Oceanus, sort the paperwork . . .'

'You don't have to take all the bad things.'

He blinks. 'I am very much giving *you* all the bad things.'

I laugh. 'Wow, perhaps we did a better job marrying each other than I thought. So, effectively, I'm taking the people and you're taking anything that involves a quill and ink?'

'That certainly works for me.'

'I don't want to be pushing you behind the scenes.'

'Please, it's both our names I'll be signing at the bottom of those documents. And at the end of each week we can still sit in our respective thrones – I doubt anyone will see one of us as more powerful than the other.'

'Okay – if you're happy then I'm happy. We'll let the court know which of us they should go to for each thing tomorrow. But if we do this then you'll have more time to yourself. You can create again.'

'I do . . . miss spending so much time in my studios,' he confesses.

'Then let's make it work,' I say. 'You may as well get something out of this marriage.'

At this he raises an eyebrow.

'What?'

'Nothing,' he says.

I am tempted to throw something at him. 'Stop saying that.'

'I do care about this realm,' he says. 'I really do. I didn't for so long but . . . I couldn't do anything and it wore on me. The reason I dislike the humans . . . the court . . . it's too much. The people and the noise and the things they talk about? It's all I can do to zone out just so I don't make a scene. I'm sorry.'

'Hades, you don't have to apologize,' I say. 'You didn't ask for all this.' *But I did.*

'Persephone,' he says. 'I . . . Gods, I don't even know why I'm telling you this. I've never told anyone.'

'That's because you've never had anyone as wonderful as me in your life,' I joke, his sudden seriousness making me uncomfortable.

He refuses to be baited and continues. 'Kronos killed his father for his cruelty. We imprisoned Kronos for his. I always assumed our children would come along and destroy our generation too. And indeed, here you are, the child of Zeus plotting his eventual downfall, in reputation if not in death.'

'Ahh, yes, well *my generation* is far more interested in . . .' I trail off because he's not laughing, not joking, not cutting me off with the expected *Screw you, we're practically the same age.* 'You're not like Zeus,' I say instead.

'Maybe. But I've done cruel things, Persephone. Undoubtedly cruel things.' Hades swallows. 'The truth is, I can't go near the humans because I'm trying to forget them.'

'I know. The war was hard for –'

'I was captured in the war,' Hades says, not managing to meet my eyes. 'Towards the end. You said you'd heard stories, right? About how I wouldn't pick up a sword and, let me guess, wouldn't hurt the people I sparred with? About how I was a coward who wouldn't devote himself to war?'

Those were the stories I'd heard, yes.

'Everyone who fought in that thing is traumatized. But it's not just that for me. In training I was forced to run laps for drawing in the sand, put on night watch for crying at the thought of killing someone. I . . . I was never cut out for it. I don't think I was the only one – other people were just better at hiding it. They'd scream at me to "be a man", like women hadn't been fighting since the war began, like other men – boys, fuck, we were *kids*, all of us.' He breaks off, whichever point he'd been making lost as he stares into the distance, apparently reckoning with all this even now. It's to the vacant air he speaks when he says: 'We were all kids waking up hyperventilating and screaming for parents we never even knew.'

He turns back to me, finally meeting my eyes with a startling intensity. 'I didn't have the emotional constitution for fighting, and I had the helm of darkness so they used to send me to spy instead. One day I got caught. The Titans knew they'd lost and my capture was their last source of satisfaction – one of Kronos's chosen, even. They made the most of it. I would have done anything for the pain to stop and I did plenty: begged, bargained, any humiliating thing they asked of me. And then it was like a switch flipped. I knew I had to kill to get out or I'd die in there.'

He's crying. Tears are welling, falling, trailing down his face, and he doesn't wipe them away.

'When I reunited with the Olympians they'd heard of the massacre – how I'd found the Titan base and decimated it – and suddenly there were all these rumours about how I really was the king of the Underworld and my touch was death. They didn't even know I'd been captured so they stuck me at the front of the battalion. I couldn't face the thought of sticking my sword in another person – and I mean that literally. I couldn't even pick the damn thing up. The thought made me shake and I couldn't breathe and . . . and so I conjured the illusion of the army of undead. The Titans saw an army twenty times the size of theirs. They ran.

'Everyone said it was over but it wasn't for me. I thought, *Okay, finally I can come down here and just drink and forget.* But I got here and they'd – Fates, the Muses had crafted this palace just like the acropolis of Olympus, and they'd stuck the swords of the fallen all over the palace to honour my legacy. Every time I see it I feel sick. And then there were all the mortal souls . . . I did so many terrible things, but all my nightmares are about me and what I went through. I can stumble through the memories of mortals who slaughtered and killed, but the ones who were hurt send me to my knees. How is that possible? How can I be more haunted by what happened to me than my own horrific actions? I'm exactly as bad as Zeus, Persephone. I'm just as selfish and cruel.'

I'm not sure what to say, not sure I can say anything that will be enough, and before I've even decided to I'm clutching his hands in mine.

I'm not even sure what I think.

If they hurt him and he hurt them back then it's war that's evil, not him. But how slippery is the slope before you reach the sort of disgusting acts the humans are capable of? All justified by war. How many acts are committed by those who think a weapon in their hands is a justification?

'It was war,' I say finally. I know the man in front of me and I have to trust that there are some lines he would never cross. 'A war you were forced to fight in and they were your tormentors. You were created in violence and now look at you – you just want to paint and . . . and you're so kind, Hades. And that's wonderful. So incredibly wonderful and I'm sorry no one ever told you that creating beauty is more noble than any war ever could be. The war has been over for years and look at what the other gods have done in that time – you're *nothing* like them.'

Hades shakes his head, still not relaxing.

'You should destroy us all,' he says.

'And then my children destroy me? No. I'm ending this cycle of violence. And it's a damn good thing you killed the people who hurt you because I would show them no such kindness.'

Despite my reservations, it's true. I'm glad Mother kept me from the war because I'm terrified of what I would have done during it. I want the names of the Titans who held him. I want to find their recycled atoms spread throughout the universe and destroy them.

'I killed my captors,' he agrees. 'Quite painfully too. I thought it might put the whole thing to rest. The ones who surrendered are imprisoned in Tartarus and I'm not sure that's right either.'

'Well, we can discuss that later. Thank you for telling me,' I say. 'It changes nothing. You're still my favourite person.'

Hades stares at me. 'You're the smartest person I know. How could you –'

'Precisely, I'm the smartest person you know. And, if I think you're a good person, perhaps you should trust my judgement.'

He looks so confused it hurts me. I can't find the right words, I can't make the right flower to fix this, and I'm lost. I don't know what to do. His tears are drying on his cheeks. I want to comfort him but I can only think to do that with touch, and I don't think he wants my hugs and affection.

Words then – something I've always thought myself good with and now I can't find any.

'Look, was it moral to kill people? Maybe not. Was it justified? Yeah, I think so. It was self-defence, right? The fact you disagree shows that you're a better person than I am,' I say. 'If nothing else the fact you are wracked by so much guilt shows that you're a good person. And I think it's time you put what happened to rest. Learn from it, repent and move forward. One of my mortal friends, Larissa, has set up these groups for people to support one another – you know, for the ones with awful memories. You could try going along? Or, if that's too much, I'm here whenever you want to talk. Either way, I think talking might be good.'

He hesitates. 'Perhaps you have a point. But . . . logic and emotion are not things that often listen to each other.'

'I know,' I say. 'But every time you need someone to remind you, I'm here.'

He squeezes my hand and manages a small smile. 'I can hardly remember a life without you.'

'Good, because it sounds like it really sucked.'

He laughs and I know it's going to be okay.

As for the swords covering the palace, they're easily handled. Some ivy here, some vines there and they're hidden.

Hades paints a wonderful picture of it.

CHAPTER THIRTY-SIX

Taking time for the picnic costs me. Back at court, Charon, Hermes and Thanatos are arguing about the influx of souls.

'Hermes, can't you at least wait until I take a boat across before bringing more?'

'Sure, let me just leave the souls floating about once Thanatos severs them. I'm sure they won't get lost.'

'And I can't very well hold off on separating souls from decaying bodies, so just fill your boat more, Charon. They're souls – they can't weigh enough to make it sink.'

But I manage to tap back into my power to push the land at the banks of the Acheron further out, creating more space for the souls to wait for passage and halting the argument, if only temporarily.

'Thank you,' Charon says, already ushering more spirits into his boat. 'Don't worry. Whatever is causing this won't last forever – mortal wars and diseases never do.'

Then I'm running on to the next stress. Apparently, now that the mortal souls have agency, not many are choosing to farm like their decaying souls once did. The gods are concerned about growing hungry as the Underworld runs out of food. At least this one's an easy fix with my powers of nature. I don't even need to send nymphs to the surface to get more; I can grow enough myself and, unlike me, the gods of the Underworld have no qualms about eating it.

I run from one dispute to the next but it's satisfying and rewarding and I enjoy every minute of it.

After a few weeks, I admit it: I'm a good queen. A really good queen, actually. It's like every one of my opinions that I've silenced over the years is suddenly important.

It's not just me saying that – or Styx or Hades. According to the nymphs who flit about without shadow or breath collecting the rumours and secrets of the court, the general consensus among the gods of the Underworld is that I'm doing a wonderful job. I can see it too: the list of issues to address grows shorter, there are smiles on everyone's faces, laughter echoes through the halls. Even more persistent problems, like the backlog of trials or the influx of souls, seem manageable.

One morning, Hades reclines in his chair, scroll perched in front of him as I gather my things to head to court.

'Have fun, if such a thing is possible in that place,' he says with a teasing smile. He's been so much happier since we divvied up our tasks.

'About that . . .'

'No.'

'I just need you to cover for a day or two,' I say. 'I need to go check on the humans. The afterlife might need tweaking.'

'I see.'

'Hades.'

He glances up from his scroll with an amused smile that makes my heart stutter. 'Oh, I'll do it. I was just hoping you might offer something in return.'

'Have I not offered you enough?'

'More than enough. That's why I was so hopeful,' he says. 'Last time you took the accursed court off me. What could you possibly offer for me to take it back?'

'My gratitude?'

He grins and Fates, that smile could be the death of me. 'And for that, Persephone, I'd do whatever you ask.'

I roll my eyes. 'Stop posturing and get to court.'

But I'm suppressing a smile too and I wonder how he's always able to draw those from me – no matter how busy or how tired I am, around him there's always happiness to be found.

When I visit Hades in his art room that evening, I find Styx with him. They both stop talking the moment I enter.

She's looking too casual, too careful, and I recognize it as her peculiar form of magic that binds secrets to her and her to them.

'Hey,' she greets me. 'Sorry, I can't stay. I have a date.'

'Pallas or Tartarus?'

'Menoetes,' she says. 'Solely to make them jealous, though.'

'Which one?'

'Whichever one hasn't asked me out after kissing me.'

'You're a mess, Styx.'

'Yes, but it's fine. I'm hot so I can get away with it.' She squeezes past me and out the door like she can't run from the room fast enough.

I turn to Hades. 'Thank you for taking my place in court today. It was so wonderful to visit paradise again. I could have done without the "we haven't seen you in so long" berating from my friends but I did get to start working on a more refined climate cycle.'

'I can attend court permanently if you need more time with them,' he says, putting his paint brushes down.

'No, that's okay, but thank you,' I say. 'Actually, I have something else I've been working on that I want to show you too.'

'Another thing? Where do you get the time?'

'Says the man with a thousand hobbies.'

'Court is considerably more time-consuming than the things I do.'

'But nowhere near as fun.' I grin. 'Besides, this was easy. Inspired by Apollo, believe it or not.'

Hades' grin falls and a hint of concern shines in his eyes. 'Those words should never be so carelessly uttered. Now you must show me.'

'Great, come on.' I rush to him, preparing to forcibly pull him to the door, but then I see his painting. 'By the Styx, Hades. This is incredible.'

'You say that about every painting.'

'Yes.'

He's painted galaxies and stars, constellations that shift on the canvas and nebulae that gleam. I can't believe it's actual paint. And the layers of it – those thick smears of paint add such depth I feel like I could reach right through it.

'Well, as much as I adore your compliments, I'm too worried about whatever Apollo has inspired you to do. Don't keep me in suspense.'

I take him outside. I have been thinking about the way Apollo strummed his lyre and vanished – he tied transport to his domain. Now, with the slightest bending of my will, flowers spring beneath my feet. And with their touch they pull me through their roots and push me out in another patch of flowers, just behind Hades. I tap his shoulder and he shrieks.

We're both laughing too hard to catch our breath. He clutches his chest and tells me not to do that again without warning, which of course just makes me do it several more times when he's not expecting it.

I appear and disappear at will until he predicts where I'll go next. As I appear I see his arm coming towards me, ready to grab my outstretched hand, and I'm not sure what happens next. I overbalance and he catches me, arm round my waist, and in the lurch of me falling he pulls back and pulls me to him. Suddenly I'm flush against him, his hand at my waist, our laughter catching into a breathlessness that leaves us staring, mere inches from each other's faces.

'Thanks,' I say. I think of our dance at our wedding, the way he was the only thing keeping me standing.

He seems lost for words and just stares at me with an odd expression. I feel that rush, the lust that shone when we first appeared to the court, the thing that jolts us apart as soon as we step away from a crowd in case it lingers. Is it possible he feels it too?

In the second before he lets go, I'm certain he's going to kiss me.

So, when his fingers slip, I don't think to catch myself. I stagger back, struggling to keep on my feet.

'Of course,' he says. The look on his face hasn't changed. I'm wrong, I must be wrong, because it looks like longing. 'I merely hope I may be there to catch you whenever you fall.'

He looks like he's about to say something else too. The words are right there, almost tangible . . . and then he shakes his head. 'If you'll excuse me, I need to go talk to Styx.'

Which is a lie because Styx is on a date.

Which means he just wants to get away from me.

At court the following week, I sit perched on the edge of my throne discussing the changes the gods of the Underworld wish to be made to the realm, things that would make it a paradise for them as well as the humans.

The day has been stressful with the usual fires to put out – including an actual fire where the Phlegethon veered too close to a bank of my flowers. I get the feeling this is a form of relaxation for them all, idle fantasies of what they might enjoy.

'I like the look of that mortal ocean,' Acheron says. 'We could make that work with my river if we – My king.'

He scrambles to bow as Hades enters, all dark smoke and sweeping robes, framed by the glow of the hearth. The dozen other gods in the room rush to their feet too, only to nod their heads as he passes.

'Forgive me for interrupting,' he says, his voice buttery smooth in that way it always is when he addresses the court. He's overly formal and I sit up straight, something tingling in my spine. 'But I'm afraid I must steal the queen away.'

I cast a panicked look at him but he offers a slight reassuring smile and then he's before me, standing at the base of the plinth. He looks up at me and takes my hand, brushing his lips against the skin like a promise of more to come.

'My love,' he greets me. 'If I might have a moment of your time.'

'Of course,' I say. I sweep from the hall before he can do anything more than say a couple of lines and kiss my hand. Apparently that's all it takes for my heart to race.

The other gods coo as we leave, Hermes' voice rather distinct in uttering that we might consider getting a room.

'What is it?' I ask the second we're out. It's no more than we've been doing the last few weeks but my pining has reached such atrocious levels that I regularly stay up half the night wondering if his actions might actually mean something, hoping they aren't just for show.

He grins slyly. 'I haven't seen you in a while.'

'I saw you this morning.'

'You know what I mean. We haven't spent any actual time together in a while. I had an excellent day today – found a bolt of fabric in the exact shade of cerulean I've been looking for. I decided if I had to steal my wife from the court in order for us to spend any sort of time together then that's what I'd do.'

'Fates, Hades, you could have simply asked,' I say but I can't shake the grin on my face. 'Okay, I actually had something planned that I've been meaning to make time for too. Come with me.'

I take him to the roof of the palace, which is not easy as there's no flat surface up there, no window that leads out to it, and he simply refuses to climb the swords, hidden as they are beneath the ivy. I make it grow thicker and we climb that instead, and after much grumbling we're up.

'This is eccentric even for you,' he says.

'Thank you.'

'I'll never be able to insult you without you taking it as a compliment, will I?'

'Stop insulting me then,' I say. 'Come on, this will be worth it.'

I moved the painting days ago and planted it on a patch of flowers. With my new transport links, I can pull it straight through to the ivy next to me.

'My painting is not the surprise you seem to think it is.'

'Is this?' I ask. I glance at it quickly but I've memorized the whole thing already and I look up to the sky.

I blast it full of stars.

Hades gasps. His hand is vice-like on my arm as he stares at the sky above us, dancing with designs he created. These are not the constellations my father made in the Earth's sky, each one a tale of his conquests. These belong entirely to us and they sparkle in the pitch-dark sky.

I hear distant cheers, mortals or gods I'm not sure, but it's nice to give something both can enjoy.

But I'm focused on Hades. Up on the roof he's framed by the galaxies and he looks so very good in starlight. His eyes mirror the stars and, Fates, the way he looks in awe at the world and then, slowly, at me.

He opens his mouth as though to say something but he doesn't, and just as I'm about to tease him for finally being speechless he leans forward and kisses me.

My brain short-circuits. I have to reach out and grab him for stability, have to find something to cling to because everything's spinning and his lips on mine are everything I hoped they'd be and this is real, no audience, no crowd, just the two of us beneath the watching stars. My fists curl so tightly in his robes I can feel my nails pressing through. When I kiss him back he gasps and the sound unravels me.

His hands tangle in my hair. He catches my lip between his teeth and I moan, which only makes him pull me closer. My own hands are searching now, finally reaching round his neck, my fingers tickling the short hair there, and it's not just his lips any more but his whole body pressed against mine and how does anyone do this and remember to keep breathing?

It's so easy, the way our lips move. A thousand fake kisses in front of a watching court and not a single one like this – not a kiss that feels like everything, a kiss that feels like I am alight.

A hand moves to my waist and now it's my turn to bite down on his lip, and his fingers curl into my side, holding me close like there is any way for us to be closer.

I break away, move my lips to his neck. I have no idea what I'm doing but something takes over. All I know is I want to kiss him there, to bite at his pulse or run a trail of kisses along his collarbone.

But then.

'Stop,' he suddenly gasps. '*Stop.*'

I pull back immediately, but his hands are still holding me in place like he doesn't want me to move away at all.

I trail my fingers along the tips of his hair, the short, wiry curls tickling, and it's all I can do not to cup the back of his head and draw him back to me. 'What's wrong?'

'We shouldn't do this.'

'Why not? It's fun.' Oh, it's so much more than that.

He laughs but it's short. He's as out of breath as I am.

'I won't pretend I haven't thought about this a dozen times.' He takes my hand and kisses my wrist, which is somehow a thousand times more intimate than the hand itself, but then he drops it and stares at it like he hadn't even thought about doing that. Now he is pulling away from me, like if he can't get distance he doesn't know what will happen. 'I can't do this, Persephone. It's all I want, believe me. But I can't kiss you like that then go back to our chaste, practised kisses for the court.'

Wait, why would we go back to that? I run my fingers through my hair, the tangles he has made of it. Why would we ever stop doing this?

'I can't – I . . . I think we're both aware that there's this . . . desire between us,' he continues and, by the Fates, his pupils are blown wide, even as they glance away from me. 'It's been an issue from the moment we started this public performance. But it's been worse recently. I've been struggling with touching you in public and then forcing myself not to want to touch you in private. I can't kiss you in both – one in faked love and one in mere lust. It's too much.'

Faked love.

My heart skips a beat. Of course, this isn't . . . this isn't a declaration of love but of desire. Eros not philia.

I nod. 'You're right. This is too complicated.'

Because I don't think I can kiss him like that again knowing he does not love me the way that I love him.

Because I do.

Of course I do.

And right now that love is a knife and it's cutting me – I'm shattering from the inside out.

Hades smiles sadly. 'I'm sure we've made a mess of things already.'

'We've handled worse messes.' My throat is tight. I need to go. I can't . . . be around him right now.

'It sounds like there's a party down there. Your stars might be a new annual festival. We could go?'

'Actually that, um, the stars kind of exhausted me. I'm going to go rest but you should go.'

The ivy swallows me before he can reply, before he can see my tears and add embarrassment to this pain.

I knew better than to fall in love with him and I did it anyway.

I have no one but myself to blame.

CHAPTER THIRTY-SEVEN

M Y COURT ARE EXHAUSTED THE next morning, having thrown quite the star-celebration party, which is a shame because I want nothing more than to throw myself into the drama of their squabbles. I certainly don't want to think about last night.

'How is Hades this morning?' Charon grins and I startle.

'What? Fine. Why?' I haven't seen him this morning, though to be fair I have been actively avoiding anywhere he might be.

'Last I saw he was throwing up in the river Styx.'

'Which explains why Styx was screaming at him while half carrying him back to the palace,' Nyx adds.

'I'm sure he wasn't the only member of the court in such a state.'

'Yes, but it's always a rare and delightful sight to see the king like that,' Hypnus says.

'Well, I think we'll call it there for today, given we've all veered off topic anyway,' I declare.

'Probably for the best.' Charon winces. 'When I went to the

shore after yesterday's meeting there were four hundred souls waiting. I couldn't have been gone an hour.'

The other gods begin grumbling with their own complaints.

'And this is normal?' I ask.

'Well,' Thanatos says, casting a look around the room, 'this is consistently higher numbers of fatalities than I've ever seen.'

There are murmured nods of agreement.

'All right, thank you,' I say, dismissing them. We can't keep going on like this. Which means I need to speak to my husband – and, after last night, that's the last thing I want to do.

I find Hades in the library, clutching a cup of nectar and looking dreadful. His eyes are bloodshot, his himation is crooked, and he is hunched over a scroll like he's using his body to shield it from the light.

'Well, I hope it wasn't kissing me that made you throw up last night.'

He laughs but it's strained. 'You heard about that?'

'Oh yes, you've thoroughly entertained every god in the realm.'

He groans.

This is good. This teasing is familiar territory. If we can do this enough, we can move past it, surely?

'I don't normally drink that much, I assure you.'

'I'm aware,' I say. 'Are you . . . okay?'

'Persephone . . .' He doesn't finish that sentence, just begins shaking his head. 'I'm so sorry about last night,' he finally manages.

There's a lump in my throat. 'Don't be. You're a perfectly adequate kisser.'

For a moment he seems offended but then he laughs. 'You don't hate me then, I assume?'

'No, I'm long past that.'

'I didn't take advantage of you?'

'I was kissing you back – you do remember that?'

'I don't remember much of last night but, yes, that I remember.' He rubs his temples. 'I'm glad everything is fine between us.'

'Yeah, all fine.' A little strained, maybe, but I can pretend. It's the one thing I can consistently rely upon. 'But the court isn't. Whatever has the humans dying in droves isn't abating.'

His embarrassment vanishes, replaced by academic curiosity, and I'm reminded of how captivating I used to find that look, fascinated by his fascination, when we first started spending so much time in the library together.

'Oh? Do we have any idea what's causing it?'

'None. What should we do?' I ask, unashamed to admit I'm out of my depth. New-found powers won't give me the knowledge about this realm that Hades has accumulated through time and research.

'Well.' He considers for a moment. 'We need to find out what's happening, and why, if we wish to pressure the other courts into doing something about it. I imagine Hermes is too busy to investigate, with the chaos of the influx of souls.'

I nod.

He takes a breath, then looks at me with an expression that says I'm not going to like what he's about to suggest. 'Then do you recall my story of the war?'

I'm taken aback. 'Yes, of course.'

'The helm of darkness, me being sent into spy . . .'

'No,' I say quickly. 'You can't go to the surface.'

'Why?'

And why can't he? Is it that I don't want him to leave me here alone? Or that, wherever he goes, I want to be by his side – though I can't, for the same reason Hermes can't. Leaving the court now would only make things worse.

But, outside of this realm, something might happen to him.

And perhaps he realizes this is my primary concern, because he offers a reassuring smile.

'Persephone means chaos bringer,' he says. 'Do you know what Hades means?'

'No, I'm not sure that I do.'

'The unseen one,' he says, twisting illusory smoke round his hand until the whole thing vanishes. 'I'll be fine. Don't worry.'

'I'll miss you,' I admit and he stares for a moment, his demeanour shifting. He straightens up like he's resisting whatever it is he's feeling. And then his shoulders fall, like he's giving into it.

'Persephone, I am sure you will be perfectly fine without me.'

CHAPTER THIRTY-EIGHT

'M SO BUSY RUNNING THE court and adding Hades' tasks to my own that I don't have time to linger on his absence. It's just something at the back of my mind, something that aches when I pay attention to it, and, when I don't, feels like a shadow following me around.

A few days later, a nymph appears at my side – Hades convinced me that sending all the storm nymphs back to Earth at once wouldn't be a great thing for the living mortals. But I am determined to source some automatons from Olympus so the nymphs don't have to keep acting as servants.

'Hades is here,' she says.

I nearly bowl her over as I run towards the palace's front doors.

Hades must have only just entered. He looks tired, helm clutched under one arm, robes dusty. I'm so impossibly happy that I practically throw myself at him, slinging my arms round his neck so tightly my feet lift off the ground.

He chuckles, clearly delighted.

'I missed you too,' he says.

'Stop reminding the rest of us how single we are!' Styx yells from a doorway where a group of court members hover, watching us.

'Not for lack of trying, apparently,' Hades says pointedly, which succeeds in something I thought impossible – a purplish blush spreads across Styx's cheeks.

Lower, so the others don't hear, he says, 'We need to talk somewhere private.'

My heart plummets.

We shuffle off to our favoured library, fireplace already roaring.

He sits down heavily.

'Are you okay?' I ask, resisting the urge to sit on the arm of his chair, to massage his weary-looking shoulders. 'You seem exhausted.'

'I am,' he admits. 'I crossed a great deal of Asia Minor. I've never seen anything like this. Wars happen on individual islands. Plagues spread in cities. This is everywhere.' He looks to me, lips pressed firmly in a reluctant scowl. 'Persephone, there's no easy way to say this. In every land, every nation I visited, there's famine. It's your –'

'Mother,' we say together – his a fact, mine a dreaded whisper.

I practically fall into the chair opposite him.

I'm torn – perversely touched that she would go to such lengths, but terrified of what her next move might be and worried about how she must be feeling to do all this. Above all, there is the dawning realization that I must do what I've been putting off for so long: talk to my mother.

I draw my arms tightly across my chest like I might be able to hold myself together.

'Persephone . . .' Hades trails off and I wonder if maybe I'm not the only one struggling with not knowing how to comfort without overstepping.

Faked love . . .

'What do you need?'

'I don't know,' I admit. Part of me is sure I've made it worse in my head by leaving it so long and giving it time to blow up into something it's not. Part of me is convinced it will be worse than I can even imagine.

'I can talk to her for you?'

I shake my head. 'No. I need to get her here and show her how happy I am. I think I need to do that alone. And I miss her.'

'I understand.'

I'll have to bring her to the Underworld, invite her into our home, show her . . . everything. And hope she can forgive me.

'There's another thing,' Hades says to my silence. 'Word of the change in the afterlife has reached the mortals. Already there are inklings that their sense of morality is shifting. A few of them are still calling you Kore. Only it seems to be more out of fear, as though saying your name might summon you or be an ill omen.'

'What?' I ask, unsure how to react to that. I gave them paradise. But they fear the punishment more?

'You're the queen of the Underworld – don't take it too personally. They call me *Pluton* for the same reason. They're superstitious of anyone related to death. But . . . as I say, that's only a few of them. The others aren't calling you Kore. They've added an epithet – you're *Dread* Persephone.'

I laugh before realizing he's not joking. And then I consider it – the fear, the *power*.

'I quite like that.'

He smiles. 'I thought you might.'

My laughter breaks. 'I don't think being Dread Persephone will make confronting my mother any easier.'

'I'm not sure about that,' he says, and he stands, crosses to me and perches himself on the arm of my chair. He places his hand on top of mine and squeezes, and, by the Fates, I'm so very glad I have him, even if it's not in the way I want. 'It won't stop it being difficult – but it should certainly remind you of all you've achieved.'

I lean into his touch. 'I need to confront her alone,' I say. 'But right now . . . I need to *not* feel alone. To feel like if she does . . . if the worst happens and she disowns me then I know I'm not by myself.'

Hades nods. 'I can help – do you want me to get Styx? Your mortal friends? You could invite them over –'

'No,' I say firmly. 'Just you. They don't get it, but you do. I've told you everything. And, well, I care most that you're there for me.'

Hades glances at his hands, his thumb brushing my skin in small, comforting circles.

He swallows.

'Of course, Persephone. I'm there for you whenever you need me. Just say the word.'

CHAPTER THIRTY-NINE

WE SPEND THE NIGHT DRINKING tea by the fire, sharing anecdotes and laughing until I forget my fear. But it doesn't put my mind at rest enough to fully remove the sting of the day.

Now I get dressed, second-guessing every little choice. I didn't put this much thought into my coronation outfit.

I spend two hours pinning every single lock of my hair in place. I look at all the crowns I have been gifted and none of them look right.

I'm terrified. I'm excited. I can't do this.

My fingers fumble on a simple black tiara. Should I choose something else? I want to look like I belong, but also like I'm the daughter she remembers, the one she loves. Or maybe I want to be whoever I am now and hope she loves that too.

I jam the tiara on my head and survey myself in the mirror. Wearing all black seemed a step too far. My gown is a hazy grey instead, like the morning mists that gather on the shores back home.

Gods, I miss Sicily so much.

I suppose if I'm not actively avoiding my mother by clinging on to how busy I am, I can actually go. I can see my friends. Maybe I can even venture off, see some of the rest of the world . . .

I shake the thoughts away. I'll see how this conversation goes first.

When I'm ready, I head to the megaron. I want Mother to see everything I have here and why I might not want to leave.

I sent Hermes with an invitation. I told her, if she wanted to come, to go to the very meadow I vanished from.

I reach through to those flowers now and find them shrivelled and weak. Even my beautiful flowers are not immune to the decay my mother has set across the land. But with my focus on them they revive. Beyond them, another presence hovers, a slow, pulsing life – weary, devastated and just a little bit hopeful.

I pull her through the flowers to the bouquet in the hall. My mother.

I don't realize just how much I've missed her until she's in front of me and something in my chest lurches.

She's not as I remember her – coiffed and polished, ready to bargain with Olympians for my hand. Her dress is torn at the hem. The soles of her shoes are worn thin. Her dark hair escapes her plait like it was tied days ago. Shadowy bags haunt her bloodshot eyes and she glances at me like, for a moment, she's not sure she can dare to hope it's actually me.

I rush from my throne so quickly I stagger over the drop of the plinth and scrape my knee as I'm hurled forward. I don't even stop to stand straight. I run until my mother is in my arms.

She clutches me tight, her bony fingers like needles, her tears wet on my shoulder but maybe they're mine, maybe I'm crying too.

'Kore.' She clasps me, eyes wild and searching. 'My child.'

'I'm all right, I'm all right, I'm all right,' I chant. My efforts to reassure her crumble in the face of the fact words are not possibly enough to fix what I have done to her.

'Come on, quick,' she says, pulling away from my hug only to grip my hand so tightly the bones crush. 'We can get away before he comes back, hide you somewhere. He won't be able to find you – you haven't eaten anything here, have you?'

'Mother, I –' I shake my head, wondering where to even begin. 'It's not what you think. I like the Underworld. I rule this realm and I have power here. I'm not leaving.'

'Power? Kore, it's the gloomy halls of the dead with a sullen brat at its helm.'

'I love Hades, Mother. The realm and the man.'

Is that the first time I've said it out loud? To my mother's crumpling face and the growing rage twitching in her brow?

'Kore, listen to yourself. You love your kidnapper? That's not love, that's you trying to survive. I'm so proud of you for that – for surviving – my darling, but you don't need to do that any more. I'm here now. It will all be fine.'

Tears sting as they gather in my eyes, my mouth dry. I need to do it – need to confess. The moment I've been dreading. But, rivers of Hell, how have I let her believe this for so long? How could I have ever thought my fear was worth her grief?

'He didn't kidnap me,' I say and I'm a coward even now because I can't look at her. 'I begged him for an audience and once I had one I forced him to give me xenia. He didn't want to do it. But then we became friends. And I . . . found power here. A domain chose me and this world bound me to it. Hades offered to marry me so I could stay. I said no –' I risk glancing up and she's pale, expressionless, unreadable even to me – 'because I didn't want to get married, couldn't bear the thought. That's why I ran here. But then I realized what Father would do to Hades if he thought he'd taken me. So I asked him to marry me. Because I care about him and I wanted to protect him. He said yes. And . . . here we are.'

My mother seems unsteady on her feet and for a moment I worry she might faint. She looks thinner than I remember. It's difficult to imagine my mother, frailer than she's ever been, cursing the harvests to fail and the mortals to starve.

'I don't know what to say, Kore,' she says at last. 'Do you have any idea how beside myself I was? Thinking of you, looking for you . . . I scoured the whole planet for you. I didn't even sleep. I travelled by torchlight.'

'I know, I know,' I say. 'I'm so sorry. I just – I couldn't get married.'

'Evidently you could. You did.'

'Mother –'

'Mother what?' she snaps. 'What are you going to say? You're sorry you hurt me but you don't regret it? My pain was worth it? Because I was going to subject you to something so terrible it justified all that?'

I don't answer. My guilt is a hole inside myself so large I could crawl inside it, perhaps even hide within it.

She buries her head in her hands. 'I'm so, *so* pleased you're happy. I'm glad you weren't forced into marriage with a monster.'

Really? That's ironic . . .

'But I can't believe you'd do this to me. I . . . You're many things, Kore, but I didn't think you were this cruel.'

'Well . . . I am,' I say finally, drawing myself back up. 'My name is Persephone now, Mother, and rumour has it they're calling me Dread Persephone on the surface. I think there's a part of me that is cruel. I certainly hope I'm kind more often, but, by the Fates, you don't live in this harsh world without your soft edges being shaved to sharp points. So yes, Mother, I'm sorry I hurt you and yes, Mother, I'm sorry that if I had the choice I'd do it again. I wish I'd told you sooner but I don't regret doing it altogether. I made a difficult choice – and it's childish to pretend there was an option where no one got hurt. I decided that it wouldn't be me.'

Well, it wouldn't be me very much, anyway.

She gives a slow, rueful shake of her head. I have never known her without a tirade of words streaming from her but now it seems she can find nothing to say.

'It was never you I was running from,' I add. 'It was Father and the marriage he was forcing me into.'

'You should have trusted me,' she insists. 'I had so many good matches on the table, Kore.'

'Persephone,' I snap.

'You would be happy up there, with me.'

'I'm happy down here,' I say. 'Please, let me show you this place.'

Mother opens her hands, palms out, acquiescing. 'Why not? Show me what it is you've decided is so much better than what I could possibly arrange for you.'

I take a moment to collect myself. I can do this, show her

everything I am, everything I always was, despite her best efforts.

I guide her through the halls, her eyes big and round as she looks at the paintings hanging from the walls, the sculptures tucked in crevices, the flowers climbing the marble columns, the ivy hanging from the ceiling.

'You didn't do all this,' she says, glancing at one of the woven tapestries.

'The Underworld is an inspiring place,' I say, hoping the sentence is vague enough to imply I might have found hidden talents down here or the gods of the Underworld are a talented bunch – anything to draw her away from suspecting Hades.

I take her to the large front doors and, when they open, even I'm impressed. I've been rushing around so much lately, pulling myself from flower to flower around the Underworld. But the garden I planted has grown rapidly. It's no longer just an orchard – plants crawl everywhere, every patch a vivid splash of colour.

My mother stops walking. Her eyes dart around like she can't take it in quick enough.

'This isn't what I was expecting from the land of the dead,' she says.

'It wasn't like this when I got here.'

'You did this? You've only been here for a few months.'

'I know.' I smile. It's quite nice, actually, showing my mother what I'm capable of. I can still hear her voice in my head: *I love you, my dear, but you are not powerful.* Proving that wrong feels like the final shedding of 'Kore'.

I take her out of the garden towards the mortal lands, trailing through flowers that tickle my bare ankles.

My mother glances down at the touch of them. 'These are new.'

She noticed. She knows my flowers – knows them so well she can recognize a new creation.

Everything will be okay. This is exciting now. I take her hand and pull her to walk quicker. 'Yes. I made them when I got here. Aren't they lovely? I had to figure out how they'd survive. The sky didn't have a sun when I first arrived.'

'Excuse me?'

I point to the horizon, where the blue sky above the human lands spills out, the sun a distant burning speck.

'That's where we're going. I built that.'

'Don't be so silly.'

'I'm not.' I scowl. 'I told you, Mother, I have power. When I got here it felt like the land was begging me to bring it to life. So I did, slowly with flowers and then with restoring the decaying mortal souls and then . . . I built that. I reached right into the threads of this world and I changed the very realm itself. I'm the goddess of life, Mother. I can do incredible things.'

She says nothing.

She stares.

She glances down to the ground then gazes in the distance.

After a while I break. 'Well?'

'What happens,' she asks, 'when you stop loving your husband?'

'What?'

'Don't be naive, Persephone. I thought you'd discarded that name. What's your contingency plan? When you stop loving your husband, or he finds another young girl in need of rescue, what will you do then?'

'He wouldn't –'

'Name a single man who wouldn't.'

I hesitate. Because he is the single man who wouldn't. And perhaps some of the other gods of the Underworld but I don't know that for sure.

'I trust him.'

'Really?' she sneers. 'You truly believe in his love enough to think it will last forever?'

I start to say yes but I catch myself. Because Hades doesn't love me, not in the way she means – not in the way that might endure.

We reach the cliff edge overlooking the humans and their glittering oasis – a whole world I created. It no longer feels like the decisive argument I thought it would be.

Indeed my mother only glances at it long enough for a flicker of shock to cross her face before she turns back to me.

'Very well,' she says. 'Let's talk hypothetically. If he found someone else, what would happen to you?'

'I . . .' I force myself to truly consider it – hypothetically. And I realize I would be fine. I'd move out, maybe, find a new home in the Underworld. Because this land is mine with or without him. I'd be heartbroken but I'd go on. I'd gather my friends. I'd feel loved without him.

If I *needed* him, if the life I loved were truly dependent on him, then I wouldn't be able to love him without hesitation, without thought – with the freedom that I *finally* do.

'I have power and the gods of this world respect me,' I say. 'I'd be devastated but I'd survive.'

'Any match I found for you would have been based on firmer foundations. More security. More stability.'

'I belong here.' I gesture to the world. 'How do you not see that?'

'You belong with me,' she retorts. 'Because I'm going to *actually* love you forever. And you're going to return to the surface with me.'

I laugh at that one. 'No, I'm not.'

'You have to,' she says. 'Or people are going to keep dying.'

I step back, thrown. 'You're going to keep killing mortals unless I come back with you? What is this?'

Mother glances around hurriedly. 'Not here. We'll talk back at the cottage.'

'I'm not going anywhere with you.'

'It doesn't have to be forever,' she says and I scoff because I recognize this. '*Just play us one song*' and all of a sudden I'm in a full recital for the goddesses who will go running back to Olympus with tales of my musical gifts. She loves to lure me in with a compromise she'll twist. 'We'll talk about it on the surface, not on this land. Not where anyone could hear.'

'I trust everyone in this world.'

'A queen should never be such a fool. Let's go back to the surface. It'll be all right, Kore.' She steps forward, and reaches for my cheek. 'Come with me and everything will be fine. Please trust me. Trust my love.'

I step back, pushing her hand off me. 'I do trust your love, Mother. I just wish you'd stop manipulating me with it.'

And, before I can do anything I might regret, I reach for the flowers she stands upon and banish her back to the surface.

Fine. I'll fix this famine another way. Life is my domain – and no one, not even my own mother, gets to bring it to an end like this.

CHAPTER FORTY

START THE LONG WALK BACK to the palace to give myself time to think. But my mind keeps flipping between my mother's cruelty towards the humans and the malice she showed when talking about my love for Hades.

And maybe she's right – maybe it will end. Maybe love really doesn't last forever. But, by the Fates, it has to start to end, right? So what if there's a middle I could love every second of?

Before I can lose my nerve I skip ahead through my flowers and go in search of Hades.

He's weaving when I find him. He's only just started but I see flowers and the edge of a waterfall from Elysium, one he designed and I created.

He's so deep in thought, just like always, that he doesn't hear me open the door. I'm struck by the yearning that's becoming more common every day. I watch his fingers fly over the tapestry and think of the man, with all this softness and gentility, who was forced into a war, forced into a crown, forced to lock himself away so the world wouldn't see his sensitivity and mistake it for weakness.

He leans in closer to strike a single thread from his creation and line up a second to replace it.

'Hades,' I say. He jumps, though for once it is not with the startled expression of someone just short of reaching for a sword.

'Persephone.' He speaks as though the word is an exhale of relief.

I find myself speaking without thinking, though I say precisely what I planned to. 'I love you.' It sounds so simple – too simple, really, for all that we are and all that we have done.

His eyebrows knit together, his dark eyes . . . lost. I imagined many responses to this declaration – one I never thought I would manage to make – but I never thought he would be confused.

'I love you too. You know this.' He watches me almost warily.

'Not just Ludus, Hades.' Playful love. That one is easy to admit. Even at the start, we verged upon it – even when I hated him still. I worry that I will fail, that the declarations I managed so boldly to my mother will dissipate on my tongue because I cannot possibly talk. 'Pragma,' I manage, swallowing round the lump in my throat. If I make it to the end of this sentence I feel like I will fall apart.

'So soon, I ...' He trails off and I know. I know it's ridiculous – pragma is a bond forged by years. But who else could I confide in? Who else has been with me through enough chaos that it should have been spread over decades?

But I'm not finished. 'Eros.' I try for a chuckle. 'Though after the other night you know about that one.' Lust. The urge frustrating me several times a day – to lean towards him, to close any and all distance between us.

'Philia, even.' And there it is: the real confession. Love on the level of the soul. 'Every love someone can have for another being, I have them all for you.'

Hades lingers in stasis for a moment. Before I can prompt him his eyes are steel and there's a rage in him I've never seen before. 'Why are you saying all this?' he hisses. 'What did your mother say to you?'

'This has nothing to do with my mother,' I snap. Gods, hasn't she done enough? Can't this moment exist without her?

'Persephone,' he says gently and I hate it. I want him to grab me and pull my lips to his. Or I want to hear his voice crack as he screams for me to leave this realm and never return. I don't want him to talk to me with pity, to say my name like his heart is breaking.

'I'm not asking for you to feel the same,' I say quickly. 'I just wanted you to know. I feel like I'm lying to you by not saying anything.'

'You can't mean this,' he says, pushing away from where he sits and walking towards me.

'Go ahead and try to tell me what I feel one more time.'

'It's not fair,' he says. 'You know that's how I feel for you and –'

'What?' I ask. The most I dared hope for was that he might return one of these loves. What is he saying?

'You know full well,' he says. 'I've made my affection rather obvious –'

'When?' I demand. I should be overcome with joy. But I won't have this, won't have him claiming he made such feelings clear before I did. Not that it's a competition but . . . no, I won't have it.

'A thousand times over.'

'Name one.'

'Designing your world, creating your entire wardrobe, marrying you,' he lists.

'Because you like me not because you love me!'

'I kissed you four nights ago and told you I couldn't keep up with the pretending and all the emotions involved. What else does that mean if not love?'

'That this situation is confusing you! And that you're a terrible actor. You *literally* told me you were faking your love, that all you felt was lust.'

'You know what, it doesn't matter right now,' he says. 'Tell me what your mother said.'

I shake my head. 'I don't want to talk about her. Now that I know you feel the same way I would quite like to head upstairs to that enormous bed of yours.'

I'm only half joking.

'We are doing no such thing.'

'See! That right there is how you didn't make it obvious at all. I kissed you and you yelled at me –'

'I thought you were doing it because you thought you had to!'

'By the Fates, why would you think that? Have I done a single thing because I had to from the moment I got here?'

'You married me out of necessity! Of course it would follow that you would believe you *owed* me such things . . . and I told you that's why I stopped it the next day. You didn't correct me!'

'Oh, what – because I was supposed to say, "No, you idiot, I really find you very attractive and would like to kiss your stupid face!"'

'Yes, that's exactly what you should have said! Well, not *exactly* but –'

I mutter something Hades doesn't find particularly pleasing and he's coming up with excuses again.

'Not to mention the fact you were drunk at the time,' he protests.

'So were you.'

'Exactly. Hardly rational decision-making on anyone's behalf.'

'You know what, while we're at it, you should probably know I proposed to you because I was scared they'd hurt you if they thought you'd ruined me for marriage.'

'What?'

'I was protecting you.'

'That's terrible logic.'

'It's literally no different from you marrying me to protect me.'

'How have we actually managed to turn this into an argument?' Hades fumes.

And he's right so I do the only thing I can think of and suddenly I'm kissing his stupid face.

Every rational thought in my head is chased clean away. It's just him and me and that simplicity has returned. He's kissing me. His hands are on the small of my back, pulling me closer, and mine are on his neck, his pulse racing beneath my fingers. His lips press against mine with urgency, with hunger, and it's so much more than everything I dreamt it to be. I feel it this time like I didn't before, everything he's saying without using words, all that love.

When we finally gasp apart he stays holding me and I'm still holding him and suddenly we're kissing again until the Heavens must be spinning.

I tug down the sleeve of his chiton and he lets me go,

staggering back and panting like if he doesn't put enough physical distance between us I will be all over him again.

And I might. My need for the sight – the *feel* – of his skin, my desire to press myself against every inch of it, is like a physical thirst.

'Tell me what your mother said.'

I'm so shocked I forget how to use words.

'Is this your idea of foreplay?' I finally manage.

'I care about you too much to . . . to take advantage of your emotional state if she said –'

'Why don't you let me worry about my emotional state?' I ask but . . . it just makes me want to run to him more. I can't believe the thought of being known has always terrified me when this is what it is instead: knowing that if I fall I will be caught.

'*Persephone.*'

'She said she's going to keep killing the humans unless I go back to her,' I say. 'Can we kiss again?'

'Persephone!'

'What do you want me to say, Hades?' I ask. 'She said she is the only one who will always love me and if I want the crops to flourish I'll go back. I would have told her to go to Hell if that weren't the opposite of what I was hoping for.'

'Will you?' he asks. 'Is all this some elaborate way of saying goodbye before you sacrifice yourself to her?'

'You're too smart to ask such questions, Hades,' I say.

Why are his lips still not pressed against mine? I don't want to talk any more. I've already processed these emotions, already locked them away. It's all very healthy.

'Persephone, I *know* you. You care an awful lot for those

humans,' he says. His voice is too stable, too grounded, when I feel like I could hardly string two words together.

'Yes and what we are doing is too important. And . . . I care about myself too. Besides, the gods aren't going to let her get away with it for too long. They all love sticking their tongues down the necks of the humans far too much to let her continue starving them all.'

'So . . . you're fine with this?'

'*Of course* I'm not fine with this. She just did her usual thing of smothering me in love while berating me and twisting me towards what she wants. And I have no idea how to get her to stop hurting the humans. It feels very pointed given I love those mortals. It's like she knows how much it means to me.'

'We'll figure it out,' he says.

I nod. 'Yes, I know we will, which is why I am fine and would very much like to go back to that kissing thing.'

'You're sure you're all right?' he asks.

'Yes!'

And finally, after what seems like an eternity, he kisses me again.

CHAPTER FORTY-ONE

WE KISS UNTIL OUR LIPS are swollen, hands reaching and breath catching, and I don't know how anyone gets anything else done, ever. His lips are buttery soft, sliding over my own, his air in my lungs, the urge to press him closer. I yearned for this so terribly I thought it might tear me apart but I never imagined this grasping need to become one, to have his heart beat inside my chest, my own pulsing beside it.

I peel layers off him and my hands run across his bare chest, trace the sharp bones of his hips. I could tug the fabric there further; I hesitate only out of fear that I'm doing this wrong, that this isn't how it goes. He grabs my hands before I can decide, entwines our fingers, kisses me like it's an art form. He breaks away only to trace his lips over my neck. My body arches like it knows what to do even if I don't.

He runs a finger over the strap of my dress and his warm breath tingles against my skin.

'Can I take this off?' he whispers. My heart is beating so quickly I can't believe he can't hear it, as close as he is.

'I . . . um . . .' Why am I hesitating? I want it off. I want everything off. But . . . but . . .

I feel safe with him.

I have no reason to hesitate.

But it doesn't change the fact that I am. Some instinct is saying *no* while every other part of me is screaming *yes!*

He lets go, smoothes my hair instead and kisses me again.

'I'm sorry,' I say. 'I just need some time.'

'Don't apologize.' He bites his lip like not kissing me is taking all of his concentration.

'It's just . . .'

'No doesn't need an excuse, Persephone.'

'Thanks for waiting.'

And now he lets go, takes a step back. 'I'm not waiting. We're not moving slowly or whatever cliché you want to throw out there. There's no end point here, no expectation. We can do what we both want, if and when we both want it.'

'And if I finally want it and we do it and I hate it then –'

'Then we stop. Then we never do it again.'

'I love you.'

He grins. 'Well, I don't think my statement warrants such a response but I will certainly never grow tired of hearing it.'

'Then can you come back over here and kiss me again, please?'

'I like this,' he says, holding me close the next morning and nestling his head into the groove between my head and shoulder.

His arms are round my waist and my hands rest on top of his. I think I could live a very happy life if we never left this bed.

'I know,' I say. 'You hug me in your sleep.'

'What?'

'Yeah, it's quite funny actually. You make little contented sighing noises.'

'And yet you dare say that *you* made your feelings known before I did.'

'Unconscious revelations don't count. You could have been dreaming about anything.'

'Oh not this again.'

'I mean, the latest rumour in the courts is that Zeus has turned his lover into a cow.'

'Zeus and I have very, very little in common.'

'Thank the Heavens.'

'I hope you had no plans to go to court today.'

'They can survive without me for one day.'

'Doubtful but we'll see.'

'They're all highly competent gods. Now roll over. I want to hold you.'

He sighs but I can hear his smile as he turns. 'If you must.'

I grab on to him, curve my body round him, think that I'll never let him go.

And with the thought I hear my mother's words: '*What happens when you stop loving your husband? You truly believe in his love enough to think it will last forever?*'

I stand by what I said to my mother. I'd survive. But, if falling in love is complicated, how much more complicated would falling out of it be? Would we fight over the realm? Hurt each other at every meeting? My mother thought she loved my father once . . .

'Hades, um . . . what happens if this doesn't work?'

'Well, your emotions sure are fickle.'

'Hades.'

He squeezes my hand. 'Neither of us are horrible people, Persephone. I'm sure we'll find an amicable solution, some peaceful coexistence.'

'Okay.'

'I do truly despise being a young god at times. All this eternity and none of the experience. But, for what it's worth, for all my creativity I can't imagine a future where I'm not in love with you.'

My panic fades. I'm going to love this man forever – how could I not?

'Um.'

'Um? That's what I get for that declaration?'

'Well, I'm torn between "I'm so glad I recklessly jumped into Hell" and "Fates, what's wrong with you? Why are you being so sappy? It's weird".'

'I'm allowed to be sappy sometimes.'

'I know.' I squeeze his hand a little tighter. 'And it's very cute but I'm much more comfortable when we insult each other to show affection.'

'That's because you have no idea what to do with affection.'

'And you do?'

'No, not at all. You laugh it off and I refute it and together we're delightfully, dysfunctionally in love.'

I'm not sure what to say to that one given 'Urgh, I hate us' is what rolls to my tongue and that only feels like it would prove his point. So I just close my eyes and breathe in the coconut scent of his hair and hold him close and hope that if I can't speak my affection I can at least show it.

*

Emerging into court feels like a revelation but of course no one bats an eyelid. They've thought we're in love for months. I suppose technically they were right and we had trapped ourselves in some triple bluff, but I want gasps and cheers and the people around me to be as excited about all this as I am.

Even Styx is a disappointment.

We both wanted to be there when she found out so we invited her over to lunch and now she's jumping around the dining room, chanting, 'I knew it, I knew it, I knew it.'

'Yes, yes, do you want an award?' Hades grumbles into his salad.

'Oh, is that on offer? Because you know I'd never say no.'

'What about your love life? How did your date go?' I ask, hoping to curb some of her smugness.

Her grin falls. 'Oh, it was the worst.'

Hades snorts. 'Of course it was terrible. You dated a cattle rancher. Of all the gods to go for . . .'

'I was desperate.'

'Well, we both knew that,' I joke and Styx glares at Hades when he laughs.

'We can't all find love with the first man we meet.'

'I had to run away from home! I went through enough.'

'Do you want to try that?' Hades perks up.

'It can't hurt,' I add.

'I can ask Hermes to give you a lift.'

'I'll help you pack.'

Styx points to both of us, glaring furiously. 'Is this what this is now? Now that you're all disgustingly in love you're going to gang up on me? That's not fun.'

'It is for us.' Hades grins.

'Persephone, come on, it's so much more fun to mock Hades together. Don't leave me like this.'

'Don't worry, I can do both.'

Hades nods sadly. 'I can unfortunately confirm that is true. The mistress of my heart is cruel.'

I choke on my water. 'Mistress of your heart? Seriously?'

Styx fake gags.

'Yeah, Styx, I'm back on your side. Help me mock him.'

'Oh, you don't need help with that one – "mistress of my heart" is a phrase that mocks itself.'

'There are other things we could do, right? Things that aren't sex?' I ask when we are alone again later. I'm straddling his lap, my lips swollen and hungry for more.

'If you want to, yes,' Hades replies, his thumb brushing the edge of my breast. We're fully clothed but what if we weren't? 'Only if you want to.'

I swallow, fumbling around the confession like admitting it is dirty, sinful – shameful. 'I want to,' I breathe and actually it feels freeing to admit to desire, natural even.

'Then tell me.' He kisses my neck between words. 'I want to hear you scream it.' His teeth graze my skin. 'If you want me to keep going, ask me to.' He trails his lips along my collarbone. 'I want to hear how it feels.' He brings his lips back to mine and whispers against them: 'And, if you want me to keep going, then let the walls shake with how loudly you urge me not to stop.'

I'm shivering, his words humming in my bones. I pull him closer, capture his lips with my own and lose myself in the feel of him.

*

I thought we could contain it, lock this new-found lust and affection up the way we have everything else, keep it behind private doors. But it bleeds out, this need, and even when we're in public it takes every ounce of self-control not to pounce on one another.

Hades comes with me to the next court meeting and we can barely keep our hands off each other. It's all the worse for the memories those touches hold, the shivers of pleasure those roaming hands have caused. Which isn't to say that I'm crawling on to his lap in the middle of a meeting but he can't walk past me without brushing my arm and I can't sit next to him without reaching for his hand, its imprint lingering on my skin. I have a sixth sense for him; I know where he is, listen a little harder when he speaks. It's like a cord is strung between us, slowly winding and drawing us back together.

I'm glad for it because court is difficult. Everyone is stressed and tired and scared.

'It's a famine on the mortal plane,' Hades tells them.

'You went up?' Thanatos asks.

Hades nods.

'That's where you were?' Styx exclaims. 'Fates, Hades – did you even think about what you were risking? What if you had been captured? A king trespassing into another court? If Zeus had found out . . .'

'We share jurisdiction over Earth,' he says, squeezing my hand as though to reassure me of this fact.

'Officially.' Styx glares. 'But you know as well as I do that Zeus wouldn't be happy with it. He's barely happy with Hermes being split between the courts.'

'True.' Hermes nods. 'A famine, you said? Is it a sun god or fertility goddess?'

'It's my mother,' I say grimly.

'Your mother?' Nemesis asks. 'Why?'

'She's not exactly a fan of this.' I nod to my hand holding Hades. 'She wants me to return to her.' I wonder if they'll scream for me to go back. I wouldn't be surprised. But I can't lie to them, and they deserve a say. If they think I should go I'll at least have to consider it.

'Well, that's stupid,' Nemesis says. As goddess of revenge, it seems she's not particularly impressed with Mother's methods.

'Is it? My respect to both of you,' Charon says, inclining his head towards us, 'but I'd be pretty upset if my daughter was kidnapped and married.'

'You know our official line on that – and the truth, in fact – is that I ran to Hell of my own volition.'

'And Demeter does not believe the official line. I don't particularly see why we should either.'

'You doubt your king, Charon?' Hades asks, the smoke he shrouds himself in pulsing. He has an amused grin on his face, as though his power is a hilarious joke. 'You doubt your queen?'

'No, of course not,' he answers too quickly to be believable and even he seems to know it because he throws his hands up. 'Look, is it the type of thing you'd do, my lord? Of course not. But, my queen, why would you run here of all places?'

'Maybe because certain powers drew her to this place?' Styx interjects before I can answer. 'We've all seen what she can do. She belongs here, with or without marrying Hades – um, Lord Hades – and she's a member of our court. And no god of the Underworld will be blackmailed into anything by an Olympian.'

There are roars of agreement from the gathered gods. If they doubted us still, their rivalry with the other courts might be enough to convince them.

'So, I'm sorry,' I say. 'It's going to be a lot of work from everyone but we can weather this. She can't keep starving all the humans – the gods of every court will riot.'

'I spoke to some of Poseidon's court at your wedding.' Styx nods. 'They're all obsessed with humans.'

'Hmm, the Olympians too,' Charon agrees.

'Exactly. They won't let her get away with this for long.'

Although if it's a question of who will win, every god on the planet or my mother, I'm not sure I'm confident in the answer.

Hades appears at the doorway of my study, impish smile on his face, basket clutched in his hands.

'I've decided to repay the favour,' he says. 'And I would finally like to see that paradise you created.'

'*We* created,' I correct. I glance at the scrolls in front of me. It's the kind of work I have no interest in doing but need to sort through if the human trials have any hope of working. 'I don't think I have time. I need to get this done.'

'I thought I was managing this side of things?'

'Yes, but this relates so specifically to what happened in the mortal-soul trials yesterday that, by the time I explained it all to you, I might as well just have done it myself. We're both so busy I didn't want to waste more of your time.'

'Well, I appreciate your efficiency. But I would very much like to spend some time with the woman I love. If I help when we get back, can we make time for paradise?'

I flick through the sheafs of parchment, trying to gauge whether, even with Hades' assistance, it's possible to get through it all. He has no idea how much there is to do, how much my mother is throwing the Underworld into disarray. There's too much – even with him. But I'm hardly focusing. I need a break.

And, as much as I'm loving everything we're doing together, I do miss spending time with him – actual time, talking and laughing, telling stories and creating stupid little jokes.

'All right,' I agree.

I allow myself a few hours. We walk through the world of the humans, and I watch Hades' eyes light up at everything he sees, catching all the details he created. We settle by a lake and pick at food until we're sleepy and full, then I lie with my head on his stomach, his fingers entwined with mine.

'I love you so much,' he whispers, pressing his lips to my forehead.

It's a reminder of what waits on the other side of all the admin. If I can get through my mother's torment, there's a life of lying in my husband's arms in paradise to look forward to.

Soon it's a struggle to find any time together at all, though we make the most of it when we do.

'Are you sure you have to go?' Hades breathes between the kisses he trails along my arm.

'Yes,' I say, even though I'd love nothing more than to wrap my arms round his neck and kiss him until I'm light-headed. But I can't expect everyone else to work hard and not do so myself. 'And more importantly so do you.'

Hades is overseeing the court again – uttering the words

I never thought I'd hear from him that 'the scrolls can wait' –
so I can put my full focus to the human trials, which are as
overwhelmed by the increasing numbers of souls as everything
else.

'I thought we were supposed to live in paradise now.'

'The mortals live in paradise. We live in a constant state of
stress.'

'Well, I can provide some stress relief.' He tugs my hand,
pulling me towards him, and I fall forward. His pupils are still
swollen, skin warm and salty with sweat. I know how that
skin tastes.

'You know what would relieve my stress?' I whisper, drawing
a finger down his chest, noting the way his breath catches in
his throat. 'If you did your job and let me do mine.'

'I believe I just did my job remarkably well.'

I flush at the memory: his roaming hands, the way he'd
growled *Do you want me to continue?* when he reached the
edge of my skirt and I'd frantically whispered *Dear gods, yes*
as his fingers slipped beneath.

'You seemed to enjoy yourself,' he continues. 'And there is so
much more fun we could have.'

The way I'd lost my breath, pressed my lips to his bare
shoulder to moan into his skin as his fingers traced places I'd
only ever explored myself and the heat built inside me like a
crescendo until, just when I thought I couldn't bear it any
more, it crashed, trembling, consuming, euphoric . . .

Now I run my hands along the soft hair of his chest until I
reach the fabric gathered at his waist. I do, desperately, want to
make him feel that way too. He arches back only to glare as I
pull his robes up rather than down.

'Another time,' I insist, the words almost a whine because I want to, I really want to, but I've already spent too much time here and there's so much chaos to manage.

Hades' eyes meet mine, his grin devilish. 'Oh, you can count upon it.'

It's not just that it's busy but that every day it gets busier. I leave earlier and come back later, falling wearily into bed. It's all we can do to hold each other as we fall asleep. Our whole relationship becomes tiny moments that we snatch away.

Like when we both get back early one evening and take to the roof to stargaze because we were too distracted that first time. We're both exhausted, nearly too tired to move, so we just lie on top of each other and make up stories about the patterns we find in the stars.

Or when we press against one another in an empty hallway, snatching kisses like seconds until we pull apart and return to work, distracted and unfocused and hungry.

Or when we both bring work home with us because we need to do it but can't bear to be apart longer than necessary. We don't talk at all but we sit next to each other, reading through documents and writing our responses and it's enough just to breathe the same air for a little while.

And when we're in bed one evening and I taste the mint tea that lingers on his lips and he's holding me close and I feel like I can't breathe until I touch every inch of him, I decide: 'Hades, I want to have sex.'

CHAPTER FORTY-TWO

'Are you sure?'

'It's okay, darling, we're married.'

'I'm not asking if the appropriate administrative procedures are in place. I'm asking if you're sure you want to do this.'

I think about it for a moment. For my whole life, sex has been this big, scary thing. Mother kept me on an island to avoid it. The nymphs called it things like 'life-changing', 'transcendent', 'everything you've ever been waiting for'. And Mother called it 'disgusting', 'sinful', 'something you only do to please your husband'. I think the reality might be that sex is none of those things. Everything Hades and I have done together has been fun – maybe a little strange – but nothing has made me feel like a different person. I think, with Hades, sex might just be nice and it could feel good. I think it might mean something, neither as good nor as bad as it's been made out to be but something wonderful nonetheless.

'Yes, I'm sure. I want this,' I say, sitting up in bed and drawing him up with me. I take his hands in mine and turn to face him.

'Do you? We've spent so long talking about what I want but do you want to have sex? It's really, truly fine if you don't.'

He gulps and I follow the movement, wanting to kiss every inch of that neck, wanting him to arch it back in surrender. 'Yes,' he says. 'I would like that.'

'I want –' I hesitate. But I've become so much better at saying what I want recently. 'I want you to tell me what you like, show me how to do things and help me realize what I like too.'

'Of course. And have you taken –'

'Silphium? Yeah.' I started swallowing its leaves the moment something like this crossed my mind. 'Contraception is sorted – don't worry.'

Hades reaches for me and strokes my cheek. I think of those hands roaming the rest of my body.

I practically throw myself at him. I climb on to his lap and we're kissing like we'll drown if we stop, as though clinging to each other is the only thing keeping us afloat. He's holding on to my waist, pulling me even closer, lips firm and desperate, catching at my earlobe, trailing down my neck and I bite into his shoulder, lick his skin, kiss him anywhere I can think to reach.

I never knew that you could want like this – with every inch of yourself.

We slide each other's clothes off, press our skin together, clutch each other like we'll perish if we can't get closer.

It is hands reaching, lips trailing, exploring one another like we can memorize each other's bodies with our tongues.

It is laughter – as he rolls me over and nearly off the bed, as pleasure unfurls within me and I jolt with such violence I nearly collide with him, as he eases oil between my thighs and the odd squelching noises have us both stifling laughter until it breaks free, washes over us, and we're back to kisses and whispers of longing.

It is need – grasping, biting, clutching. It is murmured words and panting gasps.

And, when we're moving against each other, I run my nails down his back and he moans so deeply I feel it in my core, where liquid fire builds once more.

And I am thread, unfurling, fraying, coming undone.

When we are done, we collapse in a tangled, sweaty mess, whispering our love, laughing in ecstasy.

'How was it?' he asks.

Electrifying and weird and fun and uncertain and hilarious and enchanting.

'Amazing,' I say, kissing his bare skin. 'I can't wait to do it again.'

CHAPTER FORTY-THREE

BUT WITH EVERY DAY THAT passes we find less and less time together.

Each second brings more chaos to the Underworld. There are so many souls rushing to the furthest edge of the river Acheron that Tartarus has to help Charon shuttle them across the river. All five river gods join together to control the waters, making the journey easier. And Hermes, who usually only accompanies the souls to the Underworld, now offers to help Thanatos in the act of death itself, ending the suffering of those whose bodies can't sustain them any more.

Dozens of trials happen at once and I spend whole days rushing from one emergency to the next. Hades says court is quiet, with most gods too preoccupied to attend. Those that go have genuine complaints and concerns that take hours to unpack. He hasn't touched an easel in weeks and it's getting to him, even if he doesn't say so.

I miss him. More than the feel of him and the way my body hums under his touch, I miss him – our conversations, his reassuring presence, the way he makes me feel so sure of myself.

We're so busy we barely see each other, stumbling to bed in the early hours of the morning only to wake at dawn to do it all again. We each often wake to a cold space on the other side of the bed, the other having already left for the duties of the day.

The work is exhausting. The distance between Hades and me, especially with all we have discovered these last few weeks, is fracturing. And I'm not sure how long it can continue.

'You have post,' Hermes says, dumping a bag full of letters on the table before me. There are so many I'm not sure where to start, or if I even have time.

'Later,' I say.

'The gods don't like to be kept waiting,' he says.

'I'm aware.' I pick up the nearest note and slice it open with a nail.

Hades,

What in the Heavens is going on down there? Tie Thanatos to a rock if you must. I want this killing stopped! I would have thought you'd be too busy with that new wife of yours to throw a tantrum like this but, for Gaia's sake, whatever is going on, don't take it out on the rest of us.

Poseidon

'Charming,' I say, tilting the letter to Hades so he can see.

'It's unlike him to take the time to write,' Hades says. 'Normally he causes an earthquake and lets the influx of souls get my attention. I suppose he knew that would be counterintuitive.'

431

'I recommend not reading Apollo's letter,' Hermes says. 'He wrote it in front of me and when he asks you to stop killing the humans he's rather explicit about what he would like to be doing with them instead.'

Absentmindedly I pick another.

I'm at Eleusis. Grab your mother and let's get on with this. The mortal world is dying anyway. Time to move on and become something greater.

Hecate

I would throw it in the fire if Hades and Hermes wouldn't ask questions. I settle for slipping it into a pocket of my dress instead.

'They do not know this is Demeter's doing,' Hades says. 'I trust you can accelerate the spreading of that news.'

Hermes feigns an innocent look, which simply does not work on his face. His eyes have the permanent gleam of a child whose pockets are full of stolen sweets.

'Me? I can certainly try.'

I pick up another letter, one whose script is ludicrously flamboyant. Unlike most, it's addressed to me. The others don't even have an addressee on them, such is the writer's assumption it is only Hades in control here.

Persephone,

Get it, girl. I see you've finally consummated the marriage. I don't know how you held out – I would have been all over him in seconds with even a fraction of the tension between

you two. In fact, your mutual reluctance was causing me
physical pain. Anyway, nice work. When are you visiting me
so I can get the details??

Aphrodite xx

PS Can you get Mummy to stop starving the humans? I
miss their curves and flesh. All these bony hips and vanishing
breasts are really putting a dampener on things.

I flush and again slip the letter into a pocket before the others
can see.

'Aphrodite knows it's my mother,' I say. 'The news should
spread pretty quickly.'

'I imagine that's not all she said.' Hermes' smirk is knowing.

'No, it wasn't,' I confirm.

And oh, Fates, even worse is the slight smirk on Hades' face
too and I hate it and I want to tell him to get lost but I'd also
like to pin him against a wall and –

Hermes clears his throat.

'If I might offer a suggestion, you may wish to consider
appealing directly to Zeus. An official condemnation from the
court of Hell might hold some sway in this.'

'Not when he believes I stole his daughter,' Hades says grimly.

'Didn't you?' Hermes asks.

'Hermes, is the thought of me running away to avoid an
Olympian marriage – potentially to *you* – too much rejection
for you to handle?' I counter, balancing the harsh words with a
saccharine smile.

Hermes chuckles. 'There was a time when I might have
dismissed that notion but, knowing you as I now do, I would

not be surprised if you ran down here and blackmailed Hades into your matrimonial bidding.'

'I don't know what you're talking about. I'm clearly besotted,' Hades says.

'Bewitched, more like,' Hermes mutters.

'Hermes,' I warn. He likes to see how far he can push such things.

'Yes, yes, I know. You're disgustingly in love with each other. No need to prove it any more. It's enough to put one off food for life.'

'I'll write the letter,' I offer before the two of them can start bickering. 'Father thinks I'm innocent.'

I expect Hermes to scoff but instead he gives me an appraising look like I'm running some con he can't help but appreciate.

I spend far too long crafting the letter to my father.

When I hand it to Hermes, he passes me another – one that got lost, though I'm sure he simply kept it apart for some sort of dramatic moment.

Persephone,

Come to the surface, please. If you want all this to stop then we need to talk.

Come home – I love you.

Mother x

'Thank you, Hermes. Excuse me.'

I rush from the hall to somewhere more private. I find one of Hades' libraries and lean against its dusty shelves. Should

I go? Plead with her one more time? Throw dignity aside and tell her I'll do anything she wants but I won't return home, that this is my home now?

Should I maybe even consider agreeing, if it will save all this misery?

No. That's silly. I'm not negotiating. The other gods are putting pressure on her. We just need to wait it out. I need to ignore her until she caves and then, once the humans are no longer dying like flowers in a drought, we can have a conversation.

But the thought of returning to the humans to read more names of those joining us, to arrange yet another trial, has me in tears. When I can't breathe I admit that I have pushed myself too far. I can't remember the last time I slept more than two hours in a row, the last time I ate something without rushing somewhere else.

All the doubts I felt when I first took the throne come rushing back, and suddenly I wonder if I can really do all this. I still feel like I'm pretending, wearing a costume, playing a role I have no right to be anywhere near.

Before I can curl into a ball, I make a rather clever decision I never would have made before, not even with Cyane.

I call for Hades.

When he walks into the room the words tumble free before I can think about how weak they make me sound. 'I am very stressed and very sad and I would very much like not to be alone right now.'

'Oh,' he says. There's a confused scowl on his face and I'm suddenly reminded of how I thought he was dangerous – how did he manage that with a scowl as adorable as his? 'What do you need? I can distract you or we can talk or –'

'Distract me? I tell you I'm sad and that's your response? Get your mind out of the gutter.'

His eyes widen. 'I meant with art . . . or conversation or . . .'

I laugh but it catches in my throat and Hades is suddenly holding me. I'm not sure what's going to happen or whether Mother will ever stop, but right now it feels like we'll survive this somehow.

'She wants me to talk to her,' I say, passing him the note.

He shakes his head as he reads it. 'I don't see what another conversation would possibly solve. She's killing people. She doesn't get to leverage that into you doing anything – whether that's returning to Sicily or even having a conversation. If she really cared she'd stop and then talk on an even playing field.'

I nod. It's the same conclusion I came to.

We spend the evening exchanging stories until my laughter is genuine. He toys with my hair absent-mindedly. I run my finger over the old paint that flecks his clothes and I lean into him but he pulls away, saying he is not going to take advantage of my distress. I retort that it would be me taking advantage of him as a distraction, and I'm not going to do that either, so we sit there resolutely not taking advantage of each other until we fall asleep. My final thought before drifting off is that I just want this, just this, for eternity.

CHAPTER FORTY-FOUR

'**W**E CAN'T KEEP GOING ON like this,' I say the next morning, my head resting on his chest.

'I know.'

'Do we need to head to Olympus and demand they do something?'

'That might be seen as a touch aggressive but, yes, that may be our only option. Let's give Zeus a week to reply to your letter first.'

'Fine, but you need to paint or weave or *something*. You're too tense.'

'I can think of other ways to release tension.' He coils my hair round his finger.

A shiver runs down my spine but I refuse to be distracted. 'As fun as that is, it's not a replacement. You should create even if it's just for an hour a day.'

'I'll take an hour to create when you take an hour to garden.'

'It's not the same. I'm the goddess of life – it's not like flowers are all I have any more.'

'I'm the god of illusions, not paintbrushes. You're allowed to have hobbies, dear.'

'Not in a crisis.'

'Then my studios remain locked.'

'Hades,' I plead but I don't really know how to argue that he should do something I won't allow myself to do. 'I'm tired and I'm overworked, that's all. You're going without something essential.'

'An hour,' he says. 'That's all I'm asking for – and we should give that time to the other gods too. We're already behind – it won't make much difference.'

'All right, fine. But back to those other ways to ease tension . . .' I hook a leg over him, press my body to his and push aside his cloak to run my thumb over a mark I left a few days ago, the purple so faded it's hardly visible. I push myself against the bone of his hip.

'As a negotiation tactic this is poor. You've already agreed.'

'Very well. Shall I take myself to the garden?' I feign moving away.

He grabs my wrist and tugs me back to him. I topple on to him, every line of his body pressed flush against mine. His hands hold my hips firmly in place, lest I try to leave the bed again. 'Don't you dare.'

And we waste no further time before releasing our remaining tension.

Later, somewhat dishevelled and with a mark of my own hidden beneath the high lace neck of my dress, I find myself in the garden, not sprouting flowers but harvesting from the trees. Their quick growth is no surprise but that I'm here is.

Despite the overlap between my mother and me, harvesting remains her domain.

With each fruit I pick, her words ring in my ears in a turbulent cacophony. An apple: *'You're many things, Kore, but I didn't think you were this cruel.'* A mango: *'Do you really think that if I had the power to keep you safe myself, then I wouldn't choose to have you by my side forever?'* A pomegranate: *'I love you, my dear, but you are not powerful.'*

My mother has run circles round me my entire life but I've never been more confused – too busy, too distracted by the consequences to really reckon with the fact that she's actually letting people die like this. To get me back from Hades? Yes, I could believe she would do that. But to force me to leave a world of my own, a world where I have power and have achieved impossible things? I would have thought my mother would sacrifice her happiness for mine a thousand times over – so why is she doing this?

I try to turn my attention back to the garden, the orchard so thick you could get lost inside it, the trees bursting with fruit. Beyond are the glistening mortal plains, stretching up to the very sky itself, which is splattered with my stars.

I did this.

I built a home. And I'm *not* leaving it.

The leaves above me rustle and through them flies Hermes, his hair blown into a tangled nest, a burnt red tinge to his light brown, wind-chapped skin. His winged sandals flap frantically as he comes to rest before me. From the haste and solemn look on his face, he's not bringing good news.

'Mother or Father?' I ask.

'Both.'

I sigh and flowers swallow us. We spring free in the courtyard and I march towards the library while Hermes mutters, 'I hate when you do that.'

'You're the god of transport.'

'Flowers never made my list.'

Hades is studying a document. He glances up at us and discards it – actually tosses it across the desk – and that must mean he's expecting harrowing news. If it were anyone else they'd never hear the end of treating his scroll like that.

'Well?' I ask.

Hermes pulls a furled scroll from his bag, a wax seal pressed with an eagle at its centre.

'Your presence is officially requested.'

I take the scroll with trembling fingers.

'I cannot tell you the last time my presence was requested on Olympus.' Hades stares at the seal, the golden eagle of Zeus.

'You're still not, my lord,' Hermes says with just the right amount of scathing edge that he won't be fired for it. 'Zeus only wants to speak to the queen.'

Persephone,

Come to Olympus.

'Not one to mince words, is he?' I say. He didn't even sign it. But he used my name. My actual name, not the one he gave me.

'You don't have to go alone,' Hades says. The fact he says that – not 'You don't have to go' – makes the dire reality hit hard. Zeus is the king of the gods. You don't ignore him.

Horrible things happen to girls who say no to my father.

That remains as true now as ever. My grand plan to enact change is nothing. It's a long-term ideation. It's not providing protection, just punishment. Father will never enter the halls of my realm. The king of the gods will never have his judgement day.

'What does he want?' I ask Hermes.

He shakes his head. 'I'm not sure. He demanded an audience with your mother and moments later was demanding your presence too.'

If this were a conference of the courts, Hades would be invited too.

'There's no way ...' I say, because surely not. Surely Mother can't have reach of this sort. 'She couldn't have given him an ultimatum: me or the humans. He would have stripped her of her powers and sent her to Earth for her refusal to obey.'

'Unless,' Hades says, 'he wants revenge on me for taking you and this is a convenient way to get it.'

'What about the deaths of thousands is convenient?'

'To the king of the gods? It's barely a consideration.'

I stare at the letter. 'I'm not leaving here. I'm not leaving you.'

Hades is staring at the sheet in my hands too, his eyes distant. 'Yes, but it's how we go about preventing that which concerns me.'

'Hermes, tell my father we will be along shortly.'

The messenger looks as though he is about to argue but he nods and leaves. Then it's just Hades and me.

'I think I preferred it when I was technically missing,' I say, approaching him.

'No one is going to force you to do anything,' Hades says.

'Don't worry – the court of Hell is not ready to give up its queen just yet.'

I pause, catching a steeliness in his expression that I'm not sure I've ever seen before.

'What do you mean?' I ask.

'I mean exactly that,' Hades says. 'He may try as hard as he wishes but he is not taking you from this realm if you don't want to go.'

'But if he commands it –'

'Then he will be starting a war,' Hades says.

I glare at him. 'You are not going to war for me. We'll figure some way out of this that doesn't involve dusting off old swords.'

There must be *something*. We are more powerful than Mother and Zeus must know that.

'It is an option,' he says. 'That is all I am pointing out.'

'It is not a bloody option.' I turn on him because he's scaring me now. 'Another war? How could you even suggest that?'

'I thought it would reassure you,' Hades says, leaning against the edge of his desk.

'Reassure me?' I repeat. Is he joking? 'You're still traumatized from the last one and you think the idea of another war would reassure me?'

'I'm hardly happy about the thought, but if the alternative is to allow Zeus to force you from your home then it's our only option.'

'War isn't an option.'

'Sometimes fighting your oppressors is the only choice you have,' he says grimly. 'I may be haunted by the war, might see some things we could have done differently, but the war itself? What other option was there?'

I shake my head. 'If – *if* – my father demands I return, that's hardly on par with a child-eating monster on the throne.'

'I'm not trying to be flippant, my love,' he says. 'For you I'd fight a dozen wars. But to declare the whole court at war? It would have to be something momentous – like a threat against their queen. Aside from our own feelings on the matter, symbolically you're now much more than just Zeus's daughter. You're the queen of the Underworld. Zeus would be demanding the queen of one court live in another – can you at least see that for what it is? The first step towards dismantling the fragile peace between our courts.'

I understand what he's saying – I do. I've always suspected Father wants to rule all. If we don't stand up against him at the first sign he's attempting to take power from the Underworld, why wouldn't he make further efforts? Against Oceanus too. But war is so total, so overwhelming.

'And for exactly that reason,' Hades continues, 'if he did try this, I imagine Poseidon wouldn't be happy about it either.'

'You're planning allies already?'

'Of course – it's two courts against one.'

'And that "one" is Olympus, which is far more powerful!'

'It's not as impossible as you think. Kings have been overthrown before. Twice, in fact.' Hades steps towards me and I step back.

'Don't,' I snap. 'How many died to overthrow those kings? How many people like you suffered?'

'You're the one who wants to challenge Zeus.'

'Not with violence!'

'When one side is all-powerful, it's already violent.'

'And those with the least power, the humans, will be the

ones caught in the crossfire. I don't know if you know your geography, but the exact middle point between Heaven and Hell is somewhere around Earth.'

'If it were me,' he says. 'If, I don't know, Demeter reversed her demands and said she'd stop starving the humans if I was brought to her, if I was to be punished for taking you in the first place, would you let it happen? If Zeus ordered me tortured like Prometheus or even just bound to an island somewhere like Calypso, would you just let Zeus command it? Or would you fight back?'

'I'd . . .' I trail off, growing incensed at the mere thought. I could easily see myself screaming at troops on a battlefield, manipulating my own powers – doing *anything* to get Hades back. So is it war I object to, or war *over me*?

'I don't know,' I finally say.

'Yes, you do,' he insists.

'Fine,' I snap. 'If he took you, I'd burn the whole world down. I'd be so angry I don't think I'd be able to do anything else. But I love you because you *wouldn't* do that. Because you're ludicrously powerful, but you're also kind and you're gentle and you can make the choices that would be too hard for the rest of us.'

'Don't you dare,' he hisses. 'You don't get to love me more than I love you – and you certainly don't get to turn this into a moral issue when the problem is more than just Zeus manipulating his daughter – which, for the record, I'd fight against also. It's him taking steps towards total, unyielding power.'

I break. 'You're right but, Hades, please. If there was a way to fight them without risking the humans then perhaps but –'

'I hate to point this out, but, with the afterlife you've created, mortal death isn't the deterrent it once was.'

'Afterlife isn't life, Hades – you know that as well as I do.'

It's not. As goddess of the thing, I know there's a very marked difference – the afterlife is a flickering candle, not the boldly burning flame of life itself.

'So you expect me to just stand idly by if he chooses to tear you from this realm?'

'Yes.'

'Persephone.' He steps forward again and I can hardly look at him, can't cope with that look on his face like he's already mourning for me. 'Please don't ask me to do that.'

'It's not about you and it's not about me. It's about the people the gods don't care for.'

'It is about you if you're willing to do this for them.'

'I can't be the goddess of life and cause so much death, Hades. You know how that would hurt me.'

It's the only thing I've said that's made him hesitate because he knows as well as I do that it would feel like a corruption of my very self. He stares at me instead, pleading, and I want to give in, to tell him to do anything he must to keep us together because the thought of being torn away from him is almost as unbearable as the thought of so much death.

Almost.

'We'll refuse,' I say. 'We'll leverage power, argue, fight ourselves if we must, and if we can find a way to fight on a plane without mortal lives then perhaps.'

He reaches for me, takes my face delicately in his hands and kisses me with desperation.

I cling to the taste of him, my hands curling into his robes like if I clutch him tight enough even my father won't have the power to wrench me from his side. I can't believe Mother's taken this from me too. We should have spent these last weeks doing exactly this – grasping one another, kissing until we're dizzy, breathing one another in. Instead we've been running around the Underworld trying to fix the things she's broken.

I taste salt on my lips and when he pulls away I see twin tracks of tears down his cheeks.

'I love you. There's a slight chance we're being dramatic once more, getting ahead of ourselves.' He manages a weak smile. 'But I love you.'

'I never doubted that.' I wipe one of those tears from his skin. 'But that's not actually the agreement I'm looking for.'

'I'm serious, Persephone. If you're doing this, if you're going to have the confrontation I think you're about to, then I need you to know that, despite what you may have been told, you are so very easy to love.' He takes my hands and my heart races so loudly it almost drowns out the words he's saying – words that, until they were said, I had no idea I was desperate for. 'No conditions, every version of you – I love them all. And it's the easiest thing in the world to do.'

I kiss him again and whisper declarations of my own love against his lips. This time it really does feel like it could be a goodbye. It's filled with as much heartbreak as love, with a longing that feels like losing, and it's not just his tears I taste.

He wraps me in his arms, buries his head in my hair and leans against my shoulder. I clutch him, revel in his warmth and try to memorize everything about him.

'Promise me, Hades,' I say softly, clinging to him tight. 'The humans have suffered enough over this. No war.'

'I'll promise you no battlegrounds,' he says, drawing away only so he can pierce me with the seriousness of his gaze. 'But there are other ways to fight a war, and I refuse to promise to ever stop fighting for you.'

I lean forward to kiss him again, trying not to think of each kiss as potentially being our last.

'That works for me,' I say. 'Because I plan on confronting my father and fighting for you, for this home and for myself with everything I have.'

CHAPTER FORTY-FIVE

WE CAN'T KEEP THEM WAITING; it will only make it worse. I rush about the palace, finding myself issuing orders that will only be needed if I don't return. I can't bring myself to say farewells but what if this is it and I never get another chance? But then wouldn't I have bigger problems than not getting to see the land I have created or the friends I hold dear one last time?

I find the necklace Hades made weeks ago and tighten it round my neck, trying to pretend I don't think, *Something to remember him by.*

In an effort not to spiral, I focus on what is immediate. I rush to the courtyard with everything Hades and I will need, hastily straightening the crown in my hair.

'That's your plan?' Hades asks incredulously. 'A fruit basket to save the world?'

'Appearances,' I say. And a middle finger up to my mother, about as politely as I can.

'Are you ready?' he asks.

'As ready as I suppose I will ever be,' I say, taking his arm.

It should be grandiose, this return to the surface. Instead it's a single thought for the flowers beneath our feet to pull us through and push us up to Mount Olympus.

My feet crunch on dead grass that turns green beneath me, flowers blooming where I stand. The colour doesn't stop there; it trickles out, moss growing on rocks and grass crawling down the mountain. The world aches. And it itches with familiarity that takes me a second to recognize: the Underworld. Or, more specifically, the feeling I first had there, of a realm begging for life to fill it.

'Spring has arrived,' Hades comments as the land blooms into colour, and there's something in his tone I can't quite place.

'A shame humans can't eat grass,' I say. It never used to be this easy – I had to at least think about it. But now it's like brushing near souls, the energy leaching from me.

We're on the slopes of Mount Olympus, now bright with blossoming flowers and fluttering grace, the blue sky luminous above us and clouds hovering below. I can't see much beyond but, just stepping back into this world, something lights within me – a desperate urge to find out what lies beneath those clouds.

'Are you all right?' Hades asks.

'Yes. I've just never seen anything like this. The mountains of Sicily aren't as jagged.'

'Of course,' he says. 'I'm so used to thinking of you as being from this world I forget you never even saw it.'

I'm tempted to throw this stupid basket down and wander away, to ignore my father's summons and hike these mountains and the world beyond. But the mortals would starve – and

Hades might be able to rule hell without me, but he'd be running it miserably.

So instead I loop my arm through his.

Smoke wreathes us, that dark aura of his returning to curl round me too, like a protective barrier.

'Oh well, this will work.' I laugh, clenching and unfurling my hand, mesmerized by the way the darkness clings to it.

'Don't underestimate the power a good appearance can have. It might not solve anything but it certainly adds emphasis.'

'Yes, I recall,' I say and we begin our ascent.

It takes only a few minutes of walking, my thighs burning with the steep incline, before we reach the golden gates of Olympus. They arch and twist in a gold so bright the sun itself would appear dim beside them. The horai guarding the entrance mutter among themselves as we approach. Then, without saying a single word to us, the three women hoist the gates open.

Through them, Olympus stretches up to the mountaintop – everything is grey rock and white marble and bronze foundations. Roads thread between the buildings like molten gold has been poured down the mountain. I think of the art and nature of the Underworld and wonder how the Olympians managed to make something simultaneously so bright and so dull.

Hades offers me his hand and we sweep through the city, black smoke among all this white. Gods pause to watch us pass, their whispers following us. It's so much smaller than the Underworld. Hell is a sprawling land and I've only explored a tiny fraction of it. I haven't seen where the monsters roam or the pit of Tartarus or even the full expanse of the rivers. Olympus is clustered together; the walk from the city gates to the palace of Zeus takes no more than a handful of minutes. It is a land of marble – palaces, fountains, amphitheatres, bath houses, drinking halls. It is heady with the smell of ambrosia. The occasional olive tree is all the nature that creeps into this realm.

We climb higher until the ground falls away and we are walking on the stars. The palace of Zeus looms ahead, ever larger for the approach and Hades coughs, 'Compensating.'

I choke on a laugh before grimacing. 'He's my father, Hades. But also, if the stories are correct, yes.'

The doors open and it's startling to see inside. It looks the way the palace of Hades did when I first arrived, before it was covered in soft furnishings and plastered in art with flowers in every crevice. Back when it was cold, cruel and impossibly claustrophobic for something so huge.

We walk past the singing Muses and the minor gods lounging around and laughing with one another. They barely glance at us. There is nothing of the stress that lingers in my halls, no frantic concern for what's happening below them.

We run into Hermes and he tells us that my parents are waiting in the megaron.

Outside the huge doors stand two of my father's guards who fought alongside him in the war. They are hecatoncheires, each with a hundred arms and fifty heads.

They open the doors. The huge room might be identical to the one in the Underworld, but it's full of memories ours does not contain. My eyes track to the porticoes where, at my amphidromia, gods lingered and watched. The hall is mostly empty now, but past the hearth in the centre I see my mother and my heart clenches. I want to run to her and pull her into my arms and I want to shake her, to demand to know why she's doing this, what she's possibly hoping to achieve.

And, of course, high above sits my father on his stone monstrosity of a throne.

I look back to my mother, trying to read the situation. If she looked smug or victorious, I imagine I'd be packing my bags, but she looks nervous, upset even, and that's baffling. If she hasn't got her way then why am I here?

'My king,' Hades says, and we bow about as shallowly as we can get away with.

My mother glances at Hades uncertainly, her anger mixed with curiosity, perhaps even a dash of relief. It must have been hard to reconcile what she thought she knew of him with what I told her.

'Persephone.' Zeus nods. 'Hades, your presence was not requested. You are excused.'

'With all due respect, my king,' Hades says in a tone that implies the amount of respect due is none, 'I will not abandon my wife at this moment.'

Mother's brow furrows.

Zeus tenses and I can see him weighing up his options. He could force Hades, of course, but the fragile alliance between Zeus, Hades and Poseidon rests almost entirely on the latter two pretending they are obedient and Zeus pretending they do not have to be.

'Very well,' he says. 'I suppose that is to be expected.'

'It's unusual for a citizen of my realm to be summoned before you, let alone the queen,' Hades says. 'So I'm somewhat curious as to what this is about.'

'Zeus,' my mother pleads. 'Is all of this necessary? We're family. We can take this somewhere less formal, less –'

'You,' he snarls, lightning crackling in his eyes, 'have done enough. And you aren't needed here at all.'

'She's my daughter.'

'She's not *your* anything,' Zeus says. 'You lost, Demeter. She belongs to Hades now.'

I scoff at that and my parents turn to look at me. 'Oh, do I? The man or the realm? I have questions either way.' I raise the basket I brought. 'For you, by the way. I hear there's trouble with your usual suppliers.'

They stare at the basket before Zeus nods. 'Set it over there.'

I am slow to place it and when I turn I see that Hades and my mother are watching my father with almost identical looks of contempt.

'Let's get to it then,' I say. 'Why am I here?'

Father clears his throat. 'Well, I'm sure you've noticed the humans have been dying –'

'Yes, we sent you a letter demanding action,' Hades says, barely hiding the glare he gives my mother.

'Oh, yes.'

It's not exactly the first time I've thought my father a fool, but it's the first time I've seen his foolishness in action. It's clear the rest of the gods only let him keep his power because they don't care enough for it themselves, or else they fear someone worse would pick up the crown, or maybe they just dread another war. It wouldn't be hard at all to outwit him.

Something to consider, perhaps.

I suppose I now understand where my ability to lie comes from – Father has been pretending to be competent for years.

'It needs to stop,' he says.

I turn to my mother and speak with cold fury in my voice. 'So stop.'

She looks like she might burst into tears. She starts towards me but I cut her off with a glare. Hades brings the smoke in closer, like it could protect us. Mother stumbles to a halt and shakes her head. 'It's not me.'

I turn to Hades, expecting to see my confusion mirrored but his eyes widen in realization.

'What do you mean?' I ask her. 'You said people would continue to die unless I came to the surface.'

'Why didn't you just come?' she asks quietly. 'Why couldn't you listen to me?'

'Because you were killing people.'

'Persephone,' Hades says quietly. 'The grass –'

'No, actually, she wasn't,' my father booms, so smug that he understands something someone else doesn't. 'Why don't you tell her what it is you were really doing, Demeter?'

My mother glances towards the floor, then straightens up and turns on my father. 'I was protecting my daughter, because you refused to.'

'You dare –'

'I'm already banished, right?' she asks. 'Tell me, Zeus, what do I possibly have to lose here?' My father falters and my mother turns back to me. 'I was covering for you,' she says. 'I . . . When you were taken, everything started dying. Like everyone else, I thought it *was* my doing – not purposely, you understand, but my grief radiating. It's not uncommon – Poseidon causes earthquakes, Zeus thunderstorms, perhaps my foul temper could cause a famine. But then I visited the Underworld.'

'We all saw the way Hell looked at your wedding,' Zeus sneers.

'Not all of us,' Mother snaps but then in a gentler voice she continues, 'You said it yourself, my darling: you have power. Power over life itself. I thought, well, when I visited I suddenly thought, what if it's you? What if you are the reason everything is dying?'

Of course.

The goddess of life began to live in the Underworld. And the world above began to die.

'But why didn't you say something?' I bluster.

The grass sprang to life the moment I stepped on it, like the world itself was reaching out to me, begging me . . . This is me. Oh, Fates, I'm the reason all those people are suffering – the reason so many have *died*. I'm responsible for the chaos in the Underworld – the sleepless gods, the exhaustion, the stress . . . It's me.

'I didn't know who was listening and I –' She glances at my father and stops talking. 'I pretended it was me because I thought I could get you to the surface without telling you why. I didn't want you to feel guilty about what was happening. If you thought it was me then you could blame me for the deaths instead.'

Hades rests his hand on my arm, a comfort that could never make up for what she's telling me. It's my fault – all those deaths.

'Guilty?' I demand. 'You thought me not feeling guilty about people dying was worth more people dying?'

'None of this matters,' my father interrupts. 'Your absence is clearly affecting Earth. I'll confess, I too thought it was

Demeter. The absence of the goddess of flowers was not the first place anyone thought to look for an explanation. But Pan has seen his plants dying too and Demeter has no jurisdiction in the wild. Even Poseidon has reported issues of dying populations. Artemis reports fewer prey. Life, everywhere, is vanishing.'

The world was fine before I was born, perhaps even before I claimed my power in the Underworld. Life was not tied to any deity; it flowed freely and chaotically. But now, suddenly, it's bound to me and my absence is catastrophic. There are other gods with this level of importance – life would die, too, without the sun or the air or the very Earth. But this still feels too much.

'We've also heard, um, certain rumours about the Underworld,' Father says. 'About you styling yourself the goddess of life. It seems I overdid it when I gifted you flowers. I gave you more power than I intended to.' Of course he'd try to claim that. Of course me holding power without him would be too much. 'So, you see, I need you to return to living on Earth, not beneath it.'

Suddenly I'm clutching Hades' hand with no memory of reaching for it. I stare at my parents. I was prepared for the possibility of them demanding my return. I thought it would be something I'd fight. I didn't realize me returning would save people.

'I'm sure we can come to a solution that satisfies everyone,' Hades says fiercely, gripping my hand tightly.

'This is the solution,' my father says. 'Persephone will return to Earth. You can annul your marriage – don't worry, I'll force Hera's hand. Or –' he grins viciously – 'if your wife means so much to you, Hades, you can abdicate your throne and go with her.'

This can't be happening but of course it is. Of course this is an opportunity for him to snatch all the power we took back. That can't happen – the Underworld means too much to me to let Hades leave it, to let whoever my father would set up on the throne take it instead.

'Don't be ridiculous,' I snap. 'Why would I have to permanently leave the Underworld? I can visit the surface in the day if I must and return home at night.'

'We have no evidence that would be enough to fix it,' Zeus says.

'We have no evidence to the contrary,' Hades argues.

'Life does not belong in the Underworld.'

'Life is a cycle,' I snap. 'I can live in both. Earth needs me but the Underworld needs me too.'

My father scoffs, like the thought of somewhere needing me is too much, even though that's precisely why I'm here.

'This isn't a negotiation,' he growls, banging his lightning bolt on the floor. Somewhere on Earth thunder has struck.

'Then what is it?' I ask.

'It is an order from your king.'

'It's an ultimatum, sprung on a problem that doesn't exist,' Hades snarls. 'An effort to take away the very realm we both hold dear. Is that truly a move you are willing to make? Even the very suggestion of it is an affront – I imagine Oceanus would not take it lightly either.'

My father blusters as he turns on Hades. I'd assumed he'd know this would mean war but he appears shocked at the mere suggestion. He thought Hades and I would simply part, bow to his will and annul the marriage because Hades would never even contemplate giving up the realm. Father must have been so certain of Hades' immediate agreement that he didn't even consider the implications if the suggestion were taken seriously. Only now does he realize he has issued a threat – a threat that could lead to war – so he does what he always does and doubles down.

'I have tried to be civil –' Father starts furiously.

'By stealing my wife away?'

'You stole her first.'

'Stop,' I say. 'Both of you. Let's talk about this. I could spend half the week on the surface or half the year even –'

'This is not up for discussion!' my father snarls.

'Hell won't stand for –' Hades starts.

'Without crops there won't be any people to die. Your realm will fade and stagnate and die too,' Zeus says. 'You might not acknowledge that but there are many in your court who will.'

'Is that a risk you are willing to take?' Hades asks but I can hear his confidence wavering.

'I will give you six months,' I say. 'Half a year on the surface and half a year in the Underworld.'

'Give, take, as you choose it,' Zeus says. 'You either agree and live freely within the confines of Earth or you disagree and I will bind you here. Freedom or chains is your choice, not what time you give me.'

He turns to me with such vitriol in his eyes that I realize this isn't about the supposed slight of my marriage. Tearing Hades from the Underworld was never really on the table – just a bonus suggestion to remind us all of the things he can do.

This is about me. It always has been from the moment my ambition enveloped his. Better to shut a girl down than let her grow into a woman who might pose a threat. As powerful as I am, I am not a person to be bargained with – I am a thing to be crushed underfoot.

'Do you think that's how it works?' I hiss, so angry I can barely spit the words out. 'That you can just chain me to a spot and the life will flow out? It's conscious, Father. I have control over this.' It's a bluff – I am still discovering my power – but why shouldn't it be true? Why shouldn't he believe it is? 'Bind me to the Earth and nothing will live again, I promise you.'

Zeus narrows his eyes. His knuckles whiten on the lightning bolt he holds. 'Chaining you will be better than nothing.'

Mother glances at me, fearful now. She sees the temper in me she tried so hard to reign in. Little does she know it's hardly a fraction of it.

I stare them down. 'Would you care to risk that?'

'I shall take this as a refusal to meet my demands,' he says. He turns to the door and yells for his guards.

Hades tries to block my body with his, shouting about the things Hell will do in retaliation. I reach for my sickle before remembering I have not worn it for weeks and did not bring it for fear of escalation.

Well, there's no escalation from being chained to the surface of Earth.

Hecate said I delighted in this game and she was right.

But I can't stand losing.

And what else did she say? *'Power like yours ripples through the very fabric of the magic coating the world.'*

What good is that power now?

And then a thought: *I could kill him.*

Could I? In the seconds before his guards reach me and their hundred hands hold me firm, before they drag me to Earth and bind me to a mountain somewhere, can I reach into my power, feel the beating glow of life in my father's chest and extinguish it? Can I, goddess of life and queen of the dead, continue the cycle and annihilate my father like he annihilated his before him?

Practically? Perhaps. I don't know if that's something I can do. I might vanquish every life in the room if I try.

Morally? I don't know. Maybe. I've already killed hundreds of innocents, accidentally or not. Can I kill one decidedly not innocent man? I might not make it out of Olympus alive. The gods might riot, Oceanus might join them, I might cause another war. It might be worth it.

Or –

The guards burst into the hall.

'Seize her.'

Instead of relying on the power I've discovered, I could rely on what I've always had. Before I had power I had nerve. I was resourceful. I prepared. And I grew things.

I lurch to the side, to the table where the fruit glistens in its basket. I was ready for this. There's risk, sure, but there was risk when I first leapt to Hell. This time I launch myself towards its bearings.

Fruit grown in the Underworld. Fruit I could never eat without being trapped there.

Father must realize what is happening because he shouts, 'No! Stop her!'

My hand closes on the first fruit it finds. A pomegranate. I don't think before tearing into it with my teeth as hands grab at me.

Juice drips down my chin, blood red, dyeing everything it touches.

I spit out the rind and the fruit is ripped from my hand but I manage to choke down some seeds.

Six of them.

I feel every single one as my arms are yanked behind my back.

I glance at my father but it's my mother I stare down, frenzied. Chains are slapped on to my wrists, and I wonder if I'll ever stop seeing myself through her eyes. Will I ever look into a mirror and see myself first and her second? For now I see myself, crown tilted on my head, covered in bloody juice, chained like a wild animal. And I think if she cannot love me now, like this, then I do not want her love at all.

I turn back to my father and wonder if he knows he owes his life to me, that he lives solely because I chose not to end him. And I wonder if he knows I could change my mind at any moment. He might wear the crown of the gods but it is I who hold power for the chaos I have embraced.

'Six seeds.' I grin, bright red juice staining my teeth. 'Six months. Exactly as I offered.'

CHAPTER FORTY-SIX

'UNCHAIN MY WIFE NOW OR you'll have all of Hell to contend with,' Hades snarls, his eyes entirely black, the smoke coiling from him sharpening to points.

Mother turns from me and she's shaking. 'Zeus, please, this is not the answer. She can visit. It will work.'

I turn to my father who glares at me with a level of hatred I imagine he does not even have for the Titans.

'Athena!' he yells and the goddess comes running in. She must have been waiting on the sidelines, witnessing everything, waiting for his call. I remember her at my wedding, the way she commended my choice to eat at the same time as the men and my decision not to cut my hair. I remember her on Mother's island too. She always tried to teach me things Mother said didn't matter. '*Girls should be allowed to be smart too,*' she'd say. Most women taught me how to avoid men, but Athena taught me how to fight back. She has always been one of my favourites but she's wisdom and war in one position: advisor to the king. And it's a position she'll do anything to keep.

It doesn't matter if she wants to help me. She won't. Not if siding with Zeus will mean gaining his favour.

Is this how he does it? He gives power to select women and then says, 'Yes, of course, look at all these opportunities for you.' Are we all too busy competing for the few spots to actually help one another?

Athena doesn't even look at me now, just bows to my father. 'Yes, my king?'

'Food of the Underworld. What does it do?'

I tense. I know what it does but she must know more. What if there's some loophole here?

The guards holding me relax their grip slightly when it becomes apparent I'm not trying to break free.

'Ties you to the Underworld,' Athena says. 'Mortal souls could not physically leave.'

'And ours?'

'We'd feel a pull impossible to resist. Someone could be moved by force, I suppose, but it's ancient magic, part of the weave that all our powers are tied to. If you pulled that thread the very substance that keeps us all whole would begin to unravel. None of us would stay gods for long – our powers, our immortality would slip away. I'm not even sure we'd survive as fragile mortal husks. I think that sort of power ripped from us might destroy us.'

Father fires his lightning bolt right at me and I'm too startled to even scream. It whistles past my ear, singeing my hair and slamming into the wall where I hear marble crumble and fall.

'Fine.' He bares his teeth. 'Release her.'

I expect some grand final statement – a threat to stay in line, not to push him further. But he just stalks from the room, defeated and unwilling to admit it.

Athena ducks her head, offering me the slightest of smiles before she leaves too.

If there is a way to reverse it, to undo what I have done, she's kept it to herself. She's helped me.

Is this how it begins? Small actions where we can make them?

The hecatoncheires take their chains and run the moment Hades turns his glare on them. I'm rubbing my wrists, thinking maybe there is hope even within the court of Olympus, when my mother appears before me.

We stare at each other.

'I think we need to talk,' she says.

Hades runs his hand along my arm and I squeeze it. I appreciate the comfort but I need to do this alone.

'I'll meet you back here,' I say to him.

Mother takes me to the courtyard. It's in the same place as it is in my and Hades' palace. It's not as nice. There are no flowers when the ground is curling clouds. Instead there are marble benches and singing Muses.

We find a bench and when we sit she turns to me.

'I don't want you to hate me,' she says.

'You let so many people die,' I say, unable to believe it even now. 'Because you didn't want me to face my own guilt? Come on, Mother, you know that's not –'

'It wasn't just that,' she says, glancing around the courtyard before shaking her head. 'I imagine the guards will escort me out as soon as Zeus remembers he banished me.'

'I'm sorry about that,' I say. He might have banished her

because she lied about causing the famine, but I saw his temper wearing thin with her as she searched for me.

'Don't be,' she dismisses. 'It'll be a few years at most. He can't kick me off the council without explaining how you outsmarted them all. He'll probably tell everyone Hades tricked you into eating those seeds. Heavens forbid anyone believe you make your own decisions.'

I swallow. 'Like me running to Hell.'

Mother nods. 'He's also barred Hestia from joining the council and taken xenia from her. You proved how powerful it was and he can't stand someone else having a thing like that. When the mortals started calling him Zeus Xenios, Hestia said she didn't care who the power belonged to so long as it kept people safe but I think she might have just been saying that to save face.' Mother takes a breath and gives me a look weighted with such gravity I feel immobilized by it. 'If everyone believes in your power there will be even more driving him to find a way to take it from you. So perhaps it's better to let him spread his lies about how all this came to be.'

My jaw tenses. I wanted to stop hiding behind lies.

But that's okay, I don't need to argue with Father – not when I'm already fighting him in other, more insidious ways.

Mother sighs. 'Persephone, I have another confession. I didn't keep the fact it was your power causing the famine from you solely for your conscience. Your father has only ever tried to strip power from you – from anyone he sees as a potential threat, as Hestia proves. Those who excel do so because they appease him but you've only ever wanted power for yourself. He's terrified of that. Frankly, I think he sees a part of himself in it and knows what he did to get his crown. If he thought

I was responsible for all that death then he wouldn't realize it was you. The things you've done in the Underworld alone would be too much for him. I couldn't imagine what he'd do if he realized you were impacting Earth too. And if *you* didn't realize the true extent of your power, I thought maybe he wouldn't find out either.'

I take a moment to let the weight of her words settle. Of course that's what she'd do, all she's ever done: try to protect me.

I glance away.

'You need to stop,' I say. 'I love you, I do, but please stop trying to protect me.'

'I can't do that, my child.'

'Don't you get it? It's not just Father who's been stamping any hint of power from me. My whole life you've been trying to push me into this box and . . . I feel like if I let you down the world will crumble. I feel guilty for so much as thinking something you wouldn't approve of, like you'll never love me if I —'

'I'll always love you,' she says fiercely.

'I know that, logically — but the way I *feel*? The way you've *made* me feel?' I shake my head. 'I have all of eternity and I'm not sure I'll ever fully work out how I feel about you. But your expectations hurt me.'

She reaches for my hand and I let her take it, only because even now I feel guilty for saying all this, and she looks so very sad.

'You don't remember much of your childhood, do you?'

It's not what I'm expecting her to say.

'What? Why does that matter?'

'Your first memory, Persephone. What is it?'

I consider. 'My amphidromia.'

She nods, wiping a tear from her eye. 'I thought as much. That's my doing, I suppose.' She takes a breath. 'Before that, when it was just us on the island, I . . . There was no box I wanted you in. I used to tell you that you could do anything, be anyone, find your own place in this world. And then your amphidromia happened and I realized I was raising a girl whose father would never let her live the life she wanted. I thought if I could make you want the only life available to you, it might make it all easier. I love you unconditionally but I . . . I am so sorry I stopped making you feel that. I never meant to do that. I just . . . Persephone, before your amphidromia, I used to tell you that you could have the whole world if you wanted it.'

My eyes widen. 'And that's exactly what I asked for.'

And Father shut me down. Father made clear that my mother's words were a lie, that he would never let me have something like that.

But perhaps the damage was already done. I'd never stop wanting it.

I pull my mother into a hug and hold her close. There's a lot left to work through, but I think we'll be okay.

'I have six months on Earth,' I say. 'We can talk more then. I think maybe you should talk to Hecate too.' I laugh. 'You have more in common than I realized. She told me to meet her at Eleusis.'

'Why?'

A long-term plan, perhaps. Not as Hecate wants it, but I'm sure I can persuade her towards something else – power united, power that might be enough, one day, to undo my father's world without a war.

But that's an idle fantasy.

'I guess we'll see,' I say. 'But I'll see you there?'

She nods. And then, I suppose out of habit, she says, 'You have pomegranate juice on your dress. It stains, you know.'

After I say farewell to my mother, I return to the megaron and Hades doesn't even wait for me to reach him. He rushes towards me the second I walk through the door, grasps my hands, examines my wrists, sweeps my hair out of my face to check for damage.

'Are you hurt? The chains or the lightning, did they –'

'I'm fine.'

'Your mother?'

'I am equally undamaged by her.' He looks like he believes that one less and I squeeze his hand. 'I promise, I'm fine. And I think Mother and I will be fine too.'

He nods and casts a wary glance around him. There aren't any gods here right now but there could be at any moment.

'Let's get off Olympus.'

'Let's. I can't stand these clouds.'

'Lack of soil?'

'Yes, and I know exactly where I want to go.'

I have to wait until we're out of the gates of Olympus, when my feet touch grass again. Flowers encircle us. When they clear, we're in a meadow, stalks of dried asphodel in front of us.

'This is . . .'

'Where I called to you.'

'Sicily?'

'Sicily.'

*

The meadow billows around me as the flowers spring to life once more. I can feel it echo out, life flooding back not only to this island but across the Earth. I could stay here and the world would recover, the circles rippling out across the ocean to the lands beyond. Life has returned.

The nymphs won't be happy their plants were dying. But they're not here. The meadow is empty. No doubt they are off with the dryads of the trees on the meadow's edges. Or now that I have left and the wards are gone, maybe they're off with the mortals they always wanted to dally with. I hope they're happy, wherever they are.

I sit on the ground that opened for me, where the hole formed and I leapt.

'Of course, why should I expect chairs?' Hades shakes his head as he joins me. The darkness that surrounds him retreats until it's a fine haze across his skin.

'You'll survive,' I say, taking his hand. 'And I assume you'd rather talk than see the island.'

'You bound yourself to the Underworld.'

I shrug. 'Only for six months of the year.'

'So for half a year every year for the rest of your life you're stuck in the Underworld.'

'Sure, I married you for all eternity but binding myself to the Underworld is what shows commitment.'

'Persephone.' His voice shakes like it might break at any moment. 'This is different. Even I'm free to leave the Underworld if I want to, but you'll be trapped there. That's . . . You sacrificed freedom.'

'The Underworld is my freedom.'

'I want you to choose to be there, not be stuck there.'

'And I chose to be stuck there. Please, Hades, we did it. We can be happy now.'

'Can we?'

'We won.'

'This doesn't feel like victory.'

'Is it the lack of celebratory drinks?'

'Aside from you sacrificing your freedom, you're about to leave me, right now, for months. You'll be gone half the year for the rest of our lives.'

His words strike my core. But if I don't see this as victory, don't find the good in all this, I'm going to fall apart. When I speak, it's to convince myself as much as him.

'We're gods. What's six months in a year apart? We have eternity.'

'We have *half* an eternity.'

I trail my fingers down his face, wanting to comfort him, wanting to touch him while I still can. He raises his own hand to it, clasps it tight.

'Hades, I love you.' My voice cracks. 'And I love Hell too. And flowers. And this island. And the nymphs.'

'I imagine that list goes on.'

'It does.'

'Good, because Styx would be furious if she didn't get on it.'

I'm startled into laughter and suddenly it's clear everything will be okay.

Because how could it not be? This rhythm of us – an awkward declaration followed by a terrible attempt at humour, the way we each know what the other needs to hear, the way we lean into each other just enough to know that we aren't alone – they can't take that from us. Time apart certainly won't take it either.

'Angrier than she'll be when she finds out she didn't get a goodbye?'

'Fates, I have to tell the court what happened.'

'You'll be fine, Hades.'

'Without you? It's doubtful.'

'We've managed larger problems than six months apart.'

'I know. But still.'

'All I've ever wanted is to see the world,' I say. 'I can't feel it yet. All I want right now is comfort. But I know that when the sun rises tomorrow I will wonder what is beyond the horizon. And now I'll be able to find out.'

'I know.' He sighs. 'I know this is good. You get to explore the world like you always wanted to and you get to rule Hell on the side. But I'm left in the Underworld. I can't walk this world with you – it would be encroaching on territory.'

'I wouldn't let you even if you could. You'd hate it. And who would run our home?'

'I'm not sure Hell without you is preferable to this world with you.'

'I'll explore and you'll create and time will fly by.'

'You're taking this so well.'

'I'm taking this the only way I can. I'm somehow devastated and elated at the same time but you know what I'm not? Concerned. I love you. That's all there is to it. Six months apart isn't going to stop that.'

'Six months, Persephone. You won't even be able to visit – and I certainly won't. Zeus really might start an all-out war if he so much as sees me on Earth.'

I jolt – it was something I hadn't even considered until he said that. 'Exactly,' I say, turning to him. 'Zeus couldn't *see* you.'

For someone else, I might have to be clearer. But not Hades – my clever, brilliant husband who doesn't have to leave my side at all – because Zeus gave him an item when he was a child, a helmet to be used in war, to invisibly spy on the enemy. And now he can use it for love, to visit Earth when I am here, to silently slip his hand into mine, and even if we can't say anything, if acknowledging an invisible presence might be something the Olympians notice, *we* will know we aren't alone. We won't be able to talk, to hold each other, to be together in the way we yearn to be – but we'll be together a little, and that might make the whole thing tolerable.

His eyes widen with the realization and, finally, he smiles with the success of our victory.

He plucks a nearby sprig of asphodel and pushes it into my hair, tucking it behind my ear. 'You're the best thing to ever happen to me.'

'That's not fair on Cerberus.'

He laughs. 'True. Aside from my dog.'

'Well, dogs aside then, I would have to say likewise. I never even knew it was possible for someone like you to exist. I'm so very glad I ran to Hell, that I met you – that you did all you did for me. Please take care of the afterlife. We put a lot of care into that.'

'I will,' he promises. 'Persephone, I . . . thank you. Thank you for intruding into the Underworld and demanding xenia and refusing to leave –'

'You don't sound very thankful, darling.'

'I'm trying for a dramatic and profound farewell here.'

'Farewell?' I repeat as I stand, pulling him to his feet with me. 'Um, no. You think the nymphs aren't going to yell at me until they get to meet you? You're coming with me.'

He considers. 'Zeus will be sulking for at least a day. He won't even notice I'm here.'

'Precisely. So you can come meet my family.'

He seems to realize what this will actually entail and his eyes widen. 'Oh, actually, Zeus could smite me at any moment.'

'Hades.'

'What? This is scary.'

'You're the king of Hell and you're scared of a handful of nymphs?'

'Yes.'

'Then good – you're prepared.'

'Do you know how much back and forth it took to get the nymphs to make your wedding veil? We're not going to properly be together for six months and you want me to suffer like this first?'

'Stop whining.'

'I had to fall in love with you. I couldn't just stick to my paintings and tapestries?'

'Somebody told me I'm incredibly easy to love.' I spin to face him, wrap my arms round his neck and kiss him. I imagine kissing the air might be something the Olympians note – even if they might think it's a rather tame proclivity, given their standards. The helm might offer reassurance, but it won't offer this. Six months without touching him feels distinctly impossible.

He sighs when I pull away. 'Very well. You've convinced me you're worth the trouble.'

I arch an eyebrow. 'Are you sure? Because it's been a lot of trouble.'

'If you'd like to convince me further I'm amenable to that.'

'I'm sure you are but you're not getting out of this so easily.'

'Six months apart,' he mutters. 'Every single year for the rest of eternity you're going to leave.'

'Yes, and every single year I'm going to come back.'

I link my arm through his. His steps are heavy as we trek towards my former home and he sighs, slowly coming round to the possibility that this is not an end but a beginning. With every flower that blossoms as I pass, I'm not sure how it could be anything else.

When I was in this field last, I was running for my life. I didn't know what I was looking for and definitely wasn't seeking what I found: a home, a purpose. Myself.

Now, with a crown on my head and Hades at my side, the future is a meadow I will bring to bloom. I have power now and so much more besides. I have two realms to roam, more power to find and a message to spread: all those tales of an afterlife, all those whispers against Olympus.

This is just the beginning.

I have gods to dethrone.

I have chaos to bring.

ACKNOWLEDGEMENTS

This book has been a long, messy and chaotic journey (how gloriously on-brand) and it would not exist without the many truly brilliant people who have made up Team GGQ.

Firstly, I want to thank my agent, Hannah Schofield, whose belief in this book never wavered, no matter how much my own did. Hannah was the first instance of 'my book' becoming 'our book' – something that never stopped being a delightful, heart-warming and incredible experience. Hannah, you are many excellent things and truly nothing if not tenacious.

Thank you to my wonderful editor, Naomi Colthurst, whose support, guidance and championing is responsible for making *Girl, Goddess, Queen* as good as it could possibly be. Thank you also to Harriet Venn and Stevie Hopwood, who have made publishing this book fun and exciting at every opportunity.

To everyone else at Penguin, I'm not even sure where to start. Your efforts on this book have been phenomenal, and I need you to know how thoroughly I appreciate everything you've done – if you've ever filled in a form, written copy, pitched the book or corrected my embarrassing grammar mistakes then I am eternally grateful.

It takes so many people to publish a book, so thank you to everyone whose hard work has made this possible: Candy Ikwuwunna, Shreeta Shah, Laura Dean, Claire Davis, Helen Gould, Debbie Hatfield, Rebecca Hydon, Stella Newing, Alice Grigg, Maeve Banham, Clare Braganza, Beth Copeland, Stella Dodwell, Susanne Evans, Beth Fennell, Zosia Knopp, Magdalena Morris, Rosie Pinder, Chloe Traynor, Zoya Ali, Anda Podaru, Kat Baker, Brooke Briggs, Toni Budden, Ruth Burrow, Aimee Coghill, Nadine Cosgrove, Sophie Dwyer, Nekane Galdos, Michaela Locke, Eleanor Sherwood, Rozzie Todd, Becki Wells, Amy Wilkerson, Alicia Ingram, Sarah Doyle, Desiree Adams and Jenna Sandford. Thank you to everyone at my international publishers for getting my book to so many people, and thank you to every other crucial person who has helped readers find *Girl, Goddess, Queen* – from typesetters and delivery drivers to librarians, booksellers and teachers. A special thanks for how beautiful this book is – inside and out – to my designer Jan Bielecki and illustrator Pablo Hurtado de Mendoza.

I've always found publishing to be full of the best and nicest people, and I feel so blessed to have been able to work with all of you. On that note, thank you to every author I've ever worked with in a professional capacity for inspiring me with your own talent and dedication to pursue this dream.

This book is dedicated to the members of S1, past and present, who were there for me during the most difficult years of my life. But I'd like to give a special thank you to those who have not only got me through CCHS, but also through the whole stressful and time-consuming process of writing a book:

ACKNOWLEDGEMENTS

Jessica Rome, Megan Salfairso, Eleanor Brown, Laura Ray, Dora Anderson-Taylor and Amanda Wood.

To the housemates who have dealt with me yelling 'I need to go be productive' at random intervals, forced me to take breaks (especially those involving trashy reality TV) and put up with the range of emotions publishing a book entails: Kristina Jones, Claire Kingue, Aoife Prendiville, Fraser Wing, Laura Grady and Saoirse McGlone. To you I say: there are tall ships, there are small ships, there are ships that sail the sea, but the best ships are friendships, so here's to you and me.

To my first readers, who in addition to the above include Liberty Lees-Baker, Izzy Everington and Sara Adams. Thank you for the insightful notes, pointers and constant cheerleading.

I'd also like to say thank you to Isabel Lewis, Natalie Warner and Sophie Eminson for every ego-hype, celebratory prosecco and cheer from afar.

To Daniel Fenton for taking all of this chaos in your stride, wrangling with my near-constant anxiety and making me many, *many* cups of tea. Thank you for making all of this just a little bit easier.

Thanks also to my family for the support and encouragement you have shown over the years – and for never trying to marry me off to a random Olympian. My gratitude to all of you but especially to Ben David Welsford and Amber Fitzgerald: firstly, to apologize for setting the bar so high as eldest sister, but also to say that this book was inspired in so many ways by watching you both grow up in this world. I hope you know that you inspire me so much more than I imagine I will ever inspire you, and I hope you manage to be the chaos bringers I long to see in this world.

ACKNOWLEDGEMENTS

Thank you to Cher, for teaching me to Believe.

And finally, thank you to everyone I've met on social media – every message, every like, every word of encouragement. I can't tell you how much it has all meant – and how much it continues to mean.

ABOUT THE AUTHOR

Bea Fitzgerald is an author and content creator. She has worked in publishing for a number of years and has a degree in English Literature from the University of Reading, where she also studied several classes in Ancient History. Bea is passionate about stories and fascinated by the way they endure and resonate through centuries and generations. When she's not writing, she's entertaining her followers on TikTok and Instagram with her mythology-themed comedy account @chaosonolympus. *Girl, Goddess, Queen* is her debut novel.